Nicola Matthews lives in Kirby-le-Soken on the North Essex coast. *Kitty Canham* is her first novel.

Nicola Matthews

KITTY CANHAM

Published by Hall House Press 2022
nicolamwrites@gmail.com
nicolamwrites.com

2 4 6 8 10 9 7 5 3 1

Copyright © 2022 Nicola Matthews
Nicola Matthews has asserted her right under the Copyright, Designs and Patents Act 1988 to be identified as the author of this work

A CIP catalogue record for this book is available from the British Library

ISBN: 978-1-7396698-0-5

This is a work of fiction. Names, characters, places and incidents either are the product of the author's imagination or are used fictitiously. Any resemblance to actual persons, living or dead, events or locales is entirely conincidental

Graphic design and typesetting by Dan Lovell
Cover photograph by Luke Braswell

Printed in the UK

All rights reserved. No part of this publication may be reproduced or transmitted in any form or by any means, electronic or mechanical including photocopying, recording or any information retrieval system, without prior permission in writing from the publisher

This book is sold subject to the condition that it shall not, by way of trade or otherwise, be lent, resold, hired out, or otherwise circulated without the publisher's prior consent in any form of binding or cover other than that in which it is published and without a similar condition, including this condition, being imposed on the subsequent purchaser

I would like to thank Petra McQueen, of The Writer's Company, Wivenhoe, for her encouragement and expertise which were invaluable. I would also like to thank all those who read the early drafts (you know who you are). Your honest feedback was most appreciated.

Beaumont-cum-Moze, Essex

1738

Chapter One

The basket weighed heavy at her side. Her arm ached from the carrying. She lowered it to the ground and stood awhile, gazing out across the meadow towards the backwaters. When the tide was high, vessels criss-crossed the busy estuary. But now, all was still. Kitty was well acquainted with the rounds of the tide and comforted by the familiarity each season brought. When she was a child, it had seemed to her that this is how it would always be; the summers long and hot, autumn aflame with warmth and plenty, the winters cold and harsh, and spring … ah spring. It was the season she had come to love more than any other as she blossomed through her own tender years into the summer of life. But for now the farm was busy with the harvest and the insistent smell of late summer hung in the air. Catching her wayward hair to the nape of her neck, she breathed a deep sigh. She did not want this season to end, because when it did, she sensed that everything would change.

Checking for thistles, she tucked her skirts beneath her and settled on the ground for a moment's rest. Beyond the mudflats, the afternoon sun touched the trees along the shore of Horsey Island and further still, the spit of land they called the Naze curled around into open sea. Aunt Ann's farm was there, but it had long since disappeared. The family had to move away when the sea claimed their land.

She felt the ground, hard beneath her, and shifted. This was her father's farm, safely tucked away in Beaumont-cum-Moze beyond the estuary's furthest reach. It had been her home for all of her eighteen years. She lay back beneath the meadow grasses and let her mind wander to the picnics of her childhood; she could see her father's young face as he caught her up and swung her around until she was dizzy with delight; she could hear her mother humming as she lay out the picnic. Her mother was always humming when undertaking some delightful domestic task. But that was long ago, before the great sadness took her voice.

The humming persisted. She opened her eyes and smiled; a bumble bee was lumbering nearby. The heady, hopeful, sweet perfume of the fading meadow lulled her tired body. She began to drift. But before she was lost to the world entirely, the sun was overshadowed and the coolness of the waning day touched her skin.

'Kitty?' She started awake to see Tom standing over her, his hair flopping into his eyes, just as it always had. He wiped it away with the back of his hand. 'What are you up to?' He seemed to be scowling.

'Nothing.' She sat up, rather ashamed to be found dozing when others were working so hard to get the harvest in. Tom held out his hand and with one strong tug, Kitty was on her feet. She had known Tom for so long and had never felt embarrassed around him, until now.

'And what's that you've got there?' Before she had a chance to stop him, his hand slipped under the cloth that covered the pies in her basket. She slapped it away.

'Those are for the labourers.'

'I'm a labourer,' he pleaded. She could never resist Tom; he was a year younger than Kitty and she had always looked out for him. So she relented and held out an apple, which he took and bit into. 'C'mon then.' His mouth was full. 'I've got to get this rope to your pa.'

A coil of rope was draped over his shoulder. Brushing down her skirts, Kitty scooped up the basket and trotted alongside Tom. He smelt of sweat and straw, it was not an unpleasant smell. They talked of the harvest; it had been a good year, spirits were high, though the work was hard.

Throwing the apple core aside, he asked, 'You heard about Sarah?'

'Yes.' Kitty tried to smile, but it was no good. Sarah was Tom's sister and Kitty's closest friend. They had shared dolls, stories, and the secrets of their changing bodies, in fact there was nothing they did not share. But now Sarah was courting. The news had unsettled Kitty. It seemed to her that this was a very odd match. Nathaniel Parditer was apprentice to the clerk in the magistrate's office in Thorpe-le-Soken. Kitty had met him on one or two occasions. He wasn't what she imagined for Sarah at all. He was tall and thin and stuttered slightly when he spoke. He never had anything much to say, unless you needed facts, then he was very forthcoming.

Tom stopped and turned to look at her. 'It's a good match, Kitty.'

Kitty pressed a smile to her lips in response, 'I know.'

Tom marched on. Perhaps he was right; Sarah would need to marry, and Nathaniel's prospects were good. She was a sensible girl and wanted someone who would look after her, give her children, and who brought her as little trouble as possible. Sarah would make anyone a wonderful wife. She was a happy, healthy girl with apple cheeks and wide blue eyes who made everyone smile. This could suit them both.

Tom and Kitty walked on in silence. As they reached the rise, they saw her father's field rolling away from them, golden in the waning sun. The swoosh of the scythe caused dust to rise in billows. The women and older men were gathering the corn and tying the stooks with proficient hands. Seagulls swooped among the labourers' families who were bent over gleaning what they could. Her father looked up. Seeing them coming, he turned to speak to the labourers. One by one they paused in their tasks. Some drank from great flagons whilst others just looked at her with eager eyes.

Most of them knew Kitty from her childhood. There were the Thompson boys, the Butts, the Trefalls and old Mr Morepig, who, though bent with age, never missed a harvest. And there were those she did not know, usually travellers, just here for seasonal work. Her father never differentiated, he always said that hard work deserves just reward. So she, her mother and Peggy worked hard to provide what they could to keep the labourers going through the long hot days. Laying out the cloth, she offered the food she had brought. Tom grabbed a pie and wandered away to join a group of young men sitting in the shade. Kitty's father sat down beside her; his skin was bronzed from his labours.

'How is it going, Pa?'

Her pa took a large bite out of a pie before answering. It pleased Kitty to see him enjoying her labours. 'It's going well, the weather has been kind. And these are good people, working hard.'

Kitty noticed old Mr Morepig sucking at the side of his hand. She went to him and tended the blister with the cloths she had brought for such occasion. He thanked her, his leathered skin folding into a thousand creases around his keen blue eyes. Kitty wandered back to her pa. He was lifting a flagon over his shoulder and to his lips, drinking thirstily. He wiped his mouth with the back of his hand and leant in closer to her.

5

'When the harvest is done, you know what we will do then, Kitty?'

'What? What will we do, Pa?' She mocked her father with childlike expectation.

'We will celebrate!' He took her arms and swung them awkwardly in the way of a dance. She could feel the men's eyes on them and pulled away. 'Pa, you've got work to do.'

'Indeed I have, Miss Canham, you are quite right.' Clambering to his feet, he snatched up an apple and set off to talk to Joseph, the farm foreman. He was more serious than her pa, but they worked together well through hard times and good. Joseph had come to work for her pa after his wife died, with young Sarah and Tom in tow. Kitty was always thankful that he did. They were like family to her.

Kitty shook out the cloth, watching as the seasonal labourers shared what little food they had with their families. She wished they could feed them all, but she knew that the farm could only sustain the workers themselves, so she comforted herself that her pa's generous gleaning rights would be of some help.

The men were now wielding their great blades once again. The dust of the harvest began to catch in her throat, so she set off for home. With the sun on her back, and with her basket lighter, she found herself humming as she walked. The hedgerows were full of blackberries, so she paused to gather a few in her empty basket.

'Kitty?' Sarah was calling from along the path.

Kitty didn't look up at first, not wanting to face Sarah yet, she wasn't ready, but Sarah called again. This time she looked up and smiled.

'Oh, Kitty, I'm glad I have found you.' Sarah was out of breath. 'I went to your house. Your ma told me you would be out this way.'

'And here I am.' Kitty kept on picking. She knew she was sounding churlish.

'Your ma told me that you know about me and Nathaniel.' Kitty had heard through farm girl gossip. 'I am so sorry, I wanted to tell you myself, but I've been so busy what with it being harvest and everything, and the Butts have needed attention. You know their littlest has been unwell. She is on the mend now, but I had to attend to her. There's just been so little time for anything else.'

'Except courting.' Kitty could not help herself.

'Well, yes, except …'

Wiping her hands on her apron, Kitty looked up to see the untidy bundle of vulnerability standing before her.

'You are not upset with me, are you?' Sarah could not bear to think that she had let anyone down. She just wanted everybody to be happy and Kitty was her dearest friend.

'Of course I'm not, I am teasing.'

She offered a blackberry to Sarah in red stained fingers, and popped another into her own mouth, the sweet juice bursting against her tongue. Kitty turned and set off for home, giving her friend a reassuring smile. 'Why don't you tell me all about it?'

Sarah hopped alongside, babbling excitedly about getting married and where they would live and such.

Whilst Sarah talked, Kitty's mind drifted to her own life. She was young and strong and had no intention of becoming a wife. The farm was her life and she intended to stay on it as long as possible. Father was showing her the ways of farming, and she had Joseph teaching her accounting. He said she had an aptitude for it, which pleased her father no end. Her mother had agreed to it all, so long as she learned some of the finer things like needlework. So on winter evenings, Kitty would sit with her mother and dutifully sew. She was never very good at it, but managed to glean some pleasure from the small tapestry of flowers that she had completed and which now hung on the wall by the settle.

As they approached the house, Sarah concluded her excited exposition. 'So you see, I shall be very happy and we will still be the best of friends.'

Kitty took her by the shoulders and kissed her on the cheek, looking into her concerned blue eyes. 'Of course we will, and I will be the best aunty to your children.' Sarah smiled, reassured. 'Now, I have to feed the chickens. Are you going to help or just stand there, gabbling away?' Sarah laughed and followed Kitty as she set off for the chicken pen.

As Sarah left for home that evening, she turned and waved, smiling and carefree, just as she was made to be. Kitty turned towards the house. In the evening sun, the thatch lay heavy like a young beaver's pelt. Smoke rose from the newly laid chimney in a single column; there was now no breath of wind to disturb its course. Bouncer, the ragged spaniel, trotted out of the back door to greet Kitty. She fondled him and followed him into the house.

Peggy was standing at the table preparing supper. She had come to the house when Kitty was toddling and was very much a part of the family. Kitty couldn't help smiling. Pa had always said that Peggy chopped vegetables as if they were her greatest enemy. They certainly were today. Peggy looked up from her labours. 'Did they like the pies?'

'Of course.'

Peggy nodded in response, aware that she had never made a pie that was less than perfect. 'Did you see your pa?'

'Yes, he said the harvest is going well. It should be finished in a day or two.'

Peggy offered Kitty a piece of carrot. 'That'll be in a week or so then.'

Kitty laughed and made her way into the hall; it was dark in the lowing light. Through the parlour door, she could see a candle flickering on the table in the window. Judith, her mother, was sitting in her favourite chair beside the table. Her cap was neatly tied under her chin, which lolled forward on to her chest as she dozed. She was once beautiful, Kitty could see that. Her fine features were not diminished, but her sorrows had etched their way into her skin. Usually, Kitty was irritated by her mother, but now, as she watched the rise and fall of her mother's breathing, she felt her sadness. Mother had lost all her boys at birth; she couldn't seem to keep them. Kitty was eleven when the last little one died. Mother named him Samuel, hoping for God's blessing upon him. But he died at three weeks old. She remembered cradling him there before the fire. His dear little face never looked quite right. A sadness settled over her mother that day that never left. However hard Kitty tried, she knew she could not bring her mother comfort and for that she was sorry. It was only her father who could soften her and bring out moments of her youthful past.

Mother jerked awake. 'Kitty?'

'It's only me, Ma, I'm going to get cleaned up.'

'Yes, you do that.' Judith took up her sewing. 'Your father will be home soon.'

Kitty went to leave.

'Did you do the chickens?'

'Yes, and I cleaned out the far pen.'

'Good, what about Nelly?'

Nelly was the old cow that had kept them in milk for years, but now she was too old to be of any use. Kitty couldn't understand how father allowed it. In Kitty's mind, once they stopped producing they should be slaughtered and the fodder saved for those that could use it. But mother wouldn't hear of it. Nelly had worked hard all her life and should be looked after in her old age. So that was that. Kitty assured her mother that Nelly was well and made her way upstairs to her room.

She was grateful for a room of her own where she could be alone. Pouring what was left of the water into the basin, she splashed it on her face. From her pocket she drew a small stone that she had picked up in the meadow. It was perfectly round. She turned it in her fingers. Today had been a day of moments that hung in her mind like an old melody. She placed the stone on the table under the window amongst all her other keepsakes: a feather, a glass bead, a ribbon and such like. Alongside them was the most prized of all; a small pile of lace kerchiefs, embroidered by her ma on her birthdays when she was young. Each one had a pink heart nestled in the corner among a spray of flowers. Her favourite was the last her mother had given her, when she was twelve. It was embroidered with forget-me-nots. Laying on top of the pile, was a little wooden soldier toy her father had made when she was tiny. She never really knew why she kept these bits and pieces, but she always had. Suddenly Kitty felt exhausted and flopped back on the bed. An extraordinary drowsiness came over her and soon she drifted into sleep.

Kitty awoke to hear the front door slamming and voices below. It was Father, certainly, and there was another voice. A voice she didn't recognise. Gathering her shawl, she made her way downstairs. Mother stood in the hall, needlework in hand, looking quite lost. Voices came from Father's study behind the stairs.

'What is it, Mother? Is everything alright?'

Her mother's eyes were on her, but their intention was elsewhere.

'Mother?'

'Ah, Kitty, of course … there you are.'

She was making little sense. Then, as if she were waking from a dream, she said, 'Let's help Peggy get supper. Come along.'

As they entered the kitchen, Peggy looked at Mother. 'Is everything well?'

Mother cut her off, 'Yes … yes. It is merely a business acquaintance of Robert's.' She took up the slops bucket and handed it to Kitty. 'Take that to the porker, Kitty.'

Kitty took the pail and stepped outside. The light had almost gone. It was a clear evening. A sharp breeze freshened the moment and lifted Kitty into wakefulness. The chickens, who had clucked around her feet earlier, were silent now. The old porker snuffled and grumbled as the slops landed beside her.

On the way back to the house, Kitty noticed a horse tethered by the door. He was a fine, tall fellow, but to Kitty's mind not at all well kept; his head hung low. She placed the pail by the back door, and went to greet him. 'Here, boy, here.'

Pulling a tuft of grass, she held it out in her hand. He nuzzled her palm as he took the offering. Just then the front door opened and a stranger walked out. Kitty stepped back.

'Ah, you must be Kitty.' The man was thickset and had an old hat pulled down on his head. 'Let me look at you and see if you are as beautiful as everyone says.'

He went to take her by the shoulders, but she was too quick for him and stepped back. He smiled. 'Yes, yes,' he said in a soft voice that she was sure was not his own, 'very lovely.'

Thankfully, at that moment, Pa marched out of the house. He had a determined look on his face that she rarely saw. He stood beside her, fixing the man with his gaze. 'Kitty, get inside now, it is time for supper.' She was happy to do as she was bid.

Inside, Mother was sitting on the settle with Peggy at her side. Kitty had to ask, 'What's going on? Who is that man?'

Peggy stood and brushed down her aprons. 'He's just someone your father knows and is not a nice man at all. I should stay away from him.'

Kitty shuddered. 'I can assure you, I will.'

'Now, fetch the bread to the table, Kitty, and we can all eat.'

Supper was a strange affair. Having given thanks, Father ate hungrily and talked of the harvest, Peggy spoke of the new pickles she was trying out and Mother was silent. Kitty supposed that it was not so very different from other suppers but later, in her journal, she could only describe the evening as having an air of disappointment hanging over it. After supper, when all was tidied away, Mother and Peggy went to bed. Father sat by the fire, filling his pipe. Kitty asked about their earlier visitor.

'You need not worry about him, Kitty, he was an old acquaintance. You know how it is, people see you better off than them and always want something from you. I am sorry if he upset you. We won't see him again.'

She was no longer a child and wanted to know all she could of the farm's affairs. 'But, Pa, what did he … ?'

'Let's not talk anymore about it, eh? It has been a long day. We are all tired.'

Kitty looked at her father, bent heavily over his knees as he filled his pipe, his greying hair falling about his shoulders.

After a long draw, he straightened up, pulled her close and smiled. 'My Kitty Kat.' Pa had called her that for as long as she could remember. She snuggled into his strong body. These were the moments she lived for; her and Pa, alone together. The smoke from her father's pipe drifted in the flickering light. Kitty was home.

Chapter Two

Three weeks had passed and the harvest was finally gathered. Kitty stood by the gate listening to Peggy's incessant chirping and her mother's gentle undertones drifting from the kitchen window. The sun was high. Kitty lifted her face to its warmth. She was glad to get away for a bit. She heard footsteps on the path and turned to see Sarah trotting towards her. Kitty smiled and held out her hand. Without a word, Sarah took it and together they set off towards the backwaters. First they were trotting, then they were running, and finally chasing each other in gales of laughter. They headed towards the oak where the old rope swing hung in expectation over the water.

Finding a private spot on the bank, they stood a moment, breathing heavily. Kitty was first to slip off her cloak and run into the water, her chemise billowing out as she went. Sarah was more reticent and made it clear that she was not sure it was such a good idea at all. She did not love the water like Kitty did, but she had a reason to want to be especially clean today. Her betrothal to Nathaniel was to be announced at the harvest home this very eve. There would be a binding of hands and a promise. So she reluctantly waded in. Kitty laughed to see Sarah gasping as the cool water did its worst, her arms raised to save her from each shock. After much cajoling, she plunged in. With short strokes, they swam until they could breathe more easily. Above the trees they saw a barge preparing to set sail from Landermere Quay. It was no doubt destined for London.

The city seemed a million miles away. They had heard tales of the great poverty there and of the terrible fate of the fallen women, but also of theatres and museums and dances. These were the stuff of their childhood imaginings.

'And now I may go to London one day, Kitty. The Parditers have connections there, through Mr Parditer's silver work.' Sarah had barely paused for breath over the prospects for her future. Kitty smiled patiently. When Sarah got on to the evening's proceedings, Kitty offered to bring flowers for her hair from her mother's garden.

'And you must make sure they are lasters, Kitty,' she called as she waded for the bank. 'I don't want drooping flowers all over my head.'

The tide was on the turn and with it the weather. A cold breeze was rising. Sarah now stood shivering in her sodden undergarments. 'Are you coming?'

'Not yet,' Kitty called. 'You get home, I will be over later.' Sarah pulled her cloak around her, slipped on her shoes, and scurried away.

Kitty now took longer strokes out into the deep. Pa always said she swam like a boy. She was strong, and she liked that about herself. She watched as the billowing barge released itself from the small quay and made its way towards the open sea. Soon the swell of the ship's wake beneath her reminded her that the quay side traders would soon be dispersing, so she swam hard for the shore. The silky grey muds now lay between her and dry ground. There was nothing for it but to pick her way through the purple sea heather toward the bank.

'Here, it doesn't look too bad over here.' It was Richard, the elder of the Thompson twins. He was holding out his hand. She took it and clambered on to the bank. He snatched up her cloak and offered it to her. 'Looks like you got caught there.'

He stood averting his eyes in an over exaggerated way while she wrapped herself in the dry fabric.

'Yes indeed.' She had to smile.

'You see, it is always best to swim before high tide, so you don't get caught in the mud.' He was one for stating the obvious.

'I know. I was just . . . '

'You could get into serious trouble if you are not careful.' He began to explain all the dangerous states of the backwater's mud.

She had to interrupt him, 'If you will excuse me, Richard, I must be on my way.'

'Walk with you, shall I?'

Why, oh why had she not left when Sarah did? 'No thank you, Richard, it is very kind of you.' Remembering that you had to be clear with the Thompson twins, she added, 'I am getting rather cold, so I'm going to run home anyway. You go on your way and I will be fine.' Kitty set off at a pace, leaving him blathering on behind her about being careful or some such thing. She didn't have time for this, there was still much to be done before the celebrations began. Grateful that the wind was at her back, she hurried home.

On arriving at the old chestnut, she saw Tom in the yard loading barrels on to a cart. Kitty tried to make it to the kitchen door without being noticed.

'Afternoon, Kitty.' He was giving her one of his smiles. 'Have you been leading my sister astray again?'

'If you'll excuse me, Tom, I have much to do.' She couldn't think why she was being so formal.

'Looks like washing your feet wouldn't be a bad start.' He laughed as he climbed on to the cart. 'See you at the festivities?'

'Yes, of course.' She was irritated by such an obvious question. And irritated at herself for getting so muddy.

At the well, she washed her feet as best she could. It took some time to remove the mud from between her toes. By the time she was wrapped in a dry blanket with a warm drink in her hands, made especially for her by Peggy, things did not seem so bad.

Once dressed and with all her duties performed, Kitty made her way to the garden where Mother was gathering the last of the summer flowers. Ma was at her happiest when tending her plants. It was as if she opened in her garden, in a way she rarely did elsewhere. The garden itself was dry now and obviously at the end of its season, but Mother tended every last little bud of hope.

'Look,' she said, holding out the head of a bright yellow flower, 'beautiful isn't it, Kitty?'

'It's lovely, Ma.' Kitty softened in response. Looking around at her mother's domain, she saw that it was indeed beautiful. Alongside the ordered beds were neat piles of discarded plants that had served their purpose, waiting for old Mr Morepig to remove them to the compost. In the long beds, onions, roots and the remaining greens still clung to their growing. Tall autumn flowers bobbed their heads in the breeze.

Ma turned to see her looking. 'You loved being with me in the garden when you were a little girl, do you remember?' Kitty nodded as the sense of her childhood came rushing back. Her mother's brow furrowed as she lifted her hand to Kitty's cheek and held it there. 'I don't think I have told you often enough, but you are a fine young woman, Kitty, don't ever let that fade.' Kitty wondered what she could mean. 'Promise me.'

'I can't promise that, Ma, that's for God to decide.'

'Perhaps it is, Kitty, perhaps it is.' She turned away to pick up a basket draped with the last of the summer flowers. 'Now, get along to Joseph's and adorn the cart, you and Sarah always do it so beautifully.' As Kitty took the basket, Ma lifted a little bunch of yellow and white flowers. 'These are for Sarah's hair.'

'Thank you, Ma, they are lovely.' Kitty turned to walk to the gate.

Ma called after her, 'Kitty… Sarah's young man, do you know him?'

'I've met him once or twice. He seems nice enough. Why do you ask?'

'I know his mother a little, she helps out with the collection for the poor. She's a strange little creature, uncertain somehow.' Kitty couldn't help smiling, her mother never commented on other people. After a moment her mother added, 'But perhaps we are all a little strange, in our way.' That was more like her.

Kitty hovered, reluctant to leave. It would have been good to go on talking with Ma like this, in her soft place, but there were things to be done. 'You will be coming to the feast, Ma?' But Mother didn't hear, she was already lost in her own world.

Joseph's yard was a hive of activity: young Mark was brushing down the old cart horse, Sarah's aunt Mary was chasing a chicken, looking less than amused, and a couple of girls were scrubbing unwieldy barrels, giggling all the while. Sarah was sitting on the back of the cart twiddling the ends of her unruly hair. Kitty lifted the basket onto the cart and climbed up beside her. She told her of her encounter with Richard and how she had got so muddy. Unusually, Sarah made no response. Instead she picked up the swathe of hay she had been working on. Kitty joined her in her endeavours. The familiar feel of the drying hay as it gave way to her fingers never failed to please Kitty. They worked in silence for some time. Aunt Mary caught her chicken, the young girls were now lugging the barrels into the barn, and the old nag snorted as Mark continued to brush her down with a tender touch.

Kitty remembered the flowers. 'Ma's picked some beautiful flowers for us, look.' She reached back and gathered the little posy for Sarah's hair. 'And she picked these especially for your hair.'

'Oh, they are lovely.' Sarah held them to her nose for a moment, sighed and returned them to the basket. 'Do thank her for me, but I shan't be needing them.'

'Why not?'

'I had a visit from Nathaniel's mother today.' Sarah jumped down and began draping the swathe over the sides of the cart.

'What did she want?'

'Nothing much.' Sarah was struggling to get the swathe to stay, so Kitty jumped down to help.

'What did she say?'

Sarah explained without looking up, 'She said she wanted to help me prepare for becoming Nathaniel's wife. She explained that her husband is a very pious man and set a high store on propriety.' Kitty's heart sank as Sarah continued, 'I will go to their church once we are married. It will be only right. So I might as well start learning their ways.'

'Their ways?' Kitty was bemused.

'They are Huguenots, Kitty, you know that, and apparently, for them, it is appropriate to wear a cap on such occasions.'

'Why? This is not church, it is just us, as we have always been, here in the village.'

'Mrs Parditer said ... '

'Blow what Mrs Parditer said. At the church ceremony you can wear the appropriate attire, this is just us, and besides, you have got such beautiful hair, it would be a real shame to ... '

Now Sarah was insistent, 'My mind is made up, Kitty. I have my Sunday best, that will do well enough, and anyway, it will do me good to learn from my betters.'

'Your betters!' This wasn't Sarah speaking and it infuriated Kitty. 'Is that what she said?'

'No, of course not, she was sweet, and only trying to help.' Kitty just shook her head and turned away. Sarah sighed. 'Come on, Kitty, don't make this harder than it already is. I've thought about it, of course I have, but it is a very good match for someone like me, you know it is.'

'A match at any price!' Kitty was not going to let it go so easily.

'Honestly, Kitty, sometimes I think you know nothing of the ways of ordinary people like me. It is a good match and Nathaniel is a good man, and father is delighted, which pleases me. Can that not be enough?'

Kitty was silent.

'And anyway, Nathaniel's father does not usually attend such village occasions, he is doing it for Nathaniel's sake, so I need honour him for it, you must see that.'

Kitty wasn't much comforted, but seeing, for the first time, how her girlish friend had grown into a faithful and strong young woman, she took Sarah's small hands in hers. 'Just promise me one thing ... that you won't let them change you too much.'

Sarah smiled. 'I will do my best, but I am going to need you, you know that.' Kitty nodded in response.

Joseph called out across the yard as he marched past, on his way to the house. 'They will be lighting the fires soon, you had better get that finished. We don't want to be late.'

Now they looked, they realised that the sun was going down fast. They turned their attention to the cart and were soon standing back to admire their work. They agreed that it looked particularly pretty this year, just as they agreed every year.

Once they had tidied away, Sarah picked up the little posy of flowers. 'Do you think your ma would mind if I kept these?'

'No, of course not.'

'It is only they would look so pretty in a jar on our table.'

'You keep them, they were meant for you.' Kitty scooped up the basket.

Sarah caught her arm. 'Until today, I had not really thought what my betrothal would mean.' Neither had Kitty. They stood silently for a moment, feeling together the uncertainty of the future as only true friends could.

Alone now, Kitty sat at her table arranging her own hair in a simple ribbon. She pinched her cheeks to bring some much needed colour to them when her pa called from below to announce the arrival of the cart. He was waiting at the bottom of the stairs looking fine in his better jacket and clean boots.

Ma stood in the kitchen door, smiling. 'You go on ahead, I will be along soon.' She preferred to walk and always came late to such occasions.

Kitty took Pa's arm as they stepped out into the evening air. The white flowers adorning the cart seemed to glow in the blueing light. Joseph was sat atop in the driving seat. Aunt Mary was seated behind him. Old Miss Dobson, who tended the bees, was next to her. Dairy Daphne and her gaggle of children were on the other side. Kitty took her place next to Sarah who sat at the back looking radiant, despite the cap. Pa hauled himself up next to Joseph.

After initial greetings, the little party fell silent as the cart lumbered along the earth hard track. It had been an unusually dry September. The fields were now stripped and ready for the turning. Smoke from the fires curled above the darkening bushes. Eventually the cart jolted and much laughter ensued as the old nag drew her burden into the clearing. All around familiar, expectant faces gathered.

Once the party had dismounted, Pa leapt up into the back of the cart and the crowd hushed. Pa looked for all the world like one of the noble characters in one of Kitty's books. He thanked everyone for their hard work, then invited Reverend Styles to give thanks. He was never very comfortable at such occasions. After a rather long-winded prayer, Pa welcomed everyone to take a sup of Ma's honeyed cider, and called out, as was the tradition, 'Let the festivities begin.'

There was a cheer. The fiddle started to play. Pa leapt down from the cart, took Kitty's hand and led her to start the dancing. Soon many had joined them and more were drinking. This is what they had all been looking forward to. The elderlies sat at the edges, watching with wistful remembrance. Children ran to and fro whilst the men huddled round the cider dray. Kitty noticed Nathaniel's family standing awkwardly at the back. Joseph and Sarah stood with them. Tom was nowhere to be seen. Nathaniel's father was in a black coat and fine wig with a hat perched on top of it. His mother was wearing a dark dress with a neat lace collar and matching cap. No-one was speaking. When the music stopped, Kitty suggested to her Pa that they should greet the Parditers. He suggested that a cup of mother's cider would do them good. Kitty was not so sure.

'It is good to see you, William,' Father offered as he approached the gathering.

'Robert.' Nathaniel's father nodded.

'You must excuse this informal greeting; Kitty and I always start the dancing. It has been a tradition ever since she was a little girl.'

'That's nice, is it not, my dear?' Mrs Parditer clutched her husband's arm.

Mr Parditer retained his formality regardless of the occasion. 'I trust the harvest has gone well?' This was going to be hard work.

'It has indeed, thank you for asking.'

Mrs Parditer looked hopefully at her husband's face. 'We have been looking forward to Nathaniel and Sarah's country hand-fasting, have we not, William?'

He smiled briefly. 'When might the ceremony be taking place?'

'As soon as we are all here, there are one or two stragglers, I am afraid, including my wife.' Pa laughed out loud at his poor joke.

Joseph interjected, 'A farmer's wife has much to do on such a day. I expect she is readying herself as we speak.'

'Of course.' Mrs Parditer smiled. 'Hard work is God's work after all.'

The music started up again, a gentler ballad this time. Sarah looked hopefully at Nathaniel, who looked at his parents, then at Sarah and back again. Eventually he allowed himself to be led towards the dance. He was the most awkward young man Kitty had ever come across; she couldn't help smiling at the sight of him as he stumbled towards the circle looking so devotedly at his young wife-to-be.

Joseph engaged the Parditers in conversation. Kitty drifted away, allowing the warm alcohol to soften her sight. Sparks flew up from the fire and extinguished on the breeze. Familiar faces rolled in front of her as they wove in and out in their circle dance. Young men were enjoying a joke and laughing uproariously by the fire. The poor Thompson twins looked on bemused; they never quite got the joke. Kitty perched on the end of the cart, tired now from the weeks preceding. Finally, Pa broke away and joined her.

He leant in close, whispering, 'Promise me, Kitty, that you will never, never marry someone from a family like that.'

Kitty laughed. Just then, Mother's face appeared in the glow of the fire. Pa noticed her and immediately left Kitty to greet his wife. The firelight softened her features somehow and she smiled. Her long brown hair was tied in a braid over one shoulder, with a single bloom at the nape of her neck.

For the first time, Kitty could see her ma in her father's eyes. Ma's wrap had slipped from her shoulders; Pa picked it up and wrapped it around her in the way he used to wrap Kitty as a child. There was a tenderness between them that Kitty rarely saw these days.

The cart jolted as Dairy Daphne's oldest two jumped aboard in a game of chase, quickly followed by Daphne scolding them for their riotous behaviour. She apologised to Kitty and dragged them away, but they slipped from her grasp and disappeared into the woods. Daphne gave up and joined old Miss Dobson who was cooing over the littlest babe.

Kitty sat there for some time watching familiar scenes pass before her. Everything seemed strange to her tonight, she could feel herself committing everything to memory. Just as she was beginning to relax into the evening, she spotted the Parditers talking with Ma and Pa and looking around, presumably for Nathaniel and Sarah, who were nowhere to be seen. Thankfully, Kitty caught a glimpse of Sarah as they emerged from the darkness of the trees. Her cap was not quite all it should have been; strands of hair had escaped and were tumbling about her pretty face. Kitty slipped quickly to her side while Nathaniel straightened his jacket and made his way to join his parents.

'He kissed me, Kitty,' Sarah whispered, breathing hard.

Kitty tucked the wayward curls back into Sarah's cap. 'What was it like?'

Sarah thought for a moment then said simply, 'Wet.' Kitty couldn't help laughing. Sarah added, 'I've had better.'

Kitty held Sarah at arm's length to check her appearance. 'I should not worry. He is, no doubt, a novice. Now off you go.' She gave Sarah a reassuring smile and turned her towards the awaiting Parditers. Kitty stayed on the perimeter of the proceedings, not much feeling like being a part of it all today. There was a hush as Pa addressed the crowd. Nathaniel and Sarah stepped forward. She could not hear what was said, neither did she want to.

Kitty gasped as a hand took hold of hers. It was Tom. He had his finger to his lips as he drew her back into the shadows. 'Come on, let's get away from all this.' He pulled her round the bushes and on to the path towards the backwaters. As the voices faded behind them, he let go of her hand and ran into the centre of the field, swirling around and around, arms outstretched. He had obviously found the cider earlier.

'Look, Kitty, look at the stars.' He suddenly stood still, gazing up at the sky. 'Isn't it beautiful?' She looked up. It was dark now, the air quite still.

'You are such a fool, Tom,' she said, pleased that some things don't change.

'Look,' he insisted, 'come here and look.' Kitty picked her way across the field until she stood beside him. He had the same wayward hair as his sister, and tonight it was particularly so. She craned her neck to look up again.

'Not like that.' He took her hands and lifted them till they were outstretched. The stars were beginning to show themselves. Wispy clouds veiled the moon. He was right. It was a beautiful night. Tom started twirling once more, slowly at first then gathering speed. She followed suit. It made her feel light, like a child again, watching the universe spin before her. She stumbled, but he caught her and they fell together to the unforgiving ground, helpless with laughter. This was what she needed, the fresh air of unrestrained hilarity.

They lay there for some time, in the silence of the night, breathing in the cool air. A ballad drifted on the breeze, one of the old songs which they sang every year, probably led by Jacob, the shepherd. He had a gift with the song. Kitty started to feel guilty for being away from the party and went to sit up.

Tom took her hand. 'Don't go yet, they won't miss us.'

She lay back down, deciding not to care. Though the ground was hard beneath her, everything else about this evening was soft, somehow. With his eyes set on the starry sky Tom spoke again, 'You are very beautiful, you do know that, don't you, Kitty?'

She was quite taken aback. 'Don't be silly,' she said, acutely aware that he was still holding her hand.

'Why is it silly?' His voice was flat.

'Because . . . ' she said, looking away but unwilling to say more while the feel of his touch moved something within her.

'Because what?' It was he who let go of her hand as he lifted himself to face her.

She looked at him. 'You are Tom, Sarah's little brother.'

'Not that little,' he said with a smile, 'there is barely a year between us.' The smell of cider on his breath was compelling.

Kitty studied him awhile, and realised something she hadn't noticed before, that all three of them had changed. Sarah had become a capable young woman, Tom was becoming a man, of that she was acutely aware, and she . . . was she changing too? She sat up, hugging her knees. It was cold. Tom noticed her shiver. He shook out her shawl and placed it around her shoulders, letting his arm linger.

'Kitty?' It was Richard Thompson, calling from the path. 'Your pa's looking for you.'

She jumped up, brushing the dirt from her skirts, and called, 'Tell him I am coming.' Richard ambled away. This was all wrong. Besides his youth, Tom wasn't at all the kind of man she would marry, if she was ever to do such a foolish thing. And besides that, she had her position as Robert's daughter to consider. Looking up, she saw Tom now standing before her looking uncharacteristically uncertain. 'I am sorry, I did not mean to embarrass you.'

'Don't worry,' she said, adjusting her hair, 'I expect it is the cider.'

As she walked away, he caught her hand again. 'But it is true, you know, you are very beautiful. I just wanted you to know that. I sometimes wonder if anyone tells you, that is all.'

Kitty softened. 'Thank you, Tom, that is very sweet of you, but I'd better get back.' She let her hand drop and hurried away.

By the time she had returned to the gathering, the food was being shared. Sarah and Pa were saying goodbye to the Parditers. Kitty did not join them but instead went to find Mother who was sitting with Old Miss Dobson as she told stories of giants and dragons to the delight of the children. The sound of her voice soothed Kitty's rather shaken nerves. Once the Parditers had left, Sarah came to join the storytelling. She peeled off her cap, shook out her hair and let her head sink onto Kitty's shoulder. Nothing need be said. The rest of the evening was spent in the embrace of the womenfolk of the village as they gossiped and talked of the very practical things of life, like births and deaths and marriages.

After some hours, when the fires were low and only the stragglers remained, Kitty and Pa sat by the fire enjoying the last of its warmth. She got to thinking about her mother who had wandered home earlier.

'Pa?'

'Hmm?'

'Ma seems better than she was. She is a bit better isn't she, Pa?'

'Yes, I think she is.' He picked up a stick and started poking at the embers. 'Ma and I have sorted out something that had been … ' Kitty waited as he searched for words. 'Sometimes things come between husband and wife and seem to get stuck there, like an unwelcome guest.' Kitty had rarely thought about it, but as he spoke, she realised the toll her mother's grief must have taken on her pa.

'When we met, it was on an evening just like this. Your ma was staying with her cousins. They came to our harvest gathering.

When I arrived, she was sitting on a log, the firelight dancing across her face. The first thing I noticed was her smile. Reckon I was smitten right there and then.' He threw the stick on to the dying embers and it flickered into flame. 'God, it is good to see her smile.'

They walked arm in arm on the way home. Pa suddenly stopped, looked up and said, 'Look at the stars, Kitty, aren't they beautiful tonight?'

She wished he had not said that, as embarrassment tinged the edges of a perfect night.

Chapter Three

Two hard winters had come and gone. The first winter was particularly severe; livestock were lost and the poor suffered terribly. The second was little better. Thankfully, the third winter was milder and the land and its people were beginning to heal. The awkwardness between Kitty and Tom had long since passed. He was still the Tom who liked to drink with his friends and could charm any young farm girl who lifted her eyes to him. But the emptiness that Sarah had left in her going made space for their friendship to blossom; a friendship forged in the hardships of the winters passed.

Sarah had married Nathaniel Parditer soon after the betrothal. They started out living with his parents, but once she was with child, they found a little cottage in Thorpe le Soken and settled down. It was just as Kitty had feared. The Parditers were a peculiar type of people and kept Sarah close. She was already carrying their third child. The first was a boy called Nathaniel, after his father. The second was a little girl called Jane who had the same wayward curls as her mother. Not that Kitty had seen them often, their visits together had been scarce.

Today had been a long day. The relentless rains had stopped, giving way to the March winds which would no doubt dry the ground soon enough. But until then, every task undertaken was weighed with mud. As Kitty trudged home from checking on old Jacob and his early lambers, she passed the orchard and noticed green shoots coming up under Ma's apple trees. She was happy to see that spring was on its way at last.

As she crossed the courtyard, she saw her mother standing in the back door. 'Come, Kitty, we have a visitor.'

'Who is it?' Kitty started to untie her boots.

'It's the Reverend Gough from Thorpe.' Mother started tugging at Kitty's sleeve, causing her to hop on one leg.

'Give me a moment, Ma, please.' Kitty couldn't think for the life of her what all the fuss was about. In recent years, the Reverend Gough had become firm friends with Pa and so was often on the farm. In fact, Pa said he thought that the reverend preferred it to the church.

A burst of giggles came from the kitchen. This pleased Kitty, for he had evidently brought the children with him. They were dear little things and it always lifted Kitty to be in their presence.

She turned to her mother who was anxious to hurry her on. 'You go, Ma, I'll be in in a minute.' Ma hesitated, then seeing Kitty would not be hurried, she went to the kitchen. Kitty washed her hands and looked at her skirts, which were splattered with mud, but there was nothing to be done, so she followed on.

Pa was leaning against the mantle. Reverend Gough sat at the far end of the table. His two younger boys, David and Jonathan, were on the bench beside him. Their eyes, which barely poked over the top of the table, were fixed on Ma, who was now cutting what was left of the currant cake.

'Ah, Kitty, it is good to see you.' Alexander Gough was not at all like the vicars she had known before. He was informal, some would say almost to the point of impropriety.

Kitty smiled. 'And you, Reverend Gough, you are looking well.'

'I am, thank you, Kitty, as are these scoundrels.' His youngest daughter sat on his lap and laughed as he tickled her tummy. It was only then that she noticed his older daughter sitting on the settle by the fire, fiddling with a little wooden figure. Kitty sat beside her.

'And what have you got there, Rachel?'

'It's a horse.' Her eyes shone with pleasure as she held it out to Kitty. It was a rough-hewn animal but recognisable. 'My pa made it for me.'

Reverend Gough blushed, a colour at odds with his red hair. 'It's a terrible replication, I'm afraid.'

Pa laughed. 'A noble effort, I'd say.'

Kitty reassured the girl, 'It's a fine horse, isn't it, Rachel? Made even more special because your pa made it.' Rachel looked adoringly at her father and hugged her coveted treasure to herself. 'And Michael, where is he today?'

His father replied, 'He is studying. That boy is too keen on study, I fear.'

Ma stepped forward. 'Actually, Kitty, it's the children that Alexander has come to talk to you about.'

'Me?' Kitty now realised that everyone's eyes were on her.

Reverend Gough put little Esther down, who padded towards her older sister. 'Well … as you know, Kitty, my mother has been looking after the household since we lost Elizabeth, when little Esther was born.'

Kitty responded with polite assent. He continued, 'Her health has not been so good lately, and she would like to go and stay with my sister for a while, down in Dorset, where the weather is more clement.' He looked to Mother. 'Your Ma tells me that you know well the ways of a household.'

Kitty looked at her Ma. 'Well, yes, I suppose so. But I know the farm better.'

He smiled. 'Indeed, you are a hard worker, Kitty, there's no doubt about that. But I was wondering if I might persuade you away from the farm for a while, in order to help us out, just while my mother is away, of course.'

Ma was keen. 'It would be a wonderful opportunity for you to get away from the farm for a bit.'

Kitty was wary. 'What would you need me to do?'

'I was wondering if you might come and look after the home and the children. Temporarily, of course.'

'But what about Beth, doesn't she care for the children?'

'Yes, indeed she does, and she is a wonderful help, but there are five of them and I would like the older two to take up a little learning. I've seen how well you get on with the children, Kitty, and I know you are well learned.'

Kitty looked at her father. 'But how would you manage, Pa?' Her father didn't reply but stared into the fire, his foot playing with the fallen logs.

Ma interjected, 'We would manage well, would we not, Robert?'

Reverend Gough ploughed on, 'You see, the thing is, Kitty, that if I don't find someone to help me out soon, the parish worthies will take over, and that wouldn't do at all!'

Pa laughed and shook his head.

Kitty's thoughts were flying. 'What about the village school?'

'Our school is... well, it's wonderful for the village and I am grateful for it, but there is little they can learn outside of writing and numbers and I would like my children to know a little bit more of the world.'

'Oh, Reverend Gough, I know so little of the world myself, what could I teach them?'

'Your mother tells me that you are well read and always take an interest in things.' It seemed that mother had already decided for her.

Reverend Gough continued, 'There will be pay, of course. It would not be much, but I'm sure we could come to some arrangement that would suit us both.'

Kitty was silent, determined not to fall into Mother's trap too easily, even though the offer was rather intriguing. 'For how long would you need me?'

'About four months, or a little longer if necessary.'

'Four months!' Kitty was taken aback. 'That's the whole of the summer.' What kept her going through the long winter months was the joy of summer on the farm.

Mother spoke again, 'The gardens are so lovely during the summer. And you can help with the rectory picnic.'

Kitty knew what Mother was thinking. Once or twice she had suggested that Kitty was losing her bloom, and that it was time she found a suitor. She'd be more likely to find one in Reverend Gough's company than at the farm.

Reverend Gough spoke again, 'Of course, if it doesn't suit I will put out an advertisement. I simply thought I would ask you first, Kitty, because I know how fond the children are of you. I've watched you with them, you are so easy with little ones.'

As if on cue, Esther took hold of her hand. She stroked the chubby little fingers that wrapped around hers. 'May I think about it, Reverend Gough?'

'Of course.' He stood, scooping Esther into his arms. 'Take your time, I will call again in a couple of days and we can talk further.' He turned to his family. 'Come on, everyone, let's leave these good folks to their day.' Rachel gathered the boys as Alexander led his small tribe to the door.

Father followed them. 'I'll take you on the trap, it's a long way for the little ones.'

Alexander raised his hand. 'Thank you, Robert, but we will walk, it is a fine day.' He stepped outside with Mother and Father following. Kitty watched them through the window as they said goodbye. Alexander put the little one on to Rachel's back, scooped the youngest boy on to his own shoulders and strode away. He was, without question, a good father.

Kitty did not know what to make of it all. On the one hand it would be good to be in Thorpe le Soken, which was a thriving village, and she would be close to Sarah, so maybe they could find time to spend together. On the other, to be away from the farm for so much of her time was unthinkable. She had sometimes dreamt of leaving the farm, but it had never been a dream that she particularly wanted to fulfil. She could hear Ma and Pa speaking in the hallway in whispers. She hated the thought of them talking about her. She was a child no longer and should surely have some say in her future.

Just as Ma came into the kitchen, Peggy came in from the washroom. 'I just passed the vicar and his brood marching up the lane. Been for a visit, have they?'

'Yes,' Mother replied, 'he's asked for Kitty to go and help educate the children at the parsonage while his mother is away. It's a wonderful opportunity for her.'

Peggy looked at Kitty who was fiddling with the hem of the curtain. 'Is it now?'

Mother continued, 'Of course it is, you know it is, Peggy.'

'People like Kitty have got to do what's inside them to do, and that's no mistake. If they don't it'll only cause harm.' Peggy turned away to her chores.

'Is that right?' Mother looked tired and a little defeated at fighting her cause. 'You think seriously about it, Kitty. It is only up the road, and besides, you don't know who you might meet.'

Kitty had to speak. 'Mother, I am not looking to be wed.'

'You'll have to one day, Kitty. It's all very well you working here with your pa, but you could do so much better. You are a beautiful woman, but no man will see that whilst you spend your time covered in mud. I mean … look at you.'

Pa stood in the door. 'Leave her alone, Judith. She said she'd think about it, and she will. It is up to Kitty what she does.'

'But, Robert … ' her mother started.

'And anyway … ' Pa straightened up, keeping his eyes firmly on her mother, ' … one day, the farm will be hers.'

Kitty was bemused. 'What do you mean, Pa?'

He now turned to her. 'I have been seeing to my affairs, Kitty, and have decided to leave the farm to you when I am gone, if that is what you would like.'

Mother's voice was now raised, 'But, Robert, you said … '

'I know what I said, Judith, but Kitty is our … our flesh and blood, yours and mine, and nothing is going to change that.'

He stepped close to Kitty, taking her gently by the shoulders, his brown eyes upon her. 'You think about it, Kitty. The work suits you. I think you would do well.' Picking up his jacket, which had lain on the bench, he added, 'If you decide to go to Thorpe, we will talk about it further on your return. But if you do not, then we will still have the pleasure of your company.

Either way, think about it.' He looked at Mother, a look of defiance that Kitty had rarely seen.

Mother's face hardened. 'That's not fair, Robert, you know how hard this life is, you know how much toll it has taken on us, keeping all this going through foul weather and fair. And you'd tie your only daughter to that?' Then she added pointedly, 'Our only child.' Her hand went to her mouth and she turned away. Father hesitated for a moment then marched out through the washhouse into the yard.

Mother looked exhausted. 'Peggy, I'm going to the parlour, could you bring me one of your herbal brews? I have a headache coming on.'

'Of course.' Peggy, who had remained inconspicuous in her tasks, now swung the kettle over the fire and sighed.

Kitty could barely understand what had just happened. She stood looking at the open door through which her mother had stepped moments before. Suddenly, she knew what she must do. Turning to Peggy, she asked, 'Did you see Tom on your way back?'

Peggy gave Kitty a reassuring smile. 'He is with Richard Thompson at Miss Dobson's cottage, making repairs by the look of it. If you hurry you should catch him.'

Kitty wrapped her shawl around her, tied her boots and stepped out into the mud once more. As she went, she let the cool breeze give space for her thoughts. For the first time in her life, she felt pulled between her parents. The thought of owning the farm one day filled her with excitement and fear in equal measure. It was the life she knew and loved, but would she ever manage without her pa beside her? On the other hand, there was part of her that wanted to expand her horizons and see what a different life would be like. Maybe this opportunity to spend the summer in Thorpe le Soken would help her make that decision. But the summer was coming and she loved the farm, so why would she go?

As she approached Miss Dobson's cottage, she could see Tom and Richard hanging a new door. Kitty watched them a moment. Tom was always so patient with the Thompson twins. Kitty could hear Richard droning on.

Mrs Dobson stood by, leaning on her stick. Kitty greeted her, 'Good morning, Mrs Dobson, I see you are getting a new door.'

'That I am, Kitty. The last one took a battering these winters past.'

Tom and Richard stood aside to admire their work. Mrs Dobson thanked them heartily and invited Richard inside for 'a nice bit of honeyed bread.' He took little persuading.

Kitty went to Tom's side. 'Hello, Tom.' She heard herself sigh.

Tom gave her a look. 'Let me tidy up here and we'll walk back together.' She was relieved she had found him. He always made sense of things for her, seeing life in such an uncomplicated way. But seeing Tom reminded her how much she missed Sarah, and how she longed for such female intimacy again.

Tom picked up his bag of tools and opened the gate for her. As they walked, Kitty told it all to Tom, and he listened. When she told him about going to the rectory, she hoped he would tell her not to go. Perhaps she hoped he would tell her that he could not do without her, but he didn't. Instead he encouraged her that it was only for a short time and then simply said, 'You must make up your own mind on this, Kitty. And maybe your mother is right, maybe you'll find your match.'

Kitty was despondent. 'But what if I don't want a match?'

'Everyone wants a match, Kitty, even me.'

Kitty was astonished; he seemed to enjoy the life of a young man among many a pretty farm girl. She couldn't imagine him settled down and said as much.

'Oh, Kitty, you are naive sometimes. I know I like to have a bit of fun, as much as any man, but one day I will need to marry. My pa has made his way in the world, and I intend to do the same. I'll need a wife for that.' Thinking about it, Kitty realised that she had always known it to be so, but had never let the thought dwell. Tom went on, 'And as for you, if you don't find your match at the reverend's, when you come home you can tell your pa that you'd like to inherit the farm. You'd be set either way.' Tom was ever sensible.

They walked on in silence until Tom slipped in the mud. Kitty caught his arm to steady him and he righted himself. As he did so, he spoke once more, 'There is one thing for sure … '

'What's that?'

'When I look for a wife, it is going to be difficult to find a woman who is … ' He looked at her, his brow quizzical. For a moment a thought seemed to hang on his intake of breath. But then struck a ridiculous pose like the men in the paintings they had seen at the town hall. 'Who is equal to this incredibly handsome fellow.'

'Oh, you are a fool sometimes, Tom.'

He finished with a bow and set off towards the lane. Kitty followed on, laughing hard, he always cheered her up. When Tom left her at the gate that afternoon, he made Kitty promise to do her best to find a match. She promised, though reluctantly.

That evening, no more was said about Alexander's proposal or the inheritance and, for that, Kitty was grateful.

When she woke the next morning, it was still dark. The sound of the creaking timbers announced a gusty wind. She stepped out of bed and rubbed herself all over to gather some warmth as she padded to the window. The trees were bending this way and that. She dressed as quickly as she could and crept downstairs. Firelight from the kitchen spilt across the hall and onto the old chest that had been her grandmother's. As she approached the kitchen door, she saw her father sitting by the light of a single candle. He was studying a letter with eager eyes. Others were lying on the table and, beside them, a little wooden box lay open. Kitty stood in the shadows and watched for a while. She wondered what he might be searching for in that sea of papers. As Kitty stepped into the light, Pa looked up and started to gather the letters rather too quickly to halt Kitty's curiosity. She made her way to the fire.

Pa spoke first, 'Did you sleep well?'

'Quite well, thank you, Pa, despite the wind. Are you looking for something?'

He looked at the letters in his hand. 'No, it's just some old correspondence that I've kept for far too long. It was time I sorted it out.'

He folded a few and returned them to the box. Then clutching the remaining letters tightly in his fist, he joined Kitty at the fire and after only a brief hesitation, threw them into the flames. 'Well, that's that done.'

Pacing back to the table, he took up the box and placed it on the windowsill. 'Your ma's still asleep. She suffered from one of her headaches last night, I'll leave her to rest. She asked if you could make sure that Daphne has got everything she needs for the new cheese.'

'Of course.' Kitty pulled last night's pottage over the fire and bent to stir it. Another gust of wind rattled the windows.

Pa poured a drink from the pitcher. 'It's going to be a blowy one today. I do hope the piggery roof is holding, I must get young Peter on to that today.' The sky was paling now, dawn was on its way.

Kitty gathered dishes and joined her pa at the table. 'So,' he said, 'have you thought about Alexander's offer?'

Kitty had thought of nothing else. 'I think I want to take it. Perhaps it would be good for me to get off the farm for a while.'

Father leant back in his chair and studied her. She hoped she hadn't hurt him; hurting her pa was the last thing she would want to do. 'I love the farm, Pa, you know I do, it's all I've ever known, or wanted. But I'm a woman now, and I just wonder if I've lived too narrow a life … It would be good to meet other people and do something different.'

'What people?'

'I don't know … just other people. And Sarah's in Thorpe, maybe I'll see her more often.'

Pa leant forward, his brow furrowed as he took her hand in his, just as he had done so often over the years. 'I think I've let you down, Kitty. Ma has gone on at me often enough to find you a suitor, but I suppose it's always been half-hearted on my part. I enjoy your company, my Kitty Kat, perhaps more than a pa should.'

'No, Pa … '

'And perhaps your ma is right, and you'd do better to find a husband up at Alexander's.'

'I'm not looking for a suitor, Pa.' Kitty really wasn't, the whole idea put her at odds with herself. 'I just think that perhaps it would be good for me to do something else, just for a while. And it would only be over the summer months, so you shouldn't need me so much. Then I will be back before the harvest.'

'If that's what you really want.'

'It is.' She felt more certain as she spoke. 'But I am going to make it clear to Reverend Gough that I will need regular time off to visit home.'

'You better had, or Alexander will have me to answer to.'

'Thank you, Pa.' The smell of pottage called her to the hearth.

Pa continued, 'I'll miss you, Kitty, but you are right, you are a young woman now, and seem to know your own mind. But while you are away, remember to think over what I said yesterday. The farm will be yours when I am gone, if you want it.'

Kitty stirred the pottage and spooned it into the dishes. As she placed them on the table, she had another thought, something she should have thought of before, 'But what about Mother, should the farm not go to her?'

'She's not as strong as you, Kitty. She does very well with the household and domestic animals, but you, Kitty, you were made for this. I have no doubt you would do well.'

Kitty was overwhelmed at everything that was happening. Pa must have felt it because he took her arm and drew her to him. 'I'll tell you what, you go and have a bit of fun up in Thorpe, and when you come back, if you still feel you want the farm, I'll go to Jethro and we'll get it in writing. Now, sit down and eat, we have work to do.'

Pa ate, head down, with his mind inevitably now upon the tasks of the day. Kitty's mind wouldn't turn so easily, so many thoughts tumbled through her head. 'Shall I take Ma something to eat?'

Pa stood. 'No, leave her, she needs the rest.' He picked up the little box, which Kitty had quite forgotten about, and left the room.

Kitty rose to clear the dishes, but something caught her eye. It was a little piece of paper from father's burnings. Making sure he wasn't returning, she picked it up, blowing the ash from its burnt corner. There was nothing written on it that she could make out. Chuckling at her ridiculous nosiness, she threw the paper into the flames. She turned to see sun blushed clouds scurrying across the open sky, shifting and shaping as they went. Another day was at hand.

Chapter Four

It was Eastertide when Kitty found herself sitting alongside Tom on the way to the rectory. She had asked him to take her. They were easy together and would talk freely about nothing in particular, which she thought would make the short journey most pleasant. It proved to be so. The fields were busy with folks bent over the planting. The cows stood lazily under the spreading trees. Spring flowers punctuated the countryside in hopeful anticipation as the old trap rattled along the way.

Soon she found herself climbing the stone steps to the rectory door. It was impressive, if in need of a little attention. She looked back to see Tom sliding the trunk from the trap. Before she'd had time to knock, the door opened. She must have jumped because Reverend Gough stood before her, laughing. He had a pleasant, welcoming demeanour. He was nearly as tall as her pa and, Kitty reckoned, not far off her pa's age.

'I am so sorry, Kitty, I didn't mean to startle you. I saw you arriving.' He opened the door wide to reveal a young woman standing behind him, fiddling with her fingers.

He turned to her and spoke gently but directly, 'That's alright, Tilly, this is Miss Canham. She has come to help with the children.' Tilly stared. Just then, an older woman appeared behind her.

'How many times have I told you not to answer the door? Now come with me to the kitchen and we'll find you something to do.' She turned the young woman away as Reverend Gough stepped back to let Kitty in. He saw Tom standing at the bottom of the steps with Kitty's trunk.

'Just leave that here, would you? I'll deal with it.' Tom lugged it up the steps and placed it inside the door. Reverend Gough placed a little money in his hand. Kitty was embarrassed and didn't know how to explain. But Tom just grinned, doffed his cap and walked away down the path, whistling. Kitty shook her head and smiled to herself as she watched him go. She then turned and stepped inside.

The hall was large, its ceiling high. Elegant stairs climbed away to one side. At the top, the children stood, all talking at once. Beth was with them, struggling to keep order.

Reverend Gough closed the door. 'Bring them down, Beth, let them greet Kitty.' They broke away before his sentence was out. David strained from Beth's hand as she held him tight to keep him from falling. The littlest was in her other arm.

As the children reached Kitty, little Esther immediately put her arms out to be held. Kitty took her. Rachel stood beside her father, her pretty face awash with smiles.

Reverend Gough spoke, 'I think you know Beth?'

'Of course, how are you, Beth? You have an armful of care with these little ones.'

Beth looked relieved. 'Indeed I do, miss. We've been looking forward to your coming.'

Reverend Gough took Esther. 'Come, Kitty, come to my study where we will have a little peace and I can explain everything. Mother should be here soon and we will take refreshment… in the orangery I think.' He directed this last remark to another girl that Kitty hadn't noticed, standing by an open door. 'And ask Tom to take Miss Canham's chest to her room.'

Tom? For a second Kitty was bemused, but immediately realised that it must be referring to a different Tom, the name was common enough. The maid bobbed and headed for the kitchen. Reverend Gough kissed Esther's chubby little cheek and set her to the floor. Beth gathered the children and made for the stairs.

The reverend opened the door to his study. Kitty entered. It was shabby, but comfortable and lined with books. So many books. She hadn't realised that Reverend Gough was so learned. He led her to a seat by the fire. After initial pleasantries, he sat opposite her.

'Now, before we go any further, I would be very grateful if you would call me Alexander. I have known your father for some time now and I feel it appropriate.' He looked out of the window. 'I need friends here, Kitty. It's been a difficult time since we lost Elizabeth. The women of the village tend to treat me … How shall I put it? Charitably, but perhaps too much so.' He turned to her and smiled. 'And I feel sure, Kitty, that having known your family for some little while, we will be good friends.'

She was rather taken aback by his forwardness, but also by his openness. She did not know what to say, so remained silent but nodded a reassurance. He asked after her family, then spent a little while explaining something of his parish work, but suddenly he stopped. 'Do you play backgammon?' She followed his eyes to a wooden box on a small table by the fireplace.

'I'm afraid not.'

'Then I shall teach you, if that is acceptable to you?'

'Yes, thank you, I would like that.'

He seemed to relax. 'Good. That's settled then.' His eyes, which were an extraordinary grey-green, settled on her. He gave a smile that seemed to recognise her anxiety. 'You are not to worry about your duties. Mother will explain everything before she leaves on Monday.'

'On Monday?' Kitty was shocked; three days didn't seem long to learn everything she'd need to know.

'Yes, I apologise for the speed of her departure, but a friend is travelling to Bristol and has offered to take her.' He looked towards the door. 'Ah here she is now.' The door opened and in stepped a small woman with a bonnet tied under her chin in a most unforgiving manner.

'Alexander?' she offered, with her eyes on Kitty.

'Ah, this is Miss Canham, Mother.' Kitty stood up and turned around to face her.

'I am pleased to meet you, Miss Canham.' Then to Alexander, 'Are we taking refreshment?'

'Yes.' Alexander straightened in his mother's presence. 'In the orangery, I thought.'

'Very well.' Her shoes could be heard clomping across the hall, quite a noise for a small woman. Kitty turned back to Alexander, uncertain if she should follow. He looked just as uncertain.

'I think I'll take my tea here, I have work to do, and it will give you and Mother a chance to organise everything… and, Kitty, I am very grateful to you for coming.'

Kitty felt she must encourage him. 'Thank you, Rev… Alexander.' He smiled. 'But, I think I shall enjoy it very much.'

He led her to the door and indicated a passageway leading away beside the stairs. 'If you go down there, past the kitchen you will find the orangery. I'm afraid it's been a long time since it held exotics. It was added to the house in my predecessor's time. He was rather eccentric, I believe.' With that, he closed the door and left Kitty standing alone.

The hall, which was alive with welcome when she arrived, was now silent, apart from the ticking of the grandfather clock which accompanied her steps as she walked. The corridor was dark except for the light from a semi-glazed door that stood at the far end. She opened it to a room flooded with light. Never had she seen such a thing: high arching windows, set close together, lined the walls and views of the garden could be seen all around. A number of plants, in various states of health, adorned the space. To one side, refreshments were laid out on a small table at which sat Alexander's mother, evidently waiting patiently. Kitty wondered if she had dawdled, but thought not.

'So, Miss Canham … may I call you Kitty?' Kitty nodded in response. 'You are the daughter of Robert and Judith Canham, are you not? I have met your mother several times, she is a good woman. I believe she serves on the committee for the poor?'

'She does.' Kitty did not know what to make of Alexander's mother, so decided to give as little away as possible.

'And your father?'

'He is a yeoman farmer, Mrs Gough, in Beaumont.'

'So I believe.' She seemed to be scrutinising Kitty. She questioned her about the work she undertook at the farm and her understanding of running a household. Kitty answered as best she could.

Mrs Gough placed the cup on its saucer with finality. 'Well … my son seems to think that I need to take a break for my health.' Kitty thought she looked very well. 'He says that the work here is too much for me.' Her chin rose a little. 'Perhaps he is right. The fresh air of Dorset will do me good. And so, it seems that you are to run the house whilst I am away.' She continued to explain all her duties in meticulous detail.

As the woman spoke, Kitty found herself planning how she would do things differently. But she nodded in response and asked polite questions as seemed necessary. When all was said and done, Mrs Gough showed Kitty the house. It was plain in manner, but comfortable nonetheless. Occasional paintings and small tapestries adorned the walls. She was taken to the second floor where there were three rooms, one for Esther and the boys, one in which Beth slept and the third was for Kitty. Rachel and Michael had rooms below, along with their father and grandmother. Mrs Gough watched as Kitty entered the room that was to be hers. 'You will do well enough, Miss Canham. But please remember that Alexander has a position in the parish and those of his household must be without reproach.'

'Of course, Mrs Gough, I will do my utmost to be of use.'

'I am sure you will.' And with that, she left, closing the door behind her. Kitty breathed out as if for the first time. Removing her cap, she went to the window and opened it to let the cool air in. The garden lay before her, the trees budding with blossom and spring flowers poking their colourful heads out of the dark earth. Beyond that, the countryside looked lovely in the spring light. Kitty turned into the little room which was to be her home for the next few months. She was, after all, going to enjoy her time at the rectory.

It had been agreed that on the following morning Kitty would take an hour or two to herself to settle in. She knew what she was going to do with that precious time. Heading out of the back door and into a rather grey day, she made her way up the street. She had only visited Sarah's home once or twice on rather formal occasions. Most usually, Sarah had visited Kitty at home, when coming to see her father. But today, Kitty was so full of excitement knowing that Sarah was close by, she could not resist an impromptu call. Thorpe le Soken was not unfamiliar, Kitty had been there often enough, but today it looked different, as if she was seeing it for the first time. The wide street was bustling with people going about their business, and now Kitty was a part of it. Sarah had made a journey away from her family and now Kitty was on a journey of her own. She intended to share every moment of it with her friend.

As she passed the foundry, she almost tripped over a pig running in front of her. It snuffled and snorted as it went. An old woman, bent double, ran after it, snuffling and snorting in like manner. Kitty chuckled as the pig stopped and rooted through a pile of rotting vegetables. Kitty presumed that they must have fallen from a cart. The woman caught the pig, dragged it by a rope, swearing all the while, and disappeared into an alley.

A little further down the road, she stopped at the little cottage that had been her grandmother's. She had long-since passed but Kitty remembered the sense of her, and the warm bread that always welcomed them when they visited. Kitty had been named after her. Since Grandmother's time, a large window had been added to it. It was now a little shop. Kitty peered through the window at the ribbons and bobbins, lace collars and wool. The door opened, causing Kitty to jump. Two women emerged, bid Kitty good day, then disappeared up the street, twittering away as they walked.

Across the street stood Sarah's little cottage. For a moment, she was uncertain whether it would be appropriate to call, but decided that she would not be disturbing anyone for surely Nathanial would be at work. She knocked on the door. After waiting some little while, she knocked again. The door opened. To her surprise, Nathaniel stood before her, no longer the awkward young man she once knew him to be.

'Ah, Miss Canham, I've heard that you are staying at the rectory.'

'Yes, I arrived yesterday. I have been given a couple of hours this morning, to settle in, so I thought I must see Sarah before I start. I am not sure when I will be free again.' She heard a child's cry come from deep within the house. Was it her imagination or did Nathaniel step forward to block the door?

'Even so, Miss Canham,' he went on, irritatingly formal, 'it would be best to make an arrangement.'

Kitty was insistent, 'It would be only for a few moments.' He resolutely guarded the door, but she continued, 'I have a message from her father.'

He held out his hand. 'If you care to give it to me, I will see that she gets it.' Was he calling her bluff?

'It is of a personal nature.' She had always been determined not to lie, but Nathaniel was so infuriating, she felt it was justified. He stepped out of the house, forcing Kitty to step back into the street. He closed the door behind him and became almost conspiratorial. 'Miss Canham, Sarah's confinement has left her in a delicate state. She is not up to visitors. But we will be pleased to see you another time, with arrangement.'

Sarah was a robust woman; she could never be called delicate. Kitty pressed on, 'I do hope she is not unwell.'

'No, it is simply that her condition dictates that she needs to rest. I am sure you understand.'

Kitty did not understand but continued the charade. 'Of course, but if there is anything I can do to help, please do send for me.'

'We will, now if you don't mind, Miss Canham … '

She stared him down for a while, but soon realised it was hopeless. 'Very well, please do tell her I called.'

'I will.' He stepped back and disappeared inside, closing the door behind him. Once across the road, Kitty turned back to see Sarah in an upstairs window, watching her. Her friend lifted her hand in acknowledgement and quickly disappeared.

Kitty set off towards the rectory, lost in thought. Her friendship with Sarah had changed, of course it had, but now Kitty feared that she was losing it completely. She calculated Sarah's pregnancy to be no more than four or five months along; surely she would be well enough to see her friend. But there was nothing to be done.

The sun was now pushing the clouds apart and a light breeze blew. She was disappointed, of course, but the optimism of the day enabled Kitty to put the exchange with Nathaniel behind her. She would seek to see Sarah another time. As for now, she continued her walk back to the rectory taking in all the sights and sounds of her new home.

Before she entered and faced Mrs Gough's initiation, Kitty took a turn around the garden. There was a vast lawn sprawling around the house; two or three large trees offered a full canopy over the daffodil-strewn grass. A number of flowerbeds, neatly kept, wove around the greening bushes. She thought of her mother as she meandered, and how she would spend all her time at the summer fair, wandering in the garden and smelling the roses. How Kitty would love to see her mother as mistress of such a garden. Just then, the children burst out of the door, followed by Beth. They all ran this way and that, except for Michael, who lifted his head from his book and looked at her for a moment, before turning to walk in the other direction. In the door stood Mrs Gough in a sensible deep green dress with a fine lace collar; her hands were folded in front of her and her bonnet so tightly tied that Kitty couldn't help wondering if she was afraid of losing her head. She looked at Kitty. It was time to head inside and discover her fate.

Chapter Five

It was now the fourth Sunday in Eastertide. Kitty, Beth and the children headed towards the church. Kitty had always loved this time of year when green buds bloomed in the hedges and stories of resurrection abounded. This year was no different. Mrs Gough had been gone some three weeks and Kitty was beginning to settle into her situation. The household was small, so it was not too complicated. Mrs Carter, the cook, was a gentle but firm woman who, when occasion required, made remarkably delicate iced cakes, despite her large bosom that constantly threatened to undo her work. The young woman who was at the door when Kitty first arrived turned out to be Tilly, Mrs Carter's niece, who, she said, 'was a long time birthing and never quite recovered.' When her large family couldn't cope with Tilly, Mrs Carter had taken her under her wing. Then there was the other Tom, who they named Green Tom. He lived in the woods and wasn't too good with people, but wonderful with plants, by all accounts. He worked in the garden and undertook any heavy lifting and general mending. Mrs Carter was like a mother to them both. There were two young women from the village who came and went as needed. The household had been quite busy with various women from the parish who couldn't resist calling with some excuse or another to meet the rector's new housekeeper.

As they approached the church, Kitty became aware of the position that Alexander held. She had been so busy with the household that she hadn't had time to consider it before. St Michael's was much larger than her church in Beaumont and not half as pretty, but it was impressive. At the entrance, she stopped and let her eyes follow the tall, round tower as it disappeared into a perfect blue sky. The ancient brickwork was pitted with age.

'Impressive, isn't it?' A young woman, about Kitty's age, stood beside her looking up in like fashion.

'It is rather. It makes you wonder how they built it.'

The voice responded, 'It does indeed … and so long ago.'

They stood in silence for a moment, marvelling together at the tower, until Kitty turned to look at her companion. She was dressed in a fine blue coat. The sun was shining through the most delicate lace bonnet which framed her fine features in a halo of light. It was a stunning apparition causing a gasp to rise in Kitty's throat, but to her surprise, the woman gasped first. A small girl had run full pelt into her.

'Careful, my darling.' The little one danced away. 'She's high spirited, that one. It drives my husband mad. He says that girls should be demure, but I think that it shows signs of high intelligence, don't you agree?'

Kitty smiled in response. 'I do so agree. Why should a girl not enjoy her natural exuberance and curiosity?'

'Come, my dear.' Behind the woman a tall, elegant man appeared, offering his arm. Where the woman looked soft, there was something about him that appeared sharp. Kitty recognised him at once. He was Captain James Manley-Hogg from the Manor, and the woman, she now realised, was his wife. She flushed to think how boldly she had spoken and gave a little curtsy as Captain James led his family into the church.

Beth approached with the children who were all standing good as gold, dressed in their Sunday best. Kitty led them inside.

As she listened to Alexander preach, she was impressed with the authority he carried in office. It belied the informality by which she knew him. His message was always gentle but purposeful, unlike so many preachers she had heard. Today, he spoke of the love of Christ, as if he knew it. She was quite unarmed, until little Esther started squiggling in her lap. Beth took her and the boys out into the garden. Rachel shuffled along the pew and sat close to Kitty. She was beginning to hold a special place in Kitty's heart.

After the service, Rachel ran out to join her family. Kitty sat awhile, taking in her surroundings, especially the scene depicted in the mural above her. It was painted in the most exquisite colours. And anyway, today she was in no hurry to greet the locals. They were always too ready to engage her in tittle tattle. Once everything had quietened down, she made her way outside.

Her earlier companion had been waiting for her. 'I am so sorry, I didn't introduce myself earlier. My name is Eleanor Manley-Hogg.'

'Yes, I know … I mean … '

Thankfully Eleanor interrupted, 'Of course you do.' She smiled. 'And I believe that you are the young lady who is helping the reverend whilst his mother is away.'

'That's right.' Kitty straightened her collar. 'I am Kitty, Kitty Canham.'

'Pleased to meet you, Kitty. And your family?'

She hated that question and felt herself stand taller as she spoke, 'My father is Robert Canham, he's a farmer in Beaumont. A yeoman of the parish.'

To her surprise, Eleanor asked, 'What's it like to be brought up on a farm? Is it hard?'

What could she say in response? 'Hard at times, but also … wonderful. Well, it has been for me.'

'You must come to the house and tell me all about it. There are so few younger women who think of anything but hats and husbands. When we spoke at the tower, I knew that you had much to offer.'

Kitty was taken aback. 'Thank you, I would like that very much. But I am afraid that I only have certain days free.'

Eleanor looked over her shoulder at her husband who was waiting for her. 'Of course you do. But I am sure Reverend Gough will release you for me. I will see what I can arrange.'

Kitty had no idea as to how she would do that, but agreed. Eleanor left, leaving Kitty reeling. What a strange life it was. Until recently, she had never thought of anything but the farm, and now she was being invited to the Manor House.

Alexander came out of the church, divested of his vestments and ready to leave. 'Well, Kitty, it seems you are settling in quite well.'

'I am indeed. Mrs Manley-Hogg has invited me to visit her.'

'Really? That is kind.'

'I know, I just wondered if I should go, or … '

'Of course you should, Kitty, you are an intelligent young woman and quite her equal in everything but status.' He thread her arm through his own, and led her down the path. 'Between you and me, I believe her to be quite lonely up at the Manor; her husband is often away. She is surrounded by servants who bow to her in passing and young women who defer to her at every turn. She probably just wants a conversation with someone who knows their own mind. And you certainly know yours, Kitty Canham.'

With that, he turned and chased David down the path. Kitty chuckled to herself and followed after, smiling at her own good fortune.

Some days later, Kitty was on her way to have a note delivered to her parents, arranging to visit home on Sunday week. She was surprised how little she had thought of them. Her father had come by once or twice, but she had always been too busy to entertain him. Now, as she walked, she thought of her pa and, knowing how much he would be missing her, felt a pang of her own. Kitty also carried with her an acceptance to an invitation to the Manor for afternoon refreshment on the following Tuesday. Kitty had no pretensions, but she could not deny an excitement at the prospect of visiting the Manor.

Just as she was considering how it would be, she noticed Sarah walking down the other side of the street. Her head was low and she seemed far too busy to acknowledge anyone else. As she walked, little Nathaniel trotted beside her, trying to keep up. Kitty crossed the street to catch her.

When she was close enough, she called, 'Sarah?' Sarah looked around, her eyes wide. Kitty continued, 'I am sorry, Sarah, I didn't mean to startle you. How are you?'

Sarah didn't look directly at Kitty, but rather looked up and down the street. 'I am well, Kitty, thank you for asking.'

Kitty decided that the best policy was to behave normally. 'Did Nathaniel give you my message? I am working at the parsonage for a time and would love to visit you if I may, it's been such a long time.'

'I am glad you have found something worthwhile to do, Kitty.' Worthwhile? This wasn't Sarah speaking.

'Nathaniel told me that you were not well.'

Sarah now looked hard at Kitty. 'It's the nature of being with child, it makes me feel terrible, there is nothing to be done.' Little Nathaniel hopped this way and that. She tugged his arm. 'Will you keep still.' He obeyed as best he could. 'I'm afraid that I have not been up to visitors.'

'I'm sorry to hear that.' Kitty tried to lighten the mood and bent towards Nathaniel. 'And how are you, young man?' He disappeared into his mother's skirts.

Sarah softened. 'He is very well, aren't you, Nathaniel? So full of energy, it is quite exhausting.' She did indeed look exhausted. Kitty always thought that her friend was made for light and laughter, and now couldn't help wondering if there was any left in her.

Kitty asked again, 'Let me come and see you, Sarah. We are such old friends and I have so much to tell you.'

Sarah looked about her again before speaking. 'I take an early evening walk at four pm. For my health. You could join me this evening, if you like.'

'That would be lovely. Shall I come to the house?'

'No, meet me at the back of the church. At four o'clock.'

Kitty was determined to find a way. 'I'll be there.'

Sarah straightened. 'Now, if you'll excuse me, we must be on our way. Come along, Nathaniel.' She turned back the way she'd come and, without looking back, hurried away.

Alexander had understood when Kitty explained why she must see her friend. So at the given hour, she made her excuses and found Sarah waiting for her. It was a cold evening and a fine drizzle was in the air. Both women were wrapped in cloaks as they had been a few years before when they met to bathe in the backwaters. But this time they didn't take hands and run; this time they set off, almost strangers. They took the path through the woods where it was least muddy. Little was said. As they drew deeper into the woods, and the path got narrower, Sarah took the lead. As Kitty followed, she noticed how Sarah's shoulders were beginning to drop and, despite the difficult terrain, an ease was returning to her step. The two women made their way along a little trodden path, when they came upon a small lake that opened before them. Sarah picked her way along its tangled shore to a small clearing and took off her bonnet, shaking out her lovely hair.

'This is my haven,' she said as she sat on a fallen tree by the water's edge. Kitty joined her. It was certainly a place where you could breathe deeper. In the silence, they sat together for some time watching the skeeters hover over the surface of the green-grey water. A heron took off from the far shore, leaving ripples in its wake.

Sarah spoke again, 'Nathaniel never comes here, it's far too wild for him. He says it's unsafe. But I think that's what I like about it.' She stared across the waters.

Kitty ventured, 'Are you happy, Sarah?'

'It is not for me to be happy. It is my duty to obey God.' Then she smiled. 'Maybe a bit of happiness is good too.'

The Sarah she knew was beginning to appear and Kitty didn't want to lose her too quickly, so she spoke lightly, 'Indeed. Perhaps our happiness reminds us of God's existence.'

Sarah considered, 'When I am sat here, I have no doubt of it.' Just then, the sun broke through, throwing dappled light over the murky waters. 'Nathaniel is a good man, Kitty. He just… he likes things a certain way. He is like his father in that regard. He is most devout and it is for me to please him. Which I manage … some of the time.'

Kitty was unconvinced. 'It sounds like hard work.'

She replied simply, 'It is.'

A fat old toad jumped from a nearby rock, its legs sprawled. As it disappeared into the water, Sarah laughed. Kitty laughed too, happy to see her friend enjoying the moment. They talked now with greater ease. Kitty had hoped to tell Sarah of the decision that hung over her regarding the farm, but did not want to add to her friend's burdens. Instead, she told of life at the rectory and the redoubtable Mrs Gough. And Sarah spoke with tenderness of her children, but she said little else. Kitty didn't pry.

Sarah lifted her face to the last of the sun peeking through the trees and heaved a sigh. She stood. 'I must be getting back, I will be missed.'

Kitty watched as her friend gathered her hair up into her bonnet. When she had finished, she looked at Kitty. 'Now, don't be worrying about me, Kitty Canham, I know that look. You are always looking out for people, but I am fine. It is just a different life, that is all, and I have my little ones and another one on the way. I am fine, truly.' With that, she set off down the path.

Kitty followed her. 'And I expect you have days to yourself when Nathaniel is at work?'

Sarah called back, 'That's when I have his mother.' Kitty wanted to laugh but couldn't tell how it had been spoken. As they emerged onto the wide path, Kitty could see Sarah retreating into herself once more.

Kitty spoke in the hope of keeping her friend for just one moment longer. 'May we walk together again?'

Sarah pulled on her gloves. 'I think it wise we do not, not too soon anyway.' She turned to Kitty with a kind of pity. 'You really wouldn't understand.'

Kitty decided that she understood perfectly and wished things were otherwise, but knew there was little she could do and simply replied, 'Of course. It has been so good to see you.'

Sarah turned as she was leaving. 'You too. Very good.'

They looked at one another, knowing there was so much more that could be said, but aware that in this situation, words would change nothing. Sarah walked away.

On returning to the parsonage, Kitty was greeted by Mrs Carter who was pouring water into a bowl. Tilly sat at the table folding cloths. Opposite her was Green Tom, taking a sup. It was explained that Rachel had taken sick. Earlier in the day she had been somewhat listless and it had been agreed that she was probably tired from her new lessons. Now she had a fever. Mrs Carter instructed Tom to follow her with a basket of logs, then disappeared upstairs with the bowl. Kitty hurried to divest herself of her muddy shoes and cloak and followed on. Rachel had been put in her grandmother's room where a fire had been lit. Beth and the children hovered on the landing. Kitty instructed Beth to take the children down to the kitchen and give them something to eat with Tilly and Tom.

Rachel looked very pale. Mrs Carter wrung out a cloth and tenderly soothed her brow.

Kitty was concerned. 'How long has she been like this?'

'A couple of hours, it came on quick.'

The two women stood either side of the bed studying the little girl's face. Alexander was on a visit. It was decided not to call him at this stage as it would probably pass like most childhood fevers. Once Kitty had fetched her book and was settled in the chair beside the bed, Mrs Carter took her leave to take care of the rest of the household. Kitty read whilst Rachel slept. She, too, must have fallen asleep, because it was dark outside when she awoke to hear Alexander bounding up the stairs. The door opened. He stood for a moment watching Rachel breathe. His voice was deep and anxious. 'How is she?'

'She was a little restless earlier, but is sleeping now.'

He sat beside his daughter and stroked back her hair. 'She has a fever.'

'Yes.'

His large hands moved gently across her brow. 'She reminds me of her mother. She has her eyes and her gentle ways.' Kitty watched him as he cared for his daughter. His eyes betrayed a piercing kind of love. 'She will be alright?'

What did Kitty know? How could she answer him? 'She's a strong girl, Alexander. It's most likely just a little fever. Beth and I will keep watch until it breaks.' Her words faltered at his name, she still was not used to using it, but it seemed appropriate to call him by name in this moment.

He looked at her and nodded. 'Thank you.' As he left, he turned at the door and said, 'Thank you for coming to us, Kitty, you've brought comfort to our home.'

That simple statement was reward enough for her labours. She basked in the pleasure of it for a moment before she realised how cold the room had become. Placing the book on the small chest beside the chair, she went to stoke the fire. As the fresh wood began to crackle and spit into life, she thought of her father. She could see him resting on the settle in the kitchen, smoking his pipe in the light of the flames. She had never been away from the farm this long and despite all the comfort of the parsonage, felt a pang of longing for home. Rachel stirred. Kitty wrung the cloth afresh in the cool water and lay it gently against the child's forehead, cooing soft words as she did so. She realised now, how fond she had become of the little face before her, pale now with fever. Rachel settled in Kitty's care.

Once the younger children were settled, Beth came to sit with Rachel. Kitty, tired now, made her way to the kitchen. The fire was still alight and Mrs Carter had left a plate for her. Kitty smiled at such care and poured a drink from the pitcher. On the table, a small posy of bluebells hung their heads over a little jug. Thoughts of the farm in spring danced around Kitty's head. She found herself humming as she ate.

It was a good supper and soon finished. She rose to take her plate to the basin, but almost dropped it: Alexander was sitting in the corner of the room, all but hidden in the shadows. Why hadn't she noticed him? How long had he been there?

He laughed. 'It was a pretty song.' Kitty was glad of the dark, it would hide her blush. 'I am sorry, I did not mean to startle you, I just didn't want to interrupt. You were so caught up in your thoughts.'

Kitty smiled, but kept the nature of her thoughts to herself. 'Rachel was sleeping peacefully when I left. Beth is sitting with her now.'

'That's good. I never sleep when the little ones are sick. I try to remember how their mother would care for them, and do the same. But I don't have her ways.'

'I think you do very well.'

He rose and now she noticed that in his hand he had the wooden box she had seen in his study when she first arrived. 'Shall I teach you the rudiments of backgammon?' She hesitated. He held out the box with anticipation. Although she had been hopeful of a little sleep, she looked at the rather forlorn figure before her, and agreed to play. The game was soon explained. Kitty struggled to understand, but played along as best she could and with every move the rules became clearer. Alexander was a good teacher. Sitting at the table with him was reminiscent of sitting with Pa at home. In some ways he was a very different man. His red hair was worn short, perhaps because of the wig of his office. His skin was rather pale, his face marked, but he was kind and caring of his children, which made Kitty like him immensely.

When the game was over, and securely won by Alexander, Kitty went to leave. He touched her arm. 'Wait… would you sit with me a moment longer?' He indicated the chair. 'There is something I feel I need to explain.' Kitty sat, wondering what Alexander could possibly have to explain to her. He waited for her to settle. 'Has anyone told you how we lost Elizabeth, my wife?'

'I believe it was in childbirth?'

'Yes, that is so. She had suffered from a fever during her confinement which gave her fits. Although the fever left her, the fitting did not. When the time came for the baby to be born, the birth caused her to fit so badly.' He twisted the dice in his fingers. 'Hour after hour it went on… She wasn't strong, you see. The sickness had left her weak. We watched her fading before our eyes. The doctor tried everything, but there was nothing could be done… In the end… I had no choice.' Kitty began to understand. Alexander now looked at her, his eyes deep in the candlelight. 'I prayed, Kitty, I tell you,

I prayed like I'd never prayed before, but it was no good. If I we had left it any longer, I would have lost them both.'

Kitty could hardly breath; his pain was so evident. She sat in silence until he spoke once more, 'They cut the baby from her belly.'

Kitty's hand covered a gasp, then she ventured, 'And that was Esther?'

'Yes, that was our little Esther… So you see, Kitty, when any of the children get a fever, it brings it all back. The images of that terrible night play in my mind and I find I am unable… unable to be of any use to the children, just when they need me.'

'You are their father, your presence is all they need.'

He slumped back in the chair. 'The funny thing was… we had thought ourselves especially blessed by God; we had kept all our children, not one was lost. But it never occurred to me that I might lose Elizabeth.'

Kitty hardly knew what to say. 'Esther is a fine little thing.'

'She is, isn't she?' He smiled and straightened in his chair. 'I am sorry, Kitty, you didn't come here to listen to an old man pour out his troubles.'

Now she touched his arm. 'You said we would be friends, and this is what friends do.' He patted her hand.

'I feel much comforted, knowing that you are here to look out for them. But I have said enough.' Alexander stood. 'Come, let us see how Rachel is, then we must to bed. It will be dawn before we know it, and you must get some rest.'

Rest didn't come easily to Kitty that night as she sat in the chair at the bedside. Occasionally she dozed, but more often the spectres of that terrible night moved through her thoughts. She longed now to see her family more than ever and receive the comfort that only they could give.

Chapter Six

Rachel was in and out of the fever for two days. On the third the fever broke. By the Tuesday morning, she was up and dressed and the household had returned to normal. It was early and Kitty was smoothing out her best dress for her visit to the Manor that afternoon when there was a knock on the door. It was Mrs Carter with two dresses laid over her arm. She looked Kitty up and down. 'The reverend said I should offer you these for your visit today.' She laid them on the bed. Kitty didn't know what to say. They were lovely. One was a delicate yellow floral fabric, the other a deep rust red. Mrs Carter continued, 'They belonged to the reverend's wife. He said it was time they were worn again. I've cleaned them as best I could.'

'Thank you, that is very kind.'

'He had wanted to keep them for Rachel, but by the time she's a young woman, they won't be good enough for her, I expect. No, you wear them; it'll do him good to see them used again. He picked them out himself.'

All morning Kitty worried about dressing for her visit and how it would be for Alexander to see her in his wife's clothes. When the time came, she found herself standing before the garments, half hoping they wouldn't fit. She chose the yellow floral and slipped it on. It was perhaps a little shorter than she'd have liked but otherwise it fitted well. The delicate fabric draped pleasingly around her breast. Among her belongings she found a yellow ribbon and adorned her best bonnet.

Once she was fully ready, she crept down the stairs as quietly as she could, determined not to let Alexander see her. But as she opened the front door, his study door opened and the children burst out, giving Kitty quite a start. Alexander stood behind them with Mrs Carter, Tilly and Beth. Little David spoke for them all, his round brown eyes looking up at her as he gasped and said, 'You look beautiful.' He was so grown up in his ways. Kitty smiled and thanked him. As she looked at Alexander, she was aware of the pink rising in her cheeks. She was glad that the older children were at school; the little ones would probably not remember the dresses their mother wore.

Thankfully, Mrs Carter spoke, 'It fits you very well, does it not, Reverend Gough?'

He nodded. 'It does, indeed.'

Jonathan chirped in, 'Father had us waiting specially to surprise you. We did surprise you, didn't we, Kitty?'

She crouched down to look square in his little face. 'You certainly did, and a very good surprise it was too.'

'Come on now.' Mrs Carter gathered the household towards the kitchen. Alexander hovered in the door.

She blushed. 'Thank you, it is very kind of you.'

'There's no need to thank me, I am glad it's of use.' Perhaps he could see her awkwardness as he stepped forward and all but ushered her out. 'You look lovely, Kitty. Now, get along and enjoy your afternoon at the Manor.'

As he closed the door behind her, she lifted her face to feel the sun. It had warmth in it and the promise of summer. A blackbird sang his heart out from the fresh green growth that arched above her as she passed through the gate. The street was busy as ever. A cart rattled past, filled with crates, causing her to step back in a hurry. Brushing down her skirts, she shook her head. But nothing could upset her today. Today was a special day. She made her way through the village, feeling younger than her years and beautiful, perhaps for the first time in a long time. The faces passing were becoming more familiar to her. One or two stopped and bid her good day.

The Bell Inn stood opposite the church. When Kitty passed, the innkeeper looked up from his sweeping and asked after Rachel in his lilting Irish accent. Kitty responded, 'She is doing well, thank you, Pat.'

'I'm glad to hear of it, that I am. You settling in then?' She said that she was and went to go on her way, but he carried on, 'The reverend's a good man and good company, that he is. He'll be glad to have you.' And then, chuckling under his breath, 'And glad his mother's gone, no doubt.' Kitty giggled as she continued on her way. It seemed she wasn't the only one who found Mrs Gough a trial.

As she turned into the drive at the Manor, she saw that the parkland was as it always had been, a vast sea of scrubby green where ancient trees stood in isolation. But closer to the house, a large band of men were stripping the grass to bare earth. As she approached, one of the labourers stopped to wipe the sweat from his brow and noticed her looking. He smiled, a broad knowing smile. She flushed and looked down, pretending not to have noticed him. It was only when she looked up and saw the great house standing before her, its tall gables pointing towards the sky, that she wondered if she should have agreed to come.

She gathered herself in front of the arched door and knocked. A manservant in formal attire opened the door and led her through the hallway into the great hall itself. Exquisite portraits hung high on wood-panelled walls, scrutinising her as she walked. Then up a low flight of stairs, down a corridor and finally into a room quite at odds with the dingy corridor. The furnishings were light and the walls a delicate green. Large drapes were held back in great swathes by ornate ropes. The sun streamed through the windows across the woven carpet, which was adorned with flowers. The manservant took Kitty's cloak and said that Mrs Manley-Hogg would be with her shortly.

Kitty surveyed the room. Two upholstered chairs in pinks and blues sat either side of the fireplace, which was lit in welcome. A chaise stretched between them, upholstered in like fashion. Between the windows stood an ornate writing desk, the likes of which Kitty had never seen before; it was carved with scrolls and flowers and looked most impractical. On it stood a small vase of spring flowers which overflowed their bounds. Kitty made her way to the window. She could now see the works outside more clearly. A garden was beginning to appear in geometrical shapes. A row of young men were busy planting a hedge. There was one woman among them, her skirts, though hooked up, were heavy with mud. Others were digging and heaving great sods onto a cart. In the middle of it all stood a lugubrious looking man, in a crumpled hat, holding a plan in his hands. It amused Kitty to see a smaller man with a mass of blue-black hair, stood at his side trying to engage the first in heated discussion, but he was having none of it.

Eleanor's voice called Kitty to attention. 'Ah, the garden, yes.' She stood beside Kitty. 'I would like to update the house itself, but James will not agree. He was very attached to the previous owner, you see, and won't let me change a thing. So, he's given me the garden to play with.' She leant forward to peer out of the window. 'And that … ' She indicated the arguing men, ' … the one who's flapping his hands. He's the designer, and the man beside him is the head gardener. It is not a happy coupling.' She then turned to Kitty. 'I am so sorry, I haven't welcomed you properly. Come, let us sit.' She led Kitty to a chair by the fire. 'I do hope it's not too warm, I felt it was getting chilly.'

'No, it's lovely, thank you. And what a beautiful room.'

'Do you like it?'

'Very much.'

'I'm glad. James has allowed me to decorate my own rooms, and I fear I may have gone a bit too far.'

'Not at all.' Kitty was pleased at how easily conversation seemed to flow.

'I've ordered tea and treats. I do hope that is to your liking?'

It was very much to Kitty's liking. Such things were a rarity at the farm.

'Now, tell me all about life at the rectory, how is it going?'

Kitty started by telling her about the children and the household, but there was something about Eleanor that loosened Kitty's tongue. She soon found herself telling Eleanor about Sarah and the concerns she had for her. When Eleanor suggested they ask Reverend Gough to intervene, Kitty had to persuade her that it probably wasn't as bad as it seemed. She felt terrible in the knowledge that she had broken her friend's trust. And insisted that she was probably mistaken.

Thankfully the conversation moved to Eleanor's own life. She spoke of the children, of which there were now four; three girls and, much to her husband's relief, a baby boy. Kitty was surprised at how candid Eleanor was about her relations with her husband. 'I am always rather glad when James travels away, it gives me a break from breeding.'

Tea was brought on a tray and placed on a table beside Eleanor's chair. It was served in the most delicate china Kitty had ever seen, patterned with pale blue flowers.

'James brought the set back from his travels. It is lovely, isn't it?'

As she was pouring the tea, a man's voice called from down the corridor. It was insistent. 'Eleanor? Eleanor?' Heavy footsteps were coming their way.

Eleanor rose. 'Excuse me a moment, would you, Kitty.' She made for the door but before she reached it, it burst open.

'I tell you, I cannot work with such a man!' The speaker, who was evidently French, stopped in the midst of his protestations, placed his hand on his chest. 'Oh, please forgive me, you have a visitor.' His eyes were on Kitty.

Eleanor was firm but resigned, 'Yes, Albert, I do.' She pronounced his name with a perfect French accent. 'May I introduce Monsieur Albert Robillard, garden designer and friend ... of sorts.' Monsieur Robillard laughed heartily. Now Kitty looked, she realised it was the man she had seen arguing in the garden. Eleanor was amused. 'And this is Miss Catherine Canham.'

Stepping forward, he took Kitty's hand, kissing it ever so lightly. 'Miss Canham, I am very glad to make your acquaintance.' He continued to hold her hand and stare at Kitty. She felt uneasy and slipped her hand away.

Thankfully, Eleanor spoke again, 'We will discuss your problems with Mr Trenchard in the hall.' Then, turning to Kitty, 'If you'll excuse me, I will be as quick as I can. And please, help yourself to a treat. Cook makes the most marvellous treats.' And with that she ushered Monsieur Robillard out of the room and closed the door.

Kitty sat stunned at the interruption and the familiarity with which Eleanor addressed the man. She could hear them whispering forcefully in the hallway, but couldn't hear what they were saying, so she turned to the treats. She bit into a marzipan fruit and found a nut hidden within. It was, indeed, marvellous.

Eleanor returned. 'I do apologise for such a rude interruption. Albert is an excellent designer, but sometimes rather high spirited.' She sat to pour the tea. 'Now, tell me, Kitty, all about the farm.' And with that she handed Kitty a cup. The rest of the afternoon was spent in pleasant tittle tattle.

Walking down the driveway, later that afternoon, it made Kitty smile to see the tall man working with his men in quiet harmony. Albert was nowhere to be seen. There was a chill in the air, which caused Kitty to wrap her cloak around her and hurry her step. She must not have been paying proper attention because she stepped into the road almost to be knocked down by a horse galloping past at speed. Irritation rose within her. Nobody need ride so carelessly! The horse was pulled up short, and the rider turned. She saw that it was Tom and laughed; she was so pleased to see him. But as he turned the horse around, she could see that his look was grim.

'Tom?'

He held the horse still. 'Kitty, it's your pa.'

Her stomach lurched. 'What's happened?'

'He's sick, you need to come.'

'What do you mean? I would have heard, someone would have told me.'

'I'm telling you now, Kitty. Just come, please. Your mother will explain.'

'I will get my things.' She stepped towards a run, but Tom stopped her.

'No, it's better you come now.'

Kitty looked into his eyes; they were unmoving. He held out his hand. Kitty looked towards the Manor House and down at her dress. For a moment she was unwilling to meet Tom's urgency. 'Kitty?'

Eventually she took his hand and he hauled her up behind him. As he turned the horse, he called over his shoulder, 'We will get a message to the reverend later.' She held Tom tight round his waist as the horse took off.

Chapter Seven

The light was fading as Tom and Kitty approached the farmhouse. Joseph stood in the doorway holding a lantern high. Bouncer stood beside him, barking at their coming. Kitty's heart leapt to see him. Tom dismounted and helped Kitty to do the same. The old dog ran to greet her and for a moment everything seemed as it had always been. She bent to ruffle his scruffy head, but Joseph called, 'Come now, let's get inside.'

Kitty entered the old house, taking off her bonnet as she went, and headed straight for the stairs. 'No, this way.' Joseph led her to the parlour. The room rocked as a familiar sickly smell hit her. Father was laid on a makeshift bed, his mouth open as he panted for breath. Beside him, Reverend Styles stood, holding an open prayer book and mumbling. Kitty heard a voice groan, low and strong, 'No … no … no … ' Little did she know it was her own voice. Tom supported her as her knees buckled beneath her.

Reverend Styles stood aside. 'Come, Kitty.' He placed a chair beside the bed. She sank into it and took her father's hand. 'Pa? … Pa.'

Joseph stood beside her now. 'It's no good, Kitty. Your pa is on his way.'

'He can't be. He wouldn't leave me like this, he wouldn't. Not yet. What happened?' She searched his face. 'Pa … Pa … it's Kitty, I've come to see you.' But as she watched, she recognised the signs of death upon him. She looked at her ma who sat stone-faced in a chair opposite her. 'Ma?' Her mother gave no response.

She felt Joseph take her by the shoulders. 'Come, Kitty, let the parson say the rites so that your pa can go in peace.'

How could she let him go? There was still so much to share with him, things she wanted to tell him. She needed to hear his voice. A violence rose in her chest. She pushed Joseph away and pulled her father's hand to her cheek, whispering, 'Pa, you can't leave me like this. Not now. Pa?' Nothing came in response.

Tom was beside her. 'Let the parson do what he needs to do, Kitty, then you and your ma can spend time with him before he goes.' Reluctantly, she let Tom lead her aside.

The parson opened the prayer book. She had seen it so many times and knew what must happen, but this was her pa, her closest ally. Her father's breathing seemed to soften at the reading of the scriptures, it seemed that God was easing his way. As he settled, so did Kitty. The truth was beginning to take root deep within her; her pa was dying.

When everyone had left, a silence settled around the gentle puffing of her father's fading breaths. Peggy came and went, to stoke the fire or light a candle. Her sensible manner brought comfort to the room. Ma sat in silence, as she had at the passing of all the babes. As the evening went on, Kitty found her voice. She told her father all about the rectory and her visit to the Manor, she told him of the exquisite blossom in the garden. She told him of Alexander's mother and her strange ways and all about the children. She wanted to tell him everything before it was too late. As she finished, she felt his fingers move in her palm. 'Ma! He squeezed my hand.' Mother remained unmoved. Kitty's voice weakened, 'He really did.' She leant forward to kiss his forehead. As she did so his eyes flickered open, causing Kitty to leap back. Her mother stood to look at him. A pause hung in the air. He let out one long breath, and was gone.

Kitty choked back a sob, watching as her mother bent over her husband. She let a kiss linger on his forehead, then stroked his cheek with tender touch. 'Your father has left us, Kitty.' She straightened the sheet, then ran her hand over his face, closing his eyes. Taking a deep breath, she quietly left the room.

This moment alone with Pa was precious to Kitty. It had always been her and Pa. He had been her rock, her strength, her joy. She rested her head on his silent chest and tried to grasp, one more time, the sense of him, but nothing came. She must have been laying there some time because Mother returned carrying cloths and herbs. Peggy followed on with a large basin of steaming water.

Kitty cried out, 'Not yet! Let him be, just a little while longer.'

Peggy responded, 'We are just going to clean him up. Why don't you go and see Tom? He's waiting for you in the kitchen.' Kitty gave one more long look at her pa's precious face and pulled herself away. Bouncer lay beside the door, his head between his front paws. He looked up at her and whined. She stooped to stroke his head. 'Come on, boy, let's go, there's nothing here for you.'

As she walked across the hall, with Bouncer at her heels, all emotion drained from her. A numbness was taking its place, in which questions were beginning to form. Tom was sitting by the fire. He rose to her as she entered and wrapped his arms around her. Her arms hung limp. He started to rub her shoulders, and said, 'You are cold.' She realised that she was shivering. Tom picked up a blanket, wrapped it around her and led her to the settle. He poured a drink from the pitcher and handed it to her. She drank whilst he stoked the fire. 'I have sent word to Reverend Gough.'

'Thank you.' One question fought to be answered. 'Tom?'

He looked up. 'Yes?'

'What was it that took my pa?'

Tom seemed to hesitate. 'I think your ma should explain.'

'What do you mean?'

His brow furrowed. 'It is not for me to say.'

'Was it the influenza?'

'No.' Tom looked at her. 'It was an accident.'

Kitty gasped. 'An accident? What kind of accident?' He didn't reply. 'Please, Tom, I need to know.'

Resigned, he sat beside her. 'A week ago, your pa was in Harwich, on some business or other. There was a fight in the street which he tried to stop.'

'A fight? What do you mean?'

'The men who brought him home said that it was a drunken brawl outside an inn. Your father tried to stop it. They said he was very brave. But in doing so, he received a wound.'

'What kind of wound?'

'A stabbing.'

'A stabbing!' The shock rippled through Kitty's body.

'At that time it seemed to be only a flesh wound. He said they were only lads too drunk for their own good. You know what he was like. He wouldn't let anyone send for the constable. So, your ma tended him with her herbs and he seemed to improve.'

'Why did no-one send for me?'

'At first he seemed to be healing well.' Kitty must have looked doubtful because Tom insisted, 'Honestly, Kitty, I saw him, he was in good spirits.' His voice lowered, 'Then a couple of days ago a fever came upon him. The doctor was called and he found the wound was infected. He tried everything.' Tom placed his hand on hers. 'Yesterday, the doctor cut away some flesh to clean the wound. Your pa was so brave, Kitty, you should have seen him. He seemed to be doing well. But late this morning, he suddenly took a turn for the worse. When they saw he was fading, I was sent to fetch you.'

'They should have called for me sooner. I should have been with him.' Kitty hugged her knees to her chest, her eyes dark.

'I think your ma didn't want to trouble you. She'd heard that you were caring for the reverend's daughter, and thought you were needed there.'

Anger began to rise, but hopelessness robbed it of any passion. Her head sunk to her knees, and a terrible sleepiness came over her.

They sat in silence for some time until Tom spoke again, 'I'm sure your ma will tell you more when she is able. It's late, shall I help you to your room?' She was comforted by his care, but now she wanted to be alone.

'No, thank you, Tom, I shall be alright. You go along and get some rest yourself.' He was reluctant to leave at first, but built up the fire for Kitty and took his leave.

Kitty gathered her strength and rose to bed. As she did so, she noticed her pa's pipe on the mantle. The small bowl was smooth in the palm of her hand. It was cold. She lifted it to her nose. The smell of the old tobacco caused a clenching in her stomach, but she steadied herself and set off for bed. She just wanted this day to end. As she passed the parlour, she could hear the women going about their task. Kitty wanted none of it and carried on upstairs. Her room had been prepared, and for that she was grateful. She fell onto the bed, wrapped the loose covers around her and soon blanked out the day with sleep.

Kitty awoke with a start. It was barely dawn. For a moment the forgetfulness of sleep hung over her, but in the next moment, dread bloomed. Her dress was twisted about her body. She tugged at the fabric, now crushed by sleep. She remembered how light she had felt yesterday and despite herself, felt robbed. Father's pipe lay on the pillow beside her. She set herself free of the tangled coverings and took the precious item to the little table in the window, placing it among her treasures. She was all too aware that she was consigning it to a place among her memories.

The house was quiet now, too quiet. Her father's dead face was insistent in her mind. She took up her candle and descended the stairs. Each step was so familiar to her naked feet. For a moment she was the young girl who crept downstairs in the early light, to spend time with her pa in the kitchen before he set out to work. Steadying herself against the beam, she let the memory linger. Instead of turning left into the kitchen, where the memories lay, she turned right and entered the parlour. The room was cold now. The fire dead. A single candle was all but burnt out standing on a table by her father's head. She took a fresh candle and lit it with the old, thus keeping the light burning. Her father lay cocooned in burial cloths; herbs pressed tight against his body. In the corner, Peggy was curled on a chair under a blanket, snoring gently. Kitty crept closer to study her pa's face which was barely peeking out of the shroud. His thick hair, which loosely framed his face, was now scraped back; his eyes had been coined and the sallow skin lay flat over his features. The image before her was no longer her pa. A whine from Bouncer called her gaze away. Peggy shifted but did not awaken. The old dog now stood by the door, his tail twitching, his doleful eyes searching hers. Kitty ushered him out and closed the door tight behind her.

She stood, for a moment, unsure where to go or what to do. Eventually she made her way to her pa's study. Kitty lit the candle standing on his table. Beside the small window, the bookcase stood untidily stacked with any amount of odd bits and pieces, which had always fascinated Kitty as a child. She picked up a shiny metal cog that would have been so out of place in anyone else's study, but not her pa's.

By the fireside was the high-backed chair, which was her father's place of escape when the weather closed in. Opposite sat the little chair he'd made for her when she was a girl. She would come to him there and he would tell her stories of knights and dragons and princesses. She stroked her hand along the back of his chair, hoping to feel something of him in her touch, but it was only wood. She went to the table. It was strewn with papers, just as he had left it. In the flickering light, she noticed one letter laid neatly in front of the chair, the inky quill lying beside it. On it was written one word, Kitty. Little sobs caught in her throat as she sat to open the precious document. The hand was weak, but unmistakably her father's. It read:

To my darling Kitty,
I knew that this day would come. My only hope is that it hasn't come too soon to see your precious face once more. You have been my greatest joy and companion. I am proud of you, my dearest, as I have watched you grow into a woman. But I must be brief lest my strength fail before I have told you all that I need to say.
I leave you, my darling, with many responsibilities that you will have to take up. I only wish it were not so.
We had no time to discuss the farm, so it remains as written.

After the last of our boys was lost, I put it in your mother's name. Perhaps that is as it should be. I have not always been the husband she deserved, and for that I am sorry. I cannot make up for the past but I can leave her the security of a home and a living. But she will need you, Kitty. She does very well with the household, but you know the ways of the farm. And with Joseph's help, I know you will do well. Your mother is not strong like you, my Kitty Kat. Look after her for me.

The solicitor, Jethro, will inform you and guide you. He is a good man. Look to him and to our dear friend Joseph. I know he will not let you down.

God bless you, my dearest. I say with the deepest sorrow, farewell,

Your ever-loving father.

Kitty stood a long while searching the words before her, barely breathing. These were her father's final words to her. The farm would never be hers, she knew that now. But holding the letter to her breast, she now knew what she must do and she would not let her father down. Tucking it away in her pocket, she made for the hall. Her father's coat was hanging on the peg where he had left it. She slipped it on and hugged it to herself; the smell of him hung in the fibres. In the kitchen, the embers glowed low. She knew that she should rekindle the fire and make the house warm for her mother, but instead, she carried on through the washhouse. The farm cat emerged from the servants' room, its nose low to the ground, its tail twitching, alert for prey. Kitty slipped into her work boots, opened the back door and stepped outside. The air was moist and fresh and clung to her skin as she crossed the yard. Tiny squeals came from the pigger's pen. Kitty watched as the piglets snuffled for their mother's milk, their large ears flopping over their little snouts. Kitty smiled. She then headed for the small barn, found the chicken feed, and fed the chickens as they clucked expectantly around her feet. All these simple tasks seemed to anchor her untethered soul. This was her place; her body knew it better than any other.

'Kitty?' She turned to see her mother standing in the doorway in a thin shift. Her pale skin made paler by the early light, her eyes pleading. Kitty stepped forward, but Peggy appeared behind her mother and caught her up in her arms. Peggy turned her gently and led her indoors. Kitty was relieved. She hugged Pa's coat tighter around herself and walked into the fresh air beyond the yard where a weak orb was rising in the morning mist.

Chapter Eight

The days turned into weeks and the weeks to months. The farm was beginning to settle into a new routine. Father's clothes had been given to the poor, all except for his coat, which kept Kitty warm on cool evenings. Joseph took over the running of the farm, with Kitty alongside him. She intended to learn all she needed to know to run the farm herself. But it was to be slow progress; the seasons were indolent in their turning, and each had enough work of its own. Mother managed the household and dairy, with Peggy ever at her side. Kitty's time at the rectory now seemed like a dream or passing fancy. Alexander had had her belongings sent to her with a note. He said that a local woman had stepped in to help at the rectory. He explained that although it wasn't ideal, it saved his mother from having to come home too soon. That, Kitty thought, was just as well.

Summer was once more on the wane and Kitty was exhausted. She had not seen Sarah, neither had she wanted to. Until now, she had not wanted to see anyone outside of the farm. It took an encounter with Tom to persuade her to take a rest.

At the summer's end, there are days when the cool morning belies the heat that is to come mid-afternoon. This was one such day. Kitty was struggling with a feisty ewe who'd slipped into a ditch. She had caught her and now held her between her knees to settle her before dragging her out, but the ewe was fighting Kitty's every effort. Grasping it by the horns, she tried soothing sounds that soon gave way to angry words. She heard a laugh. It was Tom standing above her.

'Woah, that's some language you've got there.'

'The blasted thing won't keep still.'

Tom came to help. 'Here, give her to me.'

'No, I can do it.' She could feel the heat of frustration rise in her face. 'You stupid animal, keep still, damn you.' She hated the fact that sometimes she needed a man's strength. Her cussing continued until it finally gave way to a sob.

Tom pulled the sheep by the horns and lugged it up on to level ground. It trotted away, unaware of the difficulty its stupidity had caused. Tom stood looking at Kitty with his hands on his hips. Her throat was tight, but she managed to thank him as he helped her up. She walked away.

'Kitty?'

She didn't turn back. 'Yes.'

Tom drew closer. 'Are you alright?'

She turned on him. 'What do you think?' He stepped back, his hands lifting in surrender. And out of her flowed a torrent of anger and sorrow in equal measure. She was so, so angry, about the little things at first; the heat, the sheep, the fact that her skirts always got in her way, why could she not wear breeches? Eventually, anger at her pa for abandoning her found voice. Rage spilled out and from within the rage, a deep, deep sorrow began to flow, first in great sobs and then, as Tom took her in his arms, in a child's tears. She wept until she was spent. He led her to the shade of the tangled hedgerow, lay out his jacket and sat her gently on the ground, his arm about her. Her head dropped to his shoulder.

'Do you remember,' he started, his voice soft, 'when we gathered wool from the undergrowth in this very spot, to make a bed for your doll?'

She remembered. 'We were so young.'

'Yes, we were. And do you remember playing chase? Sarah was always trying to catch us up, but she never could.'

'Poor Sarah, she only had little legs. Were we mean?'

'I suppose we were. You were fast, like a deer, with your long skinny legs.'

Kitty chuckled. Tom turned to her and stroked the hair from her face. 'You were beautiful even then.' She looked up at him, old feelings stirring within. He was no longer a youth. His cheeks now bristled with a man's beard. His eyes were on her until his lips met hers. Every fibre of her body felt it. She pressed in deeper to the embrace. He met her intent until, amid the heat of it, he pulled away. 'No, we cannot do this.' He scrambled to his feet. 'Kitty, I am sorry. I never should have done that; it was wrong of me.'

She was perplexed and stood to meet him. 'What? Why not?'

He turned to look at her, raking his hair with his fingers.

She knew him too well. 'What is it? Tell me.'

He could barely look at her. 'I am to be betrothed.'

Kitty staggered back; a moment before she had found her comfort and now it was torn from her.

Tom stood helpless. 'Kitty, I am so sorry.'

'What do you mean?'

'I am to be wed. There is a girl, new to the village … ' She didn't want to hear this, but as she turned to leave, Tom took her by the arm. 'Please, Kitty, let me explain.' She stood stock still, her eyes lowered. 'Her name is Miriam. You have probably seen her. Her father and brothers are good workers. She is a sensible girl and will make a good wife. I need a good wife.' Then he added, almost casually, 'I love you, Kitty, I always have, you must know that, but we both know that it cannot be.'

Kitty was calm now. 'No, I do not know that.'

'You need a husband equal to you. I could never be enough for you, Kitty.'

She started to walk away. 'You're talking rubbish, Tom, you always talk rubbish.' He followed and caught her once more, turning her to face him.

He spoke slowly and deliberately, 'You have dreams, Kitty, I see it in you every day. My dreams are simple. I want to make a way for my father's name, perhaps to own my own land. If I am to do that, I must have sons. I need to marry someone who will give me sons.'

She was tired. 'I could have given you sons.'

He looked at her. 'Could you?'

All the lost boys passed through Kitty's mind, and suddenly she understood all too well. Looking at Tom, she saw the pain in his eyes. But what use was his pain to her? She had enough of her own. She walked away. Tom called after her, but she kept walking.

At first, she drifted slowly this way and that, until she reached the water's edge. She thought of all her aunts and cousins, all girls. Could she give any man a son? And now her one solace, Tom, was leaving too. She turned towards Landermere Quay, now striding out hard and fast, weaving along each ragged inlet. She walked till her legs ached, and her mind was free of all thoughts and only exhaustion remained. Grey clouds gathered overhead and a chill wind blew. She turned along the quay and made for home, hurrying now, but before long, heavy drops of rain began to fall, catching up her tears in lament. By the time she reached the kitchen door, she was spent.

Peggy looked up from her labours and smiled as Kitty entered the kitchen. 'You got caught in the rain then?' When Kitty did not return her smile, Peggy put down her knife and came to Kitty's side. 'Let's get those wet things off you.'

Kitty sat shivering, all but naked by the fire. Peggy wrapped a blanket around her and made a brew. The old dog looked at her, but made no attempt to move. As she sank into the warmth of the room, she felt a hand stroke her hair. It was her mother. Gently, she took Kitty's hair and began to comb it, just as she had when Kitty was a child. After a few strokes, Kitty pulled away. 'Thank you, Mother, I will do it.' Mother placed the comb in Kitty's waiting palm and sat watching as she combed.

Mother sat on the settle, clenching her hands, which she always did when she was nervous. 'I want to say something to you, Kitty, if I may?'

Her hesitancy irritated Kitty. 'What is it?'

'I wanted to ask your forgiveness.' Kitty ceased her endeavours and looked at her mother. What could she possibly have done to warrant such a plea? 'I am aware that I haven't always been the mother that you needed or wanted, but I was never very confident like your pa. Life has always been something of a puzzle to me. And after the boys … I tried, Kitty, I honestly did, but it seems I had little to give. And you and your pa were so close, it seemed best to let things be. But now I wish that I had tried harder. I have let you down, and for that I am sorry.'

Mother looked so small and vulnerable, sitting there. Thankfully, she could not know just how much she had let her daughter down; the grief over her boys had become Kitty's too, but for a very different reason.

Kitty reached out and took her mother's hand. 'You have had so many trials, Ma. We will be fine. You and me and Peggy.' The old dog sat panting in the hearth. 'And old Bouncer here. I just had a bit of a bad day today, that's all, but we will be fine, won't we, Peggy?'

'Of course we will.' Peggy started her assault on the vegetables again.

Kitty gathered the blanket around her. 'Now, let me go and get dressed, and we'll have supper.' She stood, regretting having taken the comb from her mother's hand, but she could do nothing about it now, so she left the room and the weight of her mother's sadness behind her.

At supper the following evening, Joseph announced Tom's betrothal. Kitty was glad she already knew, but feigned the appropriate surprise. Even though her encounter with Tom had been painful, it had somehow woken her out of her long days of mourning. Whether it was grief expressed or the ending of a possibility that had hung between them for far too long, she couldn't be sure. As for the business with the lost boys, she put it from her mind, choosing instead the good of her encounter with Tom.

Kitty decided it was time to move forward, so she asked if Joseph could arrange for her to visit Sarah when he went to Thorpe the following day. He wholeheartedly agreed. 'I think our Sarah will be very glad to see you. This last baby has quite taken it out of her.' Mother seemed more relaxed this evening and showed concern over Sarah's wellbeing, saying that she would make a cake for Kitty to take.

It was a good supper and Kitty ate heartily. When she'd finished, she spoke on another matter. 'Joseph, I think it's time

I took over father's personal accounts.' Joseph, who had been doing them since the tragedy, straightened. 'You don't need to worry yourself with accounts, I am more than happy to continue with them.'

Kitty straightened in response. 'Nevertheless, I would like to take them on. I thought we could start next week.'

Mother interrupted, 'I think that, perhaps, it would be best to get the harvest in first. You both will have so much to do.'

'A good idea, Judith, let's do it then.' They both continued eating, the conversation evidently closed. Kitty made no fight as they were probably right; the harvest was upon them and there was much to be done.

It had been arranged that Kitty would visit Sarah the following week. Tom was taking the trap that way, so it was agreed that he would take her as she was carrying Ma's cake. She stepped out into a somewhat blustery day. White clouds skittered across the clear sky. Tom sat waiting for her on the trap.

'Good morning, Tom.'

'Good morning.' He barely looked at her as he nudged the horse into action. Neither spoke for some time. The gentle rhythm of hooves on the road always quieted Kitty, which she needed as she sat beside Tom. At last he spoke, 'Kitty, I am so sorry about what happened … '

She was quick in response, 'No need, Tom. Really.' She was determined to soften the experience. 'You simply caught me at a bad time, that was all. Let us not talk of it again.' His dark hair flopped over his brow. His eyes betrayed an uncertainty. She comforted him, as she always had. 'I am pleased for you, Tom, I really am. Let's go back to being friends like we always are. Can we do that?'

He chuckled. 'You know, Kitty, you are the most extraordinary woman ... Of course we can.' Little did he know how the sensation of his lips against hers lingered upon her as they spoke, or of how hard it was for her to be so strong. But it was better this way.

The journey continued with the usual chit chat of daily affairs. They passed the inn and the church, and finally approached Sarah's cottage. Tom drew the horse to a stand and Kitty dismounted. Sarah, who'd been waiting on the doorstep, came to greet her brother.

He looked amused. 'What, big sister? No offspring pulling on your skirts?'

Sarah gave him a wry smile. 'Father tells me you are to wed yourself.'

'Indeed, I am.' He seemed somewhat embarrassed, which pleased Kitty. Before Sarah could engage Tom any further in marital affairs, he set off, calling over his shoulder as he went, 'I shall be back by midday.'

Sarah moved towards the house. 'Come in, I shall make a brew.' Kitty followed. She had not been to the cottage since Sarah was newlywed. Little had changed. There was an addition of furniture making the small room smaller still. A bowl of blousy autumn roses sat on the table by the window. The baby lay asleep in a basket by the hearth.

Sarah saw Kitty peering at the child. 'That's our Elijah. He really is the easiest baby. I'll fetch the refreshments.' Kitty handed her the cake that Mother had made. 'That really is most kind of her.' She disappeared into the kitchen. Kitty studied the little chap further. His skin was pale and his hair impossibly blond like his mother's. A clatter of cups called her to attention as Sarah placed a tray on the table.

'It is an infusion of fennel, good for healing, and I think you will find it most delicious.' Kitty sat at one side, Sarah at the other. A formality lay between them. Sarah poured the brew, then unexpectedly reached out across the table and took Kitty's hand. 'I owe you an apology. I should have come and seen you when your pa died. I am so sorry.'

Kitty was irritated and pulled her hand away. 'Everybody has been apologising to me lately. It makes me feel like a lost pup who needs rescuing.'

Sarah recoiled. 'I am sorry, Kitty… Oh dear, there I go again.'

Kitty was contrite, 'I know, I know. Now it's my turn to be sorry. It has been a difficult time.'

'Of course it has.' Sarah handed her a cup.

'So,' Kitty said, eager to change the subject, 'where is everyone today?'

'Nathaniel is at his office. Mother has taken the older children to a church event. I told them that I couldn't go because this was the only time you had free.' Kitty made to protest but Sarah went on, 'At least that is what I said. Sometimes a little lie is the only way to get some peace.'

She laughed at herself and Kitty laughed with her. An ease entered the room and the two friends continued to enjoy each other's company. Tom's betrothal was spoken of in the lightest of terms and other news from the farm was shared. Little Elijah woke up and was inevitably damp on awakening. He really was the most delightful child, making little fuss when Sarah changed his clothes and fed him. Once the little one was returned to his bed, the friends took another cup and chatted quite freely about the lighter things of life. Neither seemed able or prepared to give away their deeper struggles, and maybe this was all that either needed. That was until Kitty twisted round and knocked her cup to the floor. It broke into a number of pieces, spilling the hot liquid over the rug. Kitty apologised and bent to pick up the fragments, whilst Sarah disappeared into the kitchen. She returned looking agitated, carrying a bowl and cloth. She rolled up her sleeves and, pushing Kitty aside, bent to clean the floor.

Kitty moved away. 'I am so sorry.'

Sarah spoke as if to a child, 'It's no good being sorry.'

'It's only a cup,' Kitty said innocently.

'It is not only a cup.' Sarah dabbed and tended the floor with resolve. 'It belongs to the family set. And this rug cost good money.' Then, added almost under her breath, 'Nathaniel says I'm clumsy, and this will just prove it … yet again.'

'You didn't break it, I did!'

'I know who broke it, Kitty.' As she stood clutching the bowl to her waist, a ray of sunlight fell onto Sarah's arm. There were bruises on her skin.

Kitty took hold of her wrist. 'What's that?' Sarah pulled her arm away and hurried to the kitchen. Before Kitty caught up with her, she was rolling down her sleeves. Kitty had seen these marks before, all too often, on the arms of the women in the village. 'Does he drink?'

Sarah laughed, a course kind of laugh. 'Drink? Nathaniel? No, never. Why would you say such a thing?' And with that she made her way to the front room to gather the remaining crockery.

Kitty stood in the door watching her friend clear the table. 'We've both seen these marks before, Sarah, you know we have.'

She pushed past Kitty, returning to the kitchen. 'Nathaniel is a good man, a pious man.'

'Then why is he doing this? A good man wouldn't hurt you.'

Sarah all but dropped the tray on the sideboard and turned on Kitty. 'You don't understand, how could you? You are not married, you have not borne children or had to deal with the daily grind of a household. You are Kitty Canham of Mede Farm with all the privileges that entails.'

Kitty was infuriated. 'What? The privilege of working morning and night to keep the farm going so that you and your father and all the other workers will have food for the table? That's my lot now, Sarah, and don't you forget it!'

Sarah hung her head. 'I am so sorry, I was forgetting.'

Kitty let her anger subside and returned to the matter being addressed. 'Listen to me, Sarah, no man should be allowed to hurt a woman like this, no man.'

Sarah lifted her head. 'Maybe not. But this is my life, Kitty, I live it the best way I can. What choice do I have?' The two women stared at each other, the truth hanging between them. There was a knock on the door. 'That must be Tom.' Sarah took off her apron and straightened her dress, then looked to Kitty. 'Don't tell him about this, ever … please.'

Kitty sighed. 'If that is what you wish.'

'It is, he must never know. No-one must ever know.' Kitty nodded, reluctant to leave it there, hating what was happening to her friend, but resigned to the fact that there was nothing to be done.

Before they travelled home, Kitty asked Tom to stop by her father's grave. He was buried at St Michael's in Thorpe, alongside his parents. It was only fitting, though she wished he had been buried in Beaumont, nearer to home. Tom stayed on the cart whilst she cleared away dead leaves that had gathered around her father's headstone. She prayed for his peace. On the way home,

Tom was quiet and Kitty was lost in thought. She longed to tell him of his sister's plight, but she had made a promise, and keep it she must.

Later that evening, as the light was fading, Kitty wrapped Pa's coat around herself to keep the breeze at bay and walked to the brow of the hill. She watched the farmhands as they lay down their tools and began to make their way home. She recognised, perhaps for the first time, that hers was a noble task; to see families fed and cared for as they worked the land. She vowed, as she had once before, that she would never marry. When she was young it had been a girlish vow, but now, it was a woman's vow; the farm would be her husband and the land her friend.

Chapter Nine

The harvest was in, celebrations past and a grey November hung over the farm. The quiet season was upon them. A mixture of excitement and trepidation filled Kitty as she stood by her bed eyeing an unopened package that she'd collected from Thorpe earlier that day. She carefully unwrapped it. Before her lay a perfectly clean and folded pair of her father's breeches that had been missed when his clothing had been given away. They had been altered for her, under strict instructions of secrecy. She slipped them on. The fabric was firm between her thighs. It felt strange. Having no idea what people would think, she decided to do her best not to care. She dressed her upper body, carefully finishing off the outfit with a long jacket. Taking a deep breath, she made her way downstairs to the kitchen, where Mother and Peggy were making pickles. Joseph was sitting at the table with an open ledger. Peggy noticed Kitty first. A smile spread over her lips as she nudged Kitty's mother. Mother looked up.

'Ah, there you are, Kitty.' She hadn't noticed Kitty's attire, and carried on stirring. 'Did you get everything you wanted?'

Joseph, who had become a fixture at the house, now looked. 'Good God, Kitty, what are you wearing?'

Kitty stood defiant. 'Breeches.' Mother turned, her stunned face almost comical. Kitty rose to her full height. 'I had a pair of father's altered. It makes sense. You can't work on a farm efficiently surrounded by skirts.'

Mother's hand went to her chest. 'But why not? Women do.' It was as if her own womanhood was being threatened.

'Because, Mother, it is not practical, and if a man can wear practical clothing, I don't see why I should not.'

Peggy gave a reassuring smile. 'That is a good point.'

Mother continued with her stirring. 'Well, if it's what you want. We know you must do as you want.'

Kitty ignored the barb. 'It is. And another thing,' she turned to Joseph, 'the harvest is long-since in and it's time I took on the accounts.' Joseph looked at her mother. 'I would like to start on Monday, if that is convenient with you.'

'Of course.'

'Good, that's settled then.' She turned and made her way outside, striding off towards the lower field. She had work to do.

On Sunday morning, Kitty was pleased to have some time to rest. The sky had brightened, which made the walk to church very pleasant. Old Mrs Dobson had received a long-awaited letter from her family, so after the service, they sat together on a bench in the churchyard whilst Kitty read it to her. Mrs Dobson listened intently and asked Kitty to re-read portions that she particularly wanted to remember. When it was finished, she tucked it away in her purse and took Kitty's arm as they made their way home. It was a slow walk, but a most pleasant one. As they walked, Kitty found herself rubbing the callouses on her hands, which she was wont to do these days. Mrs Dobson must have noticed because she stopped, took Kitty's hands and opened her fingers. She stroked an aged palm across Kitty's.

'Now look here, young lady. You may have calloused hands, that is the nature of the work you do,' she said, lifting a hand to Kitty's chest, 'but never forget you have a soft heart. Don't you be getting the two confused.' Her eyes were searching for a response.

Kitty responded as best she could. 'I will do my best.'

The old woman nodded and, seeming content, took Kitty's arm once more. She continued with her tales as they walked. Little did she know how those few words hung in Kitty's mind. Had she become hard? Had she lost the softness that her pa so loved about her? She thought of him and his gentle strength and longed to have him alongside her once more.

When they arrived at Mrs Dobson's door, she told Kitty to wait; she had something for her. The room before her was kitchen, parlour and bedroom all rolled into one, just like any other small cottage. But Kitty couldn't help wondering how a woman so bent with years could keep a home so well. A lace doily lay on the table and on the wall above it hung bobbins of every size.

Mrs Dobson, who had been fumbling in a drawer, saw her looking. 'Oh, I long-since stopped making lace. My fingers are no longer good for twiddle or tumble. My friends say as I should sell 'em, get a pretty penny for 'em. But I likes to see them hanging there, it brings good memories.' She continued rummaging. 'Ah, here it is.' She hobbled across the floor to Kitty and held out an enamel brooch. It was an iridescent blue butterfly. 'I may never have wed, but I had my beaux. There was one who I thought to marry. I would have given my life to him without a second thought. He give this to me as a token.' She placed the brooch into Kitty's hand.

'What happened?'

Mrs Dobson smiled. 'Oh, what always happens, he married someone else.' She looked knowingly at Kitty. Could she have known about Tom? Closing Kitty's hand over the treasure, she said, 'I've watched you grow, Kitty Canham, I saw you at your mother's breast. And I knows that life hasn't always been easy for you, especially now. You take this and give it a new life. And when you wear it, perhaps you'll think of me. I should have let it go long ago, I'm just a sentimental old fool, I expect.' She suddenly looked tired. Kitty thanked her, aware that no amount of thanks would be equal to such a gift.

As Kitty walked away that morning, she felt seen for the first time in a long time. Someone had been watching out for her all these years, and she never knew it. She wished that she had given Mrs Dobson more attention over the years. But as she continued home, lighter in step, she determined to be softer in her manner and to treat her ma with the kindness that she deserved.

As Kitty took off her coat, Peggy appeared in the kitchen door.

'Kitty, your mother would like to see you, in the kitchen.'

'I just have to pop something upstairs.'

Peggy insisted, 'I think you'd better come now.'

Kitty slipped the brooch into her pocket and followed on. Mother was sitting on the settle, clutching the little wooden box that Kitty had seen her father with last spring. She had been crying.

'What is it, Ma? Peggy?'

Peggy placed a chair opposite Mother. 'Why don't you sit down?' Kitty obeyed.

Mother lifted her tear-stained face. 'I'm so sorry, Kitty, I'm so very sorry.' She wiped her tears with a kerchief and gathered herself. 'There is something we should have told you, something you need to know. It should have been said years ago, but your pa didn't want to unsettle things, you know what he was like.' Kitty remembered and smiled. 'When you were little, our family was so full of life. We had a beautiful daughter and for that we were so grateful.' For a moment she looked at Kitty with a tenderness that was rare in her mother's eyes. 'But it is only right that a man should have a son. I tried, Kitty, as you know, I tried so many times. Every one I brought to birth was a boy, but I couldn't keep any of them. After the loss of our last boy, our Samuel, I knew I couldn't go through it again. I'm afraid I lost my way.'

Peggy spoke up, 'You had a lot to deal with.'

Mother was quick to cut her off. 'Nevertheless, it was a dark time.' She fingered her kerchief as she spoke. 'It seems that I wasn't able to be the wife that Robert needed. The marital bed became a barren place. And Robert … ' She looked down at her fingers. 'He met a woman.' A knot was beginning to form in Kitty's stomach. 'You mustn't blame your father, Kitty, he was a man, like any other. He had needs.'

Kitty could not make sense of it. 'What woman, where?'

'In London.'

'What do you mean? Who was she?'

'She was an actress.'

'An actress?!' This was all wrong. Her father hated London. He had no time for play acting.

'Kitty … ' She looked at her mother who held her gaze. 'She gave him a child.'

Kitty stood. 'No … no … I would have known, he would have told me.' For many men it may be so, but not her pa. She looked in desperation to Peggy who just shook her head in affirmation. Just then, Joseph appeared round the door. He had evidently been listening. Kitty glared at him. 'Did you know about this?' He nodded. 'So you all knew, except me!'

They all looked at her. How she hated their pity.

Mother's voice was flat, 'It is the way your father wanted it. He wanted to protect you.'

'From what?' They were all dumb. 'What difference did it make to me? I was here, he was my pa, I was with him every day, nothing could change that. Nothing. We were a family.'

Mother reached out to touch her. 'And we were, we are … '

Kitty recoiled. 'Then why are you telling me this now?'

Joseph sat beside her mother on the settle. 'It's the accounts. Your father has been paying for the child's education. It will be in the accounts.'

Kitty snorted as it all became clear. 'So … that's it … It's a boy, I presume.'

Mother continued, 'You were only ten when he was born. It was a terrible time for your father. I was distant and he … '

Kitty wasn't listening. 'So, I have a twelve -year -old brother. May I ask his name?'

Before Mother spoke, she knew it already. 'It's Robert.'

Kitty shook her head in realisation. 'Of course it is.' Her mind was racing. 'And do you know him? I mean, do you visit him?'

'Your father did, occasionally, just to make sure that everything was well with him. But, Kitty, you were always the most important to him, you know that. You and he were like … '

Kitty stared her down. 'Like what, Mother?' Her eyes alighted on the box, now on the settle beside her mother. 'I saw father with that box once. He was searching through letters. From the boy, I presume.'

'No, they were from … ' Mother's eyes darted towards Joseph.

He took the lead, 'The truth is, Kitty, that the woman's father, he is, well, shall we say, a scoundrel. You will see in the accounts that he took money from your father on numerous occasions, citing extra expenses for his daughter. You will see it all under the name Matthew Hodges. He wrote to your father often, claiming his daughter had lost her youth because of him and was therefore finding work harder to come by. I tried to tell him that the man was taking it for himself, but your father wouldn't listen. He was susceptible to such petitions.'

'He was a kind and generous man,' Peggy retorted.

'Of course, I just meant … '

Kitty had heard enough and sought only to be away, but Joseph spoke again, 'There is one more thing.'

Kitty's mother caught his arm. 'No, Joseph, I don't think we should. Not yet.'

'We might as well tell her now, Judith.'

Kitty steadied herself. 'Tell me what?'

Joseph looked at her mother, who nodded. 'Your mother wants to bring the boy home for Christmas.'

Kitty laughed out loud. A moment ago she had discovered she had a brother and now he was joining the family. 'No, I'm sorry, that is going too far.' She looked to her mother. 'Are you serious? Tell me you are not serious.'

Her mother now rose. 'He is your brother, Kitty. He is your blood. And the only thing we have left of your father.'

She was shaking. 'You have me! I know you've barely noticed over the years. And I know you hated the way Pa and I were together, don't think I didn't notice. But I am your daughter, I am your blood. Not him.' Her mother started crying, but Kitty felt little pity.

Joseph put his arm around her mother's shoulder. 'Come, Judith, let's get some fresh air. And, Kitty, you had better pull yourself together before we return. I am sure you have many questions. We can talk further when you are calm.' He led Judith from the room.

Kitty had hoped that perhaps with Pa's passing, she would grow closer to her mother, but as she watched Joseph lead her away, she was aware that another was already in her place.

Kitty sank onto the chair, her strength gone. The inlaid box lay on the settle. She picked it up, caressing the smooth wood, tracing the exquisite floral inlay with her finger. 'Well, Peggy, it seems that life is not at all as I thought it was.' Kitty went to open the lid.

Peggy stepped forward. 'I shouldn't.' But her plea only served to give the box heightened importance. Kitty opened it. A neatly folded pile of letters lay before her. Picking up the first, she unfolded it and read aloud:

My Darling, I miss you so terribly. How long will it be until I see you again? My longing for you never wanes…

Kitty had no desire to read further. Instead, she lifted the letter to her nose, a slight scent of perfume lingered there. It was signed Rosalind and dated 1737. That was the year that Kitty turned seventeen. Peggy's hand went to her mouth as she sunk onto the bench.

Kitty searched through the letters; they were all of a similar vein. An anger and sorrow was rising within that threatened to overwhelm her. She replaced the letters and closed the box firmly shut, breathing hard. A growl rose from her belly and grew to a roar as she threw the box to the floor. It smashed apart. She sank to her knees and began tossing the letters and the remnants of the box into the fire.

Peggy came to Kitty's side and joined her in the endeavour. 'It's a good burning, Kitty, a good burning.' They watched as the delicate inlay twisted this way and that, finally falling into the flames. Peggy put her arm around Kitty and squeezed her close. 'I'll make you a brew, shall I?' Kitty smiled through her tears. Dear Peggy, she was sure that everything was made better by a brew. Kitty feared that this time it would not be so.

Chapter Ten

Kitty never spoke to her mother about the letters, neither did she take up the accounts on the allotted day. Instead, she worked on the land until her muscles hurt. As soon as she stopped, memories of her life with her pa flooded through her mind and she found herself searching for clues; surely something must have been said or done that would have given his transgression away, but nothing came.

It was Christmas Eve and a hoar frost had settled; the whited sky was heavy over the land. Kitty trudged across the east field, spreading hay for the sheep who's plaintive bleating called from the damp mists and encouraged her on. Old Jacob was sick and his apprentice, young Peter Trefall, was so drunk the night before that he fell and gashed his leg sorely, so the task fell to Kitty. Today she was glad of it, for it was the day that the boy was to arrive. Mother asked her to be there to greet him and Kitty said she would try, but as the hour drew near, she had found a need to be working.

She was bent over one of the smaller ewes, rubbing her chilled little body with hay, when she heard the carriage approach. She gave the ewe one last rub and set off towards the house. It was late afternoon and the light was fading. A lantern was lit in the window. In front of the house, Peggy stood with Mother, Joseph a couple of steps behind. Kitty stopped by the old chestnut to watch as the coach drew up. At first, she couldn't see the boy when he stepped down, he was hidden by the coach. But once it moved away, Kitty saw that Bouncer was greeting him, wagging his tail in welcome. The boy stooped and ruffled his head. She could barely make out the figure of the boy, save for the fact that he was formally attired. Joseph ushered him indoors, followed by Bouncer and the women. The door shut behind them.

Kitty stood in the silent air. She could make no sense of the scene that had just passed before her, though it was now etched on her mind. She made for the warmth of the pigger's pen. The old fat sow lay sleeping in the corner, steam rising in great billows around her head. Kitty thrust her hand into the pocket of her father's coat and felt for the smooth bowl of his pipe. She drew it out, along with a pouch of tobacco she had found on the mantle. Often she had thought about trying the pipe and now seemed a perfect time. Sitting on a beam by the sleeping sow, she tapped it and filled it. Then, using a straw taper, she lit it from her lantern, sucking hard and tamping with a stick, as she'd seen her pa do so often. It took a few attempts until curls of smoke rose from the bowl. A sense of elation came over her as she sucked more, choked a little, and began to sink into the smell and taste of it. Her head felt light and fell back against the wall as she blew a stream of smoke up into the air.

Just then, the back door of the house opened. Kitty held the pipe low. Peggy called, 'Kitty, is that you?'

'Yes, I'll be in in a minute.' The door closed. Kitty took one more long drag. Breathing out, she let the smoke drift slowly around her. She then dampened the pipe and, uncertain if it was really cold, hid it in a chink in the wall. She stood, feeling calm now and ready to face the company that awaited her. Gathering her lantern she headed indoors, rinsing her hands in the washhouse before entering the kitchen.

Mother was sitting at the table with the boy beside her. He rose at Kitty's arrival. Mother spoke, 'Ah, there you are, Kitty. Robert, this is your sister, Kitty.'

The boy bowed a little. 'I am pleased to meet you.'

Kitty frowned at the young man standing before her. His jaw was set like her father's and his thick black hair was unmistakable. He stood erect as if starched into his clothing. She had rehearsed this moment so often. Now it had come, it seemed so ordinary. 'So … you are my brother.' He looked to her ma. She smiled and nodded. The boy sat. Kitty turned to warm herself by the fire. 'Where's Joseph?'

Mother replied, 'He went home.'

Kitty was surprised, but pleased that he had had the decency to leave the family alone. The boy didn't take his eyes off Kitty but watched as she lifted her leg over the bench to join them at the table. She faced him square on. 'What is it, young man? You obviously have something on your mind.'

He spoke without hesitation, 'We don't have ladies like you where I come from.'

Kitty almost laughed. 'And what is that like, I pray?'

'Well, you are … do you always wear breeches?'

Kitty laughed fully this time. 'Maybe.'

'Now, Kitty, don't tease the boy.' Mother turned to him, speaking deliberately, 'She wears those for her farm work, otherwise she wears skirts like everyone else.' She looked hard at her daughter. 'Why don't you go and change? Then we can have supper. It's been a long day for us all.'

Kitty studied the boy a moment longer before taking her leave. There was a bowl of warm water waiting for her; Peggy was ever ahead of her needs. She splashed it over her face, surprised how little the arrival of Robert touched her. She combed her hair, which she had always been so proud of, but it had become a tangled mess. Looking at her rough hands, front and back, they looked far older than her years. Perhaps the boy was right; perhaps she was unusual. In recent weeks, her mother had tried to encourage her to make an effort. But the more she did so, the less Kitty was inclined to take the advice. She started to undress, thinking about how tomorrow would be. She could barely remember the Christmas of last year. Her world had changed so much since then. Perhaps she, too, had changed.

Kitty rose the next morning to a white world. She stood wrapped in her blanket, staring out at the scene before her. All was still and pure and white. The Christmases of her childhood played in her mind; she could not stop the tears from forming. Wiping them away, she turned her thoughts to the day ahead. After church, they were to be joined by Mrs Dobson, Joseph, Aunty Mary, Tom and his new wife, Miriam, who was now looking more pregnant than their short marriage could sustain and which had helped to make sense of Tom's rejection of her. If she had known the state of affairs it would have made the whole affair less painful. But Kitty liked her, despite herself. She was an easy sort of girl. She didn't seem to fight with life as Kitty did, but took things as they came. Miriam seemed good for Tom, better than she could ever have been.

Kitty tried to make something of her hair, but it wouldn't yield. So she tied it as best she could and, once dressed, made her way downstairs. The Yule log, gathered the previous day, was burning bright in the hearth.

Peggy came in from the washhouse. 'Good morning, Kitty, and a very Happy Christmas to you.' She held out her arms. Kitty could never resist their embrace. Already the smell of freshly baked breads filled the room. The table was decked with nuts and fruits and a myriad of small bowls filled with treats. Quite different to the plain supper the night before. The door opened and Robert stood with his eyes popping out at the feast being laid before him.

Peggy welcomed him, 'Come in, young man, I'll get you something to eat. Did you sleep well?'

'Yes, thank you, very well.' He sat at the table, eyes darting about the room, taking everything in. 'Am I sleeping in my father's study?' Kitty didn't like the ease with which he used the term 'my father'.

Peggy replied, 'We made it as comfortable as possible. I do hope it is to your liking?'

'Yes, it is very fine. And what are these?' He picked up a nut from a bowl on the table.

Peggy explained, 'They are walnuts. Do you not have walnuts at your school?'

He studied one closely. 'I don't think so. They do look peculiar. May I eat one?'

'No, they are for later.'

Kitty stood amazed at the child's outspoken nature. Peggy put bread and cheese on the table, and the boy ate. Kitty had no stomach for food or his company so she took her leave.

She had, for some time, wanted to find a way to thank Mrs Dobson for the gift that had touched her so deeply. So she took a piece of fruit cake and one of the small gift boxes of sweetmeats that had been set aside. She thought to ask the old lady if she would like to walk with her to church. The snow was not too thick and gave way to her feet with ease. The cold air stung her cheeks as she walked. Across the field, she could see Peter tending the sheep and was satisfied.

When Kitty arrived at the cottage, she found Mrs Dobson huddled in her chair by the fire, fast asleep. She crept in, knelt at the old lady's side, and lay the sweetmeats in her lap. She started awake, but smiled when she saw Kitty, and opened the packet. 'My, how lovely. I shall look forward to these.'

Kitty was pleased with her response. 'There will be plenty more later.'

Mrs Dobson shook her head. 'I am afraid this weather is not kind to an old woman like me. I will not be coming with you today. Please give my apologies to your dear mother.'

Kitty was most sincere when she told Mrs Dobson that they would miss her company. She smiled and lay her head back, allowing her eyes to close again. Kitty stoked the fire, tucked the blanket around her and said that she would bring food from the feast. But her aged friend was already asleep.

The church was full of festive cheer. The coming of Christ lifted even the most dour of souls. Mother had not brought the boy to church, perhaps not ready to explain him yet, which meant that Kitty could enjoy the morning without complication. Once home, and the feasting had begun, Kitty relaxed into the warmth of the room and, despite herself, found some pleasure in the familiar faces around the table. It amused her to see Miriam giggling at all of Tom's jokes. Tom's Aunt Mary had a little too much cider and started telling tales of her own. But when the games started, presumably to entertain the boy, Kitty slipped away to take Mrs Dobson a basket of food. She found her in better spirits and ready to tell tales of Christmases past. Kitty was happy to keep her company until darkness fell. She helped her to her bed before she left. As Kitty straightened the covers around her, Mrs Dobson smiled and reached out to touch the brooch at Kitty's chest. 'It suits you well, my dear, I knew it would.'

Kitty smiled in return, but, obviously exhausted, the old woman sighed and lay back on her pillow, closing her eyes. Kitty tidied the small room, built up the fire and crept out. As she walked home, a soft snow started to fall. She wrapped her cloak around her, in part to keep out the cold, but perhaps, more urgent, was the need to comfort the longing within her that was still so keen on such nights as this.

Chapter Eleven

Christmas came and went. The longer the boy stayed, the easier it became. In some ways Kitty was grateful to him. He was now the centre of attention, so no one paid her much heed. She was free to come and go as she pleased. Today, on the eighth day of Christmas, Kitty stood by the window, watching mother and Joseph as they bade farewell to the boy. To Kitty it was like watching the events of someone else's life, without sense or feeling. She hadn't been surprised at the eager look her mother gave the boy the first time he called her 'mother'. Neither had she been surprised at the evident affection growing between her mother and Joseph. It all seemed an inevitable river, flowing with or without her consent. She had tried to fulfil her father's wishes, but it now seemed that her mother's care was firmly in Joseph's hands.

There was, however, one thing that had surprised and delighted Kitty. On Boxing Day, a letter had arrived from Eleanor Manley-Hogg, inviting Kitty to join her for several days in London. Mother had been horrified at the idea because of the danger and difficulty of travelling this time of year. But the ground was hard with frost, so the roads should be passable, and anyway, Kitty was determined to go. So it was agreed. The coach that was to return the boy to school would take Kitty to the Manor. From there she would join Eleanor in her carriage and carry on to London. She had often asked her pa to take her to the city but he always refused, saying that it was an unpleasant place. Perhaps her determination to go now was, in part, to spite him. Why shouldn't she see what he had evidently seen and enjoyed?

Since receiving the letter, Kitty had been busy with preparation. She mended her few good items of clothing, which she had cared little about since Pa died. She even let her mother spend hours untangling her hair. It was a good time. And now she was packed and watching as the boy finally stepped up into the carriage.

Her reverie was broken. 'Well, are you going or not?' Peggy stood beside her wiping her hands on her apron. 'Now, you be careful in London, and keep your purse close. There are many as would strip you of your skin should you let them.' Peggy slipped Kitty's cloak around her shoulders.

'Thank you, Peggy. You always look out for me.' Peggy's skin wrinkled in a smile. Kitty kissed her on the cheek.

'Go on now.' She turned back into the kitchen and her chores.

Kitty stepped outside into the frozen world. Joseph took in her appearance. 'I must say, Kitty, you look very fine, doesn't she, my dear?' He had taken to calling her mother 'my dear', in an insidious tone which made Kitty sick to the stomach.

Mother smiled. 'You look lovely, my darling.' Kitty gave no response as she climbed aboard the coach.

The boy waved as they pulled away. Once the farm was behind them, he took the blanket from his knees and held it out to Kitty. 'Here, it is cold, you will need this.' She refused it. By now he knew better than to insist. He commented occasionally on the sights that passed the window, but Kitty made no attempt to engage in conversation. She chose instead to sit in silence and watch the relentless white pass by. As they approached Thorpe, the boy pulled himself to the window. 'Is that the Manor House?' Kitty looked. Through the trees, the windows glistened in the early sun.

'Yes,' she said simply.

He looked quizzical. 'It's not as big as I thought it would be.' The boy scoured the landscape with keen eyes.

When they pulled into the driveway, he turned to her. 'Kitty?'

'Yes.'

He seemed uncertain. 'You can't know how much it means to me . . . being part of the family.'

Kitty was irritated. 'You have a family, your mother's family.'

He looked abashed. 'I know, it's just that it's not like yours. My grandfather is . . . I don't like him.'

Kitty remembered what Joseph had said of him. She had thought that he had called him a scoundrel for effect at the time, but now she wondered if there was something in it. Kitty looked at Robert for the first time not as a rival but as a boy. A boy in an uncertain world.

She fingered the enamel brooch at her chest and, gathering all the kindness she could muster, she said, 'Don't worry, you have a family now.' Even as she spoke, her own loss turned in her stomach. He beamed, a natural boyish smile which quite unnerved Kitty.

The coach jolted to a halt and the door opened. She turned to the boy. 'Goodbye, Robert. Have a safe journey.' He waved as the coach drew away.

Eleanor was standing outside, ready for the journey. 'Kitty, how perfect, I am so glad you could come. I thought we would set off straight away.' Kitty stepped aside as a carriage approached, gleaming deep red in the early sun. A manservant hauled Eleanor's luggage aboard, alongside Kitty's meagre bag. Eleanor took her hands. 'Now, you are not to worry about anything, I have got everything we could possibly need. And we have James' men to protect us on the way.'

Now Kitty looked, she saw the formidable figures sitting firmly in place. The women climbed aboard and sat back on the rich upholstered seat, a thick fur rug caressing their legs. As the coach pulled away, Kitty felt the excitement of her adventure.

The journey was spent talking about everything and nothing. The events of Father's death were spoken of. Eleanor showed much sympathy. But soon enough, Kitty's life, rather than being a topic of conversation was merely the starting point to Eleanor's many tales. She was different today, excitable. Captain James was away studying an ancient sword. His interest in weaponry bored Eleanor and took up much of his time. Eleanor spoke of him with fondness but was evidently pleased to have a husband whose many projects left her to have a life of her own. The ground was good and firm due to the freeze, making the journey less treacherous than it may have been.

After a short stop, when Kitty was rearranging the blankets over her legs, she looked up to see a mischievous smile on Eleanor's lips. 'I have not been wholly honest with you, Kitty.' Kitty wondered what on earth was coming. 'We've been invited to a masquerade party on twelfth night.'

Kitty gasped. 'A masquerade?'

'I thought if I told you, you would not come. Was it naughty of me?'

Kitty smiled. 'A little, perhaps.'

'I did so long for your company after that very pleasant afternoon we had together. I could not resist bringing you. Have you been to a masquerade before?'

'No, not really. We've done a little dressing up at home but . . .'

'They are such fun, you will love it, I know you will.'

Kitty sat back, resigned.

Eleanor looked contrite. 'You do forgive me, don't you, Kitty?' Her pleading eyes looked so very young, even though she was a few years older than Kitty.

As always, she could not be cross for long. 'Of course. But you know me well already, I should not have come had I known. What am I to wear?'

Eleanor was delighted. 'That is the best bit. We are dressing for the twelve days of Christmas. Do you know the song?' Kitty surely did. It had become a favourite at home. 'We are invited to the home of Mr and Mrs Bastion, he's in the cloth industry, a wonderful, colourful couple. You'll like them.' Kitty's heart was sinking fast, a colourful couple sounded rather unsettling. But Eleanor's joyful presence made everything bearable.

By the time they approached London, it was dark. The carriage moved slower now, as the mud thickened. Kitty had been warned of the smell, but was unprepared for the intensity of it. Eleanor held a kerchief to her nose. Kitty followed suit. Out of the darkness, hovels emerged leaning this way and that. Men and women were in the streets, huddled around small fires, drinking and laughing. Eleanor leant forward and closed the blinds explaining that there was no point in looking upon other people's misery.

Kitty had heard of the life of the poor in the city, but even so the sight appalled her. 'How can they laugh in such circumstances?'

'The poor have a great capacity for laughter.' And that was all that was said. They carried on in silence. In the darkness, Eleanor assured Kitty that although this was the most trying part of the journey, they would soon be arriving. At last the carriage rattled over the cobbles. The stench abated and after a few more streets, they came to a standstill. The door was opened and the women stepped down in front of a flat-faced building that towered above them with more windows than brick, or so it seemed to Kitty.

When they approached the door, Kitty turned to view her surroundings. A mist hung low, through which the light from lanterns bloomed. The tall houses, all joined, made a great square. It was quiet. Eleanor took her arm. 'Let's get indoors.'

Eleanor addressed the manservant who stood aside to let them in. 'Good evening, Gregory. I trust that you and Mrs Gordon are well?'

A round-faced, grey-haired woman bobbed beside her husband. 'We are indeed, thank you, madam.'

The hall had the highest ceiling that Kitty had ever seen, and from it hung a chandelier fitted with twenty candles or more. It was not lit, but nonetheless it shone in the light of the candelabra standing beneath the stairs. Eleanor informed Mrs Gordon that they would take a light supper in the parlour. They made their way upstairs to a room where a fire burned, welcoming in the hearth. Kitty was glad to sit on steady ground after the long journey.

Supper was brought and even Eleanor now had few words. After supper, Kitty was led up another flight of stairs to a comfortable and warm bedroom. Unused to such luxury, she sank on to the chair by the fire to savour every moment of her surroundings. But soon her father invaded her thoughts. This was London, where he had met Rosalind who was the beginning of all of Kitty's pains. Exhaustion from the journey overcame her and she made ready for bed. Tomorrow she would have to take part in a world that she had no frame of reference for and felt wholly inadequate to the task. However, climbing into the white sheets, she determined to enjoy every moment of this trip. She had agreed to it and wasn't going to let Eleanor down. After all, a miserable companion is no companion at all.

On rising, Kitty found Eleanor in the parlour, rifling through a writing desk beneath the window. 'Ah, Kitty, I do hope you slept well. Was everything to your liking?'

'Perfect, thank you.' In the morning light, Kitty could appreciate the room properly. The walls were a pinkish colour, with heavy floral drapes and colourful furnishings. Eleanor's exuberant style, which seemed at odds at the Manor, fitted perfectly here. A table was laid with breakfast. The smell of hot chocolate filled the room.

Eleanor found what she was looking for. 'I thought we'd breakfast here. It is so much cosier than in the dining room.' She sat and helped herself to a warm roll. Kitty followed suit. The fresh butter melted into the bread. Kitty felt sure that she had never tasted anything so good.

Eleanor wiped her mouth with the embroidered napkin. 'Now, this morning, Monsieur Robillard... I think you met him at the Manor? The designer?' Kitty remembered him very well. 'He'll be coming later this morning to help us design our outfits for twelfth night. I have the song words here.' She held out a scruffy piece of paper. 'Albert is so good at such things. Then this afternoon we will go to the dressmakers and see what Miss Wright can conjure up.'

After breakfast, Eleanor arranged for her chest of fabric and costumes to be brought to the parlour. She said that as there was so little time, it would be easier for the dressmaker to make alterations rather than start from scratch. In the meantime, she insisted that a rendition of the Twelve Days was essential for getting them in the mood. After several false attempts, the women made a surprisingly sweet sound and got all the way through to the end. Eleanor suggested that they go to the masquerade as milkmaids, but that was far too close to home, so Kitty persuaded her otherwise. The thought of laying geese had them in gales of laughter. Kitty had not laughed, really laughed, for so long. And it felt good.

When Eleanor went to attend to the household, Kitty was left on her own and to her own thoughts. It was so good to be in a different world. Gazing out of the window, she could see now that the house was not central in the square, but rather to one side, which gave a good view of the houses around. They were all fairly uniform and gave a pleasing sense of order. The sun shone intermittently through the skittish clouds. It was a blustery day. People were busy going about their business, clutching hats to their heads and holding down wayward cloaks. The gardens were formally laid out and although in its naked winter state, she could imagine how beautiful it must look in the warm weather with couples promenading in the summer sun. But today the weather caused everyone to hurry. A coach arrived at the house next door. A rather dishevelled gentleman emerged from the front door in a hurry. He hadn't reckoned on the wind and his hat blew off his head, seemingly in more of a hurry than the man himself. It tumbled down the street. The man ran after it, clinging to his clothes as if they were not fully secured about his body. Kitty found herself giggling at the spectacle. A few others joined in the pursuit, until the hat got caught in a bush in the gardens. A rather formal looking gentleman handed the hat back to the man, who bowed and retreated in the most comical way before climbing aboard the waiting coach. It pulled away and Kitty watched as the street returned to normal.

The door opened behind her. A young maid bobbed and announced in her best English accent, 'Monshur Robi-lard' She looked sheepishly at the man who stood beside her.

'Very good, Leah, your French is improving.' She giggled and scurried away. Albert Robillard stood before her, better attired than when she had last seen him. 'She will never get the hang of it.' He laughed. 'What about you, Miss Canham, can you say my name?'

Kitty wasn't going to be drawn into his antics. 'I am sure I shall once you have taught me, but until then I shall refrain.'

He smiled and raised an eyebrow. 'Forgive me, Miss Canham, you are quite correct, I must not tease.' He took her hand and kissed it. This time she was a little more prepared. 'It is delightful to see you. You are looking very well.'

'Thank you, I am.' She was not going to let him get the upper hand. 'It is very good of you to come and help us today. Eleanor and I have looked at the song, and have had a few thoughts, mostly quite silly.'

'Phla, phla.' With a flick of his hand, any ideas they may have had were swept aside. 'I shall have designs you could only dream of.'

'Albert!' Eleanor exclaimed in a perfect French accent as she swept into the room.

He took her by the shoulders and kissed her on both cheeks. 'Ma chérie! How is my garden? Is that man still interfering with it?' Eleanor reassured him that all was well, then hurried him on to the subject of costumes. She explained that they had to be fairly simple because there were only a few days for them to be created. Before long, they were all knelt on the rug surrounded by bits of fabric, old costumes and scraps of paper on which Albert was sketching his designs. Each one was exquisite, and Eleanor bobbed in delight. It was decided that she would go with five gold rings entwined in her hair and a flowing gown with golden trim. Once that was settled, they turned to Kitty. She expressed her desire for simplicity. It was going to be bad enough going to a masquerade, but to be dressed in some exotic garment would be mortifying.

Albert studied her. 'Ah, my little English rose, we will create something more subtle for you.' Kitty bit her lip as he rummaged through the oddments at hand. 'Aha!' He looked triumphant. 'A piper!' He pulled out a tartan bodice and little tartan beret.

Eleanor gasped. 'I remember that! She held the bodice to her body. 'I wore it to a Scottish reel. Miss Wright will do wonders with it for you, Kitty.'

So it was agreed.

After luncheon, the women prepared to set off to the dressmaker. They were to walk as it was only a couple of streets away. The clothes and bits and bobs that would be needed had been bagged up and sat in the hallway. Kitty went to pick it up, but a maid appeared. 'I'll take that, madam.'

Kitty was loath to let her do so, she was half Kitty's size. 'I'll manage, thank you.' But Eleanor appeared and saw Kitty holding the bag. Kitty looked at the young woman before her, all dressed and ready to go, and conceded. 'Perhaps it is a little heavy.' Then, holding it out, 'If you wouldn't mind.'

The maid took it and the little party stepped out into the

street. Eleanor whispered as they left, 'You are learning.' She gave Kitty a warming smile.

The wind had dropped. As they walked, the buildings became smaller and less uniform. Street sellers lined the way and people of every sort bustled about their business. One group of women stood in a doorway, quite unsubtle in the selling of their wares. Kitty found it difficult not to stare. Eleanor took no mind. The dressmaker's shop was small but well kept, brimming with fabrics. Mrs Wright welcomed them. In no time she had measured Kitty and alterations had been agreed. Eleanor addressed the maid who waited patiently by the door, 'Leah, take Miss Canham to the curios. She needs to find a flute of some sort.' Then she addressed Kitty, 'Leah will take care of you.'

Leah seemed to take to Kitty. She smiled up at her. 'It's just down the street, miss, follow me.' They hadn't gone far when they reached a large warehouse. Kitty couldn't help stopping at the door. 'Oh, it's not that one, miss, it's a little further down.'

The door was open. Kitty's eyes widened at the extravagant display of tableware and glassware that lay before her. 'Let's pop in here first, Leah, I'm sure Mrs Manley-Hogg wouldn't mind.'

Kitty entered before Leah could offer any resistance. There were fine tea sets and jugs, and plates of every sort. But it was the glassware that took her breath away. There were tall flutes and goblets, chandeliers, jewellery, and ornaments. She passed those that were too wonderful for her and came upon a table on which a number of perfume bottles stood. Some were engraved and some decorated with the most intricate detail. There was one, however, that took her eye more than any other. It was a ruby red perfume bottle which caught the sun as it seeped through the window, high in the cavernous building. Kitty held it up to the light, transfixed by the colour.

Leah was beside her. 'I think we'd better be going, miss, if we are to find you a flute.'

'Of course.' She replaced the bottle but halted as a thought came to her. 'Leah, do you think you could find a flute for me?' Leah looked uncertain at first, but consented as long as Kitty promised to stay there until she returned.

Alone now, she took up the little bottle once more and studied it. Delicate roses were engraved around the base, reaching up to the neck of the bottle. Kitty was sure she would not have enough money to buy it, and even if she did, she knew that she would never have use for it at home. She sighed and leant forward to replace it. As she did so she fumbled, the bottle slipped from her hand, bounced on the table, and knocked over another taller bottle. They both came crashing to the floor.

Mortified, Kitty crouched down to gather the broken pieces. A sharp pain caused her to recoil. Blood ran from the side of her hand. She felt a hand cup hers with a kerchief and an arm around her waist as she was lifted to her feet. A woman stood in front of her, looking less than pleased. She went to speak, but the man who supported Kitty spoke first, 'I'll take the lady to the office. Clear up here, will you?' He called over his shoulder as he led Kitty away, 'And bring water and a dressing.'

Kitty was feeling rather faint. It wasn't the blood; she was used to such things. Perhaps it was her deep sense of embarrassment and the overwhelming nature of the city. She found herself sat beside a fire in a small office, mumbling an apology, 'I am so sorry. Can I recompense you?'

'Let's get you cleaned up first. Here.' A small glass of spirits was held out to her. She drank the liquor and let the warmth of it settle her. The woman arrived with the dressings, eyed them both suspiciously, then left. 'Take no mind of Miss Turner, she can be a bit short tempered, but we could not do without her.'

'I really am most awfully sorry.'

The man smiled. 'No need to be, it happens quite often, as you can imagine, but perhaps not always quite so spectacularly.' And with that, he took her hand in his and unfurled her fingers. As he knelt beside her to study her wound, she couldn't help studying him. His dark hair hung in soft curls and was tied in a neat ribbon. A shock of white ran through it, far too white for one so young. His face was good, his nose quite straight. There was a faint shadow of stubble about his cheek. His eyes she could not see; they were focussed on the work at hand.

'There appears to be nothing in the wound, which is a great blessing.' He looked up at her and smiled. Her stomach flipped. She now saw that his eyes were hazel. 'Forgive me, I should introduce myself. My name is John Dalmeny, and this … ' he indicated the space around them, 'this is my workplace, as you can see.' He wrung a fresh cloth in the water and dabbed the wound. Then he set his eyes on her once more. 'May I be so bold as to ask your name?'

'Of course, I am Kitty Canham. I am not from London.'

'I rather gathered that.'

She realised that her country accent must have betrayed her. 'I am from north Essex, visiting with a friend.' As she said that, she remembered Eleanor and Leah and shifted in her seat. 'Thank you for your attendance, but I must be going, I will be missed.'

'Not until we have tended your wound. You wouldn't want it infected.' That word made her shudder. She settled back in the chair.

He gathered a small bottle of tincture. 'I have to confess, I watched you looking at the perfume bottles, from the window here. You seemed quite taken by that particular one. The ruby red, if I am not mistaken.'

'You are correct. It was the way the colour caught the light, it quite took my breath away.'

'We may have something similar?' He was evidently a salesman.

'Oh no, don't worry.' She was already concerned how she would pay for what she had broken, but offered again anyway.

'Please, do not worry about the cost. It was such a little thing.'

Kitty was curious. 'May I ask, how are they made?'

'It is a fascinating process ... ' Mr Dalmeny went on to tell Kitty all about how the glass was heated and fashioned. She could barely imagine it. She watched as his fingers expertly worked to bind her hand. 'There is a small glass jewellery maker not far from here. I could take you to see him. I am sure he would be happy to show you how it is made.'

'That would have been most pleasant. But unfortunately, I am occupied today.'

'Well then, perhaps when you are next in town.' When he finished the binding, he rose and rolled down his sleeves.

Kitty stood. 'I really must be going, I will be missed.'

'Would you like me to escort you?'

'No, thank you.' She would be embarrassed to be found with a young man. 'I am perfectly fine now, Mr Dalmeny, you have been most kind.'

She hastened out of the office. In order not to suffer the embarrassment of the eyes that would surely be upon her, she kept her head down and made her way on to the street. She had no sooner turned out of the door when Eleanor and Leah came hurrying towards her. Eleanor was looking rather cross. 'What happened? Where have you been? Leah came for you, but you weren't there.' Leah stood sheepishly aside. 'What have you done to your hand?'

Kitty explained as they walked home, failing to mention that it was a young man who tended her wounds. She knew that any mention of it would engender questions. Leah had found a flute and Eleanor was pleased with her fitting, so by the time they reached home, all was well between them and, anyway, talk of supper now seemed the most important subject.

Chapter Twelve

The following day was busy. Firstly, there was a visit to be made to James' aunt. Then another to his sister. Eleanor's own relatives lived in Herefordshire. By the time they reached home after the second visit, Eleanor was fidgety. She finally plonked herself on the chair, legs sprawled out and sighed. 'That's that done. I'm fond of James' family, but really they are so stuffy. I am sorry you had to endure their company.'

'I enjoyed it. It is such a different life to my own.'

'Oh, Kitty, sometimes I envy you, living on a farm and being free to roam.'

Kitty smiled and said nothing. How could Eleanor understand the reality of such a life? Eleanor fixed her gaze on Kitty. 'May I ask, why have you not married? You are a good-looking woman, I'm sure there must have been men calling.'

She took a moment to answer, unwilling to betray herself completely. 'Oh, there was one, or so I thought. But it wasn't to be. And anyway, father and I were happy together, I didn't need anyone else.'

Eleanor shifted her attention to Kitty for the first time since they had journeyed together. Sitting with Eleanor in front of the fire had a way of melting restraints. Kitty found herself telling her something of her recent troubles, she even spoke more of Tom. The only one she didn't mention was the boy. Too much pain shared might break down her guard completely, and that was not Kitty's way.

They spent a happy hour just talking about their lives and relationships. When supper was brought in, with it came a note.

Eleanor clapped her hands. 'We have been invited to join Albert and his sister, Florence, at Covent Garden tomorrow. Oh, what fun! There's a winter fair with entertainments. It will be such fun.' She leapt to the desk and started writing. Kitty realised that she rather more enjoyed the fireside Eleanor to the ebullient one. But even so, Eleanor's ability to turn her emotions on a pinhead made Kitty smile. It did her good to be with one who was so free of troubling.

The next morning, the women set forth into a bright, winter's day. As Kitty's cloak was woefully inadequate, according to Eleanor, she leant her a deep red cloak with fur trim and the softest muffler. The sun shone on the paving as they boarded the cab. The further it rattled from Golden Square, the busier the streets became. A bemusing array of humanity bustled about; alongside beggars, drunks and street sellers were heavily-painted men and women of substance, sporting wigs of the most extravagant fashion. She couldn't be sure that she would ever get used to the city. Eleanor explained that Covent Garden was much more fun since the gentry moved west, leaving space for artisans and tinkerers. It seemed to Kitty that Eleanor had a great capacity for fun.

Albert stood outside St. Paul's, waving. A tall, slender woman swathed in colourful drapes stood beside him. Eleanor leant forward. 'I should have explained about Florence. She is an artist.'

Soon they were perched around a table at a coffeehouse taking refreshment, and Kitty couldn't help noticing how close Albert and Eleanor were together. They were very easy, like the greatest of friends.

'Come, Kitty.' Florence took her arm. 'Lets you and I go and find the entertainment.' Kitty stood, for a moment uncertain.

Eleanor smiled and nodded some unspoken acknowledgement at Florence, who took Kitty's arm and led her into the square. 'I believe this is your first visit to the city?' Kitty nodded. 'Well, stay close. I have lived here most of my life and I love it. I can't last more than two days in the country, too much air.'

Kitty took to Florence immediately. Her accent was much gentler than her brother's. She had his looks, although not so fine in features, but she was equal to him in confidence and familiarity.

The afternoon was spent among a dizzying array of acts; stilt walkers, fire eaters and acrobats showed off their skills. And when it became too cold, there were always hot chestnuts and warm drinks to revive. Music was played in every corner and dancers jigged. One dancer was all but naked; his colourful tunic barely covered his manhood. He laughed as he danced. His skinny legs, bending this way and that, were bare but for the colourful slippers that jangled as he moved. He seemed to be aware of nothing but the music. Certainly not the cold air. A woman dressed in like colours sat drinking on a wooden box. She wore a precariously balanced jester's hat perched on her overly large wig. Kitty presumed it to be discarded by the dancing man. She would not easily forget these sights.

Every time Kitty suggested they find the others, Florence guided her away from the idea by leading her to another intrigue. But as the light began to disappear behind the buildings and a chill breeze gathered, Kitty began to grow concerned, her eyes searching the square. 'I really think I must find Eleanor, so that we may travel back together.'

Florence gave a cursory look. 'It seems they are not here. Never mind, I'll find you a cab. Perhaps it's best if you go back to Golden Square. I'm sure she won't be far behind.' With that, she led Kitty to a street where a line of cabs waited. 'And don't you worry about Eleanor. My brother will take good care of her.' She looked Kitty in the eye, as if searching for a response, but Kitty had no idea what she was meant to be responding to. Florence addressed the cabby, 'Forty-one, Golden Square.' She then turned to Kitty. 'Thank you for keeping me company this afternoon. I do hope to see you at the masquerade?'

Kitty was delighted that she had made a friend. 'Yes, I will be there.' The cab set off. Kitty was tired and glad to be heading back to the comfort of Eleanor's parlour.

Eleanor failed to arrive for tea. When Kitty found Mrs Gordon to ask her if she thought Eleanor would be alright, Mrs Gordon just smiled and said, 'Oh I shouldn't worry about Mrs Manley-Hogg. She knows how to take care of herself.' Then she addressed Kitty as though she were a child, 'You go and enjoy your evening, and I'll bring supper along soon. There is really no need to worry.'

After supper, a note came from Eleanor. Kitty opened it keenly. It said that she'd been delayed and that Kitty was not to wait up for her. Kitty sat staring at the note until slowly all the signals that Florence had given her became clear. She felt a fool. Albert's familiarity wasn't on account of him being French, it was the familiarity of fondness, more than fondness. Kitty found herself cool at the realisation. Eleanor had now made her an unwilling accomplice. She stoked the fire and stared awhile.

The wonderful day she had had seemed tarnished. But as the flames danced into life, images of all she had seen began to dance before her and made her smile again. She was beginning to understand something else. She need not make everyone else's business her own. In the village, people had to look out for one another, but in the city, it seemed that everything was different. She was not going to let Eleanor's affair rob her of her newfound joys, and the best way to keep them alive was to write about them. She would surely write in her journal before she slept. But Sarah came to mind. She had been her one true friend, and perhaps it would lift Sarah's spirits to hear of her visit to London. After all, it was the trip they had talked about so often as girls.

Sitting at the desk, Kitty started to write, carefully mind you. It must be written in a way that would be appropriate for the wife of a 'devout' husband. The writing flowed and the joy of sharing what she had seen with her dear friend soon restored her.

Kitty was sitting to breakfast in the parlour when Eleanor appeared in the doorway. Her hat hung in her hand and her hair was less than perfect. 'Kitty, I am so sorry … '

'Please, Eleanor, there is no need. I had a wonderful afternoon with Florence. We saw all sorts of acts in the square, and dancing. It was perfect.' She could feel herself trying to make her own life sound as exciting as Eleanor's.

Eleanor sat, leaning on the table. 'You are splendid. I knew we would be great friends, but I must explain.' Kitty wished she wouldn't. 'My husband and I have an understanding, you see. We are better together if we have something of our own lives.' She began to untangle her hair. 'I couldn't be cooped up, I just couldn't. James knows that. He is a good man. You do see, don't you?'

Kitty did not see, but nonetheless said, 'Of course.'

'Good. Obviously, we do not speak of what we get up to when we … Well, when we are apart. So I would be grateful if you would not mention it to anyone. It can be just between us.' Kitty nodded, resigned to her complicity.

'Good.' Eleanor jumped up and announced that today would be a rest day of reading and cards. She left with her hat in one hand and a piece of toast in the other. This was not what Kitty expected her trip to London to be like at all!

The day was spent just as Eleanor had said, playing games and eating the most delicious fancies. The outfits for the masquerade were delivered. Eleanor was quite right about Mrs Wright; the fitting was good and she'd managed to make everything look so crisp and clean.

The following day was spent in preparing. After luncheon, both women took a rest. Kitty lay on the bed looking out of the window at a grey sky. A fire had been lit in the hearth making the room cheery in the gloomy light. Her pa had taught her to read the sky, and this afternoon she could see it was laden with snow. Soon, she drifted into sleep only to be woken moments later. 'Madam said I should wake you, miss.' Leah stood inside the door. 'She said it is time to dress. Shall I help you, miss?'

This afternoon Kitty was grateful for Leah's help and companionship. She was an easy kind of girl, like the farm girls at home.

Once all was done, Kitty made her way to the parlour. Eleanor stood by the fire looking quite beautiful in a white-and-gold toga with golden rings and ribbons entwined in her high wig. Kitty was happy to look as well as she did. Mrs Wright had found her a green skirt to go with her tartan bodice. The beret sat jauntily to the side of her head. The flute was hanging on a ribbon from her skirt. That was Leah's idea. The women exchanged appreciation as they put on their cloaks and made their way to the door.

Chapter Thirteen

The coach pulled up outside a house that was not dissimilar to the one in Golden Square. It was certainly grander though; either side of the door stood fluted columns and each window was large and awash with light. The street itself, however, was a different story. It was all mud. Eleanor explained that the host, Mr Bastion, was a wealthy businessman who had the house specially built in a new part of town. The paving was yet to be added. Kitty was pleased to see that he'd had the forethought to lay a shingle path. It wasn't perfect but it somewhat kept the mud at bay. Kitty and Eleanor picked their way to the front door. It opened as they arrived. A wave of music and laughter flooded the street.

A man with a stomach the size of a barrel came to greet them. He was dressed in brown and green with a bird of some sort nesting in his wig. 'Mrs Manley-Hogg, how lovely to see you. Come in, come in.' His voice matched his stature. 'And you must be Miss Canham. Lovely, lovely, do come in.'

He then turned to greet others that were stepping in from the cold. Cloaks were taken, then they were shown to a very large and ornately decorated room, where they were greeted by a bemusing array of painted faces. There were any number of birds perched in wigs and on shoulders. One man was dressed as a drum, a large hoop hanging around his waist and drumsticks sticking out of his wig. And another wearing a beak with half an egg stuck to his bottom. She could feel herself gawping and was incapable of doing otherwise.

Eleanor's eyes were shining. 'Isn't this wonderful?!'

Kitty was not so sure. There were a number dressed as milkmaids, men and women alike. For a moment, it made her uncomfortable to see her fellow country folk so mocked. But Eleanor halted her thoughts with her bubbling laugh, her face wreathed in delight. She took Kitty's hand and dragged her around the room, introducing her as she went. But they only stopped for the briefest of introductions because it was obvious that there was only one person that Eleanor was truly keen to find. At last they spotted Albert dressed in a tasteful array of white feathers.

Eleanor took Kitty's arm. 'You will be alright, won't you?' Kitty nodded, so Eleanor hurried away.

'Well, Miss Canham, you are from the county, I hear.' It was a young woman she had been introduced to a few moments before.

'Yes, I come from North Essex,' Kitty replied simply.

The woman cried, 'Oh, how charming!' she proceeded to call her husband to her side to meet 'Miss Canham from North Essex.'

A hand took hold of her arm and drew her away. It was Florence. 'Thought you needed saving. Let's get a drink.' Florence led her to the punch table; the warm punch was most welcome. She stood back looking Kitty up and down. 'You look wonderful' Then she leant in close and whispered, 'This is a Titania costume, but don't tell anyone.' Now she looked, Kitty could see that she was dressed in a swathe of fine, leafy fabric, her hair entwined with twigs. Florence's ability to take no notice of what others thought caused Kitty to laugh at the sight.

The music stopped and the host climbed onto a chair. He announced that it was time to clear the room for dancing. Some spilled out of the room, obviously looking for a less energetic endeavour. Kitty and Florence pressed themselves against the wall while the space was cleared. When the music started up again, Florence looked keen and held out her hand. 'Will you dance?'

'With you?' Kitty was uncertain.

'Why not? You don't want to dance with any of these, do you?' The two made their way to the floor. They danced for one, two, three dances. Florence must have noticed that Kitty was flagging. 'Come, let us get some air.' She led Kitty out into the entrance hall, and to a settle by the front door.

Kitty thanked her as they sat. 'I am not used to such gatherings.'

'You must dance at home; you know the dances well.'

'Oh yes, we dance, but usually in the open air.' Florence was most amused by the idea.

Just then, a lean feathered creature approached. 'Florence! How splendid.' He kissed Florence's hand and then looked at Kitty. 'And who do we have here?'

'This is Miss Canham. Now don't you try any of your antics on her, she is visiting from the country.'

The man now took Kitty's hand and kissed it. 'How delightful. Would you care to join me in a dance?' Kitty quickly rejected the idea, citing tiredness. 'Then I shall rest with you.' He tried to squeeze himself between the two women.

Florence came to the rescue again. 'Oh no you don't, you will dance with me.' She jumped up.

After a moment, he said, 'Well if I must, I must.' He held out his arm to Florence who leant back to Kitty. 'He's harmless really, I know how to handle him. You'll be alright here?' Kitty nodded and the couple glided away.

For a moment, Kitty was left alone, but all too soon she could see a couple of men approaching. Standing as they arrived, she said, 'Excuse me,' and walked with purpose past them towards the door at the other side of the hall. A woman was warbling some incoherent song, which caused her to hesitate before moving on towards the back of the house. Pulling at the bodice that clung too tightly to her body, she found a shadowy spot beneath the stairs in which to rest. She let her head fall back against the wood panelling; the firmness of it was strangely settling.

From another door, almost opposite her, she could hear a man's voice. He was reciting something, poetry perhaps. She was intrigued and quietly pushed the door open. The man reciting stood by the window. All around there were bodies lounging in chairs or sitting on the floor. It seemed to Kitty that these were folks who took the call to dress up far less seriously. She was glad to be amongst them. The room seemed to be a small library. She found a spot on the floor by the door. Someone passed her a cushion. Another passed her a glass, from which she drank gratefully. The poem finished and another started. It was long and lyrical. The room was warm and the man's voice was gently musical. Kitty was lulled into a great sleepiness.

She started awake to the sound of clapping. A young woman beside her spoke, 'He has the most wonderful voice, don't you think?' Kitty had to agree, it was rich and deep. The woman introduced herself as Alina Scott, a friend of Mr Bastion's daughter, Beatrice. No sooner had Kitty introduced herself, than the young woman stood up and addressed the room, 'Everyone… Everyone… ' The room hushed. 'This is Kitty Canham, she is from the country, and this is her first visit to town.' Kitty smiled and stood, though her heart sank.

A large older man approached, laughing heartily. 'Ah, that great wasteland we like to call the country. How do you do, Miss Canham, we are so glad that you've joined our little troupe of misfits this evening.' He spied her empty glass. 'Drink … drink for the young lady!'

A man in dishevelled dress approached with a flagon. 'Ah, a fellow piper, I see.' There was little to tell, until he lifted the roughly hewn stick that hung round his neck and pretended to blow it. He was rather drunk. 'I'll play you a tune.' He found himself most amusing and turned to his fellows who encouraged him on.

The large man called, 'Let's have a song! Alina, come, let's hear one of your county ballads for our new friend.' Alina took her place by the window and began a ballad that Kitty knew well. It drew a homesickness from her. Not so much for the place itself, but for the warm fires of her past. Alina's voice was sweet and Kitty was soon swaying and singing to the tune.

When it was done, Alina came and took Kitty by the hand. 'Come sing with me.' There was a call of approval as Kitty was jostled to the front. 'Do you know Down in the Meadow?' Again Kitty knew it well and the two women began to sing. Harmonies broke out and others joined in. She was enjoying herself immensely and whether it was the alcohol or the warmth of the company, her inhibitions were slipping away.

'May I sing you a song?' volunteered Kitty. 'It is one we always sing this time of year at home.'

There was a whoop of approval and a settling as Alina stepped aside, leaving Kitty to her audience. She began, and with half-closed eyes she felt she could have been, for all the world, at home among her kin. The tale flowed from her lips and seemed to hypnotise the room. As she approached the final verses, she looked up. A man was leaning on the doorpost with a cup in hand, his jacket held loosely by his side. In the shadows she couldn't tell if his eyes were on her, but she felt them so. While she sang, her senses wakened at the growing realisation that the young man who had tended her in the warehouse was standing before her. She looked down to gather herself for the final verse and sang,

'When the fields are white with snow,
We remember loves lost days,
When a woman sought to hold her man,
Till he gently slipped away… Till he gently slipped away.'

The room fell to silence, until the large man spoke, 'Well, it seems that the country has produced a songbird.' He clapped and others followed. At home, everyone sang, no voice was reckoned over another. It was a strange but pleasing feeling to hear the appreciation of the room.

Making her way back to her space by the door, she was greeted with a smile. 'Miss Canham, how good to see you again.'

She smiled in return. 'Mr Dalmeny.'

'He is quite correct; you have a beautiful voice.'

Kitty blushed. 'We learn from babes in arms at home, everybody sings.'

'How is your hand?'

'Still bound, I am afraid, but it is healing nicely, thanks to you.' She fiddled with the lace glove that Eleanor had found for her. Just then, the large man proclaimed, 'Enough of these doleful songs, beautiful though they may be. Give me the spoken word. Who will give us a bit of Shakespeare?' He looked around the room, but no-one was offering. 'A room full of actors and not one offer?'

A man spoke out, 'We are having a rest.'

Another answered, 'That's nothing new.' Laughter rippled around the room.

As the banter carried on, a slow realisation dawned. Kitty saw an opportunity before her. One that she did not realise she was seeking, until this moment. Mr Dalmeny quite forgotten, she pushed forward to address the large man, 'Excuse me? May I ask, are you actors?'

'Indeed we are.' He took a bow. 'Bertram Kent, at your service, I've played the London boards for over twenty years.'

A voice piped up, 'He has, and maybe he'll get it right one day.' The woman laughed. Mr Kent jeered in return.

'Actually … ' Kitty could not let this moment pass, 'my family knew an actress once. Rosalind Hodges, do you know her?'

The man dismissed the idea with a flick of the hand. 'No, I've never heard of her.' He plonked himself down on the chaise, causing the women either side of him to bounce precariously.

Kitty found she was relieved that he did not know the woman that her father had known too well. That was until a woman called out from the corner of the room, 'I knew her.' Kitty's heart all but stopped. 'She was in that masque we did at Ingatestone Hall. A few years ago now. She was the one who never got it right. Don't you remember? We used to laugh at her, poor love.' She now addressed her friend, 'You remember her.'

'Oh yeah. Skinny she was. Head in the clouds, that one.'

Another was pleased to show her knowledge, saying, 'I remember her. Used to act as if she was better than the rest of us.'

The first spoke again, 'She was alright. Got herself in a pickle that's all.' She turned to Kitty. 'She had a kid. After that she was set up nice.'

Bertram spoke again, 'Well, are we going to have this recital or not?' Three young men pushed forward. A rather lugubrious figure declared that they would do the Mechanicals. Bertram seemed pleased.

While the actors made preparation, Kitty made her way towards the women in the corner. She asked if they knew any more about Rosalind. They were pleased to tell. 'Well, like I said, she was set up nice, had a posh room out on Rupert Street.' The other women nodded.

Kitty asked, 'Is she still there?'

'No idea, love, sorry. Lost touch with her in the end. But I'll tell you what, she used to go on about the boy's father, used to say he was coming to save her. Never did, of course. It was all in her head.'

The second woman added, 'Hounded the poor man she did, wrote him endless letters. I know, 'cause I used to help her write them. I used to say, "don't be so desperate", but she was having none of it. Don't think she got any in return.'

The first nodded. 'I used to tell her to forget him, get on with her life, but she was stuck on him and that was that.'

Another asked, 'What happened to the boy?'

'Oh, he was taken away from her, sent to some posh school, I reckon.'

The lugubrious young actor announced, 'Ladies and gentlemen; The Mechanicals.' The women turned their attention from Kitty, cheering and clapping the young men as they took their places. Kitty made her way back to her space by the door and slid to the floor.

The sounds in the room faded around her as the entertainment began. She tried to recall the content of the letters she had burned months before, but with little success. They were lovers' letters for sure, but perhaps they were not requited as she assumed them to be. Perhaps they were, as the women suggested, letters from a woman who was clinging to a hope which was not hers to have. But why had her father kept them? Kitty knew that she would never know the answer and wished that she had not given the letters up to the flames; they may have betrayed themselves if she had not.

As the entertainment went on, Kitty began to hope that perhaps her beloved pa was not the man she had feared him to be, but an ordinary man with weaknesses like any other, caught in an impossible situation. She felt a hot tear on her cheek.

A cheer brought Kitty back to the room. There was too much jollity for such a moment. She stood and found herself once more standing before Mr Delmany. 'You are a piper, I see.'

In a moment of forgetfulness she responded, 'I beg your pardon?'

'A piper.' He indicated the flute hanging at her side.

'Oh, yes.' She felt foolish now. 'To be honest, this outfit was the least I could get away with.'

Mr Dalmeny chuckled. 'Well, as you can see, I am not at all dressed for the occasion.' He was formally attired, bar the fact that his jacket was off and his shift hung loose at the neck.

'That is admirable, Mr Dalmeny, not bowing to convention.'

'Oh, I can assure you, Miss Canham, it was not a question of not bowing. I simply came straight from a business meeting.' Then he smiled. 'Although I must confess, I was glad to have an excuse.' Another cheer erupted and Kitty found herself able to enjoy the rest of the entertainment in the company of Mr Dalmeny. When the applause died down, he turned to her, holding out his hand. 'I wonder if you would care to take refreshment with me?'

'Why, thank you, sir, I would indeed.' She took his hand and let him lead her out of the room, but as they entered the hall, she heard a voice behind her, 'Kitty?' It was Alina, and she had a tired looking woman at her side. 'Kitty, this actress of yours?'

'Yes?'

'Lorna knew her, didn't you, Lorna?'

The woman sighed. 'Well, what do you want to know?' A couple of others, keen to hear the tale emerged from the room and came too close for Kitty's liking.

Alina encouraged the older woman on. 'Tell her what you told me.'

'Well, long and short is, we shared lodgings for a time.' She tilted her head and looked at Kitty, as if deciding, then carried on, 'She told me about the boy, said the boy's father was sending money to keep her. But when it stopped, which we all knew it would, she couldn't afford Rupert Street and had to move out east. Kept saying when the boy's father's business improved, he'd see her alright. He never did of course.' The woman looked around the eager gathering then added, 'At least that's what we thought.'

An excitable woman chimed in, 'What do you mean?'

'Well, what I heard, and it's only hearsay, mind. Turns out the man was sending the money alright, but Rosalind's father was keeping it to himself. Didn't surprise me, he used to turn up in clothes way beyond his station and started bringing her little gifts. I knew something wasn't right. Slimy little man he was.'

Kitty's hand went to her mouth as she remembered the man who came to their house one night when her pa was alive.

Alina asked the old woman, 'But what happened to Rosalind? That's what Kitty wants to know.' Little did she know how little Kitty cared.

'The drink got her in the end, died last year, out in Shoreditch, where she'd been selling her wares.' She now touched Kitty's arm. 'Now, don't you worry, love, her old man got his comeuppance. Apparently, and again it's just what I heard, when the boy's father heard what her old man was doing with the money, he went to challenge him. They got in a fight, the boy's father took a stabbing, it killed him. Rosalind's father had to do a runner. Jumped on a ship at Harwich, by all accounts, not been seen since … Hope he drowned, that's all.'

When the woman finished her tale, the women's eyes turned on Kitty. Alina rescued her, 'I'm sorry, love, turns out it was a sad tale. I'll get you a drink, looks like you need it.' She returned to the room, followed by her entourage all twittering after her. The old woman hovered for a moment, looked at Kitty with understanding in her eyes, then patted her arm and moved away.

Kitty could barely breathe. She had to get out.

She pushed passed Mr Dalmeny who called after her, 'Miss Canham?'

She didn't stop to answer, but rather headed for the front door and pulled at the handle.

A manservant was quickly at her side. 'May I be of assistance?'

She continued to pull at the door. 'I need air, I need fresh air.' Frustration was rising.

'If you'd like to follow me, I can lead you to the garden.' She didn't want the garden and continued her pursuit.

'Here, let me.' Mr Dalmeny opened the door, then called over his shoulder, 'Get Miss Canham her cloak … quickly.'

Kitty left the confines of the house and stumbled out, steadying herself against the pillar before staggering across the road. The cold silence enveloped her as she clung on to the railings, breathing hard. Anger rose at the thought of that night; the night her father received a fatal wound from such a man. But worse yet, if all these secrets had been told to her long ago, she may have been able to do something, to save her pa from such a fate. She may have been able to find the man and bring him to justice, but now it was too late. Tears clasped her throat, but instead of giving into the flow, she let out a low growl and kicked at the rails.

'Can I help you with that?' It was Mr Dalmeny. 'I don't think they are going to give with only one of us at it.' He lay the cloak around her shoulders.

She pulled it closer and steadied herself. 'Thank you, it was hot in there and I . . . '

'You knew the young woman of whom they spoke.'

She nodded.

'It was a terrible thing.'

They stood for some time, saying nothing. Kitty was grateful for the company of Mr Dalmeny whilst she gathered herself. 'Please forgive me, it was difficult to hear and . . . '

'You knew the lady well?'

'No, I did not know her, but my father did.' She could say no more and he was gracious enough not to ask. Instead, he held out his arm. 'Will you take a turn with me? Around the gardens?' His eyes were gentle upon her. Determined not to let the revelations ruin her evening, she took his arm. The thickening snow caused her to lift her hem as they picked their way towards the path.

As they went through the gate towards the whited square, Mr Dalmeny bent to study the ground. 'This could be the path, but then again it may not be. Perhaps we should abandon our endeavours.' Just then, he saw something and held out his hand. 'Come on, I can see just the answer.' She took his hand and let him lead her.

An old yew tree stood heavy under a blanket of snow. They bent low under its branches. The lights from the windows illuminated the snow and reflected into a little den. Stumps of wood had been set in a circle. Mr Dalmeny rolled one close to another. He helped her to sit and followed after. She wanted to thank him for keeping her company, and went to say his name, but as she did so, he spoke hers. They both laughed and Kitty could feel her cheeks reddening.

This time he spoke first, 'Miss Canham …'

'Kitty, please.'

'Kitty.' Mr Dalmeny put his hand to his chest. 'And my name is John.'

'John.'

'I was simply going to say how pleased I am to find you again. I had no intention of attending the festivities this evening, but Mr Bastion is a business acquaintance, and quite the entertainer. He will never take no for an answer.'

'I can imagine, he is certainly ebullient.'

'He is indeed.'

In the shadowy light, Mr Dalmeny's youth betrayed him; he looked like a schoolboy, blowing his hands with sparkling eyes. She blew her hands in like fashion. They sat for some time, saying nothing. The snow began to fall afresh into the silence of the night. This time it was John that shivered. Maybe it was because he looked so young, or maybe because she had grown bold, she took her cloak and spread it around his shoulders, there was, after all, plenty of it. He took the corner and pulled it around him, and she could not help but be aware of his body next to hers.

They blew their hands some more, until she muttered, 'I wish we had hot chestnuts.'

He laughed out loud, then added, 'And warm mead.'

They began to talk of Christmases past. His were far grander than hers, but family affairs nonetheless, with traditions that were shared with all of England. At least, that is how it seemed to her, in this moment. They talked of childhood memories and growing up and all the natural human things of living. It was good to think back to the days when life was simple and her pa was at her side. The minutes passed, how many Kitty could not say. John began stamping his feet.

Kitty leant forward and rolled a small log towards them. 'Here, this will help. Put your feet on there, it will keep them warmer.'

He lifted his feet onto the log, his brow quizzical. 'How do you know about such things?'

'I was brought up on a farm. It is a very practical upbringing.'

'Ah.' John leant away from her, looking at her. 'That explains it.'

'What?'

'No, I shouldn't say.'

'What?' She was laughing now as he mocked her. 'Tell me!'

'Very well, if you insist. I noticed when I tended your hand that your skin is rough.'

Just at the mention of it, Kitty pulled her hands further into hiding. She must have looked hurt because John went on, 'You see, I knew I should not have said.'

'You should not have, it was ungentlemanly.'

'Oh dear.' He was mocking her further. 'Have I ruined my chances?'

'Your chances of what?

'Of asking you to dance?' He held out his hand and stood.

'What? Here?'

'Certainly here, why not? It might warm us up.' He lifted her to her feet and began to hum a tune. Though what tune it was, Kitty could not say. They were forced to dance close beneath the branches of the old yew. She giggled as they took awkward steps.

'Ouch!' Something pulled at her hair. 'I'm caught… my hair.' Her hair was twisted in a branch.

Laughing, he said, 'Here, let me.'

His breath was upon her cheek as he worked to disentangle her from captivity. She could not see his eyes, but felt them upon her. Once she was free, he was suddenly serious. 'May I ask, who was the young woman of whom you enquired this evening?'

'Rosalind?' She nodded. Maybe it was because of the shadowy nature of their den or because she was so far from home, but Kitty found herself at ease with this young man, of whom she was barely acquainted. She spoke of her father's relationship with Rosalind; of his death and the revelations of the manner of it. She also spoke of her foolish assumptions about the letters and how she now thought her pa to be the man she always knew and loved and missed so terribly. There was much she did not say, because she knew that in John's presence, she was in danger of becoming wholly undone.

When her story was finished, she could feel John's eyes upon her. He said nothing but taking her hand, he kissed it; not once, not twice, but thrice. Just then a burst of laughter echoed across the street. A small band of people were leaving the party. Kitty pulled away. 'I had better get indoors. Eleanor will be wondering where I am.'

She went to step out of their den, but John, still holding her hand, pulled her back.

'Your hands are cold.' He blew warm breath onto her fingers. As her hands warmed, the feelings she'd had in Tom's presence, that had been dead to her for so long, began to kindle afresh. 'May I see you again?'

'We are leaving first thing in the morning.'

'May I write to you, then?' She hesitated. 'I promise not to hound you as that poor woman did your father.' How could he know her fears before she spoke them?

She smiled at his boyish earnestness. 'If you promise.'

He pressed her hand to his heart. It was warm and firm. 'I swear.' The sound of laughter rekindled. Kitty reluctantly broke away and stepped outside. As she did so, she lifted her face to the falling snow and let it settle over the anxiety that had been her constant companion for so many months. She opened her mouth hoping to catch a flake upon her tongue.

John was now beside her. 'Where do you live?'

She turned to him. 'Mede Farm, Beaumont cum Moze.'

'How will I remember?'

'Oh, you will remember.' She giggled to see him mouthing the unfamiliar name. Lifting a finger to his lips, she stopped the flow, and repeated the address, then with a flirtatious invitation, called, 'Come, dance with me, but this time in the warm.' She turned and trotted away from him fully expecting him to follow. However, when she reached the door, she was alone. Her eyes searched for John, but he wasn't there.

Eleanor called from the door, 'Where have you been? It's freezing out there. What on earth have you been doing?'

'I needed some air.'

'It's dangerous on your own, you should always be chaperoned in London, you are not in the village now.' Eleanor was evidently irritated. 'We are going home, I have a headache.' She marched off down the path.

Kitty darted a look back at the square, then Florence was at her side. 'They've had an argument. Don't worry, it happens. She will soon get over it.' She kissed Kitty on both cheeks and bid her farewell. 'You must come to town again.'

A man poked his head round the door, 'Come on, Florence, we are waiting for you.' Florence shrugged a smile and hurried back indoors.

Kitty made her way to the coach. As they pulled away, she saw John emerging from the gardens. Everything within her wanted to stop the coach and call out, but propriety stopped her. He seemed to see her for one moment, then he was out of sight. She sat back, hoping that he would not forget her.

On the journey home that night, Eleanor was so caught up with her troubles that she did not question Kitty. It seemed that Albert was spreading his affections too widely and kept leaving Eleanor at the mercy of the company of gossiping women. Eleanor babbled on, warning Kitty not to get mixed up with men. Kitty showed concern, but in truth she heard little of what Eleanor was saying. Her body still tingled from her encounter; her heart tinged with regret; she hoped, beyond hope, that John Dalmeny would remember her address.

The following morning, Kitty was packed and waiting for Eleanor in the parlour. She heard a loud knocking on the door and ran to the window. She could not see who it was, so went to the door to listen. Her heart leapt to hear a man's voice. The accent betrayed the man as Albert. How stupid she was, John could not have known where she was staying, and it was the briefest of encounters. Eleanor's footsteps could be heard hurrying down the stairs. Kitty sat by the fire listening to the lovers as they made up. Strong words were followed by soft words, soft words followed by the silence of love. The front door closed and after a few moments Eleanor entered the parlour, all smiles. She may have been hard to win over, but once won, she was most certainly all his.

The journey home was more pleasant than it might have been, now that all was well with Eleanor. Though Kitty wished she had had more time to get to know the young man she had shared a brief and delightful moment with. There was much to keep the women entertained during the long journey. They talked about everything that had happened and laughed at the extraordinary sights they'd seen the night before until the inevitable question came. Kitty had prepared for it.

'So, what were you doing in the square last night?'

'I felt faint and needed some air. I'm not used to so many people or so much punch.'

Eleanor laughed but scolded her, 'You shouldn't have gone into the square alone.'

Kitty might as well be honest, what did she have to hide? 'I wasn't alone, a gentleman escorted me.'

Eleanor seemed surprised. 'Which gentleman?'

'Mr Dalmeny.'

Eleanor repeated with some incredulity, 'Mr Dalmeny?'

'Yes. He was very pleasant and made sure I was safe.'

'John Dalmeny?'

Kitty was irritated now. 'Yes. Do you know him?' Eleanor laughed out loud; it was most disconcerting. Kitty might have told Eleanor everything if her laugh hadn't been so derisory. 'It was nothing untoward, he stayed with me until I felt better.'

Eleanor's laughing subsided. 'That's not why I am laughing. You, my dear, have been in the company of Lord Dalmeny.'

'Who?'

She repeated it slowly, 'Lord Dalmeny.'

Kitty was incredulous. 'Are you sure? He didn't seem like a lord.'

'Have you met one before?'

'No, but... he is so young.'

'Yes, he is, younger than even you, I'll wager. I am sorry, I must not tease. An attractive young man, though, is he not?' Kitty didn't answer. She sat back, astonished, and rather put out that he hadn't introduced himself as such. But when she thought of it, there was no proper introduction at all.

Eleanor continued, 'His father is a reprobate by all accounts and has made poor use of the family's finances. There is little love lost between them, I believe.' Eleanor had had enough of the conversation and moved on to more mundane subjects. All the while, Kitty was convincing herself that there was nothing disingenuous about John, though she couldn't imagine why he would spend so much time with a farm girl if not.

The women slept much of the morning away, in fits and starts as the coach allowed. As the afternoon went on, the revelations she had heard about her pa began to trouble her. She was too tired to think in any ordered way, but that didn't stop fragments of thoughts drifting through her mind, seeking a place to settle. The afternoon was long and uncomfortable, until finally, the coach turned into the driveway at the Manor. Eleanor touched Kitty on the knee. 'You will keep my secret safe, won't you, Kitty, my dear?'

'Of course I will.' Though she neither wanted nor asked for them, she had grown accustomed to keeping confidences.

Eleanor was welcomed by her husband, then the coach turned to take Kitty home. The familiar landscape gave Kitty an opportunity to adjust. Looking out into the lowing light, she could see how different her life was from the life of someone like Lord John Dalmeny. He must have known, must have guessed at the life she lived. But the stories in the romantic novels she had read helped to kindle her hope.

As they arrived, Mother stood in the door, holding a lamp, just as she always had when father returned from his journeys. Old Bouncer hobbled out, wagging his tail. She fondled his head and went inside.

Mother and Peggy made a fuss of Kitty after her long journey. Joseph was away dealing with family matters; his sister's husband had died and there was much to be arranged. Kitty was grateful. The women sat at the table whilst Kitty ate, keen to hear of her adventures. She was pleased to have them to herself. She told them of all the wonderful things she had seen, keeping from them what she had learnt about her pa. That information she stored away until it could be faced properly. Now was not the time.

Exhaustion soon came upon her, and she made her way to bed, gathering her pa's coat on the way. She lay in bed, hugging the old coat to herself, her thoughts drifting between her life with Pa and the intimate moments she had shared with John. She slipped into a deep and refreshing sleep.

Chapter Fourteen

The next day, Kitty was straight into her breeches and out on the farm. The ground was hard and the trees were pricked with ice. She went to check on a ewe that had been sickening before she left. As she approached the field, the rather bedraggled creatures bleated a welcome. The ewe was huddled under a tree; Kitty recognised her. She took a handful of hay and rubbed the animal's trembling body. Kitty talked to her and soothed her, as she was wont to do. Young Peter came across the field with a shoulder full of fresh hay for their morning feed.

'Morning, Peter. How is she doing?'

He crouched down beside Kitty coddling the ewe's soft wool. 'Not looking good, I'm afraid, but the others are fine, so there be no problem with the flock, not as I can see.'

'Let's keep an eye on her then. Where's Jacob?'

'He's been sick these past days. His stomach. Reckon he's healing now though.'

'Good, I'll visit him later.' Kitty stood and stretched her back, surveying the wintered landscape. 'This is a beautiful place, Peter.'

He looked around quizzically. 'I s'pose it is.'

She visited old Jacob that afternoon. He was indeed healing, but Kitty could see his age upon him. She could not help wondering how much longer they would have him with them.

The rest of the day was spent sitting at the table with Mother and Peggy, regaling them with tales of London. She might have mentioned her encounter with Lord Dalmeny if her mother had not been so keen to find out if she had met any nice, young men. The days rolled thus. The stresses of the past weeks were less keen somehow. Only one letter had arrived, but that was to say that Joseph would be delayed. Kitty had determined not to expect a letter from John for three weeks, the weather had been poor and letters could take time. So she let her hopes lay. She did wonder, however, if her own letter had reached Sarah and decided to pay her a visit.

Kitty set off on a rather grey day, riding Pincher, Pa's old horse. First, she visited her pa's grave, told him what she had learnt and asked him why he had kept it all from her. No answer came. She told him that she forgave him and lay upon the grave the carved soldier he had made her when she was a girl. Then she told him about John, 'You'd like him, Pa, he's like you in some ways.' For a moment she saw the two men as one. She kissed her fingertips, touched the kisses to her father's headstone, then walked away. As she walked through Thorpe, everything looked fresh somehow; the inn, the cottages, the dressmakers, the forge. Familiar faces scurried about their business as if there was no world outside their own. She stabled Pincher and crossed the road to Sarah's cottage.

Sarah opened the door, a smile wide upon her lips; the kind of smile Kitty hadn't seen on her for some while. 'Oh, Kitty, I am so pleased to see you. It was wonderful to get your letter, come in.'

The baby had grown and was sitting on the floor; a little dumpling of a thing, his blond hair now standing straight up from his head. Kitty couldn't help but smile at such a sight. Little Jane was playing with bricks on the floor beside him.

Mrs Parditer appeared at the kitchen door. 'Good morning, Miss Canham.'

Sarah seemed excitable. 'Mother has come to read the scriptures with the children, so that we may take a walk together, isn't that kind?'

'Yes indeed, it is.'

Mrs Parditer stood staring at Kitty which made Sarah look herself. 'Whatever are you wearing, Kitty?'

Kitty realised that it was her coat that caused the astonishment. 'It was my father's coat and is very practical in such weather.'

Sarah laughed, but it was Mrs Parditer who looked disapprovingly at her daughter-in-law. 'Of course it is, very sensible.' She seemed a kind woman, if not a little formal. She lifted the baby into her arms with a grunt. 'You are getting heavy, my little one.' Her brow furrowed as she looked into the baby's face. 'He seems a little flushed, Sarah, is he quite well?'

Sarah held the back of her hand to the child's cheek. 'Perhaps he was a little close to the fire. I am sure he will soon cool down in your good care.' Mrs Parditer took Jane by the hand and led the little ones to the kitchen where young Nathanial was already awaiting his lesson.

Sarah slipped on her cloak. 'Come, let's go.' As they walked, Sarah asked Kitty all about London, and Kitty was pleased to tell. She even told of her encounter with John, on strict instructions to keep it to herself. Sarah was incredulous. 'So, you weren't even properly introduced?'

'No, not really, London is not at all like you'd imagine.' She kept from Sarah John's position in life, and in so doing kept it from herself. She wasn't ready to let his position deny her her dreams.

'But he likes you?'

'I think so … I don't know. He said he would write.'

The Sarah that Kitty had known when young was standing before her once more, clapping her hands together in joy. 'How romantic.'

Kitty was keen to dampen her enthusiasm a little. 'I haven't received a letter yet. And anyway, it may just have been a passing fancy.'

'Oh, I do hope not.'

Kitty changed the subject for fear of giving the intensity of her feelings away. 'But what about you? You are looking wonderful.'

Sarah stopped to face her friend. 'I am doing well, Kitty.' For a moment she faltered. 'All that business . . . before . . . you know. Well, things are better, for the most part. And anyway, we are moving. Nathaniel is doing well and has secured a property for us that is more spacious. He will have a study. You see, he does not manage so well with the exuberance of children. A study will give him a place of retreat. It will be better for all of us.'

She took Kitty's arm and, as they set off again, leant in close. 'He has agreed to refrain from breeding, for a while. So, as you can see, I am well.' Kitty could not quite believe in such a thorough salvation. Her face must have exposed her thoughts. 'No honestly, Kitty, I am very well.'

'And I am pleased.'

They walked and talked, up and down the street, exchanging stories until the sky darkened. Sarah invited Kitty to take shelter and refreshment, but Kitty had other plans. They had passed the rectory on their walk. It had been such a long time since she had heard anything from the rectory, or the family, and longed to see the children. So she took her leave at the door, and with a kiss, the women promised to visit each other more often in future.

As Kitty headed for the rectory, fine spitting hail started to fall. On her arrival, Mrs Carter greeted her. 'My, my, Miss Canham, how wonderful to see you.' She took Kitty's damp coat. 'I am afraid the reverend isn't here.'

'Actually, Mrs Carter, I wondered if I might see the children.' At that moment, she heard a pattering of feet as the brood descended the stairs in high excitement. Beth stood at the top, as usual, helpless against the tide. The boys were now old enough to take the stairs themselves and ran straight for Kitty. She hugged them to her legs. Esther, who was tucked into Beth's skirts, was more wary; it had been a long time for one so young. And Rachel, looking quite grown up, stood formally before her, with a beaming smile. Behind her stood Tilly, beaming in like manner. Kitty was quite overwhelmed by the welcome.

Mrs Carter gathered them all. 'Come to the kitchen. Let's see what I've got for you.'

They all ran ahead. Except for Rachel who walked beside Kitty. 'It is so good to see you, Miss Canham.'

Kitty feigned shock. 'Miss Canham? Are you too old and too important to call me Kitty?' Rachel giggled. 'I wouldn't be surprised. Look at you, you are growing so quickly.'

'I am, aren't I, Kitty?' Suddenly her brow furrowed. 'But we have missed you. You haven't called.'

Kitty realised that in the midst of her own troubles she had neglected the little family of whom she had grown so fond. She took a breath and looked at the child's earnest little face. 'You know that my father died?' Rachel nodded. 'Well, sometimes when people have difficulties, they rather lose themselves. I'm afraid I rather lost myself these months, and I am sorry for it.' As she spoke, she realised the truth of her own statement.

'Oh that's alright.' The youngster looked at Kitty, and with an understanding beyond her years, said, 'So long as you are found again.'

Kitty almost laughed at her adult ways. 'I am, thank you, Rachel. I think I am.' And for the first time, she realised she was.

Rachel took her hand and led her into the kitchen, where Mrs Carter had produced cake. Kitty spent a most pleasant hour hearing everyone's news. It sounded as if the house and the parish had gone on as it always did. She noticed the sky darkening, and if she was to get home before the weather was too bad, she knew she must take her leave. Just as she was gathering herself, the front door closed and voices were heard in the hall.

'That'll be the reverend.' Mrs Carter scuttled from the room. Everyone followed.

Alexander was in the hall, accompanied by an attractive woman of about his age. Kitty recognised her immediately; Mrs Lambard, a widow from the church who had set her eyes on Alexander. When Kitty was living there, Alexander had seemed quite uninterested. Perhaps he had changed his mind.

Mrs Carter went to take the woman's coat, but she declined. When Alexander slipped off his coat, he noticed Kitty standing with his family. 'Kitty, is it you?' She stepped forward. 'We've missed you. I can't believe that you are here. Seeing you standing there with the children it is like you've hardly left.'

'I know.' She was surprised at how pleased she was to see him. 'It is so good to see the children, I cannot believe that I have been such a poor friend these months.'

He took her hands. 'As have I.' He then remembered his companion; the poor woman was left dripping by the door. 'I believe you know Mrs Lambard?'

'Indeed I do. How do you do?'

The woman looked at Kitty with some disdain. 'I am quite well, Miss Canham, thank you.'

Alexander was remorseful. 'I am so sorry, Margaret, I'll fetch the ledger.' He hurried to the study and returned almost immediately. 'Margaret has been helping me these past months and I am most grateful.'

Margaret looked hopeful. 'I could stay and we could look through them together, if you like, it is no trouble.'

Alexander ignored her plea. 'No, you need to get home and dry yourself.' He opened the front door and looked out. 'It has stopped for the time being, you'd better get home before it starts again.' Kitty couldn't help feeling sorry for the woman; he was obviously trying to get rid of her. But as she stepped on to the path he called after her, 'Thank you, Margaret, you have been most helpful today.' She seemed appeased. He closed the door and turned to Kitty. 'Take tea with me in the study, we have much to catch up on.' Then to Mrs Carter, 'Is the fire lit?'

'It is, sir, Tilly has been tending it.' She looked at the girl. 'You did tend it? Did you not, Tilly?' Tilly's eyes widened. Mrs Carter shook her head.

Alexander came to her rescue. 'Don't worry, Tilly, I'll see to it. You have so much to remember, it would be impossible to remember it all.' The way he spoke caused Tilly to grin.

The sky was dark now, and Kitty insisted, 'I am sorry, Alexander, but I really must be going if I am to miss the worst of the weather.'

'You will not get home before the storm. Take tea with me and when it is passed, I will let you go.'

It was good to be at the rectory, and Kitty was happy to be in good company. 'Very well.'

In the study, the fire was all but dead. Whilst Alexander revived it, he explained that Mrs Lambard helped with the household as well as the parish affairs. 'But,' he said, 'it is at a cost. She needs endless affirmation that her good works are being noticed.' Then almost under his breath, 'If I let her, she'd live at the rectory and become my shadow, God forbid.' He caught himself, looked at Kitty and laughed, her laughter joining his. 'It really is so good to see you, Kitty, I miss having someone to laugh with. Are you warm enough?'

She was a little cold, but nonetheless declared that she was fine.

He reached out to the familiar box on the table. 'Backgammon?' She couldn't help but agree.

Kitty stayed the whole afternoon; at first playing backgammon and eating Mrs Carter's simple but most delicious food. But then, with the room warm and a storm gathering outside, Kitty found herself settling and opening to Alexander. She spoke of her father's death and how she discovered she had a brother. She told him of how Pa had asked her to look after the farm for mother and how difficult it had been since Joseph had taken her place.

She told him of her trip to London and all she then discovered about her father's affair. Nothing was left unsaid. Nothing, that was, apart from her encounter with John. The full truth of it was her one secret, that was sweetened by being entirely hers. She talked and talked and cried a little. And when all was done, she fell to silence. Alexander sat in silence with her. He had said little while she poured out the pains of past months. Outside, the light was fading. Kitty broke the silence. 'Forgive me, I see I have taken up your afternoon.'

He chuckled. 'Don't worry, I am a priest.' Of course he was.

'You chose the right profession.'

'I think it rather chose me.' He went to the fire and stoked it afresh. Kitty knew she must leave and said as much, but with the storm raging outside Alexander insisted she stay. He said he'd have a message sent to her mother. So, with a little persuasion, she agreed.

Supper was a fine, simple affair with the family. Michael joined them. He had grown so tall; he wore spectacles and had an austerity that would suggest he was out of his grandmother's mould. Rachel sat close to Kitty and delighted in telling her all the things she was allowed to do now she was so grown up. The boys gabbled and fought, and little Esther sat peacefully enjoying every mouthful of food. After supper, Kitty offered to help put the children to bed. A whoop of joy ensued from the children, all except Michael, who seemed rather concerned that he may be put to bed. 'I play chess with my father after supper.'

Alexander reassured the boy with a hand on his shoulder. 'Indeed you do. And perhaps I will win this time.'

When, at last, bedtime was finished, Kitty made her way to the study. Alexander and Michael were sitting at the small table finishing their game. She sat by the fire, half reading a book she had taken from the shelf. Michael won the game securely. 'He beats me every time, Kitty. How the old weaken. Now, you go off to bed, son, I'd like some time with Kitty.'

'But, Father … ' Michael protested, 'we always play another game.'

'Not always. And don't make Kitty feel unwelcome, Michael, it's ungentlemanly.' Kitty didn't like being pitted between father and son. 'Say goodnight now.' Michael conceded and bade Kitty a formal goodnight as he left the room.

Alexander sat in the chair opposite her. Kitty felt vulnerable in his presence now. She had opened up to him as one might to a priest, and for the first time, their relationship felt awkward. 'You know, Kitty, what you told me earlier is … Well, it will not be spoken of to anyone. It is between you and me and will stay there.'

'Thank you.' She could think of no more to say.

A tiredness had come over her and she announced that it was time she made her way to bed. But Alexander spoke before she could make a move. 'Kitty, I've been thinking.'

He held his hands, palms together, resting his fingers on his lips, his eyes upon her. Eventually he spoke again, 'I wonder if I may have an answer to the problems that you are facing at home.'

Kitty was unsure what he meant.

'I wonder if you may come back to us?'

She hadn't considered it, although she did not know why. It seemed a reasonable request. 'It is most kind of you, but what about your mother? Is she not returning?'

'Not for some time, if at all. She is finding much to keep herself occupied at my sister's.' Kitty was silent in thought. Alexander went on, 'And, to be honest, it would be a great help. Having you here would save me from the local worthies.' He gave her a smile.

She thought of Mrs Lambard and felt for Alexander's predicament, but she was not at all sure that she wanted such a position anymore. And besides that, she may have a better offer, a far better offer. She said she would think about it and headed for bed.

Kitty slept well in her old room, but on awakening, the early light glowed cold on the bare walls. She dressed quickly and hurried downstairs to the kitchen. The fire was lit, the kettle steaming, but no-one was to be seen. She lifted the kettle from the heat and found dried mint for a warming brew.

She sat nursing the cup, wondering whether today would be the day a letter would arrive, when Alexander appeared. 'You are lost in your thoughts.'

Kitty smiled in response. 'Shall I make you a brew?'

'Thank you.' He sat at the table watching her as she poured the hot liquid into the mug.

Sitting opposite him, she placed the cup before him. It was evident that she must say something about his proposal. 'I have given your offer some consideration, Alexander. It is a very kind offer and I do hope you won't think me prideful … It is just that I don't think I want such a position, not anymore.' Alexander held her gaze. She stumbled on, 'You see, I have grown up in these last few months and have become used to being my own mistress.'

Alexander rested his head on his fingers. 'And you are sure that your position will remain, should your mother marry Joseph?' Nothing had been said about such a possibility. It had been one of Kitty's fears that had remained dormant whilst unspoken. But Alexander was giving it life. Feeling the truth of the possibility, she rose and went to the fire.

Alexander must have realised that he had caused her anxiety because he apologised. 'Forgive me, Kitty. After we spoke yesterday, I thought that that was what you were inferring.'

She stared into the fire. 'No, I hadn't given it proper thought. But of course you are right. They probably will marry.' She gathered herself and turned to him. 'Even so, I am used to being my own mistress, I could not return to such a position.'

He was standing beside her now. 'Then don't. Come back to us … as my wife.'

Kitty was astounded. 'Your wife?'

'Yes, I am asking you to marry me, Kitty.' She could not speak. This is not how she saw Alexander at all. He was not an unattractive man, and she enjoyed his company immensely but in the way she enjoyed her father's company, not a lover's. His brow furrowed. 'I can see I have taken you quite by surprise.'

She laughed. 'You have. And that is no mistake.'

'We get on so well, you and I, and if I am not mistaken, you are most fond of the children. They are certainly fond of you. There are surely worse foundations for marriage.' She looked at him with such fondness and wondered. He went on, 'I know I am a deal older than you. I know that what I have to offer is perhaps not what a young woman would want … '

'It is not that, I assure you. I am simply taken aback.' If she had not taken a trip to London, if she had not met John, perhaps she may have taken his offer. But now it was impossible, her heart was elsewhere, but she could not rebut Alexander quite so quickly. She had no intention of causing him hurt. 'I will think about it. It is a very kind offer.'

It was Alexander's turn to laugh. 'It is not kind at all, if it saved you from your problems at home and me from the interminable attention of the local women. It would be a most useful contract.' His manner always made her feel at ease, even in such strange circumstances. 'You think about it. There is no hurry.' And with that said, he instructed, 'Now let's have some food, and I will see you on your way.' They ate together like old friends, as if nothing of any consequence had been said.

Kitty arrived home that morning to find the kitchen full of dust. Mother and Peggy had already taken over the kitchen for the stuffing and mending of mattresses. The pile of hay, that had laid for some time in the corner of the kitchen, drying for such a purpose, now bulged from a sack between the two women. A mattress sagged over the table. Once Kitty's own chores were attended to, she joined the women in their endeavours. Peggy's presence was like a balm, which softened her mother … and perhaps she brought a bit of softness to Kitty too. She enjoyed the day in the company of the women. What had occurred between her and Alexander was not spoken of; it had come so suddenly, that Kitty hardly reckoned it herself.

Chapter Fifteen

Three weeks had passed and no letter came. At the end of the third week, as winter creaked towards spring, Kitty stood by the graveside of Mrs Dobson. She fingered the little brooch at her chest and thought of her visit to the old friend the week before. She had seemed well enough and had listened to Kitty's tales with delight. It was the next morning that Dairy Daphne found her in her favourite chair, a cup of beer at her side. Quite cold. There were few at the burial, all women except for Jacob who had been her closest companion these past years. The remembrance of them sitting in Mrs Dobson's garden on a Sunday afternoon was a welcome one. Familiar prayers were read as they lowered her into the ground. When Kitty turned to leave the little churchyard in Beaumont, she noticed a swathe of snowdrops ready to open. When snowdrops showed off their blooms, spring would not be far behind.

Another week passed, and still no word. Alexander had not come by, and for that Kitty was grateful. The thaw was now well on the way and the winds were drying the land. It was on a still evening, when Kitty was sitting by the old pigger, that she began to see herself from the outside; a crumpled farming woman, sitting against an old sow, smoking her pipe. She watched the smoke curl above her into the bluing light and with it, her hopes. It was time to resign herself to the truth.

John had felt the calluses on her hands when he tended her wound and he must have heard her country burr. He was probably persuaded that a relationship with such a woman would be untenable for a man in his position. And besides that, she had heard no word from Eleanor. It was as if Kitty's usefulness to her had come to an end. An end which heralded the end of Kitty's imaginings. Now she thought about it, her time in London seemed like a dream.

When Joseph returned to the farm, the pleasant evenings she had had with her little family were once again few and far between. Then the inevitable evening came. Joseph, Tom, Miriam, their new baby, and Aunt Mary had been summoned to join them for supper. At first it was a pleasant enough meal; the baby was passed around and stories were told.

At the end of the meal, Joseph stood and took Mother's hand. Kitty knew that the announcement she dreaded was about to be made. 'Judith and I would like to share with our dear family our good news. We are to be wed.'

Tom and Miriam made the appropriate noises. Aunt Mary joined in the congratulations. Peggy barely looked up, but rather busied herself with the dishes. Kitty thought it best she absent herself by helping Peggy clear the table. She said a flat 'congratulations' and stood, but Joseph stopped her,

'Sit, Kitty, please.' She reluctantly sat, irritated that already he was speaking as head of the household. 'Arrangements have been made for everyone's benefit. Tom and Miriam will stay at the cottage, Miriam's mother is coming to live with them to help with the little ones.' He looked at his son with pride. 'Of which, I am sure, there will be many.' Tom pulled Miriam close. She gave her husband a coy smile. Joseph went on, 'Miriam's mother is on her own now and I am sure will find being with the family most comforting.' He paused and seemed to gather himself. 'As you know, there is little room in the cottage, so we decided that it would be best for Mary to come and live with us here.

Kitty couldn't work it out. 'Here?'

'Yes.'

'But where will she sleep?'

He continued. 'You have plenty of room in your room, Kitty. I am sure you would be happy for Mary to share it.'

'But what about father's study, she could go in there.'

He was unmoved. 'I will need the study, Kitty, just as your father did.' Kitty's look must had belied her thoughts. 'You have been most fortunate to have such a large room of your own for so long, I am sure you will be happy to share some of your good fortune with Mary.'

The woman sat bolt upright, surveying the scene of her new home with imperious satisfaction. Then, as if with afterthought, she turned to Kitty. 'I do hope I won't be putting you to any inconvenience, Kitty?'

She could not speak an affirmation, but rose, forcing a smile. 'Is that all, because, if you don't mind, I'd like to help Peggy now.' As she rose, Peggy turned to her, shaking her head in a warning.

Joseph continued, 'There is one thing more.' Kitty turned to see her mother pulling at Joseph's arm. 'She has to know, Judith.' His attention turned on Kitty. 'With Mary joining us, we will not need Peggy's help anymore.' Kitty looked at Peggy who had turned away. 'She is going to live with her sister, in Norfolk. I am sure she will be of great help there.'

Kitty could not believe what she was hearing. 'Peggy?' The old housekeeper didn't move. 'Mother?' Mother wrung her hands in that irritating way she always did when overwhelmed.

'No, that cannot be right! Peggy is part of the family. She has always been. You don't just let her go.'

Joseph was unmoved. 'It is all arranged.'

'By whom?'

'By your mother and me . . . and Peggy of course. She will take her leave in two weeks and we . . . ' he took her mother's hand, 'we shall be wed that very day.' He lifted Mother's hand to his lips and kissed it.

'But why can she not stay? I don't understand why she cannot stay. She sleeps in the servant's room.'

Joseph was becoming irritated. 'Mary will be bringing our girl from the village. She will need somewhere to sleep. It is settled, Kitty, you may as well get used to it.'

'Joseph . . . ' Mother pleaded

Kitty shook her head as she spoke. 'You know nothing about this family. If you did, you would know that Mother couldn't survive without Peggy. She is the one who supported Mother through all her troubles . . . who supported all of us. Isn't that right, Mother?' She fixed her eyes on Judith. 'You know what she means to us, both of us. She is your support, you know it's true. Say something, please, before it is too late.'

Mother looked at Kitty, then to Joseph and back again. Joseph now stood behind his betrothed, a hand firmly on her shoulder. 'You needn't worry about your mother anymore, Kitty, I will look after her. You father may not have been able to give her all she needed, but I will make sure . . . '

Kitty thumped her hands down on the table and craned across it. 'Don't you dare speak of my father! Don't you dare! He was good man. A better man than you will ever be, and the love of my mother's life. Say something, Mother … please.' Her mother looked down at her hands.

Joseph spoke again, 'I know your mother loved him, of course, but his head for business was not as it should have been. You would have all been far better off if … '

'If what?' Kitty fixed Joseph with a glare. 'Can't you see we did not want or need anything else? We were happy. My father was the best of men, the very best, and he should never have been allowed to die the way he did.'

'We did everything we could, Kitty, you know we did.'

'Except to tell me the truth. Me, his very own daughter.' Mother looked up, her eyes full of fear. 'I know all about it, Mother.' She straightened, a strange satisfaction coming over her. 'He was murdered, wasn't he?'

A stunned silence filled the room. Wide eyes stared at Kitty as she continued, 'Did you know, Mother, did you?' She said nothing and Kitty shot her chin at Joseph. 'Or did he keep it from you, just as he did from me?'

Joseph held his ground. 'She knew, Kitty. We all knew.'

She looked around the room; even Tom and Miriam bowed their head in shame. 'So you all knew, except for me.' She laughed out loud. 'I met a woman in London who knew this Rosalind. Want to hear about it?' There was no answer, so she went on anyway, spilling every detail that she had learnt in London.

When all was said, Joseph spoke, 'Have you finished?'

She hated the way he said that. 'I am not a child, you cannot keep me as a child in this household. I live here. It is my home.' Pointing a finger in Joseph's face, she growled, 'And don't you ever forget it!'

Kitty turned to leave but Joseph was too quick for her. Leaping around the table, he caught her by the arms, his voice now raised. 'If I am to be the master of this house, I demand respect, even from you, Kitty Canham.'

Her heart was cold. 'Get … your … hands … off me.' He let her go and stepped back, hands lifted in surrender. The baby let out a loud cry. Miriam rose to take the child aside, coddling and comforting it. Tom followed. Kitty looked around the room. 'I am sorry, Miriam … Tom … I didn't mean to upset her. Mother, I am sorry.'

Mother was sobbing quietly. Peggy's back remained turned. Kitty left the room, knowing that all she held dear had come to an end.

After a fitful night's sleep, Kitty found Mother, sitting in her usual place on the settle by the hearth. She, too, looked like she hadn't slept. Peggy was kneading the bread in her usual fashion. Neither spoke. Kitty looked at them, feeling ashamed. The two people she loved best, she had, yet again, wounded with her anger. She sat beside Mother and took her small hand in hers. Mother stared resolutely into the fire.

'Ma, forgive me, I should have told you what I learnt in London. It should not have been said as it was. But why didn't you tell me about Pa … all of it?'

Mother looked at her, her face drawn. 'You were grieving so for your father. You always thought him so perfect, Kitty. You and he were … ' She searched for the right words. 'You were so close, I could not destroy your memory of him.'

'Oh, Ma, I am not a child anymore.'

'I know. I should have realised. I should have been more honest about it all.'

'And I'm sure Joseph didn't help.'

Mother pulled her hand away. 'Oh, Kitty, I wish you would try and understand him a little better.'

'I do try, I really do, but there is something about him that just infuriates me. It's like … it's like … '

Mother spoke carefully. 'Like he's taking your father's place?' Kitty said nothing. She sat back against the hard wood. 'Kitty, this is the way of things. You know it is. As you say, you are not a child.'

'But we could have managed, Ma. Pa knew I could run the farm. We didn't need Joseph to take over as he has.'

'And supposing you marry one day. What would happen to me then?' Before recent events, Kitty had been sure that she would never marry, but now she realised that the possibility was real.

She looked at her ma and saw how vulnerable she was. 'Do you love him, Ma?'

Mother laughed. 'Love is such a silly word, Kitty. It is not about love. But we do get on well, very well. And a marriage built on friendship can be a far better foundation than any notions of romantic love. Joseph is a good man, you know he is. He is trying to do his best by us all.' Kitty was unsure if the all really included her. 'And Aunt Mary has no-one else. She has been with Joseph since his wife died. He can barely be expected to cast her aside.'

Peggy wiped her hands on her apron. 'Your mother is quite right. It is only right for a man to look after his sisters. And this will give me an opportunity to spend time with mine. And as for your ma, she's stronger than you think.' Ma looked at Peggy and a smile of understanding passed between the old friends.

Kitty knew there was no point in arguing. 'Very well then. If you are content, then so will I be. And I will try not to argue with Joseph anymore.'

Mother breathed a smile. 'Thank you. You will apologise to him, though, won't you?'

'If I must.'

'Of course you must. And who knows? If Joseph's plans for the farm go well, we may be able to afford to build on another room for Mary, in time. I wish you could hear about his plans, Kitty, I think you'd be impressed.' But that was the problem. He never shared anything with Kitty. Her pa had respected her work on the farm; Joseph merely accepted it.

A couple of days later, Kitty was in the grain store when Tom put his head round the door. 'Ah, there you are.'

She stood to see his familiar form silhouetted against a weak sky. 'Get out of the light, would you?'

He stepped inside. 'How are you, Kitty? After the other night, I wondered if you were alright?'

She smiled at his uncertainty, and continued to sift the grain though her fingers. 'It's your father, he drives me mad.'

'He drives me mad too sometimes. I know this must all be difficult for you, none of it can be easy, but he loves your mother. He really does. He will take good care of her, and the farm.'

She stood and studied him. He was the same Tom, nothing seemed to change that. His hair was still flopped onto his boyish face, though fine lines were appearing around his eyes. 'You're looking older, you know that?'

He laughed. 'It's the baby, cries like a squirrel in season, all night it seems.'

'Poor you.'

He came closer. 'What are you going to do?'

'What do you mean?'

'Well, I know you, you won't find it easy with Aunt Mary. I did try to tell Pa, but she is his sister and they've always been together.'

'I know … I know.'

'And as for Father, give him a chance, Kitty, that's all. He's not your pa, I know that. But give him a chance.'

'Of course, I will. The other night, well, I have a temper on me, you know that.'

He smiled. 'Yes, you do.'

Once he was gone, Kitty looked at where he had been standing and, for a moment, she saw the young Tom before her; the carefree days of their youth together passed through her every sense, but in the next moment, they were gone. An ache of grief rimmed her eyes, until she plunged her hand into the cold grain once again.

Until the day of the wedding, Aunt Mary was ever at the house, rearranging things to her liking. Peggy worked with her, hefting furniture and cleaning. Kitty kept out of their way as much as possible. It had been agreed that Peggy could stay until after the wedding. Kitty was relieved not to have to face that day alone.

The wedding was a simple affair at Beaumont Church; only the family were in attendance. However, when Judith and Joseph came out of the church, it was to a cheer and clapping. As Kitty watched the couple being greeted by all the familiar faces, she realised, though reluctantly, that maybe this was the best thing for the farm. People trusted Joseph. He had been with them a long time, and there was no doubt that many would be happier with a man in charge.

While congratulations were received, Kitty stepped aside to take a moment by Mrs Dobson's grave. She crouched to remove dead leaves that had gathered by her headstone. Little clusters of snow drops nestled in its shade. She became aware of a presence beside her and looked up.

Alexander was standing over her, his brood at his side; a formal little row, all in their Sunday best. 'Hello, Kitty.'

Kitty stood. 'It is good of you to come.'

After a moment of reverent silence, Alexander spoke, 'Your mother and Joseph have kindly invited us to join you for victuals at the farm.'

Kitty remembered that she had promised to help Peggy with the table, and apologised. 'Please forgive me, I must get along, there is much to prepare. I will see you there.' She was pleased of the excuse not to have to face him with the question of the proposal. Not quite yet, at any rate.

Kitty trotted past Sarah, who walked arm in arm with Miriam; no doubt talking about babies. Then she passed Tom who was being talked at by Nathaniel. He gave her a pleading look, which she ignored and carried on. The newly-married couple led the party, with Aunt Mary striding alongside. Kitty couldn't help chuckling at the thought that there would always be three in this marriage.

Finally, she caught up with Peggy. 'You know they only wanted you to stay for your cooking. No-one does a spread like you, Peggy.'

Peggy scolded her. 'I am pleased they did, it is a privilege.' She was giving little away, but Kitty could see the sadness in her eyes.

'I am so sorry that this has happened, Peggy. Mother would never have done this if it hadn't been for Joseph.'

Peggy tutted. 'Come now, Kitty, I believe your mother will be well cared for by Mr Spalling. There are some as need a man. Your mother is one of them.'

'But it's not fair on you.'

'Oh, don't you worry about me. Perhaps it is time I took it a little easier, and I'll be glad to spend time with Dorothy.'

'You are always so frustratingly positive.'

'Well, I don't see as there's any point in being otherwise.' She set her grey eyes upon Kitty. 'I shall be well enough, but it is you I worry about.'

'Oh, don't worry, Peggy, I have plans of my own.'

'Do you now?' They walked a little further and could hear Aunt Mary calling after the children, scolding them for getting dirty. Peggy pulled Kitty closer and whispered, 'I just don't want to leave you with that woman.' She had not taken to Aunt Mary. 'I can't see as she'll ever get the hang of everything… and she thinks she's God's handmaid, she does. Thinks there's never been her like.'

Kitty laughed. 'Peggy, I've never heard you say such a thing about anyone before.'

'Well, there are times when it just has to be said.' She gave Kitty a little squeeze on the arm. 'And if I can't say it to you, who can I say it to?' In that moment, both women felt the comradeship of conflict.

The house looked beautiful. Swathes of hay, woven with dried flowers hung from the beams. Peggy had excelled herself, especially as it was winter's end; pies and salted ham and all kinds of pickled treats were brought out. Mother seemed happy, and perhaps, after all, that was all that father had asked of Kitty; to see her mother cared for and content.

When everyone had eaten and Joseph had thanked the party, Kitty slipped out of the back door and made her way to the pigger's pen. This had become her thinking place. She leant over the rail. 'Well, Pigger, what am I to do?'

Her reverie was broken by the snorting and snuffling of the approaching sow, its breath filling the air. Kitty held out her hands. 'I don't have anything for you.' The pig remained in hopeful proximity. The sound of children's voices caused Kitty to look up. David and Jonathan ran along the road, followed by their father. Michael and Rachel came after. Kitty headed for the gate, and called, 'Alexander?' He turned. 'May I walk with you?'

'Of course.'

'I'll fetch my coat.' Kitty passed through the crowded room slowly so as not to be noticed. She lifted her pa's coat from its peg in the hall and made her way out and up the track after Alexander. Old Bouncer followed on.

Kitty noticed that one of the children was missing. 'Where is Esther?'

'She was tired today, so I left her at home with Beth.' He called after the boys, 'Be careful, it's muddy.' Then turning to the older ones, 'Go after them and keep them in order.' Michael just looked at him. 'Please, Michael, do as I say. I would like to talk with Kitty.' The boy went after them reluctantly.

'Is Michael not at school?'

'He is home for a few days.' No more was said.

Alexander's silence didn't help Kitty at all. She simply had to speak first. 'You remember the conversation we had before I left that day?' She spoke in code, because the children were not too far away.

Alexander kept walking. 'Yes, I remember.'

'Well, I wasn't sure if it was a serious proposal. It was quite sudden you see, and I wasn't sure, well, if the proposal … '

'Still stood?'

'Yes, I suppose so.' This was all rather awkward.

Alexander chuckled. 'I admit, it was rather unconventional. Would you like it to be a serious proposal?'

Kitty heard herself say, 'Yes, I think I would.'

Alexander stopped walking and looked at her, his grey-green eyes fixed on hers. 'As far as I am concerned it is, very serious.'

Even though she had asked the question, she was surprised to hear his reply. 'In that case, the answer is yes.'

'Yes?'

Kitty nodded. Alexander smiled. 'Very well, that's settled then.' He carried on walking. 'When should we seal the arrangement?'

Kitty had found a perfect way out, why would she tarry? 'I would like to seal it as soon as we can. I see no reason to delay.'

'Very well.' He hesitated. 'Should I go back and speak to … Who should I speak to?'

'No.' Kitty did not want this to be anything to do with them. 'Let's do it quietly, please. No-one need know till it is done.'

'That would be difficult, I'm afraid. My office, you see. I will have to ask the bishop.'

'Of course.' Kitty's heart sank a little; it would not be easy to forget his office.

'I will ride over to see him first thing tomorrow. Then we can make arrangements. Would that suit?'

'Yes, that would suit very well, I will wait until I hear from you.'

Just then, Jonathan fell headlong into the mud. Alexander hurried along to sort out the boys, looking back to give an apologetic smile. Kitty watched as he comforted Jonathan and set the children off again on their walk. But instead of following, he turned and strode back to where Kitty stood. 'You have given this proper thought, haven't you?'

'I have, it is what I want.'

He nodded and took her hand.

'Father,' Michael called.

'I think we will do well, Kitty, I really think we will.' He dropped her hand and chased after his family, making them squeal as they ran up the hill.

Kitty watched them go. The sky was now a flat, steel grey and a breeze was rising. She wrapped her coat around her and walked back to the house. As she did so she couldn't help wondering what had just happened. Had she given the proposal serious thought? She couldn't be sure, but it seemed the most obvious path to take. Perhaps the contentment that had eluded her since her father died was in this arrangement. Perhaps it was to be found in submitting to the twists and turns that life brought, rather than fighting them, as she always did. And Alexander may be right; it could be that they would do well.

On her return, she entered the front door and bumped into Miriam coming out of the kitchen. 'I've been looking for you.'

'That's nice.' Kitty took off her coat.

'It was a lovely wedding, wasn't it?' The awkwardness in Miriam's voice was all too obvious. 'Peggy is a wonderful cook.'

Kitty couldn't resist it. 'It is a shame she's leaving us then.'

Her comment hit the right spot, and Miriam stuttered, 'Yes, it is a shame, but I am sure she is looking forward to seeing her sister.' Kitty didn't reply. 'And actually, Aunt Mary is quite a good cook. She makes a very good stew.'

Kitty had heard enough. 'What do you want, Miriam?'

The young woman was suitably cowed. 'Nothing, I was just . . . '

'Well, if it's nothing important, I'll hurry along and assist Peggy, if you'll excuse me.' She walked straight past her and headed to Peggy's side.

Peggy looked up. 'Did Miriam find you?'

'Yes, was she sent to check on me?'

Peggy looked around, then confided, 'Was it that obvious?'

Kitty nodded. 'I'm afraid I wasn't very helpful.'

'You mustn't tease her, she's a good girl.' Then she changed the subject. 'You been walking with Reverend Gough?'

'Yes, I'm fond of the children.' Peggy gave her a look. Kitty returned her gaze. 'What?' She knew that she could hide little from Peggy.

'You could do worse than him, you know.'

Kitty said nothing.

Chapter Sixteen

Nearly a week later, Peggy left. Mother had started in her garden since the thaw had begun in earnest and Joseph was happily installed in the house. Kitty had apologised to him. And, surprisingly, he had apologised to her for speaking so harshly. Mother was probably the catalyst to all this apology, but it cleared the air. Talk at the table was now on practical matters. Aunt Mary had moved in, and the girl from the village soon after. She was a plump little creature who could only do what she was bid. It seemed that nothing, whatever, went on in her head unless she was instructed; she was a perfect match for Mary. And there was one very great blessing; the woman didn't snore.

Kitty was out on the near field where the few cows they kept were grazing. She was wondering if yet another man had changed his mind about her, when she saw Alexander approaching on a horse. A rare sight, she thought, as he usually walked. Kitty went to meet him.

He called, 'Well, it's all done. The bishop agreed.' Kitty laughed at the way he got straight to the point. He dismounted and came to her. 'You are sure, Kitty?'

'Yes, I am sure.'

'Good.' He looked uncertain. 'But we do have to tell your mother, it is only right.'

Kitty petted the horse's nose; he was a beautiful creature. 'Is there no way we can just marry and tell them later?'

'I am afraid not. The parish would expect a wedding.' Kitty sighed. 'But we will make as little fuss as possible, I promise.'

'Very well, but I would like for us to tell Mother on her own, no official announcement … if your office allows.' She knew she was teasing him.

'I think that in these circumstances, it would be most appropriate.'

They found Mother in the garden. Alexander gave her the news. At first, she was stunned, then evidently delighted. She wiped her hands on her apron and hurried them indoors to tell Aunt Mary the good news. Kitty had braced herself for her response. The woman gave a more verbose response than Kitty had ever heard her give; she could not disguise her delight and relief. 'And when is this happy event to take place?'

Alexander looked at Kitty and laughed; a date had not been discussed. 'Will we wed before the week is out, if that is agreeable to you, Kitty?'

'Yes, most definitely.'

Mother was concerned. 'That is all rather hasty, is it not? And Joseph will have to find help on the farm.'

Alexander looked humble. 'Of course, I was forgetting. Forgive me.' Then, appealing to mother's piety, 'I am afraid that lent is almost upon us. If I am to do the sacred season justice, we must marry soon.'

Kitty couldn't help smiling to herself, as Mother stuttered, 'In that case, I am sure we will manage.'

Kitty wanted to get this settled. There would be no turning back, so why wait? 'Friday it is then.' Arrangements were made over a glass of beer before Alexander took his leave. Kitty accompanied him to his horse and thanked him.

'What for?'

'For insisting that the agreement is sealed so speedily.'

'If we waited too long, it would give the women of the parish time to make a fuss. I'm sure neither of us want that.'

'No, indeed.'

Alexander took her hand, and this time there was no-one to interrupt him. He held it in his and kissed it. Not as the London fops kissed a hand, but tenderly, like a lover. It almost took her by surprise. She was so used to his matter-of-fact ways. 'Well, it seems Miss Canham, that we are to wed.'

She enjoyed the warmth of his presence. 'It seems that way.' He kissed it again and for a moment she thought he would kiss her as a man kisses a woman, but instead he stroked a stray hair from her face and kissed her forehead, long and soft. Then he mounted the stallion. 'I will see you on Friday.' He took off at a gallop.

The days went quickly. Soon it was time for Kitty to pack. It was almost March and a typical March day; clouds scuttered across the sky at speed bringing light or dark as they willed. She put her pa's breeches deep in her chest, wondering if she would ever use them again. Over them she placed her favourite coverlet, sewn by her mother when she was young. Then she sat on her bed with the box into which she had put all her memorabilia. It was high time to rid herself of her childhood treasures; feathers and stones and beads were set aside. Only the embroidered kerchief with the pink heart nestling among the forget-me-nots, her pa's pipe, and the precious butterfly brooch remained. They were wrapped and placed safely among her things. She did not linger on memories; it was time to move on.

The day of the vows came. Whenever the occasion called, Mother could mend and beautify any garment, and now was no exception. Kitty's best dresses were those that Alexander had given her. Mother worked on another. It was green and had integral stripes in the skirt, but the lace was fraying and aged. Mother replaced it and embroidered delicate flowers on the frontal, quite transforming it.

In the spirit of simplicity, Kitty insisted they go on the cart. Young Peter sat atop, and the family sat behind. It was a windy day and everyone was clutching at their hats. Joseph went on about how they should have hired a coach, but Kitty didn't rise to it. Soon she would be mistress of her own house and wouldn't have to listen to his endless corrections anymore.

When they arrived, people were pouring into the church dressed in their Sunday best. No doubt they would all be wondering why the vicar had chosen her over their own young women. Kitty wondered herself. Alexander met the cart. He helped her down, thread her arm firmly through his and whispered, 'Let's get this over with.'

He didn't greet the family or say how lovely she looked. She was surprised and annoyed by her own disappointment. When they entered the church, it was just as she had thought; every eye was upon her. Her only comfort was to see old Reverend Styles from Beaumont waiting for them. He had known her since she was a girl. The old man smiled a familiar smile as they approached. Once or twice during the interminable hymns, Kitty wondered at her actions, but did not let the uncertainty settle. The ceremony was, as Alexander promised, simple.

Once it was done and they were outside greeting the village as the occasion required, Kitty's eyes searched for Sarah, but saw no sign of her. The wind was so strong that they were able to get away quickly. Kitty, Alexander and the children walked to the rectory, followed by what seemed like the whole of the village.

There was a cheering and banging of pans while the family made their way to the front door. Slipping inside, away from the wind and the noise, they closed the door behind them. Everyone laughed as they disrobed and smoothed down wayward hair. Little David pulled at Kitty's arm. 'Come and see … come and see. Father made me a soldier.'

Alexander ruffled his hair. 'Let Kitty settle, young man.' Beth took him and gathered the children to the kitchen, where Mrs Carter would no doubt be waiting with something to refresh. 'Come, there's a fire waiting for us in the study.' Barely two weeks ago she was in this very room, no more than a friend, now she entered as a wife. She looked around her, the familiar study now seeming unfamiliar. Alexander invited Kitty to sit, just as he always did. He poured a spirit and handed it to her. 'I think we need this.' The warmth of it settled her. She took off her bonnet.

After a moment, when neither spoke, Alexander held out the familiar box. 'Backgammon?' Kitty laughed.

An hour or so later, she began to feel unsettled. They had played a game, taken refreshment, and were now playing a second game. Alexander had not kissed her, nor had he attempted to. Would he expect his marital rights or was this to be a marriage of convenience only? As the game went on, it gave her opportunity to study him. His red hair, now paled with grey, was longer than when they first met, and tucked behind his ear; it suited him. His skin was pale, but not without colour. It was marked, from the pox no doubt, but not so badly. When he smiled, appealing crags appeared in his cheeks. He was not young, but tall and strong. Looking at him did the very thing she hoped wouldn't happen; it brought John to her mind. She tried to put the thoughts aside but, nonetheless, found herself wondering if she would ever feel with Alexander what she had felt that evening. When Kitty took to wondering, it was difficult for her to stop.

The rest of the evening was spent sitting by the fire talking of the events of the day. Eventually, Alexander stood and moved to his desk and stood shifting items on its surface one by one, in no particular order. Kitty was talking but she could see he wasn't listening. When she stopped, he turned and held out his hand. 'Come, Kitty, let us to bed.'

He led her up the stairs. In his room, the candles had been lit and a fire burned in the hearth. It was a lovely, if simple, room. Kitty was wholly uncertain as to what she should do, and even more uncertain of how the night would be. Her trunk lay open; she went to it looking for something to anchor her soul. She crouched to the chest and felt the familiar fabric of her warm wrap.

Alexander stood over her, now devoid of his jacket, his shirt loosened. Lifting her to her feet, he said, 'You can settle your things tomorrow.'

He studied her, stroking her face lightly with his knuckles and letting them run down her neck. His touch awakened something in Kitty. He let his mouth touch hers in the gentlest of kisses. But then, he kissed again, this time stronger and deeper. He tasted of rum. His breath became fast and hers rose with it. Moving her to the bed, he lifted her skirts with his hand, an urgency was upon him as he pressed in closer still. She felt his strength against her thigh. This was undoubtably a passion of the flesh. Nonetheless, because of it, Kitty was able to meet his urgency with her own. He entered her, moving his body over hers, the pleasure of it surprising. Eventually he was satisfied, and she felt the weight of his body upon her.

After a few moments, Alexander stood and repaired his breeches, then pulled her up towards him. He began to undress her, slowly, taking care with each hook as it revealed more of her body. With each revelation, he stroked her skin with his fingers. His eyes on each part, until her body was all but naked. The fire had died down. Neither spoke. She shivered. He breathed deep and, drawing her chemise around her shoulders, led her to the bed, lifted the sheets and directed her into it, tucking the blankets around her as one might a child.

Stroking the hair away from her face, he kissed her forehead, then went to speak, but he seemed to change his mind and stood; 'I will not sleep quite yet.' He took up his jacket. 'I will try not to wake you when I return.' At the door he turned. 'Is there anything you need?'

She shook her head, and with that he left the room. Kitty was alone. She turned to her side, and watched the embers glow low. Was this how it was meant to be? She felt a little sore, but that was to be expected. Otherwise, she felt nothing.

The next morning, when Kitty awoke, she realised that she had neither heard Alexander come to bed or leave it, and wondered if he had slept at all. Once dressed, she went to find him. He was at his desk. 'Good morning, Kitty, I trust you slept well?'

'I did, thank you, very well.'

He certainly didn't seem like someone who hadn't slept. 'Good. This is your home now, Kitty, why don't you spend the morning settling in. We can discuss your duties at a later date.' He rose. 'I have an early meeting with the verger, I must get going.'

'Duties?' Kitty didn't like the sound of that.

'Yes, now that you are the wife of a vicar there will be duties to perform. And we need to discuss the children, of course.'

'Of course.'

He looked at her with affection. 'You should have seen Rachel's face when I told her that we were to be wed. She was delighted. And the boys ... well, you know the boys, they were very physical in their happiness.'

She laughed. 'I can imagine.'

'They need a mother.'

Kitty hadn't thought of becoming a mother any more than she had considered becoming a vicar's wife. But now the reality was beginning to settle in.

On heading to the door, Alexander turned. 'Kitty?'

'Yes?'

'I was thinking. Why don't you take Mother's room as your own? I thought perhaps you would like that. I've asked Mrs Carter to arrange for your trunk to be taken across.' Kitty's bemusement must have shown. 'I am sorry. Perhaps I should have asked you. I simply thought that a room of your own would be appreciated.'

'It is, of course, but ... '

'I don't sleep well, you see, even when Elizabeth was alive ... ' His brow furrowed. 'I am sorry, Kitty, it is thoughtless of me to mention her so soon.'

'No, you must feel you can speak of her. She was so important in all your lives.'

He smiled. 'You really are the most generous of women, Kitty. But I think I must insist about the room. You will see, it will be for the best.'

Kitty looked into his eyes, trying to discern what might have led to the decision. All she could see there was kindness and care, nothing more. She conceded. 'Very well.'

'Good, that's decided then.' He went back to his desk and gathered the notebook he'd forgotten. 'I will see you later then.' And with that he left the room.

Kitty stood awhile; she had not spent time in the study on her own before. The shabby comfort of the room, the slight disorder, reflected the man she had married. She did not know what made her do it, but once she heard the front door close, she went to the desk and opened a drawer. There was little in it, merely fresh ink, quills and scraps of paper. Another contained letters of an administrative nature.

The third drawer was a surprise; in it were pencils, watercolours and brushes. She did not know that Alexander enjoyed such pursuits. She certainly had never seen him doing so. Opening the bottom drawer, she found a pile of sketches, some in colour, others not. They were all of the same woman. In each one her hair was tied to the side, draping her shoulder. These were informal sketches. Kitty was surprised at herself for having spent so little time wondering about the woman who had shared Alexander's life. Now she looked at the sketches, she felt sure that they must be of Elizabeth. There were so many. Some were quite complete, some barely started and some … it seemed that the pencil had cut deep into the paper as if the artist was searching for something.

One drawing particularly took her attention. It was a watercolour. The woman's head was turned, her chemise loose about her shoulders, her pale brown hair draped over her breasts. This was the most intimate of drawings. Kitty heard footsteps in the hall. She quickly returned the drawings and stepped away from the desk. The door opened; it was Mrs Carter. 'Oh, I am sorry, Mrs Gough, I heard the reverend go to prayers, I was just coming to check the fire.'

'Don't worry, I will do it.' As the housekeeper went to leave, Kitty called after her, 'Mrs Carter?' The woman turned. 'Does Reverend Gough like sketching? It is only that I came across a couple of sketches and wondered.'

'Oh no, that would've been his wife ... excuse me ... the last Mrs Gough. She loved sketching and painting. I didn't know there were any of her drawings left. I thought he threw them all out.' She stepped further into the room. 'You see, when he lost her he was in a bad way.'

'Of course.'

She obviously had second thoughts about continuing and said, 'Can I get you anything, Mrs Gough?'

Kitty didn't like this new formality that was developing between them. 'Could you call me Kitty, Mrs Carter? I'd much prefer it.'

The housekeeper looked concerned. 'Oh I don't think that would be right, not now. I'm sure everything seems new to you, but you will soon settle in, you will see.' And with a nod of the head she left the room.

Kitty remained. It was beginning to dawn on her that the relationship she had had with the household had changed. She was no longer a friend; she was now the mistress. She left the room, closing the door behind her, and berated herself for having gone through Alexander's desk. She wished that she hadn't seen the sketches. But she had. There was nothing to do about it so, uncertain of what to do or where to go, she made her way into the kitchen.

Mrs Carter wasn't there. Tilly sat at the table, sorting out linen. 'Mrs Carter has gone to the shop, miss. She said she wouldn't be long, and I was to sit here until she got back.'

'Very sensible, Tilly, I'm sure she will be back soon.' The fire looked low. 'Do you think another log would be a good idea?'

'Oh yes!' Tilly jumped to take up the task.

Kitty smiled at the young woman's innocence. 'If you need me, come and find me.'

'Thank you, miss … er misses … er … '

'Kitty will do well enough, now we are all of one family.' Tilly beamed at the idea and turned to her task at hand. Kitty made a decision; now she was mistress of the house, she felt she should have a good look at her new home. She went first to the parlour. It had the coldness of a room barely used, but it was well enough appointed. The dining room felt similar. She knew these rooms well, but looking with new eyes, she could see how neglected it all was.

Closing the door, she took a deep breath before heading to the small orangery. The plants were in a poor way; mostly dead, and one or two panes were cracked, the rest were filthy. It had been neglected for some time. Kitty found a large dead leaf and rubbed the glass in little circles until she could see through it properly. The garden beyond was as beautiful as she remembered. Daffodils were beginning to bloom and little crocuses poked their heads up out of the soft brown earth. Green Tom was in the rose bed, bent low, cutting away dead wood. A jenny wren, flicked its wings in the bird bath, saw her and hopped away into the holly tree. Kitty smiled inside and out and decided on her first project; to return the orangery to its former glory.

Chapter Seventeen

The warm days increased and the family settled into a rhythm. Michael went away to school, funded by Alexander's brother. The other children now all attended the village school. All except Esther, who was only two, and spent most of her time with Beth. She brought life to the house with her constant inquisitiveness. Rachel was not very keen on school and preferred to spend as much time as she could at Kitty's side, helping her clean and renovate the old place. She was quite useless in practical terms, but Kitty so enjoyed her company, which invariably came with singing. Alexander had made it clear that a vicar's wage and position would not be suited to extravagance. Kitty was not prone to such frippery anyway, so the house was cleaned and freshened in a way that suited them both. There was so much to do in the house, that the orangery was all but forgotten.

It was agreed that Kitty could hold her duties lightly while she settled in. However, that didn't stop the village women from calling at every opportunity to meet the new Mrs Gough. Inevitably they liked to discuss the needs of others in the village. Kitty never liked or understood the need for gossip, but soon realised that gossip was exactly what these visits were all about. She hosted each one with as much grace as she could muster, but with as little collusion as possible.

As for her relationship with Alexander, they continued to play backgammon of an evening, and the friendliness that they had once known now settled between them. There was one thing that had concerned her; that first night together was the only time that Alexander let his seed remain. On the occasions he visited her room thereafter, it was always the same; no words were exchanged between them, and he let his seed spill away from her. It was never discussed.

The only time it was alluded to was a few weeks after the event. He asked her if her women's issue was well. She replied that it was. He seemed relieved. Kitty found that she was likewise relieved. She realised then that she had no desire to be a mother, and most certainly no desire to give birth. She only wished that it could have been discussed, but found no way to begin such a conversation. So, she let it lie.

Eventually as spring became summer, Kitty began to take up her duties in the parish. It wasn't the visits where there was true need that irked her, it was visiting women that had little to do but summon the rector's wife, hoping for a gossip. The reality of her position was beginning to sink in. She should have realised that in marrying Alexander she would be marrying his office. In the days when she was housekeeper, only the household had been her concern. She now realised how naive she had been. Even so, Kitty threw herself into her parish duties as best she could.

She had agreed to join the church events committee which met at Mrs Tingwell's house at the other end of the village. She set off on a lovely morning in early June to be greeted warmly by Mrs Tingwell herself. She was a small jolly woman, who evidently took the lead. Others greeted Kitty in like fashion, all except Margaret Lambard who could not hide her displeasure. It was quite obvious that the woman had not forgiven her for marrying Alexander.

Mrs Tingwell started by announcing that the date was set for the rectory picnic on the third Sunday in August. She then went on to the subject of food. The families were to bring their own picnics, but the ladies always put on a spread so that no-one would be in want. At every suggestion, a Miss Bedwell could not help herself offering little exclamations, 'Oh, how wonderful', 'Absolutely', 'Oh, what a treat'. Kitty found herself stifling a giggle every time the little bird chirped, until it became quite irritating.

The question of blankets arose; should they provide blankets or ask the village to bring them. Last time there were those who had to sit on the grass. For some reason this was quite unacceptable to Mrs Cartwright who seemed to tut at every opportunity. Mrs Lambard said how impossible it would be to find so many blankets. The meeting went on in the same vein; every element was discussed in the minutest detail, more often than not causing arguments. Mrs Tingwell did her best to move things along, but it was a hopeless task.

Kitty attended the following two meetings, but by the third she decided that she really was not needed and announced as much, declaring that she was confident that she would be leaving arrangements in creative and capable hands.

The day after her announcement, Kitty was in the orangery, which she finally had time to clear, when she heard Alexander calling. Slightly irritated at being interrupted, she wiped her hands on her apron, and went to see what he wanted. He stood outside his study, and whispered as she approached, 'We seem to have a problem.'

Sitting in the room was Mrs Tingwell. She stood as Kitty entered. 'Ah, Mrs Gough, I am sorry to take you away from your task.'

'Oh, don't worry, I am just cleaning out the old orangery.'

She smiled. 'Ah yes, the reverend's predecessor was rather eccentric in his tastes.'

Alexander sat at his desk. 'Mrs Tingwell tells me that you decided you won't be attending the events committee any longer.'

Kitty could see where this was going, but she kept it light. 'Yes, the ladies were doing such a fine job, I felt that perhaps I wasn't needed.' Mrs Tingwell and Alexander exchanged a look.

The woman smiled, not an unkind smile, and said, 'You see, Mrs Gough, the women of the village have been without, well, how can I put this? Since dear Elizabeth, the first Mrs Gough, passed away...' Kitty could feel the heat rising in her cheeks as the woman went on, 'we have all felt the gap in our society. The rector's wife has always been such an important part of our village, you see, and I'm afraid that some of the ladies feel … well, rather let down.'

'I am sorry to hear that, Mrs Tingwell. It is simply that I still have so much to do to make the house and garden ready, as you can see.'

The woman wobbled in her eagerness to interrupt, 'Oh, we would be most happy to help you with that. Mrs Lambard in particular would be very keen to offer you any assistance you need, I am sure.'

The thought of Mrs Lambard in the house following her husband around like a puppy was too much. 'Do thank her for me, but there is really no need. I have so much help in our dear Rachel.' She realised that she had taken on the woman's tone.

'Of course, it is simply that we would like to support you in any way we can as you settle in.'

Alexander interjected, 'I am sure Mrs Gough will find time to attend the next meeting, won't you, Kitty?'

The woman jiggled in delight. 'If you would, it would be most appreciated.'

'In fact,' Alexander stood, obviously keen to get this women's conversation finished with, 'now the parlour is finished, I am sure Mrs Gough would be happy to host it here.'

Kitty stared at Alexander. Mrs Tingwell spoke, 'Well, if it's not too much trouble.' She looked at Kitty eagerly. Kitty took a deep breath and turned to her. After all, it wasn't the woman's fault. 'By all means. We will hold the meeting here, in the parlour.'

Alexander made for the door. 'Good, that's settled then.' Mrs Tingwell followed after. She turned to Kitty. 'Thank you, you have been most kind. I know our ladies will all much appreciate it. It is truly wonderful to have you with us, my dear.' Kitty couldn't help but wonder at the patience Mrs Tingwell had with the women in her charge.

Alexander led her out. But when he returned, Kitty simply had to say something. 'Really, Alexander, you forced me into that. I didn't have any opportunity to discuss it with you.'

'What is there to discuss?' Alexander looked solemn.

'Having the women here, of course. It is bad enough going to Mrs Tingwell's, but to have them here!' She flopped into her usual chair, legs sprawled before her. Alexander went to his desk, speaking deliberately, 'It is what is expected, Kitty. You have had plenty of time to settle in. It is only right that we begin to welcome the parish into our home.'

Too frustrated to hear what Alexander was saying, she went on, 'Really, Alexander, you don't know what these meeting are like. They spend their time arguing over the most trivial of things. I just don't see the point of them, and if we have them here…'

He turned on her. 'Well try… Try, will you? All they want is a little of your time. It's not too much to ask, is it?' He sat with his head in his hands. Kitty realised how exhausted he looked.

She went to him. 'Are you feeling quite well?'

At first, he shrugged her off. 'Yes, yes. I am fine.' He didn't look at her.

She felt admonished. 'Forgive me, Alexander, I have been selfish.'

'It is the pressure of the job. Sometimes it weighs heavily on me.'

'I can imagine.'

His grey eyes were suddenly upon her. 'No, you can't, Kitty.'

'Then tell me.' She perched on the small chair by the desk. 'I want to know.'

He looked at her, uncertain for a moment, then said, 'Very well.' He took a long breath. 'I buried a man this morning, a tinker. I don't think you knew him, John Spalding.' She shook her head. 'He has left a wife and seven children. The eldest son is taking charge, but I'm not sure about him, not sure at all. I feel that he may take advantage of her. And the little ones just aren't safe with him, I've seen his sort before.'

'Do they have other relatives they can turn to?'

'I don't think so.'

She came to his side. 'You should have told me. I can visit her if you like.'

He raised his eyes to her. 'Would you?'

'Of course I would.'

'That would be most helpful, thank you. But you must not go alone.'

'Very well. I am sure one of the ladies will go with me. You see, I am much better suited to helping you in your work than I am to the silliness that the women of the village seem to enjoy.'

'I see that now. I believe you are stronger than I have given you credit for. But,' he took her hand, 'there is more than one way of doing worthwhile work, Kitty, you must know that. This little group of women, that you so deride, tirelessly raise money for the poor and create occasions that lift people's spirits, when so often their days are dark. They are good women.'

She smiled a special type of smile that warmed Alexander towards her, and this time was no exception. 'If you say so.'

'I do,' he responded, with a kiss to her hand. She knew he would. 'Now go and get on with your tasks and leave me to mine.' As she left the study, she wished that sometimes his kisses would meet her lips, that she may draw him to pleasure. But they rarely did.

Kitty rose early on the day of the picnic. Opening the doors to the garden, she breathed in the freshness of a new day, then stepped outside. Her feet were bathed in dew; summer was coming to an end. But for now, one small white cloud drifted through an otherwise peerless sky, promising another beautiful day. She wandered in the garden, thankful for Green Tom, who kept it so well. There was no garden like it that Kitty had seen. Not even at the Manor.

Her thoughts began to wander, particularly to Michael. He had returned home a few days ago. His father had brought him home for the picnic. It seemed that he found the presence of Kitty irksome and barely addressed her. If he did, it was in the shortest of terms. It didn't help that Alexander insisted he 'behave like a gentleman.' The instruction just served to make him more churlish. It seemed to Kitty that school had only helped to increase the estimation he had of himself.

Just then, Rachel trotted out into the garden. How different she was to her brother. She was open faced and quite lovely, and had become Kitty's constant companion. Her excitement about the day was quite infectious. Despite herself, Kitty looked forward to it.

That morning, the church was full. It was evident that folks thought that if you came to the rectory picnic, it would only be right to attend church first. Some of the village children were unused to sitting so still, so the moment the service was over, they burst out of the doors, running this way and that. Parents followed on, trying to call their offspring to order as they made their way to the rectory. Most of the time, it was to no avail. Kitty hurried to join the committee who led the way. As she joined them, she could feel disapproval in the air. She was determined to counteract it. 'Isn't it wonderful to see the little ones so enjoying themselves?'

Miss Gantry, the confidant and champion of Mrs Lambard, was having none of it. 'Mrs Lambard was almost run down just now. You should have seen it. And the mother . . . '

Another piped up, 'Children should be taught to respect their elders.'

Kitty was perhaps too quick to speak. 'Not every elder deserves respect.' At that moment, David and Jonathan ran past, so Kitty ran after them and chased them towards home, knowing she had been provocative.

The picnic started well. The weather was fine and people seemed to be at ease. Kitty was annoyed at herself for saying what she had to the two women; it had produced a frostiness between them, and on such a lovely day. The lawn was soon strewn with picnic blankets. Long tables had been erected where a spread of fine foods lay. It was good to see families of all sorts enjoying the day together.

Alexander had invited Mother and Joseph. With them they brought Aunt Mary. In the light of a summer's day, Aunt Mary seemed less severe somehow. Kitty smiled to see her mother wandering among the roses as she always had. Kitty went to join her. They wandered together awhile, looking at the extraordinary array of blooms. They chatted about the farm and parish life, until mother turned to her. 'I wish you would visit us, Kitty, we miss you.'

Perhaps her mother did, but Kitty doubted if anyone else did. 'You know how busy I have been, Mother, I just can't get away.'

'Of course.'

'Judith?' Joseph was calling but did not see them. Mother ignored him. Instead she studied Kitty. 'You are looking older, my darling.'

'I expect I am, Mother, nothing stays the same.'

'No, you are right, it does not.' There was a sadness in her eyes. She bent to lift the head of a blousy pink rose. 'Smell this, Kitty, isn't she beautiful?' Kitty lifted the bloom to her nose; it did indeed have the sweetest smell.

'Judith?' Joseph saw her this time. 'Good afternoon, Kitty. I trust I find you well?'

'Yes, thank you.'

He took Mother's arm. 'Mary has a particularly delicious cake she would like you to try.' He led Mother away. Just then, a little hand took hold of hers. It was Esther, and with her was Rachel. She let the girls lead her. They had found a peculiar bug that they wanted her to see.

Though the picnic had gone splendidly, the days following were trying. Whatever Kitty offered in conversation over a meal was challenged by Michael. If she said that a flower was pink, he would say, 'it is, in fact, red.' If she said a dish was tasty, he would say that it lacked flavour. She spoke to Alexander about it but, as usual, he fobbed her off, saying that Michael was becoming a man now, and had opinions of his own. The most frustrating thing about it was that she was sure that Alexander would never take her side over Michael's.

The day Michael left, Kitty received a visitor; Mrs Tingwell. 'My dear, what a marvellous event the picnic was. And, may I say, you made the garden look beautiful. I have never seen it looking more lovely.'

'Actually, Tom should take the credit. I am afraid I have little skill with such things.'

'Even so, congratulations on making this, your first event, so memorable.' Kitty knew she had little to do with it, but also knew that to protest would simply engender more praise from the woman.

Mrs Tingwell clasped her hands together. 'Now, our next event, of course, is Harvest Festival. I was wondering if you might be prevailed upon to open up your home to our little group again. The ladies did so appreciate your hospitality.'

Kitty's heart sank, she had somehow imagined that she had done her duty. 'Of course.'

Mrs Tingwell went on, 'That is most kind. I will let the ladies know. I thought we would take a week to recover and start the following Wednesday. If that is convenient with you?' Kitty agreed.

At the front door, Mrs Tingwell turned to her. 'I heard that you were a little upset at a comment Mrs Gantry made on the way to the picnic. You mustn't mind our ladies, my dear, some of them have had difficult lives and it can make them rather, well, shall we say . . . at times they may not seem so charitable. But it is just their way. If anyone was in real need they would be there.'

'Thank you, Mrs Tingwell, I will bear that in mind.' As Kitty watched the little round woman scurry away down the path, she fought the anger rising within her at the thought of being the subject of gossip, but at the same time she couldn't help admiring Mrs Tingwell with her dogged determination to keep the peace.

Chapter Eighteen

The one person that had kept Kitty going, through all her parish duties, was Sarah. For a time, Nathaniel had been quite happy for Sarah to walk with Kitty now that she was no longer a wayward spinster, but rather, the rector's wife. In fact, he encouraged Sarah, saying that it would be good for her health. Little did he know how true it was. Most weeks the women would visit the little lake behind the church and find solace in each other's company. But the last time Kitty had seen Sarah, she had somewhat withdrawn again. Kitty expressed her concern, but Sarah had not been forthcoming, citing tiredness, an excuse Kitty herself had used on such occasions. Since then Sarah had not been available to walk, so Kitty walked alone. Today was such a day.

September had come in and the long dry days continued. It was a hot afternoon; Kitty had waited till the high heat had passed before she set out. The lake was still. Since Sarah had introduced Kitty to the lake, it had become her secret place, where no-one could see her or know her thoughts.

She sat on her log where a tangled web of green tumbled over the water, touching its face with thirsty leaves. Insects buzzed and lumbered over the surface. She let her thoughts wander. Since Michael had returned to school, Alexander had been busy or occupied in his own thoughts. Their times together were friendly enough, but there was little in the way for true companionship. Her mother came to mind. She knew she should visit, but somehow could not bring herself to do so.

A blue butterfly caught Kitty's attention as it landed on the log beside her, its vibrance all but taking her breath away. She slowly moved her hand towards the beautiful creature, but as she did so, it flitted away, landing here and there as it went, no doubt looking for a safer place to settle.

The time came to leave, and leave she must. So, Kitty picked her way back down the path to the churchyard. As she emerged from the trees, she was astonished to see Eleanor approaching.

Whatever she wanted, it looked urgent. 'Kitty … Kitty … ' She was waving a letter in her hand. 'It's from Florence, she sent it to me because she didn't have your address.'

Kitty took the letter. 'How did you find me?'

'I went to the rectory. They said you'd be walking here. Well, aren't you going to open it?' It amused Kitty at how Eleanor would rarely greet her in the expected way. Although she saw Eleanor from time to time, she always spoke to Kitty as if she was continuing a conversation that they were having just a moment before. Kitty was not going to be hurried and led Eleanor to a bench in the shade of the trees. She opened the letter and scanned it, not wanting to read it verbatim to Eleanor.

> *My Dear Kitty, I do hope this letter finds you, and finds you well … Albert was very sick last spring, he is spending time in the country recovering. It is a shame that he and Eleanor never quite recovered from their argument last Christmas …*

Eleanor's eyes were fixed on her. 'Well?'

'Let me have a look, then I promise I will read you anything of interest.' The letter went on,

> *Spring is beautiful in London, Kitty, I wish you could see it, but now it is far too hot …. I recently met a young man*

> *who was keen to be reacquainted with you. Apparently, you met him at the twelfth night masquerade…*

Her breath caught on the name before her, Lord Dalmeny. She could not read on, neither could she undo what she had read.

Eleanor's voice broke in, 'Kitty?'

Kitty decided to read no more until she could read it alone, and tucked it away in her pocket. 'Florence is very well and says how hot it is in London, but unfortunately Albert has been very sick… ' Eleanor's hand went to her heart. Kitty touched her arm. 'Do not worry, he is recovering well.'

'I did not know. Why did Florence not tell me? What was wrong with him?'

Kitty hadn't read that bit but had no inclination to remove the letter from the safety of her pocket. 'They do not know.'

'Oh how terrible.' Eleanor started to tell Kitty everything that had happened since London. She spoke, barely pausing for breath, 'Oh, Kitty, I have neither seen Albert nor heard from him since our disagreement. I wrote to him to invite him to come and inspect the garden, but he wouldn't come, not while Mr Trenchard was head gardener, but James wouldn't hear of letting him go, so what could I do?' She continued in like fashion. All the while Kitty fought to listen, longing for the opportunity to get away and study the precious document once more. Eventually Eleanor concluded, 'I sent a note to Albert when we were in London in the spring. I got no reply, but now I understand it. He was probably too ill to write, don't you see? It wasn't that he didn't want to see me.'

Kitty encouraged her friend, 'He has been in the country, recuperating.'

'I knew there was a reason.' Eleanor looked ecstatic. 'I have an idea.' She stood as if to take up her idea then and there. 'We will write to Florence and find out when he is returning, then we must go to London. You will come with me, won't you, Kitty?'

Everything within Kitty wanted to say yes, but she tempered her answer, 'I will have to speak to Alexander.'

Eleanor took Kitty's hand. 'I will insist.' Then she tilted her head like a little bird. 'Why did Florence write to you?'

Kitty shrugged. 'We became quite good friends during that short time together, I expect she was just being polite.'

Thankfully Eleanor's thoughts were already running ahead. 'Reply to her, Kitty, immediately, and find out when Albert is returning. He may have returned already, of course. But don't mention why you want to know. This is exciting, life has been so boring these past months.'

'I will write, I promise, and as soon as I hear, I will let you know.'

'How wonderful.' Eleanor clapped her hands together. 'Make sure you send it by messenger. We don't want it going astray. Now, I had better be going, James will think I've gone mad going for a walk, it is something I seldom do.' The women bid each other farewell and went their separate ways. Once Eleanor had walked away, past the inn and towards the Manor, Kitty turned back and tucked herself away behind the church once more, standing in the shadow of the tower. She took the letter from her pocket and read,

... a young man who was keen to make your acquaintance. Apparently, you met him at the twelfth night masquerade. His name is Lord Dalmeny. He asked if he may write to

you. What a fine young man he is, Kitty, you obviously made quite an impression on him. I said I would find you and give you his address. Then if you choose to renew your acquaintance, well and good. If not, nothing is lost.

Lord Dalmeny's address was at the bottom of the page. It was a London address. Holding the letter against her chest, she closed her eyes and leant back against the wall, allowing her thoughts to return to that night, in the snow. The church bell rang and she jumped. She could not help laughing at herself, behaving as if she had been caught in an illicit act. It was only a letter. The bell chimed for evening prayer and she had promised Alexander that she would attend this evening. She tucked the letter away and straightened her hair.

The church was cool. A stream of sunlight shone across the sanctuary touching the cross that stood above the altar. She remembered her vows. As she watched Alexander, so humbly leading his little flock, she knew she could not, and should not, seek any other life. This was her life now and Alexander was her husband.

That evening, Kitty went to her bedroom soon after supper, saying that she had a headache. She sat by the fire, took out the letter in order to hide it away with her memorabilia, but instead she held it on her lap for too long. The promise of it was too strong to let it go. Against her better nature she opened it again and studied it, hoping to find something more written within, but there was nothing. She knew that she should write to Lord Dalmeny and tell him of her situation. But she could not. And anyway, she felt sure that if she entered into a correspondence with John, it would open channels within her that must remain closed. Kitty stood and paced the floor, fighting her own conscience. Perhaps she could see him once more. Perhaps, if Alexander allowed her to go to London with Eleanor, she could see him and the whole thing would be exposed for the foolish fantasy it was.

Kitty sat again and put a log on the fire. As she did so, an idea formed. She would write to Lord Dalmeny in the most formal of terms, mention that she would be coming to London with Eleanor, and hoped to see him during her visit. She would not, indeed could not, give him her address. At the same time she would write to Florence and find out when Albert may be returning to town. Then she could let fate take its course.

She listened to the log spit and burn. Now that a plan was in place, she felt more at ease. Taking up her book, she tucked the letter in its pages, then tried to read. But it was all to no avail; thoughts of her time in London were insistent. Eventually, she succumbed to their sweetness and readied herself for bed.

Chapter Nineteen

Kitty wrote her letters and sent them by messenger the very next day. Not a week later, a letter arrived from Florence saying that Albert would be returning to London by the end of September and that she hoped to see them both when they could visit. After a little persuasion from Eleanor one Sunday morning, Alexander gave permission for Kitty to go with her to London after the Harvest Festival. They were to stay for a week. Kitty was uncertain about the trip but persuaded herself that if she were to see John, it would only serve to confirm how foolish she had been. And besides that, it would be wonderful to go to London again. The days were long in the waiting.

A few days before Harvest festival, Kitty received a note from Sarah saying that little Elijah was sick. She asked if Kitty could come and visit. When Kitty arrived at the house, she found Sarah in the parlour, kneeling beside the child, who lay on a blanket beside the fire. She looked up at Kitty, her eyes wide. The child gave a little barking cough. His mother comforted him and stroked back the blond hair that now clung to her little one's forehead. 'He was so cold, Kitty, I brought him here, by the fire. He will be warmer here.'

'What happened?'

'I took the little ones out for a walk. Mother said he looked flushed, but I thought she was fussing again, she's always fussing, but I took him anyway. We got caught in the rain. That night he developed a fever and wouldn't eat anything. He has not eaten anything since. Then today he started coughing. Oh, Kitty, why did I take him out? Why did I not listen to Mother?'

'You could not have known.' Kitty looked at his little face, the plump round cheeks now pale as milk. 'Has the doctor been called?'

'Yes, he came yesterday. Oh, Kitty.' Sarah began to cry. Kitty put her arm around her friend. Nathaniel now stood by the door. When Sarah noticed him there, she pulled herself together.

Nathaniel now spoke, 'There is nothing the doctor can do.'

Sarah gave him a fierce look. 'He's a stupid old fool. What does he know?'

'You must excuse my wife, Mrs Gough, she is upset.'

Kitty could not like the man. 'Of course she is upset. Shall I fetch my mother? She has a healing way with the herbs.'

Sarah looked round with hope in her eyes. 'Yes she does, doesn't she?' She stood and approached her husband. 'Please, Nathaniel, please, she may be able to help our little one.'

Her hand grasped his arm, but he removed it. 'God is our physician.'

Kitty responded, 'I believe that God gave us herbs with which to heal. My mother is practiced in it. I could send for her right away.'

He was firm. 'No, thank you. You must understand, Mrs Gough, that our community is a community of faith. The community is praying. The boy is in God's hands.'

'But surely…'

He stopped Kitty in her tracks. 'I think you will find, Mrs Gough, that your husband would say the same. Now if you don't mind, I think perhaps we should let Sarah get some rest.'

Sarah looked at her husband. 'Just a little longer, Nathaniel, please.'

He looked from her to Kitty and nodded an assent before leaving the room. Sarah returned to Elijah's side. Kitty sat beside her. There was nothing she could say or do to relieve this moment.

Finally Sarah spoke as if to herself, 'Why did we come here? This house is so draughty.' Kitty was surprised at the violence in Sarah's speech. 'And he won't heat the bedrooms, not unless it snows. He says we mustn't be extravagant … even at the expense of his own child.' Elijah began to cough again, a wretched barking cough. Sarah soothed him.

The door opened behind them again; this time it was Mrs Parditer. 'Good evening, Mrs Gough. I am afraid Sarah needs to rest, she was watching for most of the night.'

'Of course.' Kitty conceded and rose. 'Mrs Parditer is right, Sarah, you need to keep up your strength.' She held out her hand.

Mrs Parditer continued, 'I will stay with him, I promise.' Sarah looked from one woman to another, eventually allowing Kitty to help her to her feet. As the women made their way from the room, Sarah looked over her shoulder. 'Thank you for coming, Kitty, you will come again?'

'Of course, I will call tomorrow.' Sarah was led away. A young servant girl stepped in to show Kitty out. She took one more look at the little boy and left.

The next day, when Kitty went back to the house, the child had passed. This time she did not gain entry; the door was closed to her once more.

On Harvest Sunday, Kitty sat at the back of the church with Beth and the children. The church looked lovely, adorned with the corn of thanksgiving. Whilst Alexander preached, thoughts of home invaded her head and the joyous harvest homes of all her years tumbled among her senses. The smell of the fire, the taste of cider and the sound of singing; not the drone of the hymns she now sung, but the wistful songs of love, and the gusty songs of lust.

Today the pew was uncomfortable beneath her. She shifted, but it didn't help. Then she felt a slight sweat forming on her brow. She whispered to Beth that she was feeling unwell and was going home.

By the time Kitty closed the front door behind her, she was shivering. The only thing to do was to make her way to her room. As soon as she was in bed she slipped into a deep sleep. It was too deep; her awakenings were tortured with half realities. She was aware of Alexander's presence at one time, and Tilly and Rachel.

When she finally came to her senses, Mrs Carter was at her side. 'Oh, my dear, you are with us, how wonderful.'

Kitty's throat burned. She asked for a drink, but on swallowing, pain seared through her. She tried to speak, but it was too painful. Mrs Carter continued, 'You have been unwell for three days. It seems you have the throat distemper.' She soothed Kitty's brow with a damp rag. 'How are you feeling?' Kitty tried to speak but could not, so she just shook her head.

Mrs Carter spoke carefully now, 'Don't be alarmed, my dear, but David is also unwell. Beth is tending him. He is a strong little boy and will be fine. It is spreading in the village. More and more children are catching it.' Kitty remembered that baby Elijah had died and that she must attend the funeral. She went to sit up.

Mrs Carter tried to lay her back down. 'And where do you think you are going?'

Kitty rasped, 'I must get to Elijah's funeral.'

The older woman showed her concern. 'They buried him yesterday.'

Kitty felt a hot tear trickle down her face. She flopped back on the bed, succumbing to the weakness of her body.

Mrs Carter's voice took on a practical tone, 'Now, you must not worry about the children, we are taking good care of them. We just need you to recover quickly. We have got enough to do without you getting in our way. I will have Tilly bring something to eat.' Kitty never tasted the food; instead she slept.

As soon as Kitty was well enough, she took to looking after the rest of the family. David was improving, but little Esther soon caught it and struggled to heal. Alexander was busy making visits, people called for him at all hours. Each day that saw Esther improve was followed by one that only saw her worsen.

The night she died was a cold, clear night. Beth was at her bedside. Kitty stood with the other children at the foot of her bed. Esther's beautiful ringleted hair, which was always in motion, now lay still. She looked perfect. Rachel let out a little sob; Kitty held her close. Her father kissed the little one so tenderly and sat a moment, his head hanging heavily between his shoulders. He took a deep breath and said, 'We must pray. We will say the Lord's prayer together.'

The little gathering muttered the familiar words. As soon as the Amen was spoken, Alexander left the room and Beth went to Esther's side; she had grown so close to the little one. The boys stood staring with unbelieving eyes. Mrs Carter spoke, 'Shouldn't there be more? More prayers? Is that all he is going to say?'

Kitty could see that she was as distressed as everyone. 'I expect that is all he is able to say.'

They lay little Esther out that very evening.

The next afternoon, Kitty took a moment to sit in the orangery. The autumn sun streamed through the windows. Alexander found her there. 'May I sit?'

'By all means.'

He sat beside her. 'Kitty?'

'Yes?'

'Why did you visit Sarah's child that day?'

'What do you mean?' She knew full well what he meant.

'You knew how sick the child was.'

'I visited because that is what we do, and because Sarah is my greatest friend. I am sorry, truly I am. But I could do no other.'

He nodded, tears rolling down his cheek. He wiped them away. A combination of exhaustion and grief began to pour out of him. She put her arms around him and held him close.

That night, he came to her. As always, neither spoke, but there was a tenderness between them, an understanding somehow. They spent the night entwined in the need of each other's living breath. The next day, they buried Esther beside her mother, among a fall of golden leaves.

There was no time to grieve; the sickness continued to spread in the village. Kitty took up visiting as soon as she was able. It seemed that the whole village was fighting this disease. Days and weeks passed in a blur of activity. But by the beginning of December, far fewer were sick now and the endless stream of loss seemed to be abating.

For some time, Rachel had been pleading with Kitty to take her on her visits. Alexander had insisted that the children be kept at home. Although the boys played together, Rachel was often left to her own devices. She helped with the household tasks and so was kept busy, but Kitty could see how she longed to go beyond the confines of the walls. The week before Christmas, when they had heard no report of sickness for some days, Kitty persuaded Alexander to let her come, insisting that they would take the greatest of care. She would only enter the household of the bereaved, if any were sick Rachel was to wait outside. It had been a bright frosty day, the kind of day that at other times would have filled the world with wonder.

Rachel was evidently delighted to be out. She stopped at every cobweb, heavy with its icy coat. 'Look, Kitty, they are so strong.'

Kitty tried to keep her moving. 'Yes they are, now hurry along, Rachel, we have much to do.' Rachel would obey for a while, only to halt again at some other wondrous sight. Kitty was uncertain at the wisdom of bringing Rachel, but could not help smiling at the child's wonder. On the way home, Rachel started a song,

Though the days are cold
And the nights are long,
I will raise my head
With a happy song…

Kitty smiled, but was too exhausted to join in. 'It's lovely to hear you singing, Rachel. It is time we heard music again.'

'Kitty?'

'Yes?'

'Why does God want so many children?'

'What do you mean?'

'Well… ' A pheasant fluttered and stuttered out of a bush. 'Look, he's a fine fellow!' Her mind always flitted wherever it chose.

Kitty replied, 'He is indeed, I'm surprised nobody's had him for their supper.' The bird disappeared beneath another bush, and with it, the most difficult of questions. Kitty was relieved.

On Christmas Eve, after a round of visiting, Kitty and Rachel arrived home. They went straight to the kitchen. Mrs Carter never ceased to amaze Kitty how she managed to do everything she did without tiring, producing sustenance at every turn. At the sight of them, Green Tom slipped out the back door with a mug in his hand; he always disappeared when people arrived. The smell of fresh bread filled the room. Tilly was at the basin.

Kitty and Rachel warmed themselves by the fire, until drinks and fresh bread were laid out on the table. Rachel took a mouthful of bread and winced. She put her hand to her throat. Mrs Carter looked at Kitty. They said nothing, perhaps both hoping that it was just a passing moment. But Rachel pushed the bread away, her face pale, not with sickness, but with fear. 'I'm not hungry.' Kitty could feel the blood drain from her own face; this could not be happening, just when everyone was healing.

Mrs Carter took control. 'It seems to me, miss, that you are not very well. Let's get you to bed and I'll bring you some broth later.' Rachel looked at Kitty, who smiled reassuringly as they left the room. Kitty's head fell into her hands.

Tilly spoke, 'It's alright, miss, Esther is with Jesus.'

For the first time since the sickness first showed itself, Kitty felt overwhelmed. 'For goodness sake, Tilly, this is not about Esther, can you not keep up with anything?'

Tilly's eyes widened. 'I'm sorry, miss, I just … '

Kitty felt wretched. 'No! Forgive me, Tilly, I am just so terribly tired.' The girl looked unsure, but Kitty had little left to give, and could encourage her no further. She took her cup to the fire, where she stood nursing it.

Mrs Carter returned. 'Now, we are not going to be worrying. This horrid thing is taking the little ones. Rachel is big now and strong. She will fight it, mark my words.' Kitty knew that she was right. 'Rachel asked if you would go and see her.'

'Of course. Although, I will have to let Alexander know first.' She did not move for some time, but stared into the fire, where the world was steady.

When she arrived in the study, Alexander was sitting at his desk ensconced in his work, which he'd had little time to do until now. Kitty couldn't bear to tell him; the guilt of bringing the disease into the house still weighed heavily upon her.

'It may be nothing, but I thought I should let you know.' He looked up and she continued, 'Rachel has a sore throat. We have put her to bed, but I think we must keep the boys away from her.'

'But I thought the disease was abating? We haven't heard of a case for several days. How could this have happened?'

'I don't know.' He looked at her as if she should know. 'It may simply be a cold.'

After a moment he said, 'Very well, let me know how she gets on.' With that he returned to his studies. Evidently, the conversation was over.

Christmas came and went. The delicious food that Mrs Carter had prepared was eaten with little joy. Rachel continued to struggle against the disease. At first Alexander spent much time beside his daughter whilst she slept. But as she grew worse, he became more absent. He was agitated and worked or took walks until she began to recover. But the recovery was slow. A special chair was arranged for her in front of the fire in the parlour, so that she could spend some time out of bed.

Rachel was growing up; she would say to her father, 'Don't worry, father, I am getting better, we just need patience.'

The physician was called, but he could find nothing wrong with her. He suggested brisk walks in the cold air to awaken her body into aliveness. Thankfully, Alexander agreed with Kitty not to take any notice. Instead, Kitty sent to her mother for herbal remedies.

It was Tom who brought them. She was pleased to see him, but he did not come in, probably fearful for his own family. They spoke awhile. She told him of the loss of Esther. He told her that his own little ones had been saved from the disease. Kitty found a jealousy, that had no business being there, rising within her. She did not want Tom's family to suffer, but her own had suffered so much.

Tom studied her. 'You look exhausted, Kitty.'

'I am, it has been the most terrible time.'

He told her of the families on the farm who were suffering; the Butts had also lost two little ones. She longed to have Tom hug her, to reassure her as he always had. But instead he handed her the herbs from a distance, stood back and took his leave.

After a few days, Rachel strengthened a little. She could even be heard singing, which made Kitty's heart sing in unison. Michael was sent for; until now it had been agreed that it was unwise for him to visit. As soon as he walked through the door, it was evident that he would rather not be there. His attitude irritated Kitty no end, but he was part of the family and must be treated so. They had a special meal that evening in the dining room. Memories of little Esther were exchanged. Michael sat in silence. For the rest of his stay, he said little and continually had his head in a book.

One evening, as Kitty passed the parlour, she heard voices and peered through the door. Michael was sitting beside Rachel, talking in the most animated way, and she was laughing. His hair, usually so well in place, was awry, and she saw for the first time, the child he might have been. Rachel noticed Kitty, which caused Michael to turn. He quickly stood. 'I am glad to see that my sister is recovering.' He smoothed back his hair and picked up his book.

Kitty held up her hand. 'Don't let me disturb you, please.' She went to leave, but it was too late. Michael excused himself, walked past Kitty and disappeared. Rachel's face exposed her disappointment. Kitty was angry at herself for having interrupted a rare and intimate moment between the siblings. She sat beside Rachel and held her hand awhile.

'Will you read to me, Kitty?' The child leant her head back against the cushions. The warm pink of her cheeks had given way to a creamy white.

'Of course.' Kitty picked up Rachel's book and read until the child began to doze.

Eventually the little girl said, 'I feel terribly tired. I think I'd like to go to bed.'

'What about supper? It is your favourite. Lamb stew.'

Rachel shook her head. 'Perhaps later.'

Kitty helped her upstairs and tucked her into her bed.

The next morning, Kitty awoke to a cry. She wrapped the blanket around herself and ran toward the sound. Beth was in Rachel's room, her hands at her face, crying and calling, 'She won't wake up... She won't breathe.'

Kitty ran to her and shook her, calling her name, but it was all to no avail. Her eyes were wide and her mouth hung open. Kitty looked at Beth. 'What happened?'

Beth was shaking. 'I don't know, she was like that when I came to wake her.'

Kitty could not bear to see death upon the dear little face that she had come to love. A sob choked her as she gently closed the child's eyes. She told Beth to get some strips of cloth, but she didn't move. Alexander now stood in the doorway. Kitty looked at him, but his eyes were fixed upon his daughter's face. A long moment passed in the silence of the absence of another soul.

Finally, Alexander instructed Beth, 'Gather the household.' The young woman still didn't move. 'Beth?' She woke from her fear and left the room. Alexander sat beside his daughter and stroked her cheek. Then he said to Kitty, 'Get me my prayer book and the oil. You will find it in the cabinet.' Kitty put her hand on his. He withdrew it. His face was as stone. A coldness crept over her as she left the room.

She found Mrs Carter in the hall, clutching her stomach. 'What happened?'

'It's Rachel.' Kitty shook her head. Mrs Carter's hand went to her mouth. 'Strips of cloth, please, Mrs Carter.'

Kitty went to the study and found the items required. On her return, she found Beth standing with the boys. Mrs Carter and Tilly soon arrived. Kitty took the cloths and sat on the bed to wrap Rachel's jaw into place. Alexander pushed her hand away.

'Please, Alexander, I just want her to look well for the little ones.'

He stared at her, his eyes blank, then he nodded and let her complete her task. At last Rachel looked at peace. Alexander began to read the prayers, without passion. When he finished reading, he dipped his finger in the oil and reached to make the sign of the cross on his daughter's forehead. He stopped, and for a long moment did not move. Then instead, he stroked her face, eventually taking her small head in his hands. He bent his face close to hers, anointing his beloved child in oil and tears. Kitty led the family out of the room and closed the door. His grief could be heard behind them.

Kitty left the boys with Beth and Mrs Carter, and went to her room. She locked the door and opened her dressing chest, digging deeply until her hands found her father's coat. She pulled it free, climbed on to the bed, curled around the familiar fabric and wept.

Chapter Twenty

Michael returned to his school. The younger boys, for only boys there were now, returned to the village school. Soon the rector's wife was called upon again. There could be no special attention for Kitty, she knew that, because everyone had suffered their losses. Dreary day passed dreary day. The household was too quiet. She longed to see Sarah, but the door had remained closed to her, since that night, the night that little Elijah died.

Alexander had ceased to come to her room. Kitty was aware that he had withdrawn from her. Where once she would have challenged him, now she did not. How could a man forgive the woman who had brought such sickness into his home, and with it such grief? At times the desire to do something, anything, to cause Alexander to react to her in some way, almost overwhelmed her. But she knew she could not. He must be allowed to grieve. The little ones were his flesh and blood.

When winter turned towards spring, and the first warmth gathered in the orangery, Kitty created a corner for herself, where she could sit and watch the birds as they readied for nesting. On this particular day she sat with her face in the sun, longing for it to give of its hope, but it seemed unwilling. A robin perched on the wall outside and started to sing. Kitty could hear Rachel's sweet songs in its tuneful melody. A heat rose within her until she could bear it no more.

Hurrying from the orangery, her heart pounding, she went to her room. She drew her breeches from the chest, slipped them on and strode out for the farm. She walked hard and fast. As the rectory faded behind her, so did her passions. The awakening landscape caused her pace to slow. The constancy of the round of the seasons settled her; cows still grazed and brown fields still nurtured the seed; labourers still bent to their task. A few glanced up, surprised to see her passing by, before returning to their labours.

Old Jacob was sitting on a stump with a staff in hand, his beloved sheep around him. A small fire burned beside him. He looked up. 'Good morning, Mrs, what you doing here then?' He looked as old as he ever did, but not older. It was as if he had always been this way.

'I came to see if you needed any help.'

'We can always do with help. Waiting for some lambers here.' A sheep with a round belly fidgeted and fussed in the tell-tale way. 'She be near her time. Give her till the sun is high, I reckon.'

Kitty looked to the sky. 'I'll have a wander then.' She walked slowly, taking in the sights and sounds that were so familiar to her. She did not go to the house, but rather went down to the water's edge. The tide was neither high nor low; she realised that she no longer knew the tides and could not tell if it was on the ebb or the flow. Brant geese gathered far out over the waters twisting and turning as they gathered the stragglers before lifting into the sky. They flew over Kitty's head, squawking all the while before setting off north toward their summer dwelling. She could not help laughing at the sight, though envied their flight. When they were gone, and the vast sky lay wide before her once more, she too set off towards the sheepfold.

Jacob had his hand under the ewe, feeling her belly. 'She be ripe ready, this one.' The animal was fidgeting and let out a low bleat. Kitty gathered some fresh hay from the shelter and lay some before her.

'Do you have any tobacco, Jacob?'

'Yes, that I have.'

She took out her pipe. 'Could you spare a little?' Without a word or any judgment, he took an old leather pouch out of his pocket and offered it to her. She filled the pipe and lit it from the small fire at Jacob's side. It was good to inhale its rich smoke. The tightness she had been holding slipped from her shoulders. Jacob lit his pipe and they sat thus most of the afternoon, waiting. The lamb was reluctant to come.

Eventually Jacob said, 'I think we had better give the girl a hand.' He lay the ewe on her side and, after much coaxing, rubbing and pulling, the lubbery lamb slipped out into Jacob's skilful hands. It lay quite still. He rubbed it and swung it until its little chest started to rise and fall and it gave a little bleat. He lay it beside its mother, who raised her head and licked away the creamy fluid.

Jacob gave Kitty a proper smile. 'Wasn't an easy one, good thing you came.' She smiled in return; it was good to see a new life born. A sense of elation went with her as she walked home. She gathered spring flowers as she went.

At the front gate of the rectory, Kitty hovered, reluctant to enter. But before she could, Mrs Tingwell stepped out the front door and walked towards her.

On seeing Kitty, she put her hand to her mouth. 'Oh my!'

Alexander stood resolutely in the doorway.

Kitty became acutely aware of her attire, and the state of it. 'I am sorry, Mrs Tingwell, I didn't mean to startle you. I've been at my mother's farm. There was difficulty with a lamb.'

'Of course.' Mrs Tingwell looked relieved.

Then Kitty remembered that she had a meeting arranged with the woman that very afternoon. 'Oh, do forgive me, Mrs Tingwell, I quite forgot our meeting. I can easily get cleaned up.'

Alexander called, 'I am sure Mrs Tingwell has other things to occupy her this afternoon.'

The woman dithered. 'Well … I … '

Kitty saved her. 'Are you free to call tomorrow afternoon?'

'Yes, I could come at the same time, if that is to your convenience?' Kitty assured her it was.

Mrs Tingwell bid Alexander farewell then turned back to Kitty. 'Do not worry, my dear, these things happen.' Then she noticed the spring flowers in Kitty's hand. 'What beautiful flowers,' she said, and hurried away.

Alexander did not move, but rather stood full square in the door. He whispered, though his anger was evident, 'What were you thinking? You can't just take off like that.'

She was too tired to argue. 'I just went for a walk. Jacob needed help, so I helped him. That was all.'

She tried to pass him, but he stopped her. 'We need you here, Kitty. The boys were worried, anything could have happened. Have they not lost enough?'

'I needed to … I just needed to walk.'

He shook his head. 'We are all suffering, Kitty. We just have to get on with life, as we always do. That is the way through.' Kitty could not tell him of her suffering, of the endless tedium that drove her to distraction. Or the guilt that weighed her soul. He went on, 'And you've got to remember who you are.' He looked at her breeches. 'This won't do, Kitty. I'm sorry, but it really will not do.'

She stared back at him. 'I don't suppose your precious Elizabeth ever embarrassed you like I do.'

He shook his head. 'Kitty … ' She pushed past him and made her way to the kitchen without looking back. He called after her, his voice softening, 'There is food for you if you want it.'

Determined not to let their angry exchange ruin the day, she found a jar for the flowers, placed them on the table and helped herself to the warm pottage. Though she tried to forget it, she couldn't help hating herself for speaking of Elizabeth. From time to time, the drawings she had seen still haunted her, but she could find no way of speaking of them to Alexander, so let them be.

Spring passed into summer, and the warmth increased. The harshness of the winter began to soften, as did their relationship. Sometimes, when Kitty was in the orangery, Alexander would come and sit with her. He would read an item from a newspaper, or tell her some interesting fact that he had discovered. Of an evening, they would still play backgammon or read. A different kind of companionship had developed; it was more formal and guarded.

Occasionally, Kitty visited old Jacob in the field; she did not put on her breeches when she visited but reassigned them to her memories. And she did not revisit the house. She did, however, keep her pipe out of sight, but close at hand so that she could, on occasion, hold it and breathe in the smell of its comfort. But mainly she attended her duties in the village and gave herself to work among the poor and sick. Although Kitty took her walks, she always walked alone now; Sarah remained hidden away. Kitty was concerned for her, but she had not the energy to fight Sarah's cause.

The summer picnic took place, and although all the usual effort was made, the absence of so many children dampened the day. The committee served with the customary jollity that aimed to lift the spirits of the village folk, but it was a fragile display. Michael did not return home for the occasion.

She was sitting in her beloved orangery one grey morning, watching Tom staking the blowsy autumn flowers against the inevitable winds, when a note arrived. It was from Eleanor. Kitty had not seen her nor heard from her since the distemper struck and Captain James hurried his family to London to keep them safe. Kitty read on,

> *It was miserable, Kitty, being stuck in London with all the family. The house is far too small and James was always about my feet. However, Albert and I were reacquainted. I even persuaded him to come to the house and see how the garden was faring. He came in May when we returned. It is still so beautiful; you must come and see it as soon as you are able. My favourite rose is in bloom as I write. Albert had it planted especially for me. Its petals are the most delicate pink. If only James hadn't insisted we spend the summer visiting his relatives, you could have seen the garden in its summer glory.*

Kitty realised now how she had missed Eleanor. Her girlish ways always made her smile. Eleanor explained that she had finally come to the end of her fourth confinement and now had another little girl.

> *You know how I am, Kitty, so few seem to understand me like you. I long for adventure. It is now a year since the wretched*

day that took you ill and prevented you from accompanying me to London. I am now quite recovered from the arrival of our little Sophia and ready for an adventure.

I am aiming to travel to London before the weather closes in completely. I do hope you will agree to being my travelling companion, Kitty, I can think of no-one I would rather choose. Mr Bastion is holding a harvest party, a Mabon. I expect you will know what it means better than I. It will surely lift our spirits after such a wretched year. Do say you will come. This time, I will explain to James that I do not feel ready to visit his relatives. Then we can enjoy our time without tiresome interruptions.

The letter was concluded with an invitation to visit the following Tuesday morning and, most importantly, to bring a reply. Kitty was under no illusion that her presence on the trip would largely be to fulfil Eleanor's need to have a companion of discretion. But at the same time, Kitty longed to visit London again.

Ten days later, Kitty was packed and ready to go. She came down the stairs to see David and Jonathan standing with their father in the hall. When she looked at them, she realised how little time she had spent with the boys in recent months. Jonathan ran over to her. 'Are you coming back?'

She wondered at his question, stroked his hair, and said, 'Of course I'm coming back.' He seemed satisfied. David stayed at his father's side. She pulled on her gloves whilst Beth led the boys away.

Alexander opened the door. 'Are you ready?' She nodded, and stepped out into a cold bright day. He followed with her bag and hat box.

'Thank you for seeing me off.'

'You are my wife, I want to see you safely on to the coach.' As he stepped onto the path, he said, 'The ground is soft, you may need to stay at an inn.'

'I know.'

'If you do, take care. It would be best to stay together at all times.'

By the way he was speaking, she could tell that he was trying not to irritate her, but she could feel herself irritated nonetheless. 'And please don't go out in London alone, it can be such an uncertain place.'

'Of course I won't.' She took a deep breath, not wanting to leave with irritation on her lips.

Alexander gave the luggage to the coachman, then took her hands, his grey eyes upon her. 'Come back to us, Kitty.'

There was something about that look that drew compassion from her. She nodded. 'I will be careful, I promise.' Then he did something that he never did in public and rarely had done since the girls were lost; he kissed her on the lips, gently, but firmly.

The coachman opened the door. Eleanor sat within, smiling. Alexander greeted her in the expected way. He waved them off, a rather forlorn figure standing under the arching branches that guarded the rectory.

A night was taken at the Vulcan. She and Eleanor had to share a bed in a dingy room with a high window. There was much amusement as they lay listening to the drunken laughter from below. The weight of the past year began to drop from Kitty's shoulders. When they were dressing the following morning Eleanor asked Kitty how she would like to be introduced when they arrived in London.

'Well, as Mrs Gough, I suppose.'

Eleanor continued with a faint smile. 'You don't have to, you know. As soon as people know you are the wife of a minister of the cloth, they will behave very differently around you. It wouldn't be much fun.'

'Oh, I see what you mean.'

It was evident that Eleanor didn't want that sort of attention. 'Why don't you go by your birth name?'

Kitty didn't speak at first, but continued to clothe herself. Then, as she corrected her hair, she announced with a surprising abandon, 'Canham, then. I shall be Kitty Canham while I am in town.'

When they finally arrived at the London house the next afternoon, it was just as Kitty had remembered it. Mr and Mrs Gordon were still at the helm, no doubt making sure the household ran with the utmost discretion. So much had happened since her last visit, that in some ways it seemed an age ago, in others, yesterday. After a light supper in the parlour they made their way to bed. Kitty was pleased to be put in the room she was staying in before, the familiarity of it comforting.

The morning after their arrival, Eleanor was up early and knocking on Kitty's door. 'We've been invited to a gathering tonight at the Robillards'. Isn't it thrilling?' Before Kitty had a chance to gather where she was, Eleanor had plonked herself on the bed. 'They live together, just the two of them. They have the most marvellous rooms in Soho, you have to see them, Kitty. Florence is an artist, you know, every room is painted differently.' She went on to describe each room in detail. 'You will love it, Kitty, I know you will. Now, this morning, I thought we could go for a walk. I like to do that first, whenever I come to town, I don't know why. I think it's being among such interesting people and … ' Her hand went to her breast. 'Oh bother.' Eleanor giggled. 'My breasts seem to have forgotten that I left the baby with the wet nurse in Thorpe.' She ran from the room clutching her chest and calling, 'I'll see you in the parlour.'

Kitty, who had raised herself onto her elbows, now let her head fall back on the pillow. Stretching into the day, she realised that the fire had been lit and the curtains opened. Outside, clouds were parting beneath a blue sky.

Chapter Twenty-One

The Robillards' rooms were just as Eleanor had described, only even more extraordinary. They weren't painted particularly well, but each had a scene which told a story. In the main room, one entire wall was a forest in which sinuous nymphs played, whilst woodland creatures looked on. An abundance of soft furnishings, embroidered with leaves and bowers, adorned the room.

'Come in … come in … ' Florence stood before them draped in a similar fashion to her furnishings. She welcomed them with an extravagant smile.

People of all sorts were there, and few formally attired. Eleanor took Florence aside and whispered to her. Florence's eyes were on Kitty all the while. She nodded as Eleanor spoke. Eleanor saw Albert and immediately went to his side. He was holding court among a group of young women. On seeing Eleanor, he put out his arm and welcomed her to sit beside him on the arm of his chair, barely pausing in the telling of his tale.

Florence took Kitty's arm. 'So, Eleanor tells me that you still are Miss Canham in town.' Kitty had quite forgotten that she had written to Florence in her married name. Florence continued, 'Don't worry, your secret will not be found out here, not while I keep it.' Kitty was relieved. 'Now let me look at you.' She held Kitty at arm's length. 'Just as I expected, you are looking tired. I hear you have had the most terrible time of it. But what did I tell you? The countryside is not to be trusted.' She flung her head back with an unfettered laugh. 'Now, let me introduce you.' She scanned the room for a suitable candidate for introduction.

A tall, lugubrious man stood by the window. With him were two women, one Kitty recognised. The young woman turned and looked uncertain, so Kitty helped her out. 'Good evening, Alina. We met at the Bastions', some two years ago? We sang together?'

Alina awoke to the realisation. 'Of course, Miss Canham, is it not?'

'Indeed it is.' Kitty was pleased to be recognised and glad of a previous acquaintance.

Alina turned to her friends. 'You remember Miss Canham?'

'Kitty, please.' Now she recognised the others in the group. The tall man was the rather drunk young man she remembered at the Bastions' gathering and the fuller woman Alina's companion. After initial niceties the conversation moved away from Kitty to theatre gossip, which was quite intriguing.

Food was served and drink flowed. The evening grew mellow. She found herself emboldened to give her opinion on any subject, of which there were many. There was nothing that could not be discussed, and it seemed that no opinion was inappropriate for such company.

As the evening drew on, the entertainment began. Everyone was squeezed into that one room. Kitty found herself on a large cushion on the floor, wedged between a woman with extraordinarily large breasts and a slight young man with a clean complexion. During a song, he put his arm around Kitty's shoulders, but it was not an advance, simply a comradeship. The difference between this and her usual society caused Kitty to giggle.

The young man looked at her. 'You have the most marvellous teeth.' The evening was becoming ever more strange. She felt he was looking at her as one might a horse. He studied them closely, with gin upon his breath. 'It is good to have good teeth.' She leant away but all too soon found her head in the large woman's breast.

Now the woman put her arm around her and smiled, showing off a cavernous gap in the front of her mouth. She laughed, then put her pudgy finger to her lips. 'Shh … the poets … they are about to begin.' Kitty leant against the woman's soft body as lyrical voices drifted in the air. Some were comical, some beautiful and some beyond her understanding, but each drew from her a sweet sadness that was almost unbearable.

The evening entered into night, and the night into early dawn. The tall man was now sprawled asleep on the chaise, limbs overflowing in all directions. Others slept where they found themselves. Albert and Eleanor were nowhere to be seen. Kitty found Florence in deep conversation with a man in the dining room. They seemed to be talking about politics.

Kitty touched Florence's arm. 'I think perhaps I had better find my way back to Eleanor's house?'

'No, no, you must stay here. Find yourself a comfy spot and I will fetch you a blanket; the bedroom will be freezing at this time.' Kitty returned to her cushions. Her companion half woke as she settled beside her.

Florence soon returned with a warm blanket. 'I am so sorry, Kitty, I feel I have neglected you this evening. I do hope you found good company.' Kitty had barely nodded an affirmation before she was asleep.

The morning felt like a continuation of the night before. She awoke, cold and fuzzy headed. The only two people left were Florence, who was asleep on a chair by the fire, and an older man who sat in the dining room. A table of bread, cheese and hard-boiled eggs was laid before him. He was eating voraciously. When he saw Kitty, he stood, realised that his breeches were unbuttoned and grabbed at them before he exposed his parts. Falling back on the chair, he said, 'I do beg your pardon, I rather think I overdid it last night. Robert Calderman at your service.'

'Kitty Canham, how do you do.'

'I am quite well, thank you Miss … Mrs Canham?'

'Miss.' Kitty was surprised how easily it came.

'May I pour you a drink? I'm afraid this morning it is milk.' His fat fingers wrapped around the pitcher. 'So, how do you know our darling hosts?'

Kitty sat and took some bread. 'I am staying with a friend in town who knows them.'

'And who, may I ask, is your host?'

Kitty found Mr Calderman rather inquisitive. 'Mrs Manley-Hogg. And how, may I ask, do you know them?'

He seemed to be taken aback at having the question thrown back at him. But his pride got the better of him. 'Of course, we are old friends, I have been in their circle since … '

At that moment, Florence appeared behind him and took him by the shoulders. 'Now, Robert, I think it's time to go home, don't you?'

He rose, quite indiscreetly buttoning his breeches and saying, 'Of course, of course, I don't want to outstay my welcome. It has been a pleasure to meet you, Miss Canham.' Florence hastened him out of the room but not before he was able to take another piece of bread which he stuffed in his mouth before he left. Kitty heard Florence closing the door behind him, amid relentless apologies. Eventually she returned.

'I am so sorry that you got stuck with Robert. A terrible leach, I'm afraid. But we have known him for years.' She now sat. 'Let's eat, then we will sit by the fire, and you must tell me all about your life in the country.'

'Oh … there's not much to tell. As you once said, the country is dull.'

Florence discerned a reluctance. 'Well then, we will talk of something else.'

It was wonderful to be so easily understood. Kitty didn't question the whereabouts of Albert and Eleanor. There was something about being with these people that extinguished all of her questions and gave her space to breathe.

The rest of the day was spent in the company of Eleanor and her friends. They played silly games and talked. The intimacy between Albert and Eleanor unsettled Kitty. She found her thoughts turning often to her encounter with Lord Dalmeny. The street where the warehouse lay was close by, making his presence all too tangible.

They did not return to Eleanor's residence that night. Kitty shared Florence's bed, which was large and soft and afforded a good night's sleep.

On awakening, Kitty's companion propped herself on her elbow. 'What of that young man who wrote to you last year? Did you ever contact him?' Kitty sighed causing Florence to smile. 'I sense a story behind that sigh.'

'I can assure you, it is not much of a story. I wrote to him to tell him of my intention to visit with Eleanor, this time last year. But, as you know, I fell sick and couldn't come.'

'I remember. Did you write to him to let him know?'

'No.' She climbed out of the bed. 'He was barely an acquaintance.'

Florence watched as Kitty pulled on her underskirt. 'I think, perhaps, an acquaintance that made quite an impression on you.'

Kitty remained silent, but couldn't help a smile forming on her lips.

'Well, my dear,' Florence said, now putting on her robe, 'in my opinion, this life is so short, we must wring as much happiness from it as we can.'

Now Kitty's father came to her mind. 'But at what expense? To others, I mean. I am married to a kind and good man. It is only right that I honour him. It is God's way.'

'But does it honour him to be a miserable wife?'

'I am not miserable.' Although, as she spoke the words, she knew there to be no truth in them.

Florence raised her eyebrows. 'I believe that it is our duty to mankind, and to God if you like, to find our happiness. Life would be intolerable without people who know how to live.'

Kitty now questioned Florence. 'And have you found your happiness?'

Florence simply nodded. 'I think I have.'

'But you have no man to love you ... do you?'

'No, Kitty, there is no man.' She seemed to search Kitty for a response, but Kitty couldn't think what response was required. Florence tied a kerchief around her head. 'Anyway, I have Albert and he takes all my energy.' Kitty could imagine it to be so. 'Let's go and eat.' With that she left Kitty alone.

The sun shone through the window illuminating the vines and mythical creatures that filled the wall around the bed. In some ways, Kitty could make neither head nor tail of Florence's life, but at the same time she envied her certainty.

Eleanor and Albert stayed in bed all morning. Florence attended to household business. Kitty tried to read, but every page she turned brought thoughts of John to her mind. Not thoughts so much; she could no longer make out his features. It was the sensations of that one short encounter that haunted her. The desire to reacquaint herself with the source of such feeling overcame her every thought. And, as she reasoned, seeing him again may put an end to such foolish notions. She put her book down and went to the window. The autumn sun illumined the square. Kitty was now keen to get out and walk in its warmth and said as much to Florence, who was writing a letter.

Florence looked quizzical. 'A walk?'

'Yes, it is such a beautiful day. I know it is something you city dwellers fail to understand, but for us simple country folk, it is a pleasure.'

Florence put down her pen. 'Then I shall come with you and share your pleasure.'

'No,' Kitty said, 'do not disturb yourself, I will go alone.'

'Alone? What would your husband think if he heard I had let you do such a thing?'

'Please, Florence. I will not go far.'

She could see that her request was understood. Florence called the maid. 'Of course, my darling, you must do as you wish. Just promise me that you will be careful.' Kitty nodded.

Kitty set off towards Berwick Street, excited to be among the people of the city once more. She turned into the street and meandered among the stores, looking in windows as she went.

Every store was filled with the most intriguing things, but none could tempt her from her purpose. A woman called after her, offering lavender and good fortune for a farthing. Kitty took it knowing the smell of it would ease the still unfamiliar city smells. The dressmaker's shop now stood over the road, and beside it, the warehouse. Her footsteps slowed.

She came to the door, which hung open. The impression of the glassware was no less enchanting than it had been on her previous visit. Chandeliers hanging high caught the morning sun and sent it dancing around the walls. Dust particles drifted in the air. A woman spoke, 'May I be of assistance, madam?'

'No, thank you.' Kitty continued to browse. As she drew deeper into the room, she shot a glance at the office. It was dark inside, but she could just make out human forms within. She continued to the other side of the room, and found a group of glass animals of differing colours.

'Beautiful, aren't they?' A tall, elegant woman stood beside her. She then turned to her husband. 'Oh do let's buy one of these, Philip. Miriam would love it. They are quite adorable.' She looked at Kitty. 'Which would you choose?'

'The pig, I think.' She chuckled at herself.

'No … I think not, it is rather plain. My daughter is only ten. A swan, perhaps.' The woman found her husband had left her side and was now at the door. She scurried after him calling as she went, 'Philip?'

Just then, the office door opened and out stepped a rather large man that Kitty recognised. It wasn't until he laughed that she remembered him to be Mr Bastion, the host of the party that she had attended eighteen months before. She turned back to the ornaments, hoping not to be noticed.

'Miss Canham?' His voice echoed, causing a blush to rise to Kitty's cheeks.

'Mr Bastion.' She bobbed, amazed that he should remember her.

'How wonderful to see you. You are looking well.' He stepped back to reveal a young woman with a preponderance of teeth, grinning in her direction. 'You remember my daughter, Beatrice?'

She did not, but nonetheless said, 'Yes, indeed, how do you do?'

A man, who had been with them but had turned to speak to a shop assistant, now turned back. Mr Bastion held out his arm to include him in the group. 'May I introduce you to our good friend, Lord Dalmeny.'

The face that had haunted her for so long was now before her. His eyes were upon her. 'I believe we have met.'

Her breath faltered. 'I believe so, sir.'

Mr Bastion looked from one to the other. 'Excellent, excellent. We are to sup at the Turks Head. Will you join us, Miss Canham?'

'I fear I cannot. My hostess will be expecting me home soon.'

'Oh please do, Beatrice could do with a companion, whilst we men talk business. Isn't that right, John?'

John smiled, his eyes still on Kitty. 'Yes, I believe it is.'

She could not resist. 'Very well, I will take a drink, thank you, but then I must return.'

The party made their way to the tavern. Beatrice twittered on about the delights of London. Kitty heard not a word, but gave the appropriate noises. A table was found in the corner and soon victuals were presented.

Mr Bastion raised his voice to be heard, although it was wholly unnecessary. 'So, Miss Canham, may I ask, with whom are you staying?'

'I travelled with Eleanor Manley-Hogg, but am presently the guest of Florence Robillard. You know her, I believe?'

'Oh yes, yes, the most extraordinary woman. Quite delightful. It is the French, you see, they are liberal in their tastes.'

John was amused. 'I think you will find that they are simply better able to express themselves than we English.'

'Perhaps you are right, John, although I have little trouble.' Then he held his hands aloft. 'It must be the French in me.' He threw back his head and guffawed.

Beatrice was not amused. 'This bench is very hard.'

Mr Bastion was evidently attentive to all of his daughter's needs. 'Is it, my dear? My chair may be more to your liking.' There was a shuffling until Kitty found herself squeezed next to Lord Dalmeny on the small bench.

He turned to Kitty. 'I do hope I find you well, Miss Canham?'

'Oh yes, quite well, thank you.' She was surprised at her own boldness, as she continued, 'I intended to visit London last year.'

'So I heard.'

'Unfortunately, the distemper struck our village.'

'The distemper?' His brow furrowed.

'Yes. I fell sick myself, so I couldn't travel.'

'You were sick?'

'Yes.' Kitty became aware of the others at the table. 'We lost many of our little ones in the village.'

Beatrice now spoke, 'Oh, how terrible.'

'Yes, I am afraid that it kept me from travelling to London, otherwise I might have seen you all.'

John kept his eyes on Kitty. 'You were sick?'

'Yes … very.'

Beatrice interrupted, 'Do leave her alone, John. She said she was sick, but as you can see, she is quite recovered.'

Kitty replied, 'Yes indeed, I am quite restored.'

Beatrice went on, 'Your complexion is without fault, Miss Canham, you are blessed.' She seemed intent on changing the subject. 'Now, do tell me, where did you find that brooch? It is quite charming.' Kitty put her hand to the butterfly brooch at her chest and explained. She was all too aware that it was quite ordinary in comparison with the ornaments that bedecked her companion. The woman continued to twitter on about her love of decoration. Kitty's lack of enthusiasm must have shown, for Beatrice said, 'I am so sorry, I must be boring you.'

Kitty was quick to denounce the idea. 'Not at all, I am merely a little tired.'

Mr Bastion chirped in, 'So, do tell, what is it that brings you to town, Miss Canham?'

Kitty was amused. 'You are the reason I am here, Mr Bastion.'

'Me?'

'Why, yes sir. I am accompanying Mrs Manley-Hogg to the party.'

The old man looked ecstatic. 'How marvellous, of course, of course. It is going to be quite an event. We are celebrating Mabon. It's a harvest festival they celebrate in the country.'

Beatrice interjected, 'Of course she knows about it, father, I believe she is from the country.'

'I am indeed.'

'How wonderful.' Mr Bastion opened his arms wide. 'I shall be the green man.'

Beatrice picked up her father's excitement. 'I am so glad you are coming. It is going to be such fun.' She now addressed John,

'Now you will make an effort, won't you, John?' Then to Kitty, 'He doesn't like dressing up. He's a terrible spoilsport, but I am determined to convert him.'

John put up his hand. 'It is all arranged, I have my costume ready.'

Mr Bastion was pleased. 'Well done, well done.'

Time had passed quickly and Kitty knew she must return and said as much.

Lord Dalmeny was quick to stand. 'Let me find you a cab.'

Mr Bastion stopped him. 'No need.' He called a servant. 'Fetch a cab for this young woman, immediately.' Then he turned to Kitty. 'Well, Miss Canham, it has been delightful to make your acquaintance once more, and here, have my card.' He fumbled in his waistcoat. 'If there is anything you need whilst you are in town, do not hesitate to call on me.'

'Thank you, that is most kind.' He seemed the most generous of men. The arrival of the cab was announced.

John stood again. 'Let me escort you to the cab.' He stood aside so that Kitty could slip past him. He led her through the crowd, on to the street and opened the door of the waiting cab. 'It has been very good to see you again, Miss Canham.'

'Kitty, please.'

'Kitty.' He helped her up the step. 'I looked for you.'

'When?'

'Last year. I believed your reply to my letter was an invitation to a further acquaintance.'

'I can assure you, sir, it was.'

'But when I enquired of you at the Manley-Hogg's residence, I was informed that you were not coming and had no intention of doing so.'

'Oh, I see.'

'What was I to think? I presumed it was as you wished.' He leant in closer. 'Had I known you were sick … '

His hand rested on the window. She placed hers over it. 'Oh, John, if only you knew … '

He withdrew his hand and glanced over his shoulder. Then spoke with a quiet intention, 'Tell me one thing, Kitty, when you came here today, what were you looking for?'

She held his gaze. 'Well, I can assure you that it wasn't an ornament.' She hoped to make him smile, but he did not.

'Oh, Kitty, if only you had come to town a year ago.'

'What do you mean?'

The coachman called for the address; Kitty gave it to John who stepped back to repeat it the man.

Kitty called, 'John?' But he didn't hear. He had waved the cab on.

When Kitty looked back, he had already disappeared among the tinkers and street sellers. Kitty laid her head back, unsettled by John's words. He seemed to have grown so earnest. Perhaps he was right, perhaps it was too late. But Kitty now knew that seeing John had not laid her longing to rest. It had only heightened her senses to his presence. She comforted herself that she would see him at the party and maybe they could talk further.

When she arrived home, Albert and Eleanor had emerged and the three were taking refreshment. Eleanor looked angry. 'Where have you been, Kitty?'

'I went for a walk.'

Florence came to her aid. 'I told you she went for a walk.'

Eleanor continued, 'Florence was expecting you home ages ago. You should be more careful, Kitty, it's not fair to frighten us like that.'

Florence was now irritated, 'She is a grown woman, Eleanor. She must be allowed to do as she wills.'

'I am not sure Alexander would see it like that.'

'She is perfectly able to take care of herself. Do not I walk the streets without harm?'

'You know the city. She is a stranger.'

Kitty had had enough. 'For goodness sake, I went for a walk and have come back safe and sound. Will you both just leave me alone?' She turned to the window, wishing she could have had one more moment with John.

Albert broke the silence that now hung in the room. 'Come now, ladies, let us not fight. Kitty, come and join us. Come … come, come.' She took a deep breath and did as he bid. They ate together and the room soon settled into its usual comradeship. As they talked, Kitty made all the right responses, but her thoughts were on John; the streak of white that ran through his hair, the creases that framed his mouth when he smiled. Her feelings had not changed as she had hoped, if anything they had strengthened, but of his feelings she was less sure.

When they had finished eating, Eleanor stood. 'And now, Albert, you must let me and Kitty return home. We have stayed quite long enough.'

Kitty was relieved. She would be pleased to be among her belongings again and to have a room to herself. Albert protested and pulled Eleanor closer, but she disentangled herself.

'No, Albert. It is time we went home and got some rest. And besides, we have to prepare for the Mabon.' He looked forlorn, but after a short lover's tussle he let them go.

Chapter Twenty-Two

The following day, Eleanor was a little feverish so she stayed in bed. Kitty stayed close at hand to attend her needs. When alone, she found herself pacing the parlour floor. She tried reading, but could not concentrate. She ate a little, then mended a tear in her yellow dress. She was perched on the window seat watching passers-by, when she saw Florence hurrying towards the house. Kitty straightened her dress and waited.

There was a knock on the door, a short exchange could be heard, then Leah entered. 'Mademoiselle Robillard is here to see you, miss. She wondered if you might come downstairs to greet her.' Kitty followed the maid out of the door.

She heard Eleanor call, 'Kitty? Who is that?'

Kitty called out, 'It's only Florence.'

'Tell her to come up and see her ailing friend.'

Florence stood in the hallway, holding out a letter. 'This arrived this morning. It is for you.'

'For me?'

'Yes.'

Kitty thanked her and took it, then added, 'Please don't mention this to Eleanor.'

'It is for your eyes only, I do not need to know.'

Kitty invited Florence to take refreshment and suggested she pop in and see Eleanor, but she was evidently in a hurry and made excuses. At the door she turned. 'Kitty?'

'Yes?'

'May I leave you with one piece of advice?' Kitty nodded. 'Don't let anyone tell you how to live your life. If happiness is yours, guard it with all you've got. If not,' she patted the hand that held the letter, 'go and find it.'

Once Florence had left, Kitty stood, holding the letter in trembling fingers. She heard Eleanor calling her, tucked the letter away and went straight to Eleanor's room. She explained that Florence had only been passing and thought to return a kerchief that Kitty had left there. Eleanor was not amused, but she accepted the explanation readily enough and asked Kitty to read to her. Kitty complied, the letter burning in her pocket. When Eleanor fell asleep, she crept out and made her way back to the parlour and unfolded the letter in the light of the window.

My Most Dear Kitty,
Am I too forward to write in this way? When we met yesterday, I could not speak to you as I wished. I have much to say to you, and wondered if you might meet me that we may spend an hour together. Tomorrow, at noon, I will go to St Anne's church in Soho. If I am found in your thoughts, as you have been in mine, please come that we may spend a pleasant hour together. But if, in reading of this note, you find it to be a foolish notion, then I will be content. And you will not hear from me again.
Most affectionately,
John Dalmeny.

Kitty clutched the letter to her chest; the sweet hope of it burnishing her heart. A knock on the door caused her to jump. Leah entered. She scolded the girl. 'Please, Leah, do not knock so loudly, you cause my heart to stop every time.'

'I am sorry, miss. Madam says that she will be joining you for supper shortly, and that I was to light the fire.'

'Very well.' Kitty folded the letter into her book. What she had hoped was there before her. And yet, it was a poor hope; she was married, and, perhaps, he was married too. A notion that was new to her. Her thoughts turned to her father and Rosalind. Could he have been so unhappy with her ma that he was drawn to deceive her? Just as she now finds herself inexorably drawn. So many imaginings filled her head, but over and above them all was the beating of her heart, and the ache, the longing to feel something strong, something real again. The fire was beginning to blaze and Kitty watched as Leah stood back and admired her work. 'Well done, Leah, you are a clever girl.' The girl blushed. 'Leah?'

'Yes, miss?'

'Do you not have a boy?'

'A boy, miss?'

'Yes, someone you love.'

'It is not allowed, not in this household. Mrs Manley-Hogg insists.'

Kitty had quite forgotten the poor girl's estate. 'But I am sure you must have admirers?'

Leah looked towards the door. 'There is one, a grocer's son. I see him when I can. As soon as he is apprenticed, he is going to come for me.'

'And will you wait for him?'

'Oh.' She giggled. 'I don't know.'

Eleanor entered the room wrapped in a floral dressing robe. 'Thank you, Leah.' Leah bobbed and left the room. 'I do hope she wasn't troubling you. She can be rather too talkative.'

'On the contrary, I enjoy her company. Are you feeling better?'

Eleanor made for the fire. 'Yes, thank you, I am much restored. Perhaps you were right. It is not long since I had the baby, and to be honest, I am missing the little creature.'

Kitty was pleased. 'That is as it should be.'

Supper was taken at the small table. The two women spoke of nothing of any consequence. The sound of the crackling fire, the taste of good food, and her friend's company, lulled Kitty's unsettled soul. When supper was finished and Kitty was sitting by the fire, Eleanor went to the sideboard, opened a small door and out of it drew an inlaid wooden box. She sat with Kitty, laying the box on a small table at her side. 'Shall we play backgammon?' Kitty stared at the item on the table. 'Kitty?' It lay before her, accusing her thoughts.

'Backgammon?'

'Yes, do you not play? I could teach you.'

'No. I do play.' As Eleanor lay out the board, Alexander invaded Kitty's thoughts. All he had been through, all they'd been through together this year. As they played, there before the fire, Kitty fought to let go of her foolish hopes and to embrace the life that she had been given.

When Eleanor had gone to bed that night, Kitty stood before the embers, holding the letter in her hands. She read it once more, then placed it on the fire. It took a moment before it caught. She watched it curl and burn, her cheeks wet with tears. With a firm hand she wiped them from her face and made her way to bed.

When Kitty awoke the following morning, she found Eleanor restored. It was announced that she and Eleanor were to visit James' aunt after all. They would go for ten o'clock. Kitty dressed and assumed a cheerful demeanour, intending to drive any thoughts of Mr Dalmeny aside.

The old lady welcomed them with open arms and a kiss. She was crippled with age and sat in a large wicker chair. Kitty marvelled at how one so restricted in body could seem so content. There was nothing about the woman other than the joy of living. All she talked about were the good things: her exemplary housekeeper, the beauty of the autumn sun and her 'most comfortable chair'. She asked after Eleanor's new baby and Eleanor was happy to give a full account.

When she asked Kitty about the farm, Kitty told her of her father's accident in the lightest of terms. She was most gracious in her sympathies. But when she asked why Kitty was not married, Eleanor speedily redirected the conversation by interrupting with a request to hear about the betrothal of her cousin. Her aunt's attention immediately turned to the occasion. As they spoke, the clock ticked from the corner of the room, marking the minutes. Their conversation of domesticity faded in and out to Kitty. The small room became warm, until she could bear no more of it. She begged to be excused to take a turn in the street, citing the need for air. Eleanor responded, 'Oh, Kitty, you are always doing this.' Then, turning to her aunt, said, 'She is like a butterfly, just when you think she is settled, she is off.'

The aunt gave Kitty a warm smile. 'If she is a butterfly, you must let her fly. Off you go, we will serve something to eat on your return. Myra makes a wonderful mousse.' She rang a small bell by her side.

Eleanor looked concerned. 'You will be careful, won't you, Kitty? I can't be worrying like I was last time.' Kitty nodded.

At the front door, she instructed the maid to tell Mrs Manley-Hogg that she had a headache and would make her way back to her house, to thank her mistress and give her apologies.

The further she travelled, the faster her feet took her. She went to the end of the road and made a turn, then another. The streets were more crowded now with street sellers and shoppers. At every step another obstacle rose before her. Turning a third corner, she realised she was quite lost and stopped suddenly.

A woman carrying a filthy child in her arms careened into her. 'Oi! Watch where you're going!' Kitty asked if she knew the way to St Anne's. The woman gave a toothless grin. 'What would I want with the church, luvvy, they don't want nothing to do with the likes of me!' The woman carried on.

Kitty could feel a great sob rising in her chest. 'Stupid, stupid,' she muttered, seeking to ebb the flow. Just then, a church bell chimed. She looked all around to discern its direction. Then came a second chime. She began to walk once more towards the sound. As she turned the corner, away from the crowds, she could see a tall spire towering over the ramshackle buildings. At first she trotted and then she ran, this way and that, until before her stood an iron arch. The metal was cold in her palm as she steadied herself, breathing hard. A couple came down the path. She stepped aside and let them pass.

She walked through the unkempt churchyard and into the dingy edifice that was all but empty. A few heads were bent in prayer. She stood for some time searching the space for John. He was nowhere to be seen, so she turned and left the building, prayer was the last thing on her mind. A large horse chestnut stretched its branches over the graveyard, its leaves beginning to turn, its fruit almost ripe for the picking. Kitty stood under it, looking up into its arching branches, reluctant to return to the street.

'Miss Canham?' a voice called behind her.

She spun around to see a figure emerging from the side of the building. She could not see his face, as the sun was behind him, but his frame was unmistakable. 'Lord Dalmeny.'

'You knew about my title?' He now stepped into the light, looking abashed.

'Yes. You should have told me'

'I know.'

'I thought I had missed you. I looked for you in the church.'

'I was there, but ... '

'Yes?'

'I needed to relieve myself, so ... ' He indicated the alley beside the church.

'Oh, I see.' She said nothing for a moment, but a giggle burst from her lips. Perhaps it was the circumstance, or perhaps the release of hours of expectation. 'Forgive me, it is just ... '

His laugh joined hers. 'Oh, Kitty, I've missed your laughter.'

'And I yours.' His face now displayed all the boyish charm that had caught her so many months before.

'Shall we walk?'

He was quick to respond, 'No.' Somehow, he seemed more awkward than she had remembered. 'I do hope you will not think me too forward.' He stepped closer, his eyes upon her. 'But I have taken a room at the inn ... a side room only. That we may speak freely, away from prying eyes ... I am known in these parts, you see.'

She interrupted his halting speech, 'Yes, I'll come.' A wide, natural smile spread across his lips. He led her through the crowds and down a side alley to a small inn. A few fellows looked up with little concern, before returning to their silent drinking. A young man greeted John and led them up a small flight of stairs. He opened the door for them. A large bed took pride of place in the centre of the room.

John looked furious. 'I said no bed.'

The man sniggered. 'This is an inn, sir, we only have rooms what have beds. This is our best. I laid it out nice, just like you said.'

Kitty interceded, 'It is fine, John, let's take it.'

John reluctantly dropped coins in the man's hand while Kitty entered the room. It was a fine room indeed. The coverlet was embroidered in reds and oranges. Light from the large, if dirty, window streamed across it. Under the window was a small table laid with a pitcher, cups and a small vase of flowers. Kitty lifted the flowers to her nose; they smelt of little, but were beautiful nonetheless.

She heard John close the door. 'I specifically asked for a room with no bed.'

'It does not matter, it really doesn't. It is only a bed.'

'Kitty, you really are the most remarkable of women.' She unhooked her cloak and felt him close as his hands encircled her shoulders to remove the garment. He seemed to linger behind her. She could feel his breath on her neck. Her eyes closed to receive his touch. But it never came. Instead he stepped away to the window. 'Yesterday, when I saw you, I had never thought to see you again. I had thought that you were now firmly in my past, that our time together was all there was for us. But seeing you again … ' He now turned to her, a frown upon his brow. 'It seems that my feelings have not changed.' Kitty's heart leapt, but suddenly he spoke with accusation in his eyes. 'Last year, why did you not write to me to tell me you were sick?'

'Because I presumed that if you had come to find me, you would surely have been told.'

'No, some bumbling old fool of a servant told me that you were not expected, so I presumed that I had been mistaken, that my affections were not returned.'

'It seems we both presumed too much.'

'It seems so.' Neither spoke for some moments. Then John pulled back a little chair by the table. 'Sit with me?' Kitty did as he bid. He poured a beer from the pitcher and placed it before her, pouring another for himself.

Now it was Kitty's turn to question. 'When we met at Bastion's, that first time, why did you not write to me? I waited for a letter.'

'You want the truth?'

'Yes, please.'

'When I saw you leave that night, you were laughing with your friend. You had promised to dance, then left without a word. I presumed you had been trifling with me, so I got drunk with my friends. I thought it was as you wished.'

'I was not laughing, I can assure you. I had no choice but to leave. My friend was waiting for me. And when you did not follow me to the house, I presumed ... ' Her voice trailed off.

John now laughed. 'Oh, Kitty, it seems my bladder has twice caused us consternation.'

'Your bladder?'

'Yes, I was relieving myself. In the square.'

She chuckled and shook her head. 'If only I had known.'

He walked from the table, raking his fingers through his hair. 'And now, Kitty … now it is too late.'

'Too late?'

He nodded, his eyes upon her. 'I am to be wed.'

Kitty felt the breath go from her. Somehow her own marriage was of little importance, but his? A dawning realisation came over her. 'Miss Bastion?' He nodded. 'Why was nothing said yesterday?'

'It had not been formally confirmed. I am to see Mr Bastion this afternoon.'

Kitty's hand went to her mouth, anger rising. 'So why? Why did you summon me here?' He stuttered in response. She cut him off. 'You want a mistress? I will be no-one's mistress, John. I will not be used like this.' She grabbed her cloak. He tried to stop her but found her strong as she marched to the door.

'Kitty, wait, please, let me explain.' His words stopped her. 'I only ask that you hear me out. Then I promise I will let you go.' He held out his hand for the cloak. Instead she stood clutching it to her. She could not look at him. He went on, 'It is my father.'

'Your father?'

'Yes, he is … What can I say? He is less than he should be. He drinks and whores and gambles, the estate is in so much debt. We may well lose it, unless … unless I marry money.' Kitty began to understand; John was caught in his circumstances, just as she was caught in hers. He went on, 'Mr Bastion has agreed to help pay off our debts if I marry his daughter. I make use of their wealth, and as for them? Beatrice receives a title.'

'I see.' A hopelessness began to rest over Kitty once more.

John stepped towards her. 'It is not a marriage of love, Kitty, you must believe me.' His young brow now creased, shadowing his dark eyes. 'Please, Kitty, say something.'

The familiar coldness was creeping over her soul. 'Well, John, it seems that we are doomed.' He held out his hand. She rested hers in his, their fingers kissed in a way their lips could not. They stood thus for some time. Kitty was the first to pull away. 'I had better go. Eleanor will wonder where I am.' She made for the door.

He followed. 'Here.' He held out his hand to help her with her cloak, placing it around her shoulders. 'Kitty, if it could be any other way, I would…'

She placed her finger on his lips just as she had done so many months before. 'Let's not speak of it anymore.' She took one more look into his dear face, and walked away.

When she arrived at the house, Eleanor was already home. Kitty said that she had walked to release her headache, but it was worse than ever. She took to her bed, and the sleep of forgetfulness.

Chapter Twenty-Three

The following day was the day of the party. Kitty awoke refreshed, and although she dreaded seeing John with his future wife, she determined to enjoy the preparations for Eleanor's sake. The women dressed together in Eleanor's room. Kitty could not help being shocked at the fineness of the fabric that swathed Eleanor's body, and could not help wondering how she would keep warm. On her head was a crown of golden fruit. Under her bust was a band from which hung a sprig of hay, likewise in gold. When Kitty was offered her costume, she found it was simply a lesser cousin of Eleanor's, and just as revealing. She wasn't sure if she liked the sensation of undress at all.

They found Florence in the parlour draped in her usual autumn colours, which needed little alteration for such an occasion. Kitty admired Florence's ability to do as she pleased; she wasn't going to bow to the extravagance of such an occasion. The moment that caused the most hilarity was when Albert appeared wearing fur breeches, an impressive codpiece and a crown of grapes. 'I am Bacchus, the god of wine.' Then, thrusting his crotch forward, 'And fertility!' He scooped Eleanor up and kissed her full on the lips.

She was not amused. 'Be careful, Albert, my costume!'

He stepped aside, bowing low. 'Come, mes petites déesses, the carriage awaits.'

At their destination, the coach paused in the queue to deliver its passengers. The gardens were now completed, the old yew gone. The heavy snows of her previous visit hung in Kitty's mind, but tonight the moon was bright.

Mr Bastion, from head to toe in green, greeted the party, briefly kissing the women's hands before turning away to greet others. There was the usual array of extraordinary costumes, but this time artificial fruit abounded. When the guests were led to the dancing, Kitty made her escape and headed to the library. She was in no mood for a party tonight. The room was empty. Drawing a small stool to the fireside, she perched on it and warmed herself. It was good to be alone for a moment. A young maid came in. 'Oh, I'm sorry, miss, I came to make up the fire.'

Kitty stood aside as the girl knelt to undertake her task. The fresh wood crackled and spat. Kitty thanked her as she hauled the basket from the room. She looked around her as she resumed her seat. It was not so different from Alexander's study. She thought of him reading by the fire. She thought of the boys, chasing each other up the stairs. But the absence of ones they had lost filled every remembrance, causing Kitty to wrap her shawl closer about her arms.

She now noticed a large basket in the corner of the room; theatrical costumes spilling out of it. Images of her past visit to Mr Bastion's danced in her head. The song she had sung with Alina came to her lips. She sang once more, under her breath, right to the end, then let silence fall. Kitty knew that it was time she joined the party. She found Florence in the front room, already in heated debate with a serious looking couple. She left them to it and went to watch the dancing. She was amused to see Eleanor dancing with a bilious looking fellow in the most impractical toga. She was making pleading looks at Albert, who danced with a nymph.

Pushing through the crowd, Kitty found a cup of punch, and just as she was lifting it to her lips, an elbow jolted hers, spilling it down the front of her dress. 'For goodness sake!' She brushed at the garment frantically.

A man's hand held out a kerchief. 'I am so sorry, here.' She took it without looking up. 'Miss Canham?'

She lifted her head to return the kerchief. It was John. 'Lord Dalmeny.'

His eyes stayed on hers. 'You are looking very well.'

She smiled, determined not to allow his words to unseat her further. 'Thank you, you are looking … strange!'

'Well, indeed, I fear that I look most foolish.' He had made a poor attempt at wrapping a leafy cloak around his breeches and shirt. Mr Bastion approached. 'Ah … John, there you are.' Then he looked at Kitty. 'I must steal Lord Dalmeny away from you, my dear.' John gave a little bow, his eyes on her, and made his way through the dancers. Kitty was left alone, she made for the door to be greeted by a group of players heading into the room.

A tall man clapped his hands and the music stopped. He called out, 'This way to the entertainment.'

People were hustled this way and that as the floor was cleared. Finally, from the chaos, some kind of order was formed and chairs were laid out. She found a space near the door beside a woman who was laughing with open mouth and bad breath. But Kitty took little notice, her eyes searching for John. She could not see him.

Mr Bastion took the floor. 'Ladies and Gentleman, silence please.' It took him some time to calm the raucous chatter. 'Settle down, settle down.' Eventually the room stilled. 'Whilst our esteemed players prepare for their performance, my dear wife … Where are you, my sweet?' A slight woman scurried forward to her husband's side, making little bows as she went.

'My dear wife and I have an announcement to make. She has nagged at me to make the announcement tonight. Nagged me, I tell you.' A laugh went up. Mrs Bastion blushed. 'We wish to share our joy. Our beloved Beatrice . . . where are you, Beatrice?' The girl came forward. Now Kitty looked, she could see the young woman's love of decoration was evident; her hair was a great wave upon her head, shimmering with beads. Mr Bastion turned her to her audience. 'Our beloved Beatrice is to be wed.' A chorus of 'Oos' and 'Ahs' filled the room. Kitty felt her heart beating. 'You will all want to know who the lucky man is who is to pluck our little rose.'

A man in his cups called out, 'Get on with it.' The women around hushed him.

Mr Bastion went on unperturbed, 'The lucky man who is to marry our dear Beatrice, is none other than Lord John Dalmeny.' Kitty's heart stopped. John came forward. Beatrice giggled as her father took her hand and placed it in John's, slapping his own pudgy hand over theirs. A cheer went up. Women gathered around Beatrice and her mother. John was drowned in the embrace of her father. Kitty backed out of the room.

She stood in the hall breathing hard. She could feel a great sob rising in her chest. The strength of her emotion was all but overwhelming. She hurried to the corner beneath the stairs and stood against the wall in the shadows, chiding herself for such foolishness. But nothing would stop the flow. She was married, and had he not the right to do the same? But seeing John had uprooted her, and the pain of the past two years threatened to ride the wave of her emotions.

The sound of the revellers settled, and the voices of the players took their place. The young maid, with her basket of logs, passed by. She disappeared into the front room. Kitty took deep breaths. Just as she was about to slip into the library, footsteps approached and with them a man's voice. She pressed herself deeper into the darkness. The young maid exchanged a few words with the man, before walking past Kitty again. This time she noticed her. 'Are you well, miss? May I be of assistance?'

'No, I am quite well, thank you. Just a little warm.' The maid walked on to the basement stairs. Kitty watched her go.

'Kitty?' John's voice was low. 'I find you in the shadows once again.'

'Yes, it seems you do.' She lowered her eyes.

Drawing close to her, he said, 'You've been crying.'

'What of it?'

He now spoke with quiet insistence, 'If only we could go back to that night … if only … '

'But we cannot. You are to be wed, that is the end of it.' A wave of laughter echoed through the hall. He looked over his shoulder, took her hand and led her into the library, closing the door behind them.

He now spoke with urgency, 'You do know, Kitty, don't you, that there has never been any but you. That one hour with you ruined me for all else. I am a ruined man, Kitty. I know I must marry. But before I do I need to know if you … if you feel it too?'

Kitty nodded, a little sob escaping from her throat. Tears began to fall. He wiped them away, first with his hands, and then with gentle kisses. His lips found hers, and she was lost, this time forever. A burst of laughter in the hallway called them to their senses. It was coming closer. 'I will tell her tonight that I cannot marry her … '

'No … it has been announced. Why did you let them announce it tonight?'

'I didn't know they were going to. I was caught … but I will …'

'No!' Kitty knew, better than he, how hopeless it was. 'You cannot … your father.'

He stepped back, letting out a low growl. 'Why must life be this way?' The voices drew closer. 'Kitty, this is not the end of it. Meet me tomorrow, let me have one day with you.'

'We leave in the morning.'

'Then let me have one night, just one night Kitty.' His eyes were searching hers. 'Please.' She could not speak, but her silence betrayed her heart to him, so he continued, 'I will meet you in the gardens, where we met before. At midnight.'

Just then, the door burst open and a band of players fell into the room. John whispered, 'Please, my love, just one night,' before slipping away.

Alina was among the players. She saw Kitty and berated her for missing the performance. She was so caught up in the delights of it all that she did not notice Kitty's state. As soon as she turned back to her companions, Kitty slipped out of the room. How could she get away? One night. That was all it would be. All it could be. She would have to draw Eleanor into her confidence.

As she crossed the hallway, the clock chimed eleven. She made her way into the ballroom. Now a large woman, swathed in garlands of corn, and a tall slight man similarly attired, sang a harvest song in mocking country accents. The audience laughed. Kitty's stomach lurched at the grotesque performance. When the song finished, a loud cheer went up. Eleanor was sitting against the wall to her left, with Florence. John sat at the front, between Bastion and Beatrice, seemingly enjoying the spectacle. Keeping one eye on the clock in the hallway, she waited as the entertainment continued. The players now pushed past her, dressed as wood nymphs and fawns. The finale was announced. It was half past the hour. Kitty managed to catch Eleanor's attention and beckoned to her. Eleanor slipped along the row to join Kitty in the hallway. 'What is it, Kitty? I do not wish to miss the end.'

Kitty hardly knew where to start, but knew she must. 'Eleanor, I am going to stay away tonight.'

Eleanor was now interested. 'What do you mean?'

'I … there is someone … a man.'

'A man?'

'Yes. That is where I have been when I have been walking.'

'Of course, I knew there was something. But what kind of man?'

'I cannot say.'

'Oh come now, Kitty, you can tell me.'

'No, I can't, I am sorry, I truly am.' She would have loved a companion to confide in but knew she could not.

Eleanor now looked concerned. 'If he is married, you have to be careful.'

'He is not married. It is just difficult. We have this one night. That is all it will be. Please, let me go to him.'

'Is he reputable?'

Kitty nodded. Eleanor stepped back and looked at her like a mother looking at child who had finally grown up. 'Of course, who am I to stop you. You have kept my secret, now I will keep yours. But on our way home you must promise to tell me all about it.' Kitty nodded; she would have assented to anything. Eleanor placed a hand on Kitty's arm and added, 'But promise me one thing, you will be careful.'

'I will, I promise,'

'Very well. But remember we must leave for the country early tomorrow. You must be back first thing.' Eleanor embraced Kitty and made her way back to the entertainment.

Kitty could feel a trembling as she returned to her post in the doorway. The players were bringing their performance to a close. Kitty's eyes were on John who still sat with the Bastions. An imperious looking man sat beside Beatrice. They shared looks. Kitty presumed him to be her brother. She did not let her mind linger on the family, for if she had she knew it would be harder to become part of the ensuing betrayal.

At the last word, the audience rose and clapped. The players bowed. Kitty moved round the door into the hallway, knowing that a stream of people would soon be following. Firstly, the actors and singers came, laughing and tripping towards the library, then the audience, now in various states of dress, all the worse for wear. It was a quarter to the hour. As the stream died down, Kitty put her head through the door and saw John talking to Mr Bastion who seemed to be protesting. John gave a little bow and went to kiss his intended's hand. Kitty ordered her cloak, stepped out into the night, and across to the gardens.

It was a still night. There was no hiding place, as there had been, but the dark offered some disguise. She looked to the sky, which showed off a vast spectacle of lights, and a slithered moon. The door of the house opened and out of it walked John. He was now divested of his costume, and standing on the step, his eyes searching for her. She stepped towards him as a coach drew up and blocked her view. Stopping at the gate, she waited. The door nearest her opened; John was onboard, beckoning her. As she stepped inside, he knocked on the ceiling and the coach took off with a jolt, causing them both to slam back against the seat. Kitty let out an involuntary 'ooph'. Like two children they found themselves giggling. Turning from the square, the carriage grew darker and the laughter subsided. His hand found hers. The warmth of his touch soothed her fears. The carriage jerked and they found themselves jolted apart, giggling once more. Finally she asked, 'Where are we going?'

'To the inn we went to yesterday. It is all I could think of, I do hope . . . '

'Of course.' Kitty spoke quickly, not wanting anything to make their assignation sound sordid. 'It was a fine room.' They travelled awhile in silence, however the streets were not silent. The further they went the more alien everything seemed. The coach slowed. In the dim light falling from doorways, Kitty could see painted women, half dressed, calling the drunks that passed. The now familiar smell began to rise to Kitty's nose. John banged on the ceiling and called, 'Can't you go faster?' The coach lurched. Men swore, as they fell aside to let it through.

When they finally turned a corner into a quieter street, Kitty declared, 'I shall never get used to the city.' But John wasn't listening; he poked his head out of the window, calling, 'This will do.'

John took Kitty's hand and led her, once more, to the little inn down the alley. This time men spilled out making their way home. John found the innkeeper. Kitty couldn't hear what he whispered amongst the din, but quickly they were led up the stairs. On entering the very same room, they found a man pressing himself against a woman who lay over the edge of the bed, his buttocks naked above loose breeches. Kitty averted her eyes.

'Oi!' the innkeeper shouted. 'What are you doing in here? Get out.' He pulled the man off the woman. She rearranged her skirts and walked past them, chin in the air. 'Whore!' the innkeeper railed at her. The other man, now buttoning his breeches, staggered from the room, his head bowed. The innkeeper apologised. 'Sorry about that, sir.' He hastened to straighten the bedcovers. 'I usually keep this room locked for the likes of gentlemen like you. Someone must've left it open. Shall I light the fire?'

'No, I will do it.' John paid the man, then added pointedly, 'This room is ours until the morning.'

'Yes, sir.'

'And bring me a pitcher of beer.'

The man left, closing the door behind him. A small lantern glowed on the table. 'I am sorry, Kitty. It is not what I would have . . . '

'It is fine, John, honestly.' She was amused to watch as he fumbled to lay the fire. Gathering the lantern, she said, 'Here, let me.' Aware of his eyes upon her, she skilfully laid the fire and put it to light. The man returned with the pitcher and two mugs. When he left, John closed the door and locked it firmly. The fire crackled and flamed. John took her hands in his. 'Your hands are cold.' He lay his over them to warm them. Then opening her palm, he stroked it. 'Do you have a scar?'

Kitty remembered their very first encounter. 'Only a faint line.' He lifted her palm to his lips and kissed it, then moved it to his bristled cheek. He then unhooked her cloak and slipped it from her shoulders. She felt him draw the hair aside from the nape of her neck, then kiss it so gently. Kitty yielded to his touch. He ran his hands down her arms and turned her towards him. The firelight caught the amber of his eyes. Her name escaped from his lips as he kissed her tenderly. He kissed her eyes, her face, her neck, then kissed her palm once more. 'I shall ever love this hand.' He kissed it again. She shivered. 'You are cold.' Pulling the coverlet from the bed and folding it, he lay it before the fire. Kitty piled more wood in the grate, until it burned high. When she turned, she saw John divested of his coat and waistcoat, his shirt open, displaying the soft welcome of his chest. As her garments fell about her, every sensation of her body was alive to his touch.

They lay together that night, by the fire. Making love, talking, making love some more, until the blue light of dawn touched their skin with its coolness. John drew her cloak over them, then his coat. They curled together, there on the floor, before the dying embers. Kitty felt the floor hard beneath her as a tear ran down her cheek.

Kitty awoke with a gasp. The sun had risen. She shook John awake. 'I have to go.' Scrambling into her clothes, she berated herself. 'I didn't mean to sleep.'

John stood with her pulling on his own clothes. They did not speak until he made for the door. 'I'll call for the coach.' Once he had gone, Kitty finished dressing, slumped onto the edge of the bed, and found herself staring at the dust playing in the early sun. John returned. He lifted her to her feet and kissed her. 'Kitty, come to me again. When you can, when you are in London.'

She pulled away. 'No! No, I will not become your mistress.'

He held her hands firmly in his. 'Then become my wife.'

'I cannot.' She pulled her hands from his and took up her cloak.

'Why not? I will put a stop to the betrothal. Don't you know, Kitty, how I feel about you?'

She now drew on her anger, 'John, stop it. Stop it, please.' His dear face looked crushed, but only she knew why she must wound him so. 'It cannot be, I cannot be the cause of your family's misfortune.'

'Kitty ... please.'

'No, John, let it be as you said, one night only.' She studied his hazel eyes, drawing from them all the love they could give, and kissed him.

There was a knock on the door; the carriage was waiting. John led her into the street, which was just waking to the morning. He helped her into the carriage. She gave the coachman the address and climbed aboard. John closed the door after her. Kitty was alarmed. 'Aren't you coming with me?'

'No. It is best you return alone.' Now she looked, she realised this was a different carriage. She felt herself panic that this was the last time she would see him, but he went on, 'Kitty, I cannot believe that this is all there is for us. I will disentangle myself from the arrangement with Bastion. I will find another way for my family. Then I will come for you.'

'You cannot!'

'I must. I am lost to you, Kitty, spoiled for any other.' His kiss was so sweet that Kitty could feel her resolve slipping away. 'You may write to me, not at the farm ... my step-father ... ' She had told him that her life was a misery at the farm because of him. The lies had run easily from her lips. 'You can write to me at Eleanor's, she is a good friend and will keep our council.'

He kissed her hands. 'I will write. Watch for my letter.' With that, he nodded to the coachman. As they set off, she remembered and called, 'Wait! Stop!' The coach came to a halt. She opened the door to see John trotting towards her. 'The address!' Laughter was once more their friend.

'The Manor, Thorpe le Soken. It is in Essex.' She repeated it, then said, 'And don't forget this time.' He smiled; the small creases forming round his mouth had become so dear. She hurried aboard, looking back as she went, at the one who now held all her hopes.

The sun was bright and giving off a surprising warmth when she arrived at the house. She stepped onto the front step to hear a voice calling behind her. It was Leah, beckoning urgently. Kitty followed her to the servants' entrance. It was explained that they were to have a travelling companion, and she mustn't see Kitty 'in a state of undress'. The young maid giggled as she said it. Kitty looked down at her dishevelled state and smiled at the remembrance of the cause of it. She let herself be led by Leah. At every corner the young woman looked this way and that before beckoning her charge on.

When they got to Kitty's room, Leah said, 'I'll tell the missus that you are here.' She shut the door behind her. The sun streamed into the room. Kitty splashed her face and began to remove her costume, sensing John's touch at every turn.

The door opened. Eleanor slipped inside looking concerned. 'Now, Kitty … '

Leah followed.

'I know, I know.' Nothing was going to rob her of her happiness today.

'We have a travelling companion.'

'I will be as quick as I can. I promise.' She thanked Leah as she started to assist her in dressing. 'Who is it that is joining us?'

Eleanor stepped forward. 'A Miss Parditer.'

Kitty stopped in her tracks. 'Miss Parditer?'

'Yes,' Eleanor continued. 'She is the niece of our Mr Parditer in the village. Come on, Kitty, do hurry up, I have been keeping her occupied for ages. I told her that you had been unwell and needed to rise slowly.'

'Why is she accompanying us?'

Eleanor explained that her father was a business acquaintance of James' and that he thought his daughter to be a foolish girl who would benefit from time with her aunt and uncle. Kitty could not imagine the Parditers from Thorpe the Soken being of any good to anyone. Eleanor went on, 'He heard that we were travelling to Thorpe and brought her to the house this morning at some horribly early hour. It's been a nightmare, Kitty.'

'I am sorry.'

Eleanor now had a twinkle in her eye. 'Never mind, did you have a good night?'

'Yes, yes I did.'

'Good, you must tell me all about it another time. Now let's go and face her together. Remember, you have been unwell. A headache.'

In the parlour, a young woman in an impossible lacy bonnet was waiting for them. She stood as Eleanor introduced them. 'Laura, this is Mrs Gough.' A shock went through Kitty. Of course. She had to become what she truly was, but she hadn't been ready for it.

'How do you do, Mrs Gough, it is very kind of you to allow me to travel with you. I will be as little trouble as possible.' Kitty somehow doubted that it would be so.

The beginning of the journey was quite tolerable; the young woman had plenty to say, which meant that Kitty had to say little. Instead, she watched as they passed through the city and out into open countryside. Kitty felt herself doze in the freshening air. But by early afternoon, clouds had rolled in and the rain had started to fall. It fell lightly at first but soon became a torrent. The women huddled together on the bench to steady themselves. The coach slowed to a stop. The coachman told them that he would try and make it to the Vulcan. Laura saw the whole thing as a big adventure. Eleanor was irritated. But Kitty was just pleased to put off her arrival home. After a trying hour with the coach bumping and rocking, they arrived. A room was found for all three of them, in which they took a light supper.

It seemed that Laura's enthusiasm was wearing off; she was not amused by the state of the room. 'If Father had known where I was to stay, I feel sure he would have made better arrangements.'

'Unfortunately,' said Eleanor, 'your father could not have foreseen the rain.' There was one large bed.

'Where are we all going to sleep?' The young woman's pretty blue eyes were wide.

Eleanor had little sympathy. 'It is all they have, we will manage.' In the end, it was agreed that they would sleep crosswise. Kitty had to agree to sleep in the middle, otherwise the argument would have gone on all night. She waited until the young woman's breathing settled into a steady rhythm. 'Eleanor … are you awake?'

'Yes.' Eleanor turned to her, but she could barely see her in the shadows. 'So, who is he?'

'I cannot say.'

'Do I know him?'

Kitty could not tell. 'No. I met him when I came to London two years ago. We were reacquainted, and … ' The girl beside her shifted. Kitty watched for her breathing to settle, then continued. 'The truth is, I didn't mean for it to happen. We just came across one another, that day when we went to the dressmaker's. I went to buy a flute. Do you remember?'

'Yes, I remember.'

'Oh, Eleanor, when I am in his presence, nothing else matters. I did not know it could be like this.'

Eleanor's voice betrayed none of the excitement that Kitty expected. 'Does he know you are married?'

'No.'

There was a long silence before Eleanor spoke again. 'Do you love him?'

'Yes, I think I do.'

She heard Eleanor sigh. 'Oh, Kitty, an affair is one thing, but you must be careful. If you give yourself away too much, you could lose everything.'

'I think it is too late. Do you not love Albert?'

'No, not in that way. With Albert it is ... there is a passion between us, certainly, but that is something quite different to love. You see, I love my husband, Kitty, I am his wife.'

In that moment, Kitty realised that her situation was so very different to Eleanor's. She wished that she hadn't told her, but she needed her help. 'Eleanor?'

'Hmm?'

'He is to write to me. In my haste I told him that he could write to me at your address. I do hope that I did not do wrong?'

To Kitty's relief, Eleanor sounded warmer, 'No, of course. This is my fault after all. I brought you to London, to a very different society to your own.'

'Thank you, Eleanor, I am in your debt.'

'Have I not been in yours these past two years? You have been a faithful friend, Kitty. I shall be the same to you. The secrets we keep will remain ours only. Should a letter arrive, I will send for you.'

'Thank you.'

The women fell to silence. Just as Kitty was sinking into sleep, Eleanor spoke again, 'Kitty, may I give you one piece of advice?'

'Of course.'

'Love can be a fickle thing. Many have been ruined by it. Take care.'

Eleanor's unusually sombre tone arrested Kitty. 'I will.'

The way home was slow; the rain steadily fell. Laura was mostly silent and the effort to keep her spirits up kept both Eleanor and Kitty busy. It was early afternoon when the coach pulled up outside the rectory. As the coachman opened the door, a bitter comfort met Kitty as she looked through the gate to the familiar door beyond.

Mrs Carter was there to greet her. 'You poor dear, what weather! Come in, come in, I will fetch you a brew.' The dear woman led Kitty to the kitchen, where Tilly sat. 'Look who's home. We weren't expecting you for another few days.'

Kitty explained Eleanor's desire to return to see her baby. Sitting by the fire with a warm brew seemed like a dream; her body still felt the rocking of the coach. Mrs Carter brought food to the table and instructed Tilly to go and make the fire up in Kitty's room. The young woman gathered a basket of wood and did as she was bid. Mrs Carter asked about the trip, but Kitty answered little, not ready or able to share it. Once she had eaten a little, Kitty went to her room. Tilly had set the fire well and it was crackling into life. She lay upon her bed, remembering the warmth of John's body around her. She smiled at the ease with which they spoke and the foolish jokes they shared. Curling into the warmth of the memory, she drifted into sleep.

When she awoke, it was dark. Alexander was sitting in the fireside chair, reading. She watched him for a moment, his face lit by the orange glow. He looked up. 'Ah, you are awake.'

She pulled herself up. 'I'm afraid I must look a terrible mess.' He came and sat beside her, taking her hand.

'Not at all. The journey must have been tiring?'

'It was rather.'

'Well, I am glad you arrived home safely.' He kissed her gently on the forehead. 'It is good to have you home. I have missed you. We all have.' His eyes seemed to be searching hers and she looked away. 'Freshen up and come downstairs. I've ordered supper for us in the study. Then you can tell me all about your trip.' He left her alone.

As Kitty changed out of her travelling clothes, she realised that she had not asked about the boys. It saddened her that her affections were not the same for them as they had been for their lost, beloved girls. Over supper she asked after their welfare. Alexander told her of scrapes and arguments, the usual boyish antics. Then she painted a picture of her time in London that was, for the most part, honest. He laughed when she described the scenes she had seen at the Mabon. He seemed content with her account. When supper was finished and Alexander reached for the backgammon board, her heart sank, but nonetheless she played.

Chapter Twenty-Four

The next morning when Kitty was in her beloved orangery, clearing dead leaves and listening to the rain, Alexander came to her. He seemed uncertain. 'What is it, Alexander?'

'While you were away, I received a letter.'

'A letter?'

'Yes, Mother is returning.'

'What do you mean?'

'It appears that my sister cannot have her any longer.'

'Why not?'

'Her husband has been unwell, and she needs to devote her time to him.' Kitty could hear the excuse in those words.

'What about your brother?'

'He travels continually and has made it clear that he is likewise unable to accommodate her.'

Kitty felt indignation rising. 'So we have no choice.'

Alexander took a clergyman's breath. 'It is only right that we take care of her. We have room, and she can help with parish visits and the boys. I thought you would like that as they are such a burden to you.'

Kitty found she could not protest.

He continued, 'And the boys have lost so much this year, it would be good for them to have the comfort of their grandmother.'

Kitty could not imagine Alexander's mother being a comfort to anyone, but she also knew that she could bring little comfort to them herself and conceded. 'Very well. Am I to vacate her room?'

'No, you are still the mistress of this house, Kitty, nothing is going to change that. Mother will take Rachel's room.' He hovered as if there was more he wanted to say, but simply added, 'Thank you, I will make her position clear when she arrives.' Kitty nodded. As he was leaving, he turned to her. 'I am pleased to have you back, Kitty. We all are.'

There was a sadness about his smile.

Kitty called after him, 'When is she to arrive?'

'At the beginning of next week, if they can get through.'

As Alexander walked to his study, she noticed how he had aged; his upright stature had a heaviness about it, his walk slower. Perhaps the years had brought too much grief.

As the days passed, Kitty took up her duties once more. A letter arrived to say that Mother had been delayed. Kitty was grateful. She spent much of her time in the orangery, listening to the rain fall upon the glass. And when the sun came out, she would sit with her face towards it, gleaning the last of its warmth. Her desire to hear from John had not waned and it kept her alert to every knock on the door. It was almost two weeks later that a note came from Eleanor asking Kitty to visit her. She stepped out to the Manor that very morning. The sun was unusually bright, illuminating the trees as they showed off their final glory before the fall. The formal gardens either side of the drive were now complete. Gardeners were bent over browning plants, tidying and tying the ragged foliage.

Eleanor met Kitty in the Great Hall. She was invited no further. Eleanor smiled, but was formal today. She held out a letter. 'This came for you yesterday. The messenger said to take care with it.' Eleanor lowered her voice, 'Remember, Kitty, it is your marriage that will keep you, guard your heart.' Kitty thanked her and took her leave, but Eleanor's advice did not touch her; her heart already beat for the treasure she held.

Kitty went straight to her room and sat at the desk with her back to the door, lest she be discovered, and opened the letter.

My Dearest Love,
Every day away from you is a day too long. But every day will have been worth it, if it is leading me to my greatest joy; a life spent with you, my own beloved.
I told Bastion that I could not marry his daughter. He was outraged, as was my brother. It will be some time before my family forgive me for making fools of them, and for turning away the opportunity to take my part in saving the estate. But I could do no other, I could not marry knowing that my heart belonged to you, you alone.

A breathless joy bloomed within Kitty. She held the letter to her lips, remembering the touch of his upon them. Opening it again, she read,

What I am to tell you next, I ask you not to judge me too harshly. By the actions of Beatrice's brother you would think that I had brought murder into his household. He is intent on setting society against me. More than that, he has presented me with a challenge, a duel. But how could I risk my life when it is only just beginning? In finding you, I found my life, surely it would be wrong to end it so lightly. In the light of all this, a most dear friend, Charles Thorn, has offered me refuge in his rooms out in Epping Forest. I go there this afternoon. And this, Kitty, is where I will need you to trust me. I have decided to flee to Europe, until the heat is over. It hardly seems a noble course, but what else can I

do? What I am asking, my most dear love, it that you would accompany me. Why should two people be so unhappy and cause the unhappiness of others, when we can be together and multiply the happiness already ours?
I cannot wait until I receive a reply, so I will come for you, Kitty. Charles has found a seaman who knows the waters at Hamford water. He will bring me to you. I will arrive on Saturday, October 14th, on the early rising tide. Come to Beaumont Cut at first light, I will find you there. Thereafter, we will away to France, where I will make you my own.
I will remain whilst the tide is in full swell. When it wanes, I will go with it, and if I do not find you there, I will assume that my passions are unmatched in you and it will be the last time you shall see me. But if you agree to come, you will make me the happiest man, and the most devoted husband.
Yours forever, John.

Kitty sat in the still of the moment, hardly able to breath. How could she simply leave? She looked up and saw Green Tom working in the garden. Alexander walked across the lawn and exchanged a few words with him, evidently admiring his work. Kitty held the letter in her lap watching their exchange. Alexander was always so kind to everyone, whatever their position. She folded the letter and put it safely away.

The rest of the day, Kitty followed her duties as she must. And the next. Whenever she had recourse to talk with Alexander, she could hear herself giving cheerful responses whilst another conversation was taking place within her, judging and weighing and wondering. Every duty became a special effort to show normality, whilst a storm raged within. After great effort and seeming success at a meeting with Mrs Tingwell and the ladies, Kitty sat in the parlour by the last of the fire.

She heard a carriage arrive. Going to the window, she saw Mrs Gough step down. Her bonnet, as ever, was tied tightly under her chin. She stumbled a little and the coachman put his hand out to steady her. She slapped it away. Kitty turned from the window and hid against the wall. She heard Mrs Carter's footsteps cross the hall and the front door opening. She could hear her mother-in-law complaining about the terrible journey. Alexander's voice now joined the women. He called her name.

She knew she could not put off the meeting any longer. Bracing herself, she entered the hall, apologising for having dozed. The old woman looked at her, unbelieving. Kitty continued, 'I do hope your journey was not too trying?'

'It was most trying. The roads were all but impossible and you should have seen the dreadful inns we had to stay in, always amongst the most undesirable company. I tell you, Alexander, that is the last time I will be forced from pillar to post on the whim of my family.'

Alexander took her arm. 'Of course, Mother, come into my study and Mrs Carter will fetch you some tea.' The old woman's tirade lasted until Mrs Carter brought a warm brew and fruit cake. For someone who complained about how the journey had left her sick to the stomach, a surfeit of cake was easily consumed.

When she was wiping the crumbs from her mouth, Mrs Gough addressed Kitty for the first time. 'Now, what am I to call you? I cannot call you Mrs Gough.'

'Call her Kitty, Mother, that is her name.'

'Of course.'

Kitty responded, 'And what am I to call you?'

'Why, Mrs Gough of course.'

Alexander leant forward. 'I think that may be confusing for the household. I wonder if you might let Kitty call you Mother.'

She looked at Kitty sidewards. 'But that is ridiculous, I am not her mother!'

'But she is my wife.'

The old woman bowed her head towards Alexander. 'Forgive me, it has been a long journey.' Then to Kitty, 'Let us see, shall we, let us see how things go.' The sound of the boys bursting through the front door reached them. 'Oh, the boys, my poor boys.' Leaping up, all weariness forgotten, she strode from the room.

Kitty looked hard at Alexander. He rose to follow his mother. 'It is going to take time, give her time.'

Kitty stood in the door watching the family greet one another. Grandmother was all affection with the boys, who looked somewhat bemused and stiff in response. When she had finished fawning over them, Beth took the boys to the kitchen.

The old woman watched them go. 'They have grown so much, Alexander, but Jonathan looks pale. Are they getting enough fresh air? Poor little things, what heartache they've been through.' She looked to Alexander. 'You have all been through.'

Kitty slipped back into the study and left them talking. She heard her mother-in-law's voice raise as she said, 'Rachel's room? But Elizabeth never needed a room of her own!' Alexander lowered his voice, but Kitty did not bother to listen. It was as if the whispers, which were inevitably about her, had little to do with her now. Outside, grey clouds moved quickly across the blue sky, running their course. She ran her hand along the smooth, hard edge of Alexander's desk, until it rested over the drawer in which Elizabeth's images lay. Kitty had barely thought more of them until now. She cracked the drawer open to see the same image she had seen some two years previously, still laying there, unmoved.

She pushed the drawer closed as she heard Alexander returning. 'Mother is happy to take Rachel's room.'

The old woman stood in the doorway, her face suggesting otherwise. 'But I insist on having my own furniture.'

Alexander was keeping the peace as best he could. 'If that is what you wish. I am sure we can find furniture to suit Kitty, can we not, my dear?'

Kitty stepped forward. 'No, you take your old room, Mrs Gough, I will take Rachel's.'

Covered in the confusion of an unexpected kindness, she responded, 'No, not at all, you are the mistress of this house now, it is only right … '

'No, I insist.'

Alexander was irritated. 'But, Kitty, I have agreed with Mother.'

Kitty held her ground. 'Rachel's room is a fine room, I will be most comfortable.' She was enjoying her small victory. And so it was agreed.

Once the room was prepared, Kitty went to gather her things. Tilly came to help. 'Well, Tilly, you have grown up a lot since I have been here.' Kitty had become fond of the girl. 'You are such a help to Mrs Carter.'

She gave a wide smile. 'I like Mrs Carter.'

'I am sure you do.'

'She looks after me and gives me cake.'

The simplicity of the young woman made Kitty smile. 'That she does, Tilly.' Kitty went to her drawer, took out the small butterfly brooch and placed it in Tilly's hand. 'This is for you.'

Tilly looked over her shoulder. 'Mrs Carter says I shouldn't touch what isn't mine.'

'Well, it was mine, now I am giving it to you. It will look very well on your Sunday dress.'

Tilly smiled her wide, artless smile. 'Thank you, miss. Can I go and show it to Mrs Carter?'

'Of course you can.' Kitty watched as the girl hurried away. It was now only three days until John arrived.

Alexander's mother was quick to make her place in the household. At every opportunity she spoke about the need to look after Alexander and the children, always calling them, 'her poor boys.'

Two interminable days passed when Mrs Gough pointed out that Kitty had 'failed to make sure that the boys were appropriately dressed for school.' She added, 'Of course, when Elizabeth was alive … '

Finally Kitty snapped. Perhaps it was not simply her mother-in-law's insensitivity that caused her to act the way she did. Perhaps it was simply the desperate need for a cease of the war within her. She stormed to the study, swinging open the door.

Alexander looked up, startled. 'Kitty?'

The familiar heat was stirring in her chest. 'I cannot take this any longer, Alexander. I cannot take it!'

He leapt to the door and closed it. 'Sit down, Kitty.'

'I don't want to sit down.' She was pacing now, speaking deliberately. 'I've tried, I've tried so hard, I honestly have. And now, with your mother.'

'I know she can be difficult but … '

'Ha!' Kitty shook her head. 'It's not just her. It is everything.' Alexander tilted his head in his usual listening response, which irritated her all the more. 'I am not what you expected, I know that. I have tried to be, I have honestly tried, but I cannot be a rector's wife any longer. I cannot do it, I am sorry.' Tears began to fall. He stepped towards her. She turned on him, holding up her palm. 'Don't! I do not want your sympathy.' He withdrew. She gathered herself, knowing that she was robbing him of the one thing he knew how to do. 'You don't understand, Alexander. You do not know what it is like for me being a rector's wife. All those meetings with those petty women. All the endless tittle-tattle you have to listen to day after day.'

'Kitty, I'm sure we can find a way … '

'No … no. Don't you understand? I don't want to find a way, not anymore. What I am telling you is that I cannot do it. I just can't.'

Alexander paced to the window. A soft rain was falling. After a moment, he turned to her. 'My brother, Jonathan, tried to tell me that such a position would not suit you.'

'Your brother?'

'Yes.'

'But he doesn't know me.'

His grey eyes on her were full of pity. 'That week, the week you agreed to marry me, I was away, talking to the bishop about our arrangement. When I returned, Jonathan was waiting for me. He had made enquiries about you in Beaumont.'

'He did what?!'

'He sent his man to find out about you, Kitty.' Kitty shook her head in disbelief. Alexander continued, 'I was angry with him, of course I was, so angry that I sent him away. I told him not to come to the wedding.'

'Why did you not tell me?'

'I don't know, I suppose I did not want to lose you. Maybe I should have listened to him. Maybe I should have saved you all this pain. But I could not, I wanted you to be my wife, Kitty. I wanted you more than you can know.'

'Then why don't you come to me anymore, Alexander, as a man does to a woman?'

He closed his eyes for a moment, as he did so often when a question was too difficult to answer.

She went on, 'Even when you did, in the early days, it wasn't complete, was it? Why not? If you didn't want children, why could you not tell me? Why could you not share yourself with me fully?' Alexander leant heavily on the chair, his head low. Kitty searched for answers. 'And since we lost the girls, why could you show me no affection? There should be some tenderness between husband and wife, should there not? And perhaps even passion?'

'You are young …'

She hated the way he brought up her youth at such times. 'You knew that when you married me.' He said nothing, the pain evidently heavy upon him, but Kitty felt little pity as the one thing she had not wanted to rail against him fell from her lips. 'Is it her? Is it Elizabeth?'

Alexander shook his head, his eyes wide. 'No! Kitty, no. You've got it all wrong.'

'Have I?' She went to the desk, opened the drawer and grasped a handful of drawings. She held them before his face. 'If it is not, then why have you kept these?'

He took her wrist, snatched them from her hand and now held them aloft. 'These … these are not my drawings. They are the drawings of a young boy, a boy who had lost his mother.'

'A boy?'

'Yes, Kitty, these are Michael's drawings.' He leant on the desk, smoothing the precious drawings with his hand. 'Michael was very close to his mother, too close perhaps. When she died, I could not help him. He shut himself away for weeks. All he did was draw, image after image. He barely ate or spoke.' Alexander turned to her. 'I failed him, Kitty.' He placed the drawings lovingly back in the drawer. 'I failed him. I could not help myself and had no idea how to help him.'

'But the drawings, they are like that of an adult.'

'Yes, they are. He had an extraordinary gift. But when he finally stopped drawing her, he never picked up a pencil again. It seems the gift was to be buried with his mother.'

Kitty stepped away, her mind on the boy she had failed to touch. Alexander continued, 'And, Kitty, you have it all wrong about Elizabeth. Yes, I did love her, of course I did. But that is not why … why I have been distant, too distant for too long. It is because I could not see you go through what Elizabeth went through. I could not see another woman I loved perish in such violence. I had to protect you, don't you see? The only way to keep you safe, was to keep you from me. I could not let our intimacy grow because I could not trust myself.' He took her by the shoulders, with a passion she had not seen before. 'If you knew, Kitty, if you knew how much I have longed, how much … '

He pulled her closer. She felt the air around her, thick, and pulled away. 'Oh, Alexander. Why are you telling me this now? Why?'

He tried to take hold of her again. 'I should have told you. I should have ...'

'No, no ... I can't ... Let me go.' She struggled out of his arms.

He gathered himself. 'I am sorry, Kitty, I have been a coward, I know that now. But I can make amends, I can change.'

She reeled away, shaking her head. 'I need to think. I need ...'

'Kitty, please ...'

Holding up her hand, she made for the door, then steadied herself against its frame. She could not look at him. 'I shall be walking today, Alexander. I will return before dark. Please don't come looking for me.' She slipped from the room.

Within a few minutes, Kitty stepped out of the front door, ready to walk, to think, to stop her own pain. She was wearing her breeches and her father's coat.

The rain had stopped and a chill wind was rising. Kitty's skill at reading the weather had not left her. She walked towards the farm, her feet leading her. Rather than take the road, she took the track behind which weaved among the trees. Behind Mrs Dobson's cottage, a young woman was gathering nuts under a nearby tree with a little child at her side. Kitty walked on towards the farmhouse. All was quiet. She carried on around the back of the house. Just then, the dairy door swung open and the laughter of women could be heard from within. Kitty hid in the shadows.

Mother came out with a basket over her arm, putting it down to pick the last of the autumn flowers. The sound of Mother's humming came to Kitty on the breeze. How she longed to speak to her ma, to tell her everything, to ask her forgiveness, but she knew she could not. Suddenly, the humming stopped and

Mother looked up. Kitty hid herself behind a great oak, her heart beating against her chest. She heard her mother's voice calling, 'Kitty?' Kitty did not move, but clung to the tree so deep that her fingernails hurt. Eventually, when she heard the dairy door close, she looked. Mother had gone.

Kitty slid to the floor, the damp leaves beneath her hands. The sound of the little woodland embraced her. Dried grasses lay along the border of the garden. Kitty gathered them and sat awhile weaving them together. Soon a little heart was forming in her hands. Her earliest memories, when her mother was soft, played in her mind. A tiredness was upon her, but it was not for her to rest, not yet.

Kitty set off again along the path away from the house. She did not look back. All day she walked, aware of little but the ground beneath her. When her thirst became too great, she turned towards the hamlet of Beaumont to take a drink at the well. But on the way, a couple recognised her and bid her good day, so instead she carried on past, not wanting to face anyone she knew too well. The sun was beginning to dip. Her stride slowed into the inevitability of her thoughts as she approached the village. The Bell Inn was a welcome site.

A couple of old boys sat within, drinking. With difficulty, she exchanged pleasantries with Pat, then thirstily downed a beer before making her way home. The village was quiet now, all bar the sound of the blacksmith who was working late. She passed the familiar sights: an old woman sitting outside her door plucking a chicken, young boys kicking stones. She hovered at Sarah's cottage and for a moment longed to speak to her friend, but the door was shut tight. Kitty moved on, past the cottage that had been her grandmother's and on to the rectory.

As she approached, Green Tom headed toward her. 'Evening, missus.' He was making his way home; he was unusually engaging tonight.

She had to respond to his effort. 'It is a fine evening, Tom.'

'It is that.' He bowed his head and plodded away.

She committed it all to memory, and made her way indoors.

Supper was about to be served. Kitty changed quickly and joined the family at the table. Keeping the conversation light, she asked the boys about their day at school. She did so want them to think well of her. After supper she gave her best performance yet, playing cards with Alexander and his mother in the study, just like any other evening. After a couple of games, Kitty stood. 'I am tired after such a walk. I think I will go to bed.'

Alexander took her hand as she rose to go. 'Goodnight, then, my dear.'

'Goodnight.' She never quite knew why, but she bent to kiss him, on the lips. He smiled.

Later that evening, she heard Alexander knock on the door and whisper her name. She did not respond. He knocked again and tried the handle. 'Kitty, are you awake?'

She kept her silence, all too aware of the suffering she was inflicting upon a man who had already suffered so much. Eventually, his footsteps disappeared down the hallway.

All night, Kitty lay on the bed, watching the firelight play on the ceiling. When she was tempted to doze, she awoke herself fully and paced a little. As the coldness of dawn crept into the room, she tucked her letters from John and Florence deep in her bag, with her pipe and kerchiefs. Then she crept downstairs, slipped on her pa's coat, and stepped out into the blue of first light.

Kitty walked out of the village and over the rise. The backwaters sprawled before her. The lean of the land took her and caused her to stumble and trip towards the destination of her longing. Her feet were light, her head lighter still. Stopping a moment to catch her breath, she looked towards the eastern sky. It was blushing pink. The tide would be high when the sun was full over the eastern horizon.

A cock crowed from a homestead nearby, causing her to set off again at pace. She would need to be gone before the farm awoke. Running now, as she used to with Sarah so long ago, she saw the sun catch the tops of the trees that separated her from the Cut. A figure emerged from the trees. She knew, she hoped, it would be John. As she drew closer her hopes were realised and, stumbling the last few steps, she fell into his arms. Afraid of being seen by early risers, she tugged at his arm until they were under the cover of the trees. Once they were in the shadows, he pulled her back and kissed her, freely, openly and deeply. Nothing was said between them, nothing need be said. He looked at her, stroked the hair from her face, then took her hand and led her through the trees which opened to the water's edge.

A skiff bobbed in the shallows. A man leant against a nearby tree, smoking a pipe. When he saw them coming, he damped his pipe and heaved a great plank across the mud. 'C'mon then, the tide be fast on the rise. Best be goin'.' He walked across the plank and jumped into the boat. John threw Kitty's bag to him, then led her across to the safety of the little vessel.

As they pulled away, the sun was rising, breaking open the clouds that sought to keep it from its course. The boatman pulled hard against the tide in long strokes. At some distance, a small ship lay to anchor. Beyond her, in the far distance, the traders' vessels, in full sail, were making their way towards them. Kitty looked back at the familiar landscape drifting away, the rope swing, the brown fields and ragged inlets. The farm stood as a distant memory, so small in the vast landscape. A noise caused Kitty to turn, it was a bob of seals basking on the muddy bank.

John laughed and said, 'They've come to see you off.' Pulling Kitty to him, he added, 'You are sure? This is what you want?' Kitty nodded and dropped her head to John's shoulder. At last the tears began to flow.

Once aboard ship, the lovers stood at the bow, amid much calling and heaving, as the sailors pulled anchor and released the great sails to the breeze. A trading vessel passed, causing a conflict of waves. She had heard of the boiling, where winds blew keen and the estuary gave way to the sea, but now she felt it herself as the vessel jostled over the uncertain waters. They turned into open sea, the ship finding its course and picking up speed.

Kitty had boarded a ship in dock with her pa, but she had never stood under the full-bellied sails as they abandoned themselves to the wind. Nor had she felt the great swell beneath her; with each rise, an exhilaration rose in her belly, and with every fall, her unfettered feet caused her to stumble into the laughter of her lover. Softening her knees, she quickly learnt to ride the waves. The coastline faded behind them as the sun rose, a full orb over the east.

Chapter Twenty-Five

They were awoken by a calling and a knocking from on deck. John stumbled from the cot to see what was happening. The rasping whisper of men in heated discussion brought Kitty to attentive wakefulness. She sat in expectation of John's return. When he lurched through the door, his voice was urgent. 'We need to go. There is a boat waiting to take us to shore.'

It was dark but she could feel his anxiety. They emerged from below deck to a dark sky, bruised with blue. Kitty was surprised to see that no lamps were lit. Casks and crates were being hauled aboard. Once it was done, they were ushered, without ceremony, over the side and into the waiting boat. An old tar pulled hard against the chill breeze. Kitty and John were given no mind. They clung together against the elements until the boat hit the sand and they clambered out into the shallow water. Two men ran out of the shadows of the cliffs and hauled the boat ashore.

John approached one of the men, exchanging a few words in French. He then flung his bag onto his back, lifted Kitty's bag and led her away along the sands at pace. Though they hurried, they seemed to make slow progress; each footstep sinking into the soft sand. At the far end of the cove they found a small path that climbed away from them. It was no easy climb in the early light, but after some effort they took a final haul to the top of the cliff. Kitty stopped to catch her breath and looked back. The ship was turning into open sea. She could barely believe that she had travelled in such a vessel.

John tugged her hand. 'We had better keep going.'

Kitty was used to walking, but this was different. John didn't speak, but pulled her along with an urgency. The wind dropped and a small hamlet opened before them. At last, John stopped by a stream. He dropped the bags, breathing hard. 'Forgive me, Kitty, those men ... Charles assured me that he had found an honest sailor. I had no idea that they were smugglers or I should never have brought you this way.'

She interrupted his apologies, just as she always did, with a finger to the lips and after that ... a kiss. How could she tell him that the danger of it all only heightened her excitement?

He was placated and returned her kiss. 'I was told that the folks of this village would find us a warm fire and decent food.'

They had taken but a few steps when Kitty pulled John back. 'But how will we explain ourselves?'

John laughed. 'Don't worry, my French is quite good.'

'No, I mean our situation. What will we say?'

'Oh, don't worry about that, the French love romance. When they know we have eloped, they will surely take us in. Come on.'

They walked over a wooden bridge and towards a little stone hut standing quite alone among the fields. A farmer stood shielding his eyes from the rising sun, trying to discern the figures approaching him. As they drew close, he called behind him, 'Femme, femme.' A woman in aprons and a folded kerchief covering her hair came to the door. John stepped forward and spoke to the man, who seemed not to understand him at all. The woman joined them, speaking in a strange tongue, so very unlike the French she had heard at home. After a number of gesticulations and slow entreaties from John, the woman seemed to understand and opened her arms wide. 'Entre, entre.'

John and Kitty were soon sitting in the warmth. The woman had taken their filthy stockings, washed them, hung them in front of the fire and stood their boots likewise. She then smiled and babbled and busied herself preparing food whilst John managed to express what he needed to the man. He nodded in agreement, except when he asked for his wife to interpret. Once they had eaten the most delicious fish stew that Kitty had ever tasted, John explained, 'They have offered to take us to a village, not too far from here, where we can stay, and from there I can arrange a coach.' Kitty was pleased that their journey would finally be underway. John looked down. 'But there is one thing.'

'Yes?'

His expression was uncertain as he took her hand. 'These are good catholic folk.' He looked at the man who smiled and nodded. 'They want us to set things right before we make our journey.'

'What do you mean?'

'I told them that because of a family disagreement, we are running away together.' John now fixed her with his hazel eyes. 'They know a protestant priest in the village who will marry us.'

'Marry?' Kitty looked at the man who stood by the fire and seemed to be explaining something to the woman. He was nodding earnestly. John continued, 'I did not intend to ask you like this, Kitty, but after all this is what we are doing, is it not, my love?'

Kitty felt the blood run from her face. What could she do? The expectation of the old couple was upon her now, their eyes eager in the firelight. In front of her was the uncertain face of the one who was the source of all her happiness. The words now tumbled from her lips, 'Of course, of course I will'

John smiled in relief, the little creases framed his mouth once more as he said, 'You will marry me, then?'

She nodded and found the tears streaming down her face. He kissed her hands, then her lips. The woman laughed and, with flailing arms, batted John away from Kitty, took her face in her ragged hands and kissed her firmly on both cheeks.

The men were ushered out of the house amidst much babbling. Kitty sat on the bench in the little hut, watching the old woman take a kettle of steaming water and pour it into a great basin in front of the fire. She added some from the jug and swished it around with a large wooden spoon. She then undressed Kitty, laying each piece of clothing aside. She had her stand in the warm water whilst she gently washed her arms, her legs and even her most intimate parts. Her babbling had given way to a reverence. Kitty felt thoroughly exposed, but gave herself to the fullness of the process. Standing there, before the fire, water dripping from her body, it became, to Kitty, a baptism; a thorough turning of her life. She knew she must trust its course.

Once Kitty was sat in a chair, wrapped in a drying sheet, the woman picked dried herbs hanging on the wall, muttering to herself. She now sat beside Kitty, and with the smile of silent memories, she gently rubbed the herbs over Kitty's arms, down over her breasts, between her thighs and to her feet. The smell of lavender filled the air. When all was done and Kitty was dressed, an exquisite, embroidered shawl in reds and yellows was placed around her shoulders. The final piece was a kerchief, piled high on her head. The old woman went to the door and beckoned the men. John stopped when he saw Kitty through the door, looking as stunned as she felt.

Once everything was gathered, they sat together on the back of the cart, clutching the bread and jar of wine that the old woman had given them. She followed the cart through the village, calling women from their homes. Soon a small band of women and children were following on, waving, calling, babbling, until the cart reached the edge of the hamlet and stopped. The old woman climbed up beside her husband and they made their way through the open fields.

Men and women who had been bent to their task, stood and waved and nudged one another as the cart went past. Kitty told John about the ritual she had undertaken, though the weight of it remained her own. He said that he had been most unfortunate and had been forced to wash in the freezing water of the stream. They laughed together as they bumped along the way. It seemed to Kitty that she was once more in that stream of life that took her where it will. But this time it was a soft stream, a sparkling stream.

On the approach to the village, they stopped before a small cottage all but hidden in a wood. The man went to the door and knocked. It was some time before a most dishevelled gentleman answered the door to a narrow crack. His face was covered in hair. A long exchange took place. Eventually the woman jumped down, pushed her husband aside and let a tirade of words shoot from her lips. When she stopped, the man peered at the couple and closed the door. Kitty was beginning to doubt that all would be well. But the woman ushered them from the cart and around the back behind the shack.

As she did so, John tugged at her arm. 'Wait, we must choose a name. My name is known and there are so many English travellers these days.'

'Woods,' Kitty said without hesitation.

John looked around at the carpet of fallen leaves before them, and the tall arching branches above. 'Woods it is.'

The woman beckoned. 'Venez, venez.'

The priest, now wrapped in a long cloak, stumbled out of the house, a plain cross in one hand, a book and a bottle in the other. He took a great swig from the bottle and placed it on the floor, then straightening himself he said, 'Welcome, my friends.' He was English. John thanked him and started to explain, but he simply held up his hand. 'Let that be as you will, for now. Let's get you wed.' He lifted a colourful, if dirty, stole, kissed it and placed it around his shoulders.

During the simple ceremony, Kitty's previous vows became just a part of the life she had barely learnt to live. These vows to John were said with every fibre of her being. And anyway, the strangeness of the day, the eccentric priest, the old couple, and the birdsong that accompanied the ceremony, all conspired against her. She found all the pain of her yesterdays gathered together into the healing balm of the moment.

When the ceremony finished, they thanked the priest who hastily retreated to the safety of his shack. Kitty and John mounted the cart and were taken to a house in the village where they were shown to a room where they could stay. With much smiling and waving, the old couple trotted away. Kitty committed the scene to her memory. She would never forget their kindness.

Kitty's days were now spent journeying beside the husband of her heart. Together they laughed at the strange sights they saw. They were struck dumb by the mountains and bickered when the journey was tough. But, most wonderful of all was when, after the fullness of their love had found expression, they lay deep in each other's arms.

Alexander sat beside the fire reading morning prayer. It had been some weeks since the village had given up their search and the constables indifferent investigation had been deemed inconclusive. The familiar prayer book lay open in his hands. Words formed on his lips, but took no place in his heart. Michael's drawings burned in the grate.

Eleanor sat at the table in the window. She feared for Kitty, but would say nothing, for fear that her own indiscretions would be revealed. James' position and the happiness of her entire family were in her hands. Looking out at the garden with its geometric forms, she wished she could turn the clock back.

Sarah sat nursing her baby, another boy. She remembered Kitty for a moment and wondered. But she was long past tears or any deep feeling. The infant, overwhelmed with the flow of milk from her breast, choked a little. She patted his back and looked at him with unseeing eyes.

Judith knew Kitty better than anyone. She sat on the end of her bed fingering a grass heart she had found on the gatepost and that now lay in her lap. Through the window, the sun streamed across the fields, causing the high waters to show off their blue. She whispered, 'Be happy, Kitty, happy enough for all of us.'

Chapter Twenty-Six

After many days of travelling, Kitty had ceased to count how many, she awoke high up in a Venetian villa. Going to the window, she flung open the shutters to see the red-roofed city shrouded in the mists of encroaching winter. A Venetian voice called out, another called in answer. Kitty opened the window to see a man gesticulating across the canal below. The pungent smell of it caused her to close the window fast.

John laughed. 'Come back to bed, my love.' She padded back, her feet cold on the hard floor, and curled once more into the warmth of her lover's body.

Kitty could not help being entranced by the city, with its waterways, little bridges, ornate arches and alleyways. For weeks Kitty and John spent their days wandering the streets as spectators, neither wanting nor needing to take part in the revelry in which the masked Venetians were evidently intent. But it was the churches that filled Kitty with wonder. At Christmas they attended a concert of children's singing in St Mark's Basilica. The images of all humanity that hung above her in the great dome all but transported her. Only once, when a procession of the Virgin Mary passed them in the street, did Kitty feel a consternation rising in her protestant heart.

Once the sun began to give of its warmth, Kitty sensed a restlessness in John. She would watch him sitting in the window, looking out at the world beyond. If she asked what he was thinking, his reply was invariably, 'Nothing.' But she could see a stillness about him that was full of intent.

Today, she watched him as he clothed himself; his fingers moved with an elegant efficiency as he buttoned his waistcoat. He tied back his hair, which had grown long and fell in soft curls at the end. Every little move he made pleased her. As he pulled on his coat, she noticed that he was formally attired. Smoothing back the loose hair about his face, he said, 'It is time I found an occupation, my love.'

'An occupation?'

'Yes, there is a perfumer in the city, not far from here. I will visit him this morning and see if he has any contacts that may be of use.'

'But, John, I do not want to live in the city. I thought we might find a small villa and settle in the country.'

'What would I do in the country, my love?'

She shot back, 'And what would I do in the city?'

'That is quite different.'

'Is it? Why?' She stood before him wrapped in a blanket and wished she was dressed if they were going to have a disagreement.

The face before her, always so soft towards her, now hardened. 'A man has to have an occupation, Kitty. I cannot be as others and spend my days in frivolous pleasures.'

'I am frivolous, am I?' She knew she was being provocative.

'That is not what I meant. You know it isn't.'

And so began their first real argument. He told her that she did not understand the needs of a man. She told him that he could not understand the needs of a country woman and added that he should not have married one if he wanted to settle in the city. But he insisted their finances would not last forever and he would need to find work. So she told him that she would make money off the land.

'I do not need you to make money, Kitty, you are being ridiculous.'

'Then what do you need me for?'

John did not respond, but rather gathered himself and spoke deliberately, 'I am going to see the perfumer. When I return, we will discuss this further.' He headed to the door.

Kitty did not like the tone he was taking and lurched after him, but stumbled on the blanket wrapped around her legs. 'I want to discuss it now!'

John turned, his brow low over his hazel eyes. 'No, I am not going to discuss it, not with you in this state. Look at you. Why don't you get dressed?' He closed the door firmly behind him.

Kitty pulled the blanket from beneath her feet, growled and plonked herself down on the bed. She looked around at the hard whitewashed walls that had been their home for some weeks and realised, for the first time, how she missed the feel of the soft earth beneath her feet. A crack ran down the wall by the window. A spider emerged from its dark recess, stopped in its tracks to consider her presence, then scurried away and disappeared into the window frame.

She sat listening to the rhythmic trickling of water as a solitary gondola passed beneath the window. Just then, a warmth spread between her legs. She thought her flow had finished and for a moment was irritated by its presence, but it got her to thinking. Though her regular blood had not faltered, perhaps one day it would, and she would find herself with child. For the first time, the idea didn't horrify her. She let herself imagine carrying John's child. The idea took on weight as she stroked her belly. With the argument quite forgotten, Kitty curled on the bed, letting her thoughts drift.

When John returned, he found her sleeping. 'My love?'

Kitty awoke to the smell of fresh bread. John sat beside her tearing the crust from a warm loaf. His cheek showed the shadow that always thrilled her to the touch.

He handed her a piece of bread; it was soft in her mouth. She watched as her lover ate, the pout of his lips moving around each morsel. Then he spoke, 'Come, my love, get dressed, I want to take you out.'

'I cannot, my flow is still with me.'

He looked disappointed. 'Could you not come? I will help you.' Without another word he gathered a bowl of water and her clothes. She could not resist him.

Once she was cleaned and clothed, John led his wife down the stairs, through the courtyard to the canal's edge. The smell of it still caused Kitty to hold her kerchief to her nose.

He held out a small box. 'Here, this will help.'

Kitty held the offering in her hands. It was a green leather box with gold inlay and a tiny clasp which she now opened. Inside, a small ruby red glass bottle was held safe in the snug recess. She smiled in remembrance of their first encounter. She opened the golden stopper and lifted it to her nose. The most exquisite perfume filled her senses. Her eyes filled up though she knew not why.

John helped her on to the waiting gondola. Once inside, the lovers apologised to one another and enjoyed the sweetest of kisses. John started to tell her about the exquisite perfumes that Signore Bartoni produced. His eyes were alight with possibility as he talked of the contacts he had been given. He would find work in export, Signore Bartoni would help him. The hard edges of the city seemed to soften as Kitty listened to John's boyish enthusiasm. Maybe she could find a way in such a place.

They spent the day in the spring sun, watching the world go by from Caffe Florian in St Mark's square. That night, they did what all lovers do after an argument, they succumbed to the ardour of their passions.

John agreed terms of work with Signore Bartoni, and agreed to take on a small villa in San Palo. To one side the lazy canal ran by, to the other was a rather neglected courtyard. Kitty put herself to the renovations, though she only had pots with which to work, but soon the courtyard was full of hope. And when she held her first waxy lemon to her nose, the scent of it fair transported her to God's own garden. Sometimes, in the rising heat of summer, she would sit in the shade of her leafy glade and remember the plants that languished in her little orangery at home, and would chuckle. But at other times, she would lean out of the window and long for the open skies of home. Kitty learned enough of the native language to buy what she needed and to exchange greetings with neighbours, but otherwise she spent most of her time alone, waiting for the sound of John's footsteps at the door. But in the high heat of the summer months, Kitty felt her energies draining in the rising heat.

On one particularly hot day, at the end of August, John came home to find Kitty resting in the shade of the beloved vine that she had tended to full health. Her hair lay loose about her shoulders, her dark lashes kissed the small creases under her eyes. John smiled to see her and whispered, 'Hello, my love.'

She smiled a sleepy 'Hello' in response.

He sat beside her and, opening her fingers, traced the small scar that had first brought them together. 'I have something for you,' He often brought her little gifts, but something about his look made her sit up. He slipped a small item out of his pocket, and placed it in her palm, closing her fingers over it. It was cool to the touch.

The little creases around John's mouth gave way. 'Well, are you not going to look?'

She obeyed. There, lying in her palm, was an old key. 'John? What is it?'

'I've taken a villa out on the mainland.'

'A villa?'

'Yes, it is not much, but you will have a garden.'

'But what about your work?'

'I am not needed so much, so it has been agreed that I will come to the city twice a week. But you might have to use those country skills of yours to make a little extra.'

'But, John, you said you need to work.'

'I know, but I was wrong not to consider your needs, and besides, it turns out that the work is rather dull.' He smiled, a wide natural smile.

'When can we go?'

'It is ours as soon as we can get there.'

'Come on then.' Kitty jumped up.

'Where are we going?'

'To pack, of course.' She laughed and led John inside.

Not a week later, Kitty found herself standing in front of the little stone building that was to be their home. A neglected herb garden lay before her and beyond that a grove of olive trees standing in the dry ground. A goat stood among them looking at the couple looking at them, then returned to its munching. Above the trees, in the far distance, a range of purple mountains disappeared into the haze. And above it all was a vast, peerless, cobalt sky. Kitty breathed in the heady scent of the late rambling rose that clambered over the roof of the veranda. The summer here was so different to the summers of home, but just as sweet.

A warm breeze touched Kitty's cheek and with it, the lips of her lover. 'Are you happy?' She nodded as they swayed gently in unison, his arms around her waist. At her feet were the numerous pots that she had insisted on bringing.

There was much to be done. Too much for Kitty alone. She taught John what she could of the land, but he had no aptitude for it. A young man was brought in to help. He reminded Kitty of Tom with his brown forearms and wayward hair. Marco was a hard worker and although he knew no English, they managed to communicate through nodding and pointing. The soil was so very different to her own at home, dry as dust, but Kitty knew soil and it seemed to respond well to her care. Marco soon tamed the rose that had been left far too long to weigh on the timbers. She liked his company. She took to teaching him English. They would laugh often at his poor attempts. He was good company when John was away.

Kitty trusted herself to her young husband so completely that when the weather turned cold, she dug deep in her chest and brought out her breeches. At first when John saw her, he laughed, but then he drew her close and said, 'You are wonderful, Kitty Woods.' The name had become easy to her. And when John came home late one evening to find Kitty sitting on the veranda step, smoking her pipe, he simply held out his hand and took it. Taking a long drag, he said, 'There, now when I kiss you, we will taste the same,' which he proceeded to do without delay. It seemed that whatever she did that might provoke his displeasure, was met with kindness.

When winter came on, John stayed at the city more often, but Kitty now understood that as much as she needed the fresh air of the country, he needed the interest of city life. Some days Kitty would accompany her husband so that she might visit a museum or the little English bookseller, who sold books from his villa on Ruga Veccia. Through the winter months, she continued to make sense of the garden with the help of Marco. His father joined him in the work. He spoke a little English and helped Kitty to understand the soil better. Plants and little packets of seeds, labelled in both English and Italian, would often arrive at her door.

As the months went by, Kitty's flow did not falter, and so no little ones came to keep her company. But the easy rhythm of her days with John and her work on the land, became enough balm to soften the moments of sadness that visited her.

The high heat seemed to come early the next year. The vegetables began to give of their yield and flowers bloomed. The early summer was busy with harvesting. Marco's father sold some of her produce at the market. It pleased Kitty to be earning even a little from the land. But once the heat was at the height of its intensity, it sapped her of all energy once again. In the afternoons she would lay on her garden chaise, watching as Marco worked in her precious garden. Sometimes she sat beside John as he worked at a makeshift table beside her, at other times he read to her until she dozed. She awoke from one such doze with a start. She thought she saw her pa leaning against his rake, his long hair flowing over his shoulders, but when she came to her senses, she realised that it was Marco's father; she had never noticed the likeness before.

Kitty awaited the cooler days when her energies would return. As each day came to an end, she fully expected the next to bring with it a new vitality, but each morning refused to yield its strength. As the days grew colder once more, Kitty found herself colder still. She wore a blanket around her shoulders most of the day and when John noticed her appetite waning, he called in the apothecary. The tall, cloaked stranger stood at the table of their kitchen mixing potions that would 'bring light back to her beautiful eyes and colour to her silken cheeks.' John and Kitty were amused at his extravagance of phrase and laughed together when he had gone.

Kitty did not want help in the villa, it was her special place, her secret place. But John insisted. He employed Marco's sister, Amelia, to keep house. She was a pleasant enough girl with skin as dark as her brother's, but Kitty missed the quiet of keeping her own home.

The potions brought little relief, and when her flow ceased, a physician from the city was called. How she wished it was a sign that she was with child, but she knew better. He poked at her and prodded her and when John took him to the door, the physician was shaking his head.

John ceased going to the city, but sat by his wife, reading to her and comforting her. He reminded her of the sights they had seen on their journeys, of the old couple who had taken them in at the first. And she would smile. John wanted to know everything about his wife, but when he asked about her previous life, she would simply close her eyes and turn her face away. He stopped asking. Day and night, John watched and hoped, even when hope was without cause. Sometimes she would rally and he would hold her hand, and stroke the hair from her forehead. At other times she tossed and turned in semi-sleepfulness, calling for her pa or speaking inaudible words.

It was at one such time that she suddenly awoke and grasped John's sleeve. 'Get me a priest, John. I want to see a priest.'

'But, Kitty, you are not a Catholic. I may not be able to find a protestant priest.'

Her eyes were desperate upon him. 'Please, John ... please. Just find me a priest.' She fell back upon the pillow, exhausted.

John's stomach tightened as he went to the garden to find Marco. The young man put down his tools and hurried away to find a priest. It took some time for Marco to return. Kitty now seemed particularly restless. Amelia brought warm water and cloths, so that John could bathe his beloved's face. The moment the priest entered the room, Kitty rose to wakefulness, calling out. The old man hurried to her side and soothed her to silence. He made the sign of the cross over her face and uttered a few words. Kitty spoke again grasping at the old priest's arm, 'Tell John I am sorry.'

John soothed her. 'I am here, my love.'

Kitty tried to pull herself closer to her confessor and rasped, 'I am the wife ... the wife of Reverend Gough.'

John pushed the priest aside and came to comfort her. 'No, my love, you are married to me ... to John.'

A tear ran down her face. He wiped it with his finger. Every word was now an effort on her dry lips. 'Forgive me, John,'

'What for, my love?'

'Tell Alexander ... I am sorry. I am so sorry.' Her frail hand grasped at John's clothing. 'Take me home, John, please ... Take me home.'

John barely knew what he was saying, 'Of course, my love, I will take you, I will. Now hush … hush.'

She quieted in his arms, though her lips moved. Then, on the slightest of whispers, she said, 'Forgive me.' And breathed her last.

Chapter Twenty-Seven

Alexander stood in the orangery. At first, he had Tom keep it for Kitty's return, but he didn't have the way with it that Kitty did and as the months passed it fell into disrepair. Dust-dry pots housed plants now skeletal with neglect. Mother always said that the orangery should be taken down, and now, standing there, Alexander had to agree. A thump startled him. A bird must have mistaken the glass for the sky. He watched the small creature as it staggered a little then flew away into the pink blushed sky of early morn.

Something caught his eye. Tucked away in the corner of the high shelf was a small knife. Lifting it to his fingers he felt the smooth handle that Kitty had held so often. He could see her now; her soft dark hair hanging loose over her shoulders as she tended her plants while he read to her. He ran his finger along the rusted blade, dull now. The argument they had had before she disappeared still played in his mind like an unfinished symphony. Today was no exception.

He replaced the knife on the shelf, and turned to make his way to the study, but was halted by a loud knocking on the front door. He let Mrs Carter answer it. It was probably a woman from the village. These past years he had learnt not to give in to a moment of weakness in their presence. If he had done so, they would no doubt have suffocated him with care. But instead of the usual female twittering, Alexander heard a man's voice, and in response, the disapproving tones of Mrs Carter. He left his ponderings and went to see what was going on. A man stood in the hall with a satchel hung across his shoulder, and a second man behind him.

Mrs Carter was the first to speak. 'Excuse me, Reverend, but this gentleman has a letter for you. He said he has been told to give it to you in person.'

Alexander held out his hand, but the man kept the letter close. 'Are you Reverend Alexander Gough?'

'I am.'

The man glanced at Mrs Carter as he spoke, 'Good, I was told to give this letter into your hands only.'

'I see. Well, I can assure you that I am he.'

The man continued to retain the document. 'And I am to await a reply.'

Alexander held his patience. 'Mrs Carter, take the gentlemen to the kitchen and find them a beer.' He held out his hand once more. This time the man was all too keen to release the letter. The housekeeper led the men away. Alexander went to his study and closed the door. He sat at his desk and opened the letter,

Dear Sir,
As the customs officer officiating at Hythe Quay in the boundary of Colchester, I write to you with the utmost respect. Of late, we have been on the lookout for smugglers in our waters. In the midst of a pick-up, we came across a young man accompanying the body of a woman.

Alexander's stomach lurched.

He refuses to tell us his name or the name of the woman in his care. He says that he will only speak when you have been summoned. It would be most helpful if you could make your way to the Hythe office and help explain the circumstances

of this unfortunate young man. I would be grateful if you would come as soon you are able, that we may conclude this sorry affair and see the poor woman given a Christian burial.
Philip Mayhew
Customs Officer.

That morning, John had asked for water, a razor and comb. To his surprise, the officer brought them. The water was cold, but it was enough to wash the ordeal of the past days from his face. His hand trembled as he moved the sharp blade across his skin. When he had tidied himself as best he could, he sat on the hard bench, watching the sunlight as it crept along the wall of the dingy room into which he had been put some long hours before. He could make no sense of the meeting that was to occur, he only knew that it must be done.

Once the sun had moved beyond the window, leaving gloom in its wake, the exhaustion of the past days swept over him. He lay back on the bench, hugging his coat around himself against the cold, and closed his eyes. No sooner had he begun to drift than he awoke again to find an officer standing over him; the time had come.

John was led from the room, down the dark corridor and into a room filled with light. Once his eyes adjusted, he saw another, taller man standing before him. The man nodded in recognition. John did likewise.

Alexander had expected to find himself faced with a young cockerel, but instead a rather cowed young man stood blinking in the sun. Alexander spoke first, addressing Mr Mayhew, 'I would be glad of a chair, if I may, it has been a long journey. And one for Mr . . . ?' He inclined his head to the young man, who replied without hesitation.

'Dalmeny, John Dalmeny.'

The men sat, but the question that burned to be asked soon fell from Alexander's lips. 'Mr Dalmeny, I have to ask you, who is the woman ... ' he took a breath ' ... the body of the woman in your care?'

John spoke, again without hesitation, 'She is your wife.'

'My wife?'

'Yes ... and mine.'

'Yours?'

Mr Mayhew stepped forward to intervene, but Alexander held up his hand, thus giving John space to speak. 'I did not know, I swear it. I did not know that she was married. If I had I would never have taken her as my wife.'

Alexander studied the earnest young man before him; there was nothing of the rogue about him, and besides, he knew Kitty well enough to know that she was perfectly capable of deceit, and with a smile, he said as much. That simple kindness enabled John to continue. He told the tale right from the beginning, from the moment he held a kerchief to her hand, there in the workshop in Soho, to their escape from Beaumont Cut. He spoke of the little ceremony among the trees in France, of their journeyings and of the happiness Kitty found in her garden before her demise. It was only when he spoke of seeing her embalmed body laid in the casket that would bring her home, that he struggled to speak; the tears that had threatened to overwhelm him so often now fought for release. He fell to silence.

Alexander went to the window. The winter sun caught the water in a thousand ripples, each one carrying a memory of his own years with Kitty and all the conversations they should have had. He knew now that the love he'd had for her would never have been enough for her, and he was sorry for it.

There was a splashing and a squawking, as a swan flapped and stumbled across the water, seeking flight. Alexander watched it as it found its wings, then turned once more into the room. He addressed the young man whose ashen face was spent from telling his tale. 'Well, Mr Dalmeny, shall we take Kitty home?'

Kitty's remains were taken to the rectory that very evening. Alexander stood in the dining room with his little household whilst John anointed Kitty's body with perfume. For a moment, the scent of summer surrounded her once more before it dissipated into the cold air. Replacing the stopper of the little ruby-red bottle, he lay it next to her heart. The reverend opened his prayer book and spoke the familiar words over the body of his wife, words that he had been caused to speak too many times over those he had loved and lost. When all was said and done, Alexander took John to the inn where a room had been prepared. They drank together and remembered, laughed and cried, until dawn.

At noon the next day, the two husbands walked side by side behind the cart that carried Kitty's body to her final resting place. The boys followed on with their grandmother. Judith, supported by her husband, came after clutching the little grass heart she had kept close these years. Tom and Miriam, Aunt Mary and old Jacob walked behind. All the village lined the way. Eleanor stood by the lychgate, her head bowed as the procession passed through. The silence of the day was made more keen by the absence of Sarah. She had lost hope the year before and now lay awaiting her friend. Kitty was laid beside her beloved pa, there in the graveyard under the old oak tree. The tide was on the turn and a cool breeze was rising. Kitty was home.

After Kitty's death, John returned to the family estate in Scotland. He died three years later at the age of thirty one. Alexander lived for another twenty years.

Kitty's birth in Beaumont, her marriage to Alexander, her elopement and bigamous marriage to John, Lord Dalmeny, are well documented in the accounts of her life. The nature of the return of her body to Thorpe and the unlikely event of the two men following her coffin, some say hand in hand, are all agreed on. The rest is of the author's imagination.

The Bell Inn continues to stand at the heart of the village of Thorpe-le-Soken. It is said that Kitty's presence can still be felt in its ancient timbers.

Printed in Great Britain
by Amazon

80005190R10185